"So, what do we do now?"

"I can't . . ." Davida stole a glance at her watch. "It's six thirty, and I need to . . ."

He leaned forward and pressed his lips to her cheek, kissing her as gently as he'd ever kissed anyone. When her head tilted in silent acceptance, Marc followed the urgings of barely concealed desire. . . .

"I wish I could say I was sorry for that," he said quietly.

Me, too, Davida thought, *but I'm not. Not even a little bit.* It had been a long time since her body had reacted like this to a man. She was suddenly, stunningly aware of how deprived she was, how hungry she'd become.

"Boo?" He sounded like he needed an answer. "What do we do now?"

She took a deep breath and made a decision. "I take a walk on faith, and you put your face a little closer to mine, and ask me that question again in exactly the same way."

Marc hesitated for the first time since they'd actually met.

"Ask me," she whispered.

"What do we do now, Boo?"

BOOK YOUR PLACE ON OUR WEBSITE AND MAKE THE ARABESQUE ROMANCE CONNECTION!

We've created a customized website just for our very special Arabesque readers, where you can get the inside scoop on everything that's going on with Arabesque romance novels.

When you come online, you'll have the exciting opportunity to:

- View covers of upcoming books

- Learn about our future publishing schedule (listed by publication month and author)

- Find out when your favorite authors will be visiting a city near you

- Search for and order backlist books

- Check out author bios and background information

- Send e-mail to your favorite authors

- Join us in weekly chats with authors, readers and other guests

- Get writing guidelines

- AND MUCH MORE!

Visit our website at
http://www.arabesquebooks.com

WHEN LOVE CALLS

GAIL A. MCFARLAND

ARABESQUE

BET
BOOKS

BET Publications, LLC
www.msbet.com
www.arabesquebooks.com

ARABESQUE BOOKS are published by

BET Publications, LLC
c/o BET BOOKS
One BET Plaza
1900 W Place NE
Washington, D.C. 20018-1211

First Printing: August, 1999
10   9   8   7   6   5   4   3   2   1

Printed in the United States of America

*In memory of my mother Mildred,
because she would understand.*

*And with love to my father Leon,
because first, last, and always you have family.*

Special Thanks to:

Denise G. and Ruth for making me aware. To Avery Harris, and all of the LIFE Center crew for holding my hand and being patient. To Shanika, Pam, Tandra, Yamina and Abbo for your unselfish reading. To Regina and Chiquita, and who knew the words to the song when I needed them most. To Truvie and Laura for the best smiles in the western world. To Brenda, Ira, and Wylene for their medical expertise. Thank you all for being my special angels.

CHAPTER ONE

The switch clicked a third time before the antique lamp on the bedside table cast a warm amber glow across the highly polished cherry wood of the bedroom furniture. Thunder rolled by with a low sound that might only be matched by Barry White's baritone, as Davida Lawrence tugged her ancient Cleveland Browns T-shirt over her head. Pulling the big old shirt lower, past the tops of her thighs, she caught sight of herself in the oval mirror across the room.

Phat. That was the word the kid used when she passed him on the way to the bus stop this afternoon. When she swung past him to catch the number twenty-three bus, his eyes suddenly came up from the ground and traveled on, up past her ankles to the bending curve of her legs. It seemed she felt the insolence of his gaze like the hot sweep of a broad hand as it touched her—sweeping from the solid roundness of her hip right up to the plump swell of her breast, and back down. He had the nerve to look at her *and* take his time doing it.

"Ooh, Mama," he breathed, shaking his head to the rhythm of his words. "Girl, you know you *phat.*"

"Fat?" Girl? Davida's eyes moved first, followed closely by the rest of her body. The hand hit her hip in record time.

"What did you say to me?" *And, who are you calling fat?*

The kid recognized attitude in action when he saw it. *"P-h-a-t,* shorty," he explained, using his hands to do it. The bold grin wavered, then renewed itself. "You major *phat.*"

Phat? It must have been a real word, he'd used it in a sentence—sort of.

The grin that slid over his knowing brown face was so wise it made her break her stride, stop, turn, and look at him—hard.

"What?"

Wishing for the full glory of the conquest, but knowing he was out of his league, the teenager mustered all the nerve his energetic sixteen years bequeathed him. "I said." He jigged a nervous step or two. "I said, you are *phat:* pretty, hot, and temptin', you know. You are one fine lady, and you look real good today, and I just had to say something . . . something to let you know that I'm admirin' all you are. Tha's all."

Hard words danced on the tip of her tongue, and in the brown eyes Davida hid behind her dark glasses. There was something dangerously sensual and brazenly insolent lurking behind the compliment—something embarrassingly intimate, unduly personal about such outrageous flirtation from one so young, and it made her more than a little nervous.

What are you, anyway? she wanted to demand. *Fifteen? Sixteen? I'm old enough to be your . . . your . . . well, your mother's younger sister, and you're out here saying the kind of things to me that I haven't heard from a grown man since . . .*

. . . and for what? What did I do to make you think I needed compliments from a child? It's just a good thing I'm not out here fishing for men, 'cause I'd have to throw you back for being under the legal limit!

Davida pressed her lips together and neatly clipped off the thought. Why punish this boy for making her question herself? And, the good Lord knew, he had certainly done that. She made her lips form a tiny smile and tried not to drop her gaze before this arrogant child. "Thank you," she said, angry at herself for the quick blush she felt heating her skin.

As for the man-child, he spun on his heel, looking over his shoulder all the while, and nodded, showing more teeth than the law allowed. "I'm just admirin' is all," he said, again using his hands for emphasis as he headed down the street, turning toward Olive.

"*Phat.*" Davida wondered if that informal term meant the same as *brickhouse.* "I should have asked him," she whispered to the empty room. *Brickhouse*—she knew, for sure, what that meant. That was what men used to call her back in the seventies—back when she was little and sassy—a tall sleek size nine, never larger. Back then, her body was high and tight, her legs long and shapely, neatly rounded at the calves, with full thighs. "Back in the days before gravity took over," she whispered to her still neatly curving size-fourteen reflection.

"Come on, 'Old School.' " She could hear Anne's teasing voice, laughing in her ear. "You're way too serious and mature about this turning forty thing."

Man, the women in her little "Sister Circle" were having a ball with that one: Turning forty—being officially mature, no longer credibly phat. Anne and Mel had already cooked up some kind of scheme for her birthday, and it no doubt, involved Quita. Not that they'd said anything; Davida could just feel it coming.

Quita Walton, as usual, suggested the party. Davida had moaned and then graciously, she thought, declined. "I'll be forty, and there just isn't that much to celebrate."

"Girl, turning forty is not the end of the world," Melanie promised over a rushed lunch. "You might as well use it as a good excuse for a party. A few things may sag, and others are coming to an end, but trust me, it's not all bad, and life does go on."

Quita scooped cheesecake and savored it with a smile. "Yeah, girl"—she lifted her fork—"you may not look as good after forty, but you care less."

"Oh. Gee, thanks."

Anne had nodded and winked.

In her bedroom, Davida turned slightly and checked her reflection from the corner of her eye. Mel was right, whether "things" sagged or not, life did go on. "I don't care what Quita says, I'm always going to care what I look like." Moving slowly, letting her hand slide along the soft line of her hip, Davida refused to give in to the sigh she felt rising in her chest. It had been a long time since a man, even a very young one, had complimented her without an ulterior motive—just because. She turned again, thanking goodness and her mother for a lifetime of good posture.

A lifetime. Davida tried not to think enough about what the term really meant. Defining it would be a mistake. If she did, she'd have to think about Skip. His full lifetime had consisted of only forty-two years, and when it ended, it left her alone. Now here she stood, teetering on the precipice of forty herself.

"Girl, get over it," Quita kept telling her. "If life is a mountain, then forty is its summit."

Easy for her to say, she'd already survived it. Davida used her hand to press at her hip, gauging the softness she found there. Actually, it felt more like life was a clock, and forty was high noon—time for the showdown.

A swift thought made her bite her lip. No, they wouldn't do that. But the thought persisted—strongly. No. But, it was an awfully determined thought. "Lord, please don't let them send me a stripper for my birthday. And please, please, God, if they do, don't let them send him to the office!" Knowing what her friends were capable of made Davida draw a deep breath and blow out hard. "They won't," she said, with more confidence than she felt, and determinedly dismissed the thought.

. Turning back to the mirror, tilting her head, she critically pinched the skin at the top of her thigh. It was never too soon to spot check for cellulite—she'd read that in *Heart and Soul* on her last trip to the dentist. She rolled her foot to the side and looked again. Okay, from that angle, Davida Lawrence didn't think she looked all that bad. Rolling the hem of the T-shirt higher, she stopped at the band of her white cotton panties to squint at her legs. Not bad, the smooth skin the color of the Hershey's chocolate bars she'd learned to crave while carrying Destiny wasn't sagging, *yet.*

The flat of her palms pressed critically against the slight roundness of her belly—Davida continued to take stock. She pressed harder and felt the defined resistance of muscle beneath the softness—at least the sit-ups were working. She sighed. There was a time when Skip used to be able to fit her little waist right in the circle of his thumbs and fingers. She pinched a narrow band of flesh at her waist and sighed again. "Guess those days are gone."

Bending slightly, giving a simultaneous twist to her hips and back gave her a full view of her bottom—always an area for concern, and hours on the Stairmaster. Davida searched for softness, found what she was looking for, and vowed to work harder. Everything she'd read promised skating made this better. She poked again. *Apparently it works for every body, but mine. It's bigger than I want it to be,* she thought, grimacing, still poking. There was no need to let it sag until it slid down the back of her legs.

Forty was starting to look mighty scary.

Anne Laird still told horror stories over lunch about how she'd had to take to her bed for days both before and after her fortieth. She survived it, complete with an "Over the Hill" party, but not without a ton of trauma. Davida shivered. Those parties—not for her. She was running the other way if anybody brought a black balloon within fifty feet of her. She thought of Quita's love for theme parties. It would be just like Quita to have everybody dress in black and get together to celebrate the "death" of her youth.

And, if Quita did, why was she so very unprepared for it? What was it about "youth" that she was so afraid to relinquish? Or a better question still, what was it about "youth" that she was so desperate to find before she surrendered it? She'd had a wonderful marriage to a wonderful man. She had a terrific daughter, whom she wouldn't trade for anything in this world or the next. She had a lovely home, a good job, financial security. *What else is there to want?*

She was a real woman, living in the real world, and, she intended to spend her "middle-age" years just like her mother, and Aunt Wesie and Mama Lou. She was going to read, and take classes, and shop, and travel, and do lunch, and ... Yes, she was going to shop until she had everything she and Des needed and wanted.

Are you going to get a little doggie or a kitty to keep you company, to make you feel wanted when Des is older and on her way? a little voice quizzed.

I don't need those things I'm secure, she thought.

And the little voice piped in with, *Are you, really? How about the warmth and security of companionship? The touch of a warm hand on a cold night? The strong sound of a man's laughter over a silly, shared joke? The love that only a man and a woman can share?* The voice in her mind was so clear and sharp it made her look around the room for another person. The voice sounded suspiciously like her brother's.

"I have got enough on my mind, Butch. Get out of my head," she said, checking the mirror again. Didn't somebody, some philosopher or other, say that self-examination was good for the soul? She looked closer.

Her breasts, when she pulled the T-shirt tight against her chest, were still perky. They were smaller than she would have chosen, given a choice, but stood proudly at attention when she threw her shoulders back. Was that enough to qualify for a phat rating? *Phat and forty— is that really me?* Unsure, Davida squinted at her reflection, and wondered if a grown man, let alone a man who loved her, would ever seriously call her "fine" again—forget phat—and treat her the way Skip used to ... She should have asked that kid if *he* was interested.

She heard the thunder roll around her house again as she took three steps closer to the mirror. The house shook, and nervousness almost made her tiptoe. "At least something still rocks my world," she whispered. Feeling silly, almost giggling, she bent closer to the mirror to examine her face. No real wrinkles yet, but a few slight "character" lines were etched into her brow and framed her small pouty-lipped mouth—her face didn't seem to mind, though.

Lifting her brows and widening her eyes, she tried to see more clearly, but it didn't seem to help. Maybe it was the light. Somehow her face seemed younger and more tender than her age might imply. Squinting slightly at the flat oval she appeared to be, Davida reached for her glasses on the dresser. Slipping the wire frames over her ears and settling them on the bridge of the broad nose her mother still kissed every time she saw her helped a lot. No matter how young she looked in this light, there was no way that kid could have thought her young enough to be considered phat.

Maybe attractive in a mature way. She tilted her head, watching the subdued light play against the gloss of her short, sculptured haircut, and sighed. Raking both hands through her hair, she stood like she saw the girls do it in the BET videos, and swung her hips seductively from side to side. "Lady," she whispered to her reflection, "you may be turning forty, but you're still *phat.*"

The telephone rang at almost the same moment that the lightning glazed her vision, turning the world negative for a few seconds. Ensuing thunder rocked her house again. The assaulting sound was so loud and forceful it shook the walls and rattled the windows. Davida clapped her hands over her ears in reflex action. She wasn't even sure she'd heard the phone until it rang again. Sliding across the floral-sheeted queen-size bed, she snatched the phone from the bedside table, and half-listened for her daughter.

Destiny made no sound, and Davida shook her head in wonder. All this thunder and lightning, and a ringing telephone—that child could sleep through anything.

"Cookie?"

"Butch!" Aunt Wesie used to say, "Speak of the devil, and the imps appear," and while her darling brother didn't quite qualify as an imp, here he was. "I was just thinking of you!" Davida smiled with pleasure at the call from her brother. Eleven months older, he'd called her by the same pet name for as long as she could remember. "This connection is terrible," she said, "I can hardly hear you." Raising her voice with an eye on her daughter's door across the hall, she asked, "Can you hear me?"

"Yeah, I just wanted to check on y'all. Can you hear me, am I coming through?"

"Yes, I can, but where are you calling from? Are you back in town?"

"No, I'm still in Atlanta."

"Atlanta?" What was he doing there? She frowned and pushed the phone more firmly to her ear. "You sound a little funny, all this static on the line, I guess."

"Yeah, that and I've got a little sinus thing going on," he said. "It's got me a little stuffy."

"Headache? Right in the front? Like right between your eyes?"

"Yeah, how did you know?"

"That sounds just like sinus, and with all these weather changes, I'm not surprised. Have you tried goldenseal, maybe some echinacea, and . . ."

"Save the home remedies, Mom," he answered teasingly. "I've got it covered."

"Okay, if you say so. Besides, I guess that's your lady's job, anyway. Babying you and all," she teased back. "And having invoked her spirit, I guess from this point on, nothing more need be said."

Glenn knew exactly how she felt about pretentious, flaky, wanna-be-a-socialite LaDonna Crane.

After a too brief pause, his voice came flatly over the sizzling phone line. "That's over. I'm taking care of myself these days."

"Really?" Davida loved her brother too much to pretend sorrow or other emotions she could never feel for the woman who treated him with the same cavalier regard she used for her eel skin purses and discount-store shoes. LaDonna, the woman who hoped to parlay Barbie doll looks and Glenn Morrison's St. Louis city political and legal connections into a real life, was a grade-A witch. Davida shivered. Glenn truly deserved better, he just didn't seem to know it—until now. "Over?" she asked.

"Done. In the wind, history, over and out."

Thank you! If she clapped her hands, he'd hear her, but she'd known LaDonna would blow it one day. She'd known it couldn't last forever. She couldn't fool him forever, not the way things were going. *Thank God, it didn't last forever!* If she'd ever had to refer to that woman as her sister-in-law . . . Ooh! Or see her over one more Thanksgiving or Christmas dinner, sitting there acting, like the Queen of Sheba . . .

Davida settled on the corner of her bed, and drew her knee under her. It wasn't fair for her to be so glad that Glenn was out of that dismally one-sided relationship. She pulled the Browns shirt over the bend of her knee, and tucked the slipping phone more tightly against her chin. "I'm sorry, Butch. You know, I know how it is to be left alone. Especially when you had no way of knowing it was coming. What happened?"

"Long story."

"Like, you think *I* wouldn't have time to listen?" *Weren't you there for me when I lost Skip? Weren't you there every time I thought that his death was my own?* Unconsciously, her hand folded over her own strong heart, and she sighed. Forty-three was terribly young to die from anything, especially a heart attack, she thought. And no one, including Skip, had seen it coming, but her brother had been there to help her through her loss. Now he deserved her support. "Come on, Butch, you know better than that—tell me what happened."

The edge of an almost bitter laugh preceded his words. "You could say I finally saw her, really saw her for what she was."

"Oh, that's telling me a lot, Butch. She doesn't deserve you and she never did. As a matter of fact . . ."

"I appreciate your loyalty, Cookie, but you're prejudiced. It didn't help that this mess involved an intricate series of lies and another man. I guess I got so tied up in work, I didn't see what I didn't want to see. Being emotionally available and sensitive can wear a man out, you know." He paused again when he heard her breathy, wordless reply. "No, don't go, 'I told you so,' not now, Cookie. Save it for when I'm feelin' better, okay? I don't feel like trying to defend myself right now."

Davida made a face on her end of the phone. He did sound a little tired and careworn. No, she amended, he actually sounded ground down by life and rotten ol' LaDonna Crane. He sounded a lot like he really did need a bit of a break, right then. "I wasn't going to say that," she improvised. "I was going to say, if you want to come and spend some time with us, maybe for my birthday," she hinted broadly, "you're more than welcome. It would be good to have some adult conversation around here, for a change."

"Nah, I think I'll just hang out at home and lick my wounds."

"That's why I'll always love you, Butchie, you're so emphatically pitiful when it comes to women."

He sniffed, as if to prove his defenseless status. "I'm just a gentleman, is all. On top of that, I guess when a man reaches our age, he wants the security of knowing where he stands and who he stands with." He sniffed again. "I didn't want to jump to stupid conclusions about my lady, not even with evidence, but you know, there are limits . . . anyway, what's happening with you? You're not getting whatever's going around are you? You sound a little funny to me, too."

"Not me. Guess this is just the end result of a long day of toiling in the IRS salt mines." That, and turning forty! A series of electronic sizzles and pops made her wince and hold the receiver a few inches away from her ear. *Boy, what a storm,* she thought. *All this electricity, no wonder Butchie sounds so funny!*

"In the *what* mines?" he asked when the noise faded. "Sounded like you said, 'IRS.' "

"Yeah, I did."

"Why're you doing your taxes now?" He sounded genuinely puzzled. "Cookie, you didn't file for another one of those extensions, did you?"

"Butch," Davida said slowly, wondering what the name of *this* game was. "Come on, Glenn. You know I work for the Internal Revenue Service, been there for fifteen years. Right downtown in the Robert A. Young Building."

"Renee, I can hardly hear you. When did you start working for the IRS? . . . *Did you call me Glenn?*"

Static crackled through the phone line again, immediately followed by a seemingly sympathetic, neon-bright flash outside Davida's windows. Confused, she pulled the phone from her ear and blinked at it. *My brother has lost his mind!* The thought made one heck of a lot of sense right then; shoot, the man was acting as though he didn't know his own name.

"I thought I heard you call me Glenn," he repeated through the ragged remnants of static. His voice, a slightly roughened baritone, suddenly came clearly through the line. Davida immediately detected two things: his voice was warm and comfortable—and not at all familiar!

"Start over, Renee. What were you telling me about the IRS?"

Davida gasped when she finally remembered to breathe. *"Renee?"* There was a long, blank moment. Finally, "This isn't Renee, is it?"

"No." Davida wondered how she got the word out without stuttering. "I guess this means you're not my brother, Glenn, are you?"

"Oh, man." The voice on the other end of the line groaned. "Man, this is seriously embarrassing. I am so sorry, I must have dialed the wrong number. I thought you were my sister . . ."

"Renee." Davida hid the lower half of her face behind her hand. "I thought you were my brother . . ."

"Glenn." His low laugh made her smile in spite of herself. "I was trying to call 555-7583, uh, area code 314—did I even get close?"

"Close, and who knows, maybe it was the storm." She ducked just a little to peek through the lacy curtains at her bedroom windows— the storm had eased into a steady glittering sheen. I'm 3857, but you did get the right area code for St. Louis."

"I got this all wrong." He laughed. "Then, I talked to you all that time . . . and it wasn't until you said you worked for the IRS. Man, Renee is a school teacher, wanted to be one for as long as I can remember . . . and when you said IRS"—he laughed again—"I really did think you were Renee, and I don't even know your name."

"And remember, I thought you were Glenn," she echoed, her smile widening, "and I don't know your name either." Too funny! Davida shook her head at the absurdity. This was one of those things you saw on television, something from *The Outer Limits* or *The Twilight Zone.* The women she knew would never believe this one, she decided.

"Maybe it's better that way—gives you a kind of freedom, don't you think?"

"A freedom to what? Talk to a stranger about things that we just happen to have in common?"

"Sure. I don't suppose your brother lives in Atlanta, does he?" he asked, chuckling.

Davida's laugh chimed musically over the now clear phone line. "No, he lives here in St. Louis, but he travels a lot. This month, he's in Toronto, and he spent the past two months in St. Croix." *Like this man could care,* she told herself. He was calling long distance, trying to get in touch with his sister, and here she was holding him up. "If you dial the operator, maybe you can get them to connect your call correctly and credit you for this call.''

''Yeah,'' he said slowly. ''I guess I could do that. Uh, well, I guess I should try Renee again.''

''Yes, is she expecting your call?'' *Dumb*.

''Probably not, but she's always after me to stay in touch. I just wanted to touch base with her, and . . .'' Davida heard his breathing thicken as he shifted position. He seemed to be trying to find a way to continue the call, and odd as it seemed, so was she. ''. . . and it was good to hear a caring voice. I guess your husband will be wondering who you're talking to for so long.''

''I'm not . . . he's not . . .'' She took a deep breath. ''I'm a widow.''

''Oh, I'm sorry.''

The awkward silence they shared was deafening. *I hate when people say ''I'm sorry,''* Davida thought. How did you respond? Why were they sorry about something that was out of their control? And if they could have controlled it . . . well, how many of them . . . ? She closed her eyes and rejected the thought as unworthy even as it occurred to her that it might be easier to say she was divorced or separated instead of widowed, but that would have made healing next to impossible. After all, there was no chance for reconciliation: Skip was gone forever. And this was an awfully nice man, he hadn't meant anything wrong. ''It's okay,'' she said.

''I only meant it must be hard, sometimes.''

''You know, Des and I have managed together. Being together, sometimes, that makes it easier.'' She hoped she sounded strong.

''And Des is . . . ?''

''Oh! I forgot you don't really know me.'' Davida laughed, thinking, *It just feels like I know you . . . really know you.* ''Des is my daughter, Destiny.'' Hearing the tone of her voice brought her up short. Was she flirting with this man? Davida had to wonder, since the skills and responses were rusty—it had been that long since she'd really dealt with a man outside of work. The few dates she'd had since losing Skip had been disappointing, to say the least—men who invited her to dinner and thought she owed them sex in exchange for food. Men who figured a young widow needed intimate charities, and were far less than gracious when they found out otherwise.

But, this man was different. She could feel it right through the phone lines. He didn't seem hungry, or needy. He seemed funny and downright charming. Maybe that was why she was finding this wrong number call so entertaining, and why she was so reluctant to let go of this man she only knew as a voice in the night. 'Cause she was hard up for adult companionship, or because she might never hear from him again?

"You have a daughter, must be nice."

"Oh, believe me, there are some days when 'nice' is an understatement. She's good company, but eight-year-olds can be a real challenge, and Des is eight going on twenty-nine."

He laughed, remembering his own sister at eight. Renee had been funny, for sure. "I'd like to have kids someday." Maybe a son to shoot baskets with, one who would watch him while he shaved, and a little girl who would adore him without reserve. How bad could that be?

"No kids of your own?"

"Not so far," he said. "I've got a nine-year-old, almost ten-year-old nephew I borrow from time to time. Call me old-fashioned, but the way I figure it, I need to get married first, then have the kids."

After you work out that girlfriend problem, right? Davida was glad the words stayed safely in her mind.

"Are you, uh, seeing anyone right now?"

"Why?" she asked flippantly. "Are you going to ask me out on another one of these long-distance dates?" His laugh was delightful, and Davida brought her hand to her own cheek in imitation of the touch he might have offered had he been there.

"Not quite. I was just thinking that you sound far too nice, and way too young, to be alone. Maybe you should give some lucky guy a chance. We can't all be toads, can we?"

"What makes you think I'm alone?" Davida challenged.

"Something in your voice. Don't get me wrong, I'm not calling you some kind of hermit or anything like that. You just don't sound like you let a lot of people go tramping through your life. You sound"—he thought before continuing—"You sound very private. Even private people need to make contact with others from time to time."

For half a second, Davida remembered the kid who called her *phat.* Now this stranger was telling her to get out into the world. Aunt Wesie always said, "When advice comes pouring down on you, there's a reason." Maybe she was right, because enough of it sure seemed to be coming her way, lately. Rather than taking offense at the unsolicited advice, Davida smiled again. What could be so bad about a man who could make her smile so much?

"Maybe I am." She bit at her lip and struggled to find a way to change the subject. "So, what do you do when you're not dialing wrong numbers?"

He chuckled into the receiver. "Oh, I play a little ball, run a lot, and follow the Braves on TV. How 'bout you—when you're not 'mommy-ing,' that is."

Davida grinned, then screwed up her face: turnabout was fair play. "Inline skating."

"You're one of those maniacs with the helmets, and the nine-wheeled skates, and all the pads, doing ninety miles an hour down the street?"

"Guilty, except I don't go much faster than about seventy."

"Seventy?" He laughed. "That's a good one. Anything else?"

Thinking of her work in the gym, and all that time on the StairMaster, Davida shook her head. There was no way she was going to admit having to work overtime on her butt, and she was sure not going to tell it to a stranger! "That's about it," she said sweetly.

"About it," he echoed.

"Yes' " she repeated, feeling their conversational thread fray.

"Well," he said, "I guess I'd better try Renee again. It was nice talking with you, and I'm sorry about dialing the wrong number."

Outside her window, night had settled, the remaining rain leaving just enough mist and softness to make her wishful, and Davida knew she wasn't ready to be left alone—not by this nice man with the voice that made her smile. "Please. Please, don't apologize. I actually . . . I enjoyed it," she admitted.

"Me, too." He paused, and the phone line crackled lightly, reminding them both of the felicity of the call. "Are you sure you don't want to tell me your name?"

Defenses she'd almost forgotten she possessed rose to bind her lips and Davida shook her head. "I don't think so."

"Should I call you, 'Cookie'?"

"Only if you have to, but don't expect me to call you 'Butch,' because I'm not going to. I don't think the names are necessary."

"Well, if that's the way you want it." She could picture him shrugging it off, a kind of "what the heck" gesture, what was the harm in his asking. She'd done the worst she could do, she'd said no. " 'Bye, then."

"Don't forget to try the goldenseal and echinacea," she said hurriedly—he still deserved to be taken care of properly, after all, he was *someone's* brother.

"Thanks, I will. 'Bye, again."

" 'Bye." She listened for the disconnecting click, and reluctantly replaced the receiver. Musing, she sat with her hand on the still-warm phone, wondering if it was just her imagination. Had he really seemed as unwilling to hang up as she was? Standing, she pulled the covers back. A quick check on Des, and she'd turn in herself.

The phone rang again.

"I had one last thought," the now-familiar voice said.

Davida smiled. "Really? What is it?"

"Your brother's still dating that troublesome person, the one you don't like."

Her mouth opened in surprise. She'd completely forgotten mentioning anything to do with LaDonna. "You're right," she groaned.

"Hang in there, she's bound to shoot herself in the foot if she's as bad as you think she is. Then, you'll get to have your I told you so. I know my sister's going to thoroughly enjoy hers."

Davida was still laughing when the call ended as abruptly as it began.

CHAPTER TWO

Marcus knew he was fighting a losing battle right from the start. Concentration never stood a chance, even as he moved the new set of pens across his drawing board for the fourth time. His roving eyes wandered to the phone, still lying on the gray and blue patterned futon cover where he'd tossed it.

"C'mon, Marc, you can do this" he admonished himself. "Focus, man, focus." Jamming the tip of the charcoal stick against the manila sheet, he sketched lines, and watched the familiar face of Bro'Man appear. That was better, the art work was comforting, even if the artist wasn't in high creative mode this evening. If Bro'Man had a face, then maybe there was motion and a story to go with it, and Marcus Benton had plans for that story. He was hoping that Bro'Man's adventures would secure the funding he needed to mass-produce and market the comics.

Bro'Man was a childhood fantasy, nursed through adulthood. A big, strong, black, do-good, righteous talking superhero, Bro'Man had thus far garnered praise from educators, churches, entertainers, and most importantly from J.B., his nine-year-old nephew. Praise, but not a lot of cash, but Marcus Benton wasn't worried. In his heart of hearts, Marc knew that if J.P. considered Bro'Man, along with his friends and foes, "fly," then Saturday morning cartoons and action figures wouldn't be far behind.

It was just a matter of time.

So, Marcus Benton needed to work on this project with a vengeance—and get over his urge to place a certain long-distance phone call. He already knew the call would be totally inappropriate. To make a telephone call was to invite himself into a place where he was not necessarily wanted, and she had a right to her privacy. Doing what he wanted would mean a call to someone he'd never met, whose name he didn't know, whose face he'd never seen, whose habits he didn't know, and whose number he couldn't forget. Her voice had haunted him for a week.

Aware that his hand was still moving, Marc looked down at his loose sketch. Bro'Man had somehow gotten to a phone and was busily dialing. There was a broad smile on the cartoon man's face while he waited for his call to be answered. The corners of his broad lips turned up, showing the shine of his teeth. "Why fight the feeling?" he seemed to be saying, though Marc hadn't given him the line. Marc blinked at the page—he didn't remember giving Bro'Man the phone, either.

But, *why fight the feeling, indeed,* Marc wondered. It was not like it was working. He moved to the futon and scooped up his own phone, and dialed. She said she was widowed, but that didn't mean she didn't have a man in her life. What if she . . . ? The phone was already ringing in his ear when Marc realized he already had a plan and knew the drill: if a man answered, he would just hang up.

"Hello?"

It wasn't a man—definitely not a man. He congratulated himself when she answered on the first ring. He had enough time to hope that that was a good sign, even as he fell into the sweetness of her voice. Her voice had tones like rich whipped cream, feminine and breathy. Satisfying, with just enough throaty authority to wrinkle a man's imagination, and he savored her one word. He closed his eyes and tried to see a face that matched the voice he had waited so long to hear. That she'd be attractive, he had no doubt, but his artist's eye couldn't conceive of a collection of features that would do her justice.

"Hello?"

"I don't suppose you'd believe I dialed the wrong number again?" He looked at the floor, jammed his hand into the pocket of his jeans, and hoped she wouldn't laugh in his face.

She paused, and he held his breath. "If you did, we need to enroll you in a remedial telephone class."

She didn't laugh. He started to breathe again. She didn't sound annoyed at all—in fact, she sounded rather pleased. Marc liked the idea of giving her pleasure. Settling back on the stool at his workstation, he was happier than he could have imagined. "Would that be a class *you* teach?"

"Why, yes. As a matter of fact, I've been quite successful in teaching five-year-olds to dial both local and long-distance calls."

The casual banter felt good. "How's life in the fast lane?"

"You mean my skates? Fine." On her end, Davida checked the hall, and assured Destiny's light was out, she settled on the tufted chenille–covered chaise in front of her bedroom windows and looked out. Her reflection, grayed and half-transparent against the night, smiled back at her, and she felt her skin warm. She felt like a woman with a secret. "Your voice sounds much better," she said.

He cleared his throat confidently. "Yes, thanks. I'm feeling much better, now. That ikky . . . ekky . . . that stuff you suggested, it worked real well. Tasted like uck, but it did the trick."

"You actually used it, I'm touched. I usually can't convince Glenn to try as much as a cough drop."

"Maybe he already knows how that stuff tastes . . . uck."

"How kind of you to call and tell me that." The woman paused delicately, then asked, "Is that why you called?"

Davida heard the clock on her bedside table tick off the passing moments.

"I don't know," her caller finally admitted. "I just, well, I just enjoyed our conversation last week." He swiped a hand across his face, and was struck by inspiration. "I was a little worried about you," he improvised.

"Me?"

"You said you were alone, and there was the storm, the phone lines were so messed up and all." Okay, so it was weak, but you had to work with what you had—the army called it "appropriate technology". "Did you, ah, ever get to talk to your brother?"

That was a slick "about-face," Davida thought, unsure of how to treat his concern. "No," she said, "not yet."

"Hhmm." His hum of concern was a deep-throated rumble in her ear. "You know, the nice thing about talking to a stranger, especially long distance, is that you don't have to worry about what you say. You probably won't ever meet me."

Her silence expressed her surprise. "Probably not," she said slowly. "I don't even know your name."

"No, Boo, you don't." His voice phrased an intimately playful invitation, a seductively masculine challenge, something she hadn't known since Skip, and it made her sit a little straighter. "I don't know yours either, if it makes you feel better, and maybe I can offer you a change in conversation that an eight-year-old can't. So, if you feel like talking, now's your chance."

He called me Boo. Davida ran a hand over her bare arm, and shivered. *He called me Boo and invited me to talk. He's too good to be true.* His words sounded too much like what she wanted to hear—

almost as if she'd written a script for him to follow. "Do you remember everything I said last week?"

He did. Idly moving the sponges he sometimes used for washing backgrounds, Marc would have sworn he recalled every word, every nuance of their conversation. How could he forget when he replayed that all-too-short, too-sweet-to-forget conversation over and over again in his mind? "Some," he replied. "Whatever you have on your mind, I'd like to hear it."

Holding the telephone between her cheek and her shoulder, Davida wondered what might possibly interest her caller. *I'm not going to tell him I've started dying my hair!* Though it was the first thought to cross her mind. Her eyes shifted as she thought. When her considering hum stroked his ear, Marc happily realized she was still listening, not hanging up. "I don't know what to say," she said softly.

Refusing to let the conversation die, he thought quickly. "Talk to me like we've known each other for years, like I was an old friend, or . . . talk to me like I was your brother. Tell me something you'd tell Glenn. Something you find funny."

"I can't think of anything offhand."

"Tell me something you've already told him, then. Something, . . . oh, I don't know . . ."

"Something," she echoed. "Something . . . oh, I know! I already told you I work for the IRS, right?"

"Right." Marc liked the lift to her voice as she marshaled her thoughts.

"I work in telephone assistance, and I manage a group of fifteen people who are charged with answering taxpayer questions. On the whole, they're very efficient and professional—they know their jobs, and they do them. Well, this morning I walk in and Pam Britton has this really funny look on her face. She's talking slowly and fanning her hand at me, trying to get my attention. When I get closer, I can hear her saying something like, 'I'm sorry ma'am, but this department doesn't handle that.' And then she fans at me again.

"I stand there by her desk, trying to figure out what's going on for, like five full minutes. Finally, Pam formally refers the call to me, and I pick up, identify myself, and try to get to the bottom of the situation. Turns out the call is from the governor's office. It seems a little old lady called us to get her cat out of a tree a couple of weeks ago, and not only did we fail to render appropriate service, but the silly cat ran away from home once it got out of the tree. In my most professional tones, I asked why this call had been referred to us in the first place." She paused, then said, "Ask me why."

"Okay. Why?

"It was our job," Davida said pleasantly, "because we're listed in the telephone book under 'problem resolution.' "

"Under . . ." He burst into laughter, and when she joined in, he laughed all the more. "You spend a lot of time on the phone," he said when his laughter simmered to a chuckle. "You ever get the really angry people?"

"All the time. Irate taxpayers are proof that you can't fool around with people's money indiscriminately. When I first took this job . . ." She blew out a pressure releasing blast of air. "When I first took this job, fifteen years ago, I was pretty naive and took it all very personally, and I had hurt feelings all the time. Skip nursed me through so many tears, so many nights . . . Thank goodness it's like they say, 'time heals all wounds.' I have some distance, some perspective, now."

Skip. Marc snatched the name out of the air, like some kind of verbal frisbee. Her deceased husband's name was Skip. Wondering briefly how a grown man got and kept a name like Skip, Marc concluded he was probably a jock who continued to bask in his own former glory well past high school and college, and he didn't like him very much. He wondered briefly if the woman on the other end of the line had once been a cheerleader, complete with short skirt and pom-poms, for the man named Skip.

Nah. They didn't have cheerleaders for sports like tennis and cricket, did they? Those were the kinds of games guys with names like Skip and Chaz and Biff played. Nothing manly like football, where they have cheerleaders. Right?

Nah, I'll bet he never played football, or basketball, or anything like that, Marcus simmered, remembering his own glory days as a tight end, and then as a small forward. You grew up, took the lessons of group sports forward, and got an adult name. You didn't hang on to nicknames like "Skip" all your life, unless you were some kind of egomaniacal . . .

That's jealousy talking, man. Marc gave himself a little shake, clamped down on the mean thought, and tried to check what passed for his own reality. Okay, so it might be a little envy in action, he realized. His ego was healthy enough to accept the fact that maybe Skip hadn't been a bad person, even if she did know him first. Marc wished again that he knew what she looked like, this very self-possessed lady, who had once been married to Skip. Had she loved him? Everybody who got married didn't necessarily fall in love, did they?

No. Of course, they didn't. People got married for all kinds of reasons. People got married for security, for companionship, and some just because they had nothing better to do. *But not Boo. She wouldn't have married for any of those reasons,* he promised himself, knowing it with an unspeakable certainty, and realizing something else at the same time. He wanted to believe she was the kind of ''one-man woman'' who would marry for love. He almost laughed out loud—he really wanted to believe.

Obviously, she was bright, poised, and deservedly well respected, she also had a great sense of humor. She deserved to fall in love. *Bet she's real sexy, too.* Marc nudged the errant thought away, but it refused to go quietly. *Talk about being judgmental,* he scolded himself. *Who told you you had a right?* Something about her though—he couldn't quite put his finger on it, but there was something beyond her sultry voice and throaty laughter that was so attractive it carried over the phone lines.

''Perspective is important,'' she said.

''Do guys ever make passes at you over the phone?''

''What?''

His mouth snapped shut, and his eyes rolled skyward. He couldn't believe he'd actually said the words out loud. Closing his eyes, he tried to regroup. ''It's just that you have such a sensational telephone voice, and you seem so competent. I'd guess that the males you encounter are bowled over without ever meeting you—in the flesh, so to speak.''

She sucked her teeth. ''How very hormonal.''

''Don't you mean 'just like a man'?''

''We-e-ll,'' she drawled the word deliberately, making him laugh again. ''I'm going to give *you* the benefit of the doubt.''

''Man, Boo,'' he moaned. ''Now, you *really* sound like Renee.''

Davida didn't know whether or not to be insulted. She finally took the high road, and decided to be flattered. Why be insulted? He likes his sister—she thought. ''Is that a good thing?''

''Most times, but . . . ooh, when she decides she knows better . . .'' The masculine voice on the other end of the line went up several octaves, faking a passable alto. ''You've just come out of a bad relationship, and here you are on the telephone with a strange woman, asking her just any little thing you think you want to know. Like you've got a right! Just like a man—dumped on, burned to a crisp, but you'd walk through fire to get to someone like Halle Berry. In a heartbeat! Umph!'' he imitated.

''That's supposed to be your sister? How right would she be about your Halle Berry fixation?'' Surprised at her own boldness, Davida bit her lip and was glad this man didn't know her name.

''Actually, I prefer my women taller, and with fuller figures. But, that's okay, 'cause see, I figure I've got normally active hormones, so when there's something to see, I look. How are yours?''

''My whats?''

''Your hormones, of course. You didn't say how long since, you, ah ..." The pause, though narrow and indelicate, spoke volumes. "Anyway, you couldn't have sworn off men altogether."

Pulling the phone from her ear, Davida stared at it, then shook her head and pressed the instrument back in place. "I haven't sworn off men . . . at all," she said, "and my hormones are perfectly fine, thank you very much. But, we were talking about you and this woman your sister believes you were so crazy about that you were ready to . . . to do what with?"

Kenya Witherspoon? For a while there, I'd have tried to walk on water if she'd asked me to, he thought. But he couldn't have made himself say it, if his life had depended on it. Feeling caught, on his end, Marc ran a hand across his close-cropped hair and reached for one of his pens. Bro'Man suddenly looked like he could use a little more definition. The pen in Marc's hand moved quickly. A thin line of sweat now gleamed on Bro'Man's strong forehead. "I have to admit that when I met her I wasn't looking for commitment or anything like that. It was the falling in love that took me by surprise."

"Did you fall in love or did you fall in lust?"

He grimaced when he thought of Kenya, a woman who was nowhere near as pretty on the inside as she was on the outside. "Lust," he admitted, "but . . ."

"She was gorgeous," the woman said flatly. "She looked good at your side, knew a few interesting bedtime tricks, said all the things you wanted to hear at the beginning, and to top it all off, she made you hot from across the room."

"Whoa! Wait a minute, Boo." This woman sounded like she knew Kenya personally, and had a full accounting of her measure. Would she listen if he tried to tell her that what he had with Kenya was never really under his control, and that he'd learned a lot about love in a relationship from what his affair with Kenya had lacked? No, this woman would probably accuse him of thinking with the wrong part of his anatomy. "Like I told you before, she's a part of my past. And you don't let the past tangle up around your feet and trip you in the future."

His hand covered the phone, allowing a small private space for deep breathing. Would this woman understand if he told her that Kenya was too much of the wrong kind of woman for a man who had finally learned that his heart and mind agreed—a woman of emotional and moral integrity was worth more than a stereotypical *babe* any day of the week? He wished for the words to explain what it was he really wanted, then held back. That, he decided, was too much to learn from a stranger on the phone.

She sighed and he heard the slight press of her lips as she prepared to speak. "My Aunt Wesie always says, 'be careful what you ask for, because you just might get it.' "

"She's a regular fountain of information."

"She's my aunt, and I love her very much."

"Okay." Knowing instinctively that he'd somehow stepped into the deep end of this conversation, Marc felt he had to be very careful, instead he said what was on his mind. "I guess Aunt Wesie is right then, and that means that what you're really looking for is a reasonably well educated man with a good heart and sincere intent. Nothing else matters to you. Good looks, deep pockets, and smooth talk mean nothing at all to you—am I right?"

"Please. I'm not asking for anything, besides we are not talking about me, and I am not trying to judge you."

"Really? So you say—I have the sneaking suspicion that you're tall, right?"

"What's height got to do with anything?" She had no intention of admitting that she stood five nine in her stocking feet.

"You've got that royal attitude that tall people automatically assume. Kind of noblesse oblige." When she didn't answer, he went on without her. "Tall people always look down on the rest of us average mortals. How do you feel about Munchkins and Gary Coleman?"

"I think Munchkins are adorable, and even with gray hair, Gary Coleman is still as cute as he can be."

"Cute." The man on the other end of the phone groaned miserably. "See, I had a feeling you'd say that." Marc closed his eyes, and tried to swallow around the lump of pride in his throat. He attempted to ignore the discomfort her words roused in him.

"So," she hazarded, "I take it cute is not a favorite word?"

"Definitely *not* a favorite word," he said heavily.

"So, tell me why—since we don't have a need for secrets . . ."

He drew a deep breath, and then another. "My first serious relationship, you know, the one where you start thinking of putting something aside for the future, and children, and stuff like that. For me, it was when I was a senior in college. It started out great, then she dumped me because I was too short. I confess, I did a lot of weeping and wailing over that one. She looked just like Robin Givens, too." He sighed at the svelte memory.

"Nnnoo. Why would she dump you because you were too short? Was Miss Thing suffering from some kind of sensory deprivation? Didn't she notice how tall you were when you two started dating?"

"Yeah," he admitted glumly, "but she thought I was *cute*. It was a part of my charm. Then I guess her sorors started teasing her . . . In heels, she was about four inches taller than me." He hummed a tuneless comment, then continued. "Being Homecoming Queen made it all too clear that as far as she was concerned, I was just one little joker. She dumped me for a six foot four inch basketball player.''

"What a pig," Davida crowed.

"Hey, it's the potential earning power of the NBA and genetic favoritism—but I ain't mad with her, I'm still *cute*. At least she knew what she wanted, and being dumped is better than being divorced. Right?''

"Right, but it's still awfully lonely, isn't it?''

It was because she was a widow, and still missing her husband— that's why she zoned in on loneliness like that. It was because she was so familiar with it. Missing someone, maybe even feeling a little betrayed and abandoned by someone you've planned a life with, sworn to love forever, brought a child into the world with—that had to leave a hole in your life. It had to leave a wound in your soul that could only be healed with love and tenderness, not a breezy, no strings affair. *I only called her to talk,* he reminded himself. *It's not like I'm the cure, or setting up some kind of psychological assignation.*

"I guess," the woman said, "we've all fallen for the wrong person for the wrong reasons at least once in our lives. Sometimes we do it with open eyes, closed hearts, and a pocketful of good intentions and protection against pregnancy and disease.''

"Is that a hormone-driven observation?''

"Nooo," she drew the word out so that it sounded like a child's wish. "The important thing is to understand forgiveness, for ourselves and others. That and the fact that the wrong person doesn't make us less—only we have that power over ourselves.''

"You ever do anything like that?''

"What? Date a Homecoming Queen? Never!''

"Don't dodge the question." He laughed.

"What do you mean, 'dodge the question'?''

"I mean, don't do the 'girl thing', don't claim a 'woman's right to change her mind'.''

"You know, that is a woman's prerogative," Davida offered sweetly.

"Yeah, right," Marc snorted. "Shame on you, Boo. After all we've shared, all we've talked about, you want to change the rules?''

"Change the rules? Why not? We're adults, we can be flexible.'' Davida lowered her lashes and held the telephone closer, flirting across the telephone lines separating them.

Marc's hand cupped the lower half of his face, a finger curling across his lips, barely concealing his grin. "Why not," he echoed. "Because every time we talk, I learn a little more about you, and it's not fair if you hide and I don't." He let his voice go warm, low and confidential. "I like getting to know you, and I want to know more. So, come on, Boo. You can tell me."

And, she wanted to. Davida fought the urge to curl up and purr like a kitten, refusing to admit or access the satisfaction just talking to this man always seemed to give her. "We've been talking for quite a while now," she challenged, "and you've been sincere in everything you've said to me? Every time we talked?"

Hundreds of miles away, Marcus Benton nodded as much for her as for himself. "Every time, Boo." He could feel her smile and wished for about the ninetieth time that he could actually see it; the change in her mouth, the curve of her lips, with his own eyes. Settling more comfortably into his own body, Marc leaned farther back on his futon to ask again, 'You ever do anything like that?"

"Like what?"

"Boo." His voice held enough accusation to make her lift her eyes to the ceiling.

"Be with the wrong person because it was easier . . . because it seemed better than being alone?" He hummed assent, and on her end, Davida paused, then pulled in a deep breath.

"Actually, I did, once," she admitted. "Almost. He was an old friend of Skip's. They'd been teammates in high school and college—football, basketball, stuff like that, and I guess he just felt . . . he just felt comfortable to me. Our first date was . . . it went pretty well. Maybe that was what led him to expect more."

"More?"

Clearing her throat gave Davida a moment to chose proper wording. "Let's just say that our second date ended when I had to pull my clothes together, and he was left nursing a lot of lower body swelling." She paused again, long enough to draw a deep breath and press her hand to her own warmly flushing cheek. "And praise Jesus I'm never going to see you, because I absolutely *never* talk like this with people I know!"

"It's kind of fun to talk to a stranger though, isn't it, Boo? To not have to guard your words or worry about what someone else thinks of you, kind of freeing?"

"You know"—her laughter chimed lightly in his ear—"it is fun. Think maybe we've stumbled onto something here? Dial a stranger and give vent to all your deeply secret thoughts. We could call it . . ." She hesitated. She had almost given him her name—part of it, anyway. "We could call it something alliterative and sexy and provocative, something like 'Lady Lust Listens,' " she covered quickly.

He chuckled. "Sounds like a winner Boo, but *I* called *you*, remember?"

"You're right, so I guess we'd have to name it after you—fair's fair. How about''—she dropped her voice in seductive imitation of the late-night sirens she'd seen on television—'' 'The Lusty Live Listening Man Line'?''

He hooted on the other end of the line. ''Too long, but you're really hung up on that 'lust' thing, aren't you?''

''Okay, okay—so the idea needs work. Have you got any more sensual secrets, or deep-seated anger, or heavy frustrations you want to get out of your system while you have me on the line—just to make this call worth while?''

''Not tonight, and between you and me, I don't think there's any chance we'll ever replace the phone sex lines.'' Pleased at the smile he detected in her voice, he was glad he'd made the first phone call by mistake. *E-mail will never replace the amazing beauty of a woman's voice,* he thought. ''This call was interesting, to say the least. I think I got my money's worth.''

''By the way, did your sister get to make her, I-told-you-so speech?''

The memory of Renee's extensive rant made him cringe. ''Oh yeah, Boo. She explained in intricate and explicit detail how she'd known from the very beginning that I would arrive at my present sorry state— it was just a matter of time, she said. And hadn't she warned me, she said, that I would find myself having a pity-party if I didn't take her advice? It didn't help that I told her I didn't remember.

''Believe me, that really set her off. She went on and on for more than fifteen minutes, talking about how she just knew I should know better and what was *really* good for me. She said awful things, like when was I going to figure out what it took to make me happy. Then she had to add insult to injury. Why, she wanted to know, why didn't I let *her* find a good woman for me?'' He made a gagging sound into the phone.

''So,'' the feminine voice teased, ''why don't you?''

Bro'Man was now dressed in the casual clothing of his alter ego, and heading off to his real job. Marc continued his sketching as he talked. ''Renee got married her second year in college, and she and George are, like, the original loving couple. Now, she's convinced that her mission in life is to get me married off, and she has to save me from myself—long distance.''

''She loves you and wants to see you happy,'' Davida said, thinking of her own brother, Glenn—a happy, LaDonna Crane-less, Glenn.

''The last woman Renee hooked me up with had the IQ of rice, and the one before that had dollar signs in her eyes and hot wings on her lips. Then the one before that was *really* bad. She . . .''

''I get it. I get it.''

''Oh, no, Boo. I've got to tell you, the worst was when she . . .''

''Really, I get it—I truly feel your pain.'' She was laughing. ''Butch has had almost the exact same complaints with the women I've tried to pair him up with—even though, if he would just give them half a chance . . ."

"Must be a brother thing, pardon the pun. I keep telling her to let me do it myself, but Renee just seems to be driven. It's like she has this compulsion . . ."

Davida nodded to herself. "That sounds an awful lot like an I-told-you-so."

"No, no, no, Boo. I wouldn't even try to go there, it's not worth the ultimate humiliation—for any of the parties involved." He took a deep breath and spoke from deep within his chest. "Brothers, you see, are more noble than sisters. From the high aspect of our masculine superiority, we do not feel the need to rub your noses in it when we're right."

"Yeah, 'right,' indeed." The woman's chuckle came across the line as a puff of air. "If you only had a clue as to how many times *he's* gloated when he found out he was right and I was wrong."

"Ah, well," the man sighed into the phone. "There's one in every bunch, and I guess I can't help every brother out. Anyway . . ." He leaned back on his stool and stretched broadly, feeling the pull deep in his lower back. "It's getting late."

Knowing that the call was drawing to a close made Davida reluctant to even look at the small china and brass bedside clock. When she did, she was surprised at the late hour. Well past eleven in St. Louis, and he was calling from Atlanta. She did quick mental calculations; he was on Eastern Standard time, and on his time, it was past midnight. Somehow, even knowing that she had to be up at six in the morning, it was still nice to have a man who called you Boo on the phone, since she didn't have one in her bed—even if she didn't know his name.

"Guess I'd better let you go."

"Yeah." The word came out as an embarrassing sigh. "These calls are going to add up, and you're going to have a pretty healthy telephone bill this month," she said.

"That's okay, I make a pretty healthy salary," he admitted.

It didn't surprise her. Intuitively, she'd known he would be successful at whatever he did. She didn't ask him to amplify his statement.

"I guess that might have sounded like bragging. I didn't mean it to."

His humility was endearing, and Davida felt her lips twitch in response.

"It's just that, well, we didn't grow up poor, but my mother had a real thing about what she called, 'paucity of spirit.' "

The twitch rippled across her lips. "Our mothers must be kindred spirits. My mother still lectures and cautions my brother and me about cheapness . . .''

"Of the soul," her caller finished. "Just based on my experience, I have to say I think there might be a good bit of truth to the idea. You ever notice that people who are cheap monitarily—and I mean cheap, not thrifty, because there is a difference . . .''

"I know exactly what you mean. People who are cheap with their money are cheap with their emotions, their souls, and their time." Davida nodded agreement in her St. Louis home. "Sounds like we were raised a lot alike."

"It does," the man on the other end of the line seconded. "Would you mind, . . . I mean, would it be okay if I called you again some-time—just to talk?"

Licking her lips bought her a few seconds to think. Call her again? No, of course he couldn't. That was beyond unthinkable. They didn't know each other and had no real plans to change the situation. *Of course, you absolutely cannot call me again.* Davida knew those were the words of a sane and logical woman, but she couldn't seem to get them out of her mouth. Finally, her lips parted with a slow question. "You don't think that would be a little . . . well, strange?"

"No, I think it's more like a pen pal relationship."

"Oh, I don't know . . ." Under other circumstances, she would have had a name to insert in this blank conversational space. But here? She rather liked him as a fantasy man. Somebody fun and intellectually stimulating, who had no way of tracing her except through the tele-phone. He was the ultimate confidante, the man she could say anything to. "Pen pals . . .''

"Okay, so we're not really writing to each other, I'll give you that. But, in this electronic age, there's not a lot of difference outside of the speed of communication—is there?"

"No, not much."

"If we promise to maintain anonymity . . .''

"No names, no descriptions."

"You don't ask, and I don't tell . . .''

"Neither one of us will." His voice touched her ear with the same kind of prickly sensation a new growth of beard would bring to her cheek, and Davida felt warmth surging through her body, lower than she wanted to admit. "I guess so," she agreed quietly.

"You know, I could give you my number. If you ever decided . . .''

"I don't think so," she interrupted gently. "We have kind of a 'don't ask, don't tell' agreement, remember?" Knowing would spoil the illusion, cut into the fantasy of her encounter with the stranger. He'd called her Boo, and sounded like he meant it—that was enough. "Thanks for the offer, though."

"I don't think I've ever been turned down quite so nicely. Well . . ." He stretched again, and caught sight of his watch. After midnight.

"I guess I'll wait to hear from you, then."

God, he hoped so! "Well," he said again, wondering why he couldn't seem to get more than the one word out of his mouth, "g'nite. Be good, okay?"

"You, too."

"Thanks. See y . . ." Marc bit down on the reflexive, casual words he'd almost uttered. "See you," he'd almost said. Of course he wouldn't. Not sooner, not later. And if she had her way, not ever. " 'Bye," he closed.

"Bye."

CHAPTER THREE

Had she really sounded wistful when they said goodbye, or was it just his imagination? Just what he wanted to hear? *Hey,* Marc confronted himself, *projection is a powerful thing.* It was true. He'd read a couple of articles on how people could project their feelings onto another person, and wind up thinking that what they thought was what they thought somebody else thought they thought ... "Too big a circle," he concluded, "I need to quit reading *Psychology Today.*"

Reaching across his drawing board, he clicked off the high-intensity lamp and began restoring his supplies to some form of order known only to him. Bro'Man's fearless face, bent on reckoning with evil-doers, disappeared beneath a muslin drop cloth. Leaning his weight on his folded arms, Marc promised to cancel that magazine subscription—the darned thing was making him too introspective: obviously a bad thing if you indulged in anonymous long-distance flirtation.

But, he was handling it—wasn't he? "I mean, I dialed her. I'm the voice of sanity in this madness, the one who realized the time and got us off the line, this time. I've put this whole relationship into its proper perspective," he said aloud, wiping his hands on the color-stained towel he kept near the drawing board for just that purpose. In thirty-four years, he'd learned a thing or two, and it wasn't like this was the beginning of a real or enduring relationship or anything.

And right now, the truth of the matter was, he needed a relationship like he needed a hole in his head. Seeing Kenya down at Bertucci's last night had proven that. Seeing her on the arm of another man pretty much killed Marc's desire for his favorite dish, Chicken Domani. In her wake, the tender, lemon-touched chicken and pasta had tasted like sawdust—old, moldy sawdust.

If he'd been in the mood for puns, Marc might have said Kenya left him with a bad taste in his mouth. Sitting across from Milt, watching her strut through the door in her clingy, high-slit, turquoise silk dress made his hands itch with memory. He could almost feel the flow of soft fabric and firm flesh as she moved impatiently and unseeing past their table. *Didn't need her then, don't need her now,* he promised himself, even as he probed the soreness of his heart for raw memories.

I'm lyin', he admitted without rancor. He might not need her, but he sure as heck wanted her. Pumping his fist against his lips, Marc took a hard look at his last thought, and as tough as it was, the bottom line was almost too easy to read: *You're thinking with the wrong part of your anatomy, brother.* Kenya was the wrong one. Boo on the phone was a much better choice.

Now, how did he know that, when he didn't even know her name?

Standing, he kicked his stool out of the way and headed for the kitchen. Maybe a sandwich would make things clearer, help him digest this annoying fixation he had on whatever-her-name-was. She said she's in no hurry to hook up with another man, and after Kenya, being with another woman was sure the last thing on his mind. It was not like Boo was the girl next door. She didn't trust him enough to tell him her name. Even though she said she didn't mind him calling, he'd probably never talk to her again in life. So, why was he sorry the conversation ended?

"Time I'm spending on the phone, I could have been finishing up some of the copyright stuff Milt brought by earlier." Marc muttered. "Shoot, I could have spent that time filling in background frames and rechecking my story lines. I could have . . ." *But, I wouldn't have,* he thought *I would have spent the time doing exactly what I did, trying to figure out how else to get in touch with her—how to learn her name.*

Marc looked at the jar of mayonnaise that had mysteriously appeared in his hand. What had he wanted from the refrigerator, anyway? "Talking to this lady can't be good for me. Look here," he told the cool glass jar, "she's got me talking to condiments. Now, how normal is that?"

He closed the door and headed down the hall toward his bedroom. After midnight, time for bed—at least that made sense. Pulling his Oxford cloth shirt free of his jeans, Marc continued his ramblings, working buttons all the while. "What she needs," he told his reflection, "is someone very special. Someone willing to take time with her pain and loss, someone selfless enough to help her work through her loneliness." He shrugged free of his shirt and draped it over a nearby chair. "Matter of fact, that's what we *all* need. But, see now, what Boo needs is an *extraordinary* person, and me, I've got too many problems of my own to be *extraordinary* for anybody else.

"Besides, by nature I'm just an ordinary man." Flopping onto his back in the middle of his king-size bed, Marc took stock. "I'm about as ordinary as they come," he told the white ceiling. "Okay, maybe I'm not completely ordinary, but I'm about as medium as you can get." Medium height, medium weight, medium brown skin, Marcus even came from a middle-income family, and had moved South to get away from "middle America." "Medium, all right," he agreed with himself.

"Wonder what I'll look like by the time I reach middle age." He puffed out his bare stomach and patted the pretend paunch. Nah, that would never be. He had run too many miles for too many years to ever stop. Besides, he already assumed he'd look like his father and grandfather: he had since birth. Like his father, Marc knew that at fifty, he would still be slim and boyish, with a full head of hair, and probably hiding behind a mustache he would cultivate in a vain effort to look mature and sophisticated.

Folding his hands over the tight flatness of his belly, Marc remembered what Tannie, his best friend Milt's teenage daughter, said about him. "If I don't get a date for the prom next year," she gushed, "I'll ask you. Nobody would believe you were any older than eighteen, and you'll look so cute in a tux!"

Milton swore his kid meant it as a compliment. Marc was terrified she meant exactly what she said.

Renee was no help, either. His thirty-two year old baby sister accused him of staying young looking just to spite her. She took after their imperious-looking mother, right down to the premature gray streak and the two little vertical lines between her brows. More than once, Marc had wished his soft dark curly hair and dimples on his sister—where he figured they rightfully belonged. His rounded cheeks had been known to bear the peach tones of a summer blush, long past his twenty-first year, and he longed for the oval of his sister's beautifully elegant countenance. Renee's face had the kind of character and grace that lent bearing to everything she said and did.

He, on the other hand would never be a major hunk, no matter what Tannie thought, and he might as well get used to it. Silently ticking off all the things he knew any woman would look for in a qualifying "hunk," Marc cursed his dimpled cheeks, thick curling lashes, and the mouth that curved and pouted in the center, like a girl's. Just this morning, a strange woman stopped him in the grocery store—right there in the middle of Publix, and with her arms full of

groceries, announced that he, "just had 'bout the longest lashes in
the world, up over them pretty eyes!" Then she'd giggled with the
pleasure of her discovery, and cooed over his, "smooth, pretty skin,
and sweet li'l dimples!"

He had to be born with candybox looks, instead of rugged, chiseled,
flashing manliness. It was galling, even though the woman ran out of
the store behind him waving her telephone number scrawled on the
back of some coupon or other.

Rolling onto his side, Marc decided bed, and most definitely sleep,
was out of the question. He scooted to the edge of the bed. Sweeping
a foot under his bed, he snagged a battered Reebok with his big toe
and thought about taking a run. "Yeah, right," he told himself. "Go
running this time of night and wind up a statistic. Not a good idea."
A second foot sweep sent the shoe back under the bed where it settled
toe-to-toe with its mate.

He found his shirt and ambled back into the direction of his work-
room. Punching his arms into the sleeves, he left the shirt open, unsure
of why he'd bothered to put it back on. The only thing he knew for
sure was that she was still with him. Boo was probably seriously
fine. Whatever-her-name-is was probably drop-dead gorgeous, and
not looking for a "cute" little man like himself.

Throwing his hands into the air, he walked faster through the unlit
hall. "It's not about ego," he explained to the air around him and
the sketches on the wall. "I like the way I look, just fine. I'm comfortable being me. I don't even have a real problem with somebody else
liking or not liking it, but it's about types." He slid his hands into
his pants pockets. "Everybody has a type, and they just tend not to
stray from it, so unless her father was five ten, and one seventy five,
I'm probably not her type."

But she sure as heck sounded like she could be his type. Smart and
funny, had one child, so he already knew she liked the family things.
Then, too, there was that voice. Women who sounded like that usually
had faces and bodies to match.

Oh, man! What was that? he reproached himself. *Now, I've got
myself paired off with a woman whose name I don't even know.* "Gotta
stop doing that," he said. "I don't know her, not going to meet her,
not trying to meet her, never will meet her. She's on the telephone,
and that's where she's going to stay. Let it go, man!"

Still trying to put her out of his mind, he sat in front of his drawing
board and uncovered Bro'Man again. Reaching for his charcoal stick,
Marc bent over his work. He anticipated the shadows and lines that
would tell his story, then followed them with the well-used charcoal.
It was better, and if not better, then at least it was safer to lose himself
in his work. *This is the work that makes me smile,* he thought. *This*

is my love, and it's faithful and true. The carefully scaled detail and innovation that marked his work, from the smallest sketch to the wall-sized fresco he'd completed for Big Bethel AME last Christmas was more than pleasure for him. It was pure, unadulterated passion, and he liked it that way. Always had.

But Bro'Man was more than art born of passion—he was his creator's heart, and very real in his imagination. The freelance work Marc did for other companies would always pay the bills, but Bro'Man was a labor of love. He was the fantasy that could make a different reality possible, but li'l ol' what's-her-name? She was something else. She was a fantasy that would probably only lead to disaster and disappointment.

Using a sharpener, Marc brought the end of his pencil to a sharp point, and with deft strokes, used it to bring a gleam to BroMan's eyes. And, darn if he couldn't still hear the rushed whisper of her voice: he didn't even have to listen very hard.

"I have one for you," she'd said. Marc scratched idly at his ear, still feeling touched by the mere memory of her throaty voice. "Tell me a fantasy."

"A fantasy," he'd repeated, charmed. "I guess I have the same fantasy as most men. Something like being Michael Jordan at the hoop during the playoffs . . ."

"No, no, no, honey. Come on, don't play me cheap. I've been honest with you—the least you can do is give as good as you got. Give me a fantasy—one of yours—a real one." Her voice slid through him like iced vodka, and was every bit as heady.

"I could tell you how I'd like to . . . to . . . go parasailing off the coast of some beautifully tropical Caribbean island with nothing but air between me and all of eternity."

"Is that really what you dream of? What you hold as fantasy?" Had she caught the tiny, pregnant pause in his words? For a moment, it seemed she had, and Marc was tempted to tell her the truth—the complete truth.

"No," he wanted to say. "What I really fantasize about is making long, hot, sweaty, mind-shattering, all-night-into-the-next-afternoon love to a woman who is as beautiful as you sound right now. I want to hold her so tightly I don't know where she ends and I begin, and know that she loves me as much as I love her. I want to use my hands, my skin to read her in braille and print her indelibly into my life. What I fantasize about now is living a Teddy Pendergrass or Babyface love song—and taking you with me—how about you?"

Afraid of scaring her off, he never said it, but that didn't stop him from dreaming it.

A slight shake of his head did nothing to clear it. She was still there.

Marc rubbed a slow thumb against Bro'Man's cheek, intentionally smudging and softening it. Manila paper was rough beneath his skin, and he wondered again what she looked like. He wasn't sure of what he wanted her to look like. Vague images swam through his brain, sifting like smoke, forming features that were slow in settling. His artist's brain drew mind pictures that made him pass a hand across his damp brow, and reminded him to breathe. Near full tumescence brought him back to where and what he was. His hand, still working on Bro'Man, had rubbed a hole right through the paper.

"Let it go, man," he whispered to the surrounding night just outside the glowing circle of his lamp. "Let her go."

Davida sat holding the phone for long minutes after the call ended. Torn, she could no longer lie to herself. She'd cavalierly ignored their agreement and rushed to K-Mart the day after his most recent call and bought the Caller ID unit for just this occasion. She'd called Southwestern Bell and changed her service the same day, just because he might call again. And, though she'd felt no fear from the man, she liked knowing that if she wanted it, she would have a little information about him on hand.

So, do I look or not? She turned the phone in her hands and sat still, debating her next move. A little move, just one slight inclination of her head, would tell her so much . . . What must he think of someone with so little discretion and so much desperation that she'd hold long, in-depth, personal conversations with a stranger? Her eyes strayed to the small unit resting on her bedside table. And what would he think if he knew how much being called Boo meant to her—and from a stranger?

She'd be forty years old in less than a month, and she was reverting to teenage actions. She was giggling on the phone with a strange man who called her by a pet name because he didn't know her real one, and now she couldn't make up her own mind as to how much she needed to know about him. *Get a grip, girl.*

Her eyes found something else to fix on, and she crossed the room to glance at Iyanla Vanzant's *Faith in the Valley.* Fingering the hardcover, Davida flipped it open and squinted slightly to read the first few lines. It was almost as though they'd been written for her—written to give her just a little more insight into her loneliness. Turning more pages, she read words that felt like little directed arrows of wisdom, and every one of those arrows hit its mark. She closed the book over her finger, holding on to the last page she'd read. "You trying to tell me something?" she asked the pastel covered book. Though she waited, the pages remained silent and waiting, keeping their wisdom safe for another time. Turning the book face down, Davida's eyes found the Caller ID unit, again.

She couldn't believe some of the things she'd said and shared with that strange man, that strange man whose name she didn't even know. Her skin warmed as she thought of telling him what it had been like to sleep without Skip: how even her skin had cried out for him in those empty nights, and the hungers she experienced on finding herself alone. She covered her mouth with her hand, too late to hide or call back the secrets she'd held for so long.

And he listened. He listened with a quiet persuasiveness that kept her talking for longer than she would have ever imagined possible. He kept her talking about a man who had once been the center of her life, and now, was no more. He kept her talking until she'd worked through that last little bit of hot, denied anger—talking until the anger broke through and crumbled beneath his care and concern. He kept her talking, like a friend.

And, that's what he is to me, she thought, satisfied that she finally had a name, and a place—sort of—in her life, for the stranger. Davida thought of an old song, something she remembered her mother humming and singing through the house when she was young. "... If they could see me now, that little gang of mine ..." Davida and Butch had always wondered who their mother's "gang" was, and what she wanted them to see.

Now here she was, about ready to sing the same song. Yeah, the sisters in her circle would be shaking their heads, looking at her from the narrow sides of their eyes, and trying to figure out who was going to keep Des while Davida went quietly crazy in her office downtown, singing songs about the man on the telephone. "That's what comes of holding your secrets for too long," they would say. "You wind up on the phone, telling your business to a strange man, just because he calls you Boo."

And they would be right.

Feeling a touch of guilt, Davida glanced at the phone again. He'd already called; he wasn't going to call again tonight. Though, if he did call, the conversation would be good—not really what you could call "juicy," but satisfying. Satisfying. The word was so right for what she felt for the stranger that she couldn't help smiling.

"Satisfying," she whispered to the empty room. "Satisfying. He satisfies me. With him, I am satisfied—and all he had to do was talk to me. He had to talk to me in a voice like soiled satin." She liked the description because that was how it was with him; a sleek, darkly male strength that never came off as dirty, but made you feel like he'd been somewhere, knew something that you didn't—and she liked it. Feeling vaguely wanton, Davida looked toward the Caller ID unit again. "It's not always what you say, but how you say it," she whispered to the absent man, wishing she'd had the courage to send the words across the telephone lines.

They'd been carrying on these lengthy, sometimes astonishingly frank conversations for weeks and she'd told him about embarrassing moments, private fantasies, lost dreams, and past disappointments. In return, he'd given her the same: he'd given so much, Davida was startled to find that men's private thoughts were not so very different from women's, once the constraints of face-to-face conversation were eliminated—thanks to the telephone.

What has gotten into me! Melanie would call me a fool for even putting my business out in the streets like this, Davida chided herself. *She would call me a fool, and she would be all too right. You don't let your life get out of control like this. I've told a stranger things I've never told another living soul. And, I don't even know this man's name.*

Bending slowly, her eyes never leaving the intimidating bit of whim-purchased technology, she lowered herself to the chaise. Caller ID. Innocuous little thing, the tiny plastic box held the answer to at least two of the questions in her mind. If she read it, she'd know his name, and how to reach him. She'd have his phone number just like he had hers. But did she really want the information that lay just inches away?

He won't mind, she rationalized. *Why should he? He would tell me if I asked, and besides, he always wants to know things about me. He's always asking questions* She could still hear his voice, asking questions.

"What's your favorite color?"

She'd thought it over. "I don't know . . . I guess I'd have to say blue. A deep, not dark, maybe cerulean shade of blue."

"Picky, but definite, and you have to admire someone who can be so specific."

"Are you laughing at me?" she'd challenged.

"Hardly. I'm asking. What's your favorite food?" he'd asked, and she had a ready answer.

"Seafood, other than something like squid or Sushi, any kind of seafood. And it doesn't matter how it's prepared."

"What's your favorite movie?"

When Davida hesitated, he'd hummed the theme from *Jeopardy* until she felt pressed for an answer. *"Lady Sings the Blues,"* she blurted. "Either that or Spike Lee's *Malcolm X.*"

"You are, without a doubt, a true eclectic."

"No, I just know what I like," she said defensively.

"Do I take that to mean you favor 'pretty boys'? Handsome leading men like Denzel Washington, and Billy Dee Williams at his most sartorially splendid?''

"I *like,* what I *like.*" She let her tone paint her words with innuendo. "And what about me, Boo? Do you like me?"

Why ever had he asked her that? He had no right to ask that— knowing that they were going to forever remain strangers. *Why did he ask me that?*

She crossed her arms and tried to get angry with him—anger was the most useful emotion she could imagine.

Anger was an emotion that would turn down the heat of her imagination, make it easier to stop watching strange men on the street from the corners of her eyes. Anger might let her stop smiling back into the faces and eyes of strangers—smiling like she had a secret pressed just behind her lips. Anger might let her get back to wearing her usual practical, dark blues and charcoal grays and blacks—nothing like the lime green suit with the short, short skirt she'd bought today. Anger might even let her get over feeling she was even a little bit, phat.

Why did he ask her that, when he already knew the answer?

Anger might have made her able to walk past Victoria's Secret without going inside to find out more about how those "secrets" really worked. Anger might even make it possible for her to tame the musical little extra swing she'd caught herself putting into her walk today. Shoot, even Des had noticed and commented on it. Anger might make her able to deny her attraction to this voice in the night.

But, anger wasn't knocking at her door this night.

I need to know more about him. I need to know who he is, just to tame my own curiosity.

Twisting the slender white gold band she still wore on the third finger of her left hand, Davida listed the things she would never forget about this strange man she'd found too easily compatible on her telephone. He was funny, sensitive, kind to a fault, and he offered exactly the kind of emotional cave she longed for on frustrating days and lonely nights.

He seemed to be a man who not only knew and understood the differences between love and romance, but also between sex and intimacy, and was willing to open himself to all of the possibilities. He was almost the perfect fantasy man.

What if it's an act? her internal guardian argued. *What if it's just something he's doing to rope a lonely widow in?*

Davida slipped her wedding ring from her finger and looked at the fine engraving on the inside. "My Destiny, My Life, My Eternity, My Wife" it said. The words ran around the band in a continuous circle, making powerful statements no matter how they were read. Davida closed her eyes and reminded herself to breathe. So many words in such a small space, so much empty space in her heart. She held the ring tightly in the warm, moist palm of her hand, and thought of Skip's big broad grin the day he put it on her finger. Shaking her head, she returned the ring to her finger and stared at it.

Rope a lonely widow in to do what? Steal my family jewels?

Covering her eyes with her hands, she tried to rest there, hidden in the dispassionate darkness, but the slight glint of light on her ring denied Davida her peace. "Skip," she whispered to the ring, "I know I'm entitled to a life after you, and I know that Destiny wants and needs a father, but whoever he is, he needs to be the right one." She folded her hand over the ring and pressed both hands to her heart. "Whoever he is, he's got to be the right one."

Whoever he was, this mystery man was not "the one," forget about his being, "the right one." He couldn't be. First of all, he was crazy, and you don't knowingly get involved with crazy people—of that, she was certain. Davida laughed, thinking of his general madness. He was crazy alright, and she knew she could prove it. When she asked him about his favorite movie, he sighed happily and announced, "Almost any Disney animated feature." She pulled the phone from her ear to stare at it. That couldn't be right, could it? Cartoons. For a grown man. That was crazy—right?

When she'd finally returned the receiver to her ear and carefully repeated, *"Disney?"* she was sure she'd misunderstood. He giggled. *Giggled!* Then went on to chronicle all of the great animated features of the twentieth century, listing his favorites by name as he went along. Admittedly, he knew more about the chronology of Mickey Mouse than most humans would ever have a need to, including the names of each of the original Mouseketeers and all the words to the theme song, but there were limits. The man knew the names of all seven dwarves, for pity's sake.

Second, she tried to remember exactly what he'd said, but failed. Still, she remembered him saying something that told her he couldn't be more than thirty-three or four. And, she was not looking for a younger man. Not at this point in her life. Oh, sure, some women thought it was alright to grab up some young kid and bend him to their will . . . Davida knew the kinds of stories women, and even some of the men, told. She'd heard them at work over lunch or coffee and in the ladies' room.

Fiftyish Anne Laird was still giggling over the young twenty-something guy she met when she took evening classes at St. Louis University. The classes seemed like a good idea when Anne decided she needed to "age-proof" her career, so she enrolled with the intent of just picking up what she needed to enhance her degree. What she got was an enhanced life.

Anne told all kinds of stories about her "baby" in the break room and around her desk at work. Some of the stories were pretty hot, too. The tame stories told of watching his jeans and his dreds swing as he strode down Lindell Boulevard on his way to class, and about how she'd followed him from the building to get a chance to meet him. She piggy-backed on his big Harley, and wore black leather on weekends. Then, last year, Anne got a tattoo to commemorate one of the wilder weekends, and was all too willing to show it off and provide details, given the opportunity.

And, that's what happened when you messed with younger men.

After two years, they were still together, sharing an apartment out in U. City, and he called Anne, "Mommy." She called him "Teacake," after Janie's young lover in Hurston's *Their Eyes Were Watching God.* And Anne never hesitated to say, "When you need something sweet, ain't nothin' like a little Teacake."

Davida shook her head in thoughtful denial. *That's not for me.* But, at thirty-three, or-thirty-four, she grudgingly admitted, he wasn't really a kid, was he? In fact, if she'd met him in church or at a PTA meeting, and didn't know his age, he might be a likely candidate.

Candidate? For what?

Girl, give it up, she cautioned herself. She didn't have a clue as to what he looked like. He might look like a twelve-year-old. Or, what if . . . she shuddered. What if he wore high-water pants pulled all the way up to his armpits! The telephone wasn't an adequate marketplace, you just couldn't see around the corners, and a telephoning stranger . . . well, it just wasn't right.

Davida twisted her ring again, and refused to wonder why she'd never thought to remove it completely.

But, if she ever married again . . . There would be another ring, another gift, another pledge from another man. What would he be like?

Part of her already knew. The man she might someday let into her heart and home would have to be somebody she could see and touch, not a disembodied voice over the phone on lonely nights. He would have to be a strong, supportive father for Des, and a . . . a what for her? Didn't matter, because the man on the phone was not, would not ever be "the one."

But he tried so hard, and the sensitivity, the generosity of his spirit—touched her so deeply, she . . . Davida dropped her eyes to her knotted fingers. What was it he'd asked her? Then she recalled the conversation. It was the night he'd asked her about her favorite movie. Somehow, *Waiting to Exhale* came up. They agreed they'd both enjoyed it, but liked others better. Then, he said . . .

"I don't think the women were very believable."

"Why do you say that?"

"Think about it. Women that talented, that beautiful, that well educated, and that capable. None of them could find a man?"

"Maybe they were looking for more than just, 'a man.'"

He seemed to think about that. "You mean, maybe they didn't need fathers and providers and directors and sperm donors as much as they needed mature, caring, balanced, empathetic companionship? You think, maybe they were looking for that 'equal yoke' that the bible talks about?"

"Exactly."

"Like you?"

Davida looked at the phone then laughed gently. "Are you teasing me?"

"No," he said solemnly, "I'm trying to learn. I want to know."

And I believed him, Davida realized. It never occurred to her to wonder if he was setting her up for some kind of weirdness in the future. She bit her lip as she tried not to look over at the Caller ID unit. He really seemed to enjoy talking with her though, and his second call was not an accident at all. And, he still called her Boo.

But knowing, having a name to attach to the man she kept secret from everyone, including herself . . . she didn't know. Even with the cute nickname, knowing too much about him would take away from the mystery, and reduce the delicious tension that made her head turn and her skin tighten at the sound of her telephone. Knowing his name was like having too much information: it would make him too real, too prone to human frailty. Mindful of her option, Davida moved slowly from the chaise to the bed, but was somehow unable to let her eyes fall to the digital readout of the small beige tracing unit.

Besides, they had something of a pact, didn't they? He'd asked . . . suggested, and she'd said no. Davida braided her fingers into a tight knot, and wondered how much of what she shared with this stranger would be sacrificed if she glanced at the Caller ID unit. To look, wouldn't that be a betrayal? Hadn't they agreed on the security of anonymity? But she really wanted to look. He knew all about her, and she had rights, too.

Never mind that he knew so much because she sat right here and told him almost everything about herself. But, who else was she going to tell? She couldn't recall the last time she'd spoken so openly and honestly to anyone, including Glenn, mostly because other people had real lives.

All that honesty, that's another reason she looked forward talking to him; another reason she thought of him as a friend. And another reason not to ever meet him, no matter what fantasies were beginning to weave themselves into her dreams. Dreams where his now-familiar voice murmured just the right pretty words while his hands stroked her starved body and he looked down at her with a smile bracketed by soul deep, and utterly endearing dimples.

". . . soul deep, and utterly endearing dimples"? Mel would call me a fool for even trying to think like this, I know she would. Melanie Baker, her best friend since seventh-grade cheerleader tryouts, was running for the state senate this year. That was a long way from Vashon High School and those little short skirts they used to roll up even shorter before the football games, Davida thought. Mel had good intentions, and she loved her like a sister, but with speeches and strategy meetings, the girl was busier then a one-legged woman in a butt-kicking contest. She didn't have time to listen to trying-to-be-in-love stories. Anything more than the occasional lunch or quick phone call was out of the question these days. No way could she bother Mel with the story of her mystery telephone caller.

Glenn would listen if she could track him down. He always listened, but his law practice kept him moving around the country when he wasn't chasing behind LaDonna Crane, and he needed to focus all his attention on the business at hand. That left Destiny. An eight-year-old, she wanted to offer her mother all the support she could, but hugs and chocolate chip cookies had their limits. No wonder she talked herself silly when her mystery man called. All those words had been building up for a long time, and he'd gotten as much from the calls as she had, Davida was sure of it.

He'd never call again, of course. Why should he? He knew enough about her to have satisfied his curiosity, and even the second call—the impulse call—was probably to ease his mind. He said he was worried about her.

What a nice man, to be worried about a perfect stranger. Davida eased closer to the bedside table, her eyes never leaving the miniature electronic device. *He sounded so nice,* she thought as she pulled back the comforter and smoothed the cool sheets with the palm of her hand. Lots of men sound nice, and weren't once you get to know them. And lots of men could call you Boo, too—if you let them. For the first time, she noticed an annoying buzz behind her eyes.

Why was she stressing over this? It wasn't as if the calls were dates or anything. Perhaps it wasn't such a good idea to speak so frankly with a stranger. *Perhaps?* She could already hear the things Glenn would say if he ever found out. He would have a fit. He would have a natural lay-down-dying fit was what he would do. She sighed and looked over at the Caller ID unit again—she couldn't read it from here, not without her glasses, anyway.

She'd be more careful from now on. Careful was exactly what she'd be, and not allow herself to be corrupted by a stranger's wit and sedulous charm. She was supposed to be a responsible, mature individual who was supposed to know better—she owed that to Des. No more chatty little calls with strangers, no matter how charming and harmless they seemed. Get on and get off—answer the call and then move past it, that was the way to handle the telephone these days. Let the cranks and obscene phone callers get their kicks somewhere else.

Her pajama leg had managed to crawl up around her calf, and she shook it down before swinging her leg under the covers. Tacky little pale blue cotton jammies, probably washed fifty times, and as familiar as an old friend's face, they were a good choice—for nights with Des. They weren't what a woman wore unless she was alone. If there were a man in her life, Davida knew she'd be wearing something else, something soft and sheer, something designed with removal in mind.

The Caller ID unit sat silently waiting. The little beige box seemed to know her name, and held her attention like a miniature hypnotist. Spellbound, Davida climbed into her empty bed, telling herself that she really didn't mind sleeping alone in her blue cotton jammies, and that it had nothing to do with the man on the telephone, who cared enough to call her back, and called her Boo. A little knowledge to give her an edge on whoever called her home. It was safer this way.

Lonely, but definitely safer.

Reaching for the light, temptation finally pulled at the last thread of her resistance. She owed it to her daughter to look at the Caller ID, to know who the man was. She ought to be responsible enough to know the name of the man she'd thus far allowed to enter her home via the telephone lines. Dropping her hand, she lifted the unit and brought it close enough to see clearly.

"Private name/private number," it read.

"Damn."

CHAPTER FOUR

No. Davida ran her thumb over the raised buttons of the remote, then shook her head and sighed. There is no way that could ever happen in real life. It could only happen in the movies. Real women didn't lose their husbands to death and then toss out their children to run merrily off to glamorous lives in exotic cities like Paris or Istanbul, where they donned designer "glad rags" and survived in endless luxury with hot and cold running millionaires at their beck and call. Did they?

Of course, they didn't, she answered herself. Real women anchored their lives in the real world. Real women didn't stay an eternal size two like Susan Lucci. Did they?

No way, she decided flatly. Past forty, they turned into whoever they were going to be, and modeled themselves on people like Maya Angelou and Oprah. They faced their lives in whatever condition they woke up with, and things were fine—even with post-forty ups and downs. They faced it all and emerged scarred, but stronger. Didn't they?

Sure, they did and that's what made them beautiful. Wasn't it?

That question only succeeded in raising another. Did real women continually watch their telephones and answer them in breathless whispers—waiting for calls from a deliciously witty and intelligent man with a sexy voice, and God only knew what motives, whose name they would never know?

No. Davida shook her head firmly and worked her way through

the remote, glad to finally locate the ten o'clock news. It was that stupid movie that had her thinking such mushy thoughts. She didn't even know why she bothered to watch junk like that. Maybe she watched it just to convince herself that her life was right, right for Des and her. That stranger on the telephone? He was like a dessert. Something sweet to finish off with—not meant to be real or fulfill the kinds of hunger life leaves you with.

Gathering her bowl and glass, she tsk'd at the mess she made when her hand tipped the glass, spilling chips and bits of melted ice across the pecan veneer of the small table in front of the sofa. Kneeling, she caught the slippery ice chips, then mopped at the water with the tail of the shirt she wore. It was one of Skip's. An old, too-big, white oxford cloth button-down, frayed at the collar and cuffs from so much washing, but so comfortable—even though it no longer smelled of him, she still wore it around the house.

Skip. Davida almost smiled, even at the thought of his name. He always could make her smile. Big, broad, and willful, with skin the red, rubbed color of sweet Georgia pecans, Douglas Lawrence always knew what he wanted, and he almost always got what he wanted. From the first time he saw Davida, coming out of the old White Castle over on Natural Bridge, he'd known he wanted her. He was loud and bold enough to make sure she knew it, too.

Watching her cross the heavily traveled street, carrying that white bag full of those little square burgers, he even seemed to know they would be together. Watching her long legs and free swinging walk in that little red plaid kilted miniskirt she used to wear, he seemed to know they would one day marry.

The first time he looked down from his mountainous height, gazing into her brown eyes like they held all the best secrets of the universe, he'd smiled and said, "I want to love you forever. However long forever is, that's how long I want to be with you." And Davida understood exactly what he meant, because she felt that way, too.

Pushing his long sleeve higher along her arm, she was glad she'd saved a few of his old shirts, and marveled that she still had these thoughts, and even more amazingly, these feelings. Skip passed more than four years ago, and she still reached for him in her sleep. When did that end? Davida rolled the paper towels she'd been using as napkins and tucked them into the glass.

Walking to the kitchen, she listened for Destiny. Thinking she heard the child moan, Davida hoped for the best. Setting the dishes in the sink, she crept toward her child's room. Des refused dinner, and that worried her. Destiny simply did not pass up Micky D's—unless she was sick. *Lord, please don't let her be sick.* When she was sick, the flare-ups could be so frightening, but they came with the package.

And Des was quite a package: Unpredictable from the start.

When they married, Davida and Skip had planned on having children, wanted them desperately. After five years of diligent planning, temperature taking, and assiduously scheduled sex, they were still childless. Even the trips to all those "Solution" meetings seemed a wasted effort. The support group, and its monthly meetings over at the Brentwood Community Center left them both feeling a little guilty.

Or, maybe it was the rain of images that invaded her thoughts at unpredictable and unguarded moments. Images of herself holding a small, wriggling bit of humanity that had his eyes and her nose, and gurgled and cooed, and recognized her as Mommy. Skip felt it, too, mostly when he thought she wasn't looking. The images, pleasant as they were, left her desolate, holding her head, sniffing back tears, unable to sleep. They left Skip angry and impotent.

On reflection, pushing the sleeves of her dead husband's old shirt higher on her arm, Davida realized something she'd never been able to identify before. The images that tortured both her and Skip should have told her long ago what their guilt really was—a cover for the absence of the complete family they'd always believed they both deserved.

Mama Lou and Papa Carter had been wonderful parents to Skip, proudly and indulgently raising their only son. Jewell Morrison, a single mother had done her very best, and successfully raised her son and daughter on her own. That Davida and Skip had come from two traditionally different kinds of families was never an issue for either of them. All they knew was that family was a good thing. Once married, Skip and Davida had to find their own way—the way to making a family of their own.

It didn't help that everybody they knew seemed to watch her waistbands and the front of his pants. "When y'all gon' make some babies?" seemed to be the well-meaning question everybody, including strangers, seemed to feel they had a right to ask. Every one of the women she knew and loved best had an idea and a suggestion, guaranteed to get Davida, "in the family way". It was beyond embarrassing and only added to the guilt both she and Skip carried.

The counselors they talked to seemed to have such pat answers. "Infertility," Linda Gowmer said over and over again, "is defined as the inability to achieve pregnancy after a year of trying." Having the knowledge and definition of what infertility was didn't seem to be enough. Linda worked for Solution, and she was supposed to be something of an authority on the subject, but her knowledge was not the power Davida and Skip needed. What they needed, what they both wanted, was a baby.

Well, it had been five years, and Davida and Skip were as healthy as horses, and childless. Still, when Linda pushed her glasses high on her nose and recited the fact that, "in the United States, it's estimated that one in six couples experiences infertility," it didn't help.

The day Davida introduced the subject of adoption, Skip was adamant and it led to a fight—a big one.

The fight began simply enough. Davida said, "We want a baby, and adoption is a viable option. I think we should look into it."

Then, Skip said, "Oh, hell no!" And it was on.

Finally, tired of a battle he saw no way of winning, Skip laid out a low blow. Eyes tight and lips pouting, he laid aside the screwdriver he'd been using on an upturned dining room chair. As he walked to the counter, it was obvious he had something on his mind. He picked up the phone and punched in numbers while Davida watched.

He held a brief, whispered conversation, nodded, then triumphantly handed the phone to his wife. Stunned and appalled, she took it from his hand. Her voice shook as she tried to speak.

"H-hello?"

"Davida? Girl, what is this I hear about you wantin' to take on somebody else's child?" He called his mother! Mama Lou, usually convivial and patient to a fault, was thoroughly perturbed. Pressing the phone more tightly to her ear, Davida refused to give Skip the satisfaction of meeting his eyes or moving her neck.

"Davida? Davida, what are you thinkin'? I mean, you do know, you adopt, and all you get is someone else's problems. You do know that, don't you?"

Something about her mother-in-law's tone broke through the anger. Davida looked directly at Skip as she spoke to his mother. "I'm only going to say this once, Mama Lou, because I don't think I can ever say it any better. When we came into this marriage, Skip knows, we both agreed that we wanted to raise a family, and a family means children. We have to start somewhere to build that family, and there are hundreds of children out there waiting to be loved. We can start with one. Whatever that child brings, problems or otherwise, in a family, we agree to accept our child as a whole package.

"Between us, Skip and I make more than enough money to feed, clothe and house, and educate a whole passel of children. We've been married for five years and we're still childless—nobody's fault, but still childless.

"Mama Lou, that's five years of hugging other people's babies— smelling the powder and the milk, feeling the soft tender skin and the warm little bodies. That's five years of big, beautiful Christmas trees in this house with no toys beneath them. That's five years of buying somebody else's child's Girl Scout cookies and school raffle tickets, and five years of listening to other people's children's Sunday School speeches.

"You and Skip had both better understand, I don't want somebody else's child. I want mine. I want ours. Children don't come into this life stamped with ownership like 'his and hers' bath towels. When a child comes here, with whatever baggage they carry, they are never 'somebody else's problem.' They belong to whoever loves them, and I intend to love this child with all my heart, whether it's born of my body or not." Finished, Davida calmly handed the telephone back to her husband.

Trying not to hear the remainder of the conversation, she went back to folding clothes in the laundry room. As hard as she tried, it was harder to miss the rumble of Skip's submissively low-voiced, "Yes, Mama. Yes, Mama" replies. Two days later, he put on a dress suit and accompanied his wife to the adoption agency.

So many years later, she still swore that was the night their daughter was conceived. Standing at her child's door, Davida closed her eyes and took a deep breath, then slowly turned the knob. To her great relief, Destiny slept deeply and easily.

Trying not to wake the child, Davida neared the bed to slip her hand beneath the weight of the colorful patchwork comforter, a relic from her own childhood. Maybe it was the air-conditioning, but Davida had never understood her daughter's cocooning urges. The child insisted on sleeping beneath the heavy comforter both summer and winter. Davida moved carefully to lift it aside. Still holding her breath, she moved her hand gently over her child's body. There was no evident swelling in Destiny's hands or feet.

"Thank you, Lord," Davida whispered, releasing her held breath. Her daughter's skin, though warm and slightly moist, was like that of any other healthy sleeping child.

Unaware of her action, Davida brought a hand to rest at her breast and let her own breathing fall into the sleeping child's rhythm. It was hard to believe how very afraid she'd been. Even before Skip's death left her having to do everything on her own, the sickle-cell crises had scared her. Knowing that she could lose her child to something she couldn't physically fight back against, or hold off, terrified her. Tonight, she said another small prayer of thanks that this one had been a false alarm.

"There are no small prayers, child, just necessary ones." Aunt Wesie told her shortly after Des's birth. Davida had confessed that she hoped all of her tiny prayers while caring for her baby might help her to somehow escape all the inherent childhood agonies and dangers of her disease. "Sweetie," her great-aunt comforted, "you take the

good with the bad, and trust Jesus for the rest.'' That was where
Davida left it, and offered her prayers as often as they felt right.

And Destiny thrived.

Wandering back to her place on the sofa, Davida pretended to watch
the news, then thumbed the remote again. Somehow, tonight she didn't
want to feign interest in the Middle East, and she couldn't have cared
less about the levels or the conditions of the muddy water flowing
through the Mississippi. She stretched and looked at her watch. Ten
thirty. Maybe she'd just go on to bed.

The phone rang.

Half rising from her place on the sofa, hesitating because her body
rocked with the jumping of her heart, Davida looked numbly at the
phone. It couldn't be him again. This time it almost had to be Mel,
or Glenn. It could be Quita or somebody from work. Or, it could be
him. Why would that man, who didn't know her from Adam's house
cat, call her again? she reasoned. It had been two weeks since the last
time he . . . Yes, she decided, it was Glenn, probably calling to get a
last minute idea for Aunt Wesie's birthday next week. That boy, as
otherwise responsible as he could be, he was always forgetting the
little things, then playing catch-up. Calmer, grinning, Davida plucked
the phone from the end table. ''Hello.''

''Hey, Boo.''

Something hot and sweet melted a sinuous path through her body,
and Davida let her knee drop to the sofa cushions in front of her. Her
arm shook slightly as she supported her weight before sliding into
a seated position. Two weeks did nothing to dull the effect of his
voice, even with only two little words, and he hadn't forgotten the
name she'd answered to. Her grin bloomed into a full smile. ''Hey,
you. There's no storm this time, and the remedial dialing class isn't
in session tonight. You don't have any homework from our last session . . .''

''I just had some questions.''

''For me?''

''Renee always said it was a good thing I wasn't born a cat. I'd
have lost six or seven of those nine lives by now.''

He sounded a little sheepish. Davida imagined him running a hand
across his face, trying to find a way to mask his interest. She heard
a shuffling sound and a muffled squeak. Picturing him leaning back
in a deep leather chair, she tried to put a face on him. Was he dark
and brooding, with smooth, tight-fitting skin the color of night, or a
bright, freckle-faced ''red-bone''? Was he tall and lean, or short and
round—maybe fat? He didn't sound fat. She smiled at her foolishness
and asked, ''What are you curious about, this time?''

''Did you ever hear from Glenn?''

"Glenn? My brother Glenn? Funny you should ask, because I did, and I thought you might be him—calling back to figure out what to do about our great-aunt's birthday." But, she was so glad he wasn't.

"Oh." He paused, then nonchalantly asked, "How are you? Everything okay?"

Davida paused, unsure of what to say next, wondering where the conversation was meant to go. "Fine. How's Renee?"

"Doin' fine," he drawled.

"And the woman who broke your heart? Has she been replaced—in your heart, if not your bed?" Davida bit her lips shut. She had to get out more! Why in the world had she asked him that?

"Oh, no, Boo? No, you didn't ask me that! Not a woman who hasn't, uh, *been* with a man for a while . . ."

Her cheeks heated and she was grateful he couldn't see her—him with this flawless memory and unavoidable curiosity. She shrugged, hoping the bluff found its way through her voice. "Haven't you ever heard the saying, 'do as I say, and not as I do'?"

"Yeah, Boo. Heard it and ignored it." He paused, seeming to think through his next words. "Are you asking because you want to know what it would take to replace her in my life? Or are you asking me if I'm good in bed?"

Implied arrogance, drenched with provocation hung in the air, flowed through the telephone line and surged, swollen and ripe between them. She'd come this far, she couldn't back down now. "I . . . suppose I am," Davida finally acknowledged, taking the dare. What the . . . what in the world got into her when she talked to this man?

"Which?" he challenged.

"Both," she bit her lips to hold back the embarrassed giggle. *Ooh, Lord!* Here she was, somebody's mother, on the phone, talking with a strange man like this! Flirting like she didn't have the sense . . . Her mother would kill her—if she knew. She pressed her lips tighter.

On his end, he moved again, she heard the chair squeak. "Hmm . . . It's kind of hard to rate your own performance," he said. "But I haven't had many complaints."

Davida's eyebrows rose, and she watched her eyes blink into the night reflected through her living room windows.

"And," he continued, "I guess I should admit I'm not into one-night stands—too unpredictable. We both know that sort of behavior is too dangerous, these days—for everybody concerned." He cleared his throat. "So, to answer your question, let's just say, I'm no novice."

What would it be like to just meet this man on the street? How would he approach a woman . . . *like me?* What would he say to get her to be this open, in person? How "okay" would it be to . . . Davida sighed. "It's so different for men."

"You say that like you sat out the sexual revolution. How is it so different for men?"

Here she went again ... "You, as a man, can admit to having experience, even a whole lot of experience, and it's considered admirable. A woman, especially a woman with a child, has to worry about her reputation with every step she takes. I mean, if you're thought of as being loose or easy, then you're an adventurer. With a woman, there's no allowance for missteps or mistakes: all that double-standard stuff comes into play."

"I don't think it's that bad anymore."

"Really?" Her voice rose and quickened. "When's the last time you were a woman?"

"Oh, come on, Boo. I'm not trying to be offensive, it's just that I don't see what you see."

"Maybe because you're not on the receiving end of it. How seriously, no, how big a liability would a female supervisor be if she slept with every man on her staff? Her professional value—regardless of her area of expertise—would drop immediately, and I guess the jokes would tell you how to get an easy promotion, wouldn't they? But that and a dollar would never buy respect."

"And respect is important to you?"

"Yes, it is." She paused. Marcus felt an emotional shift that rushed through the telephone. "What would you think of me if I told you I'd been with dozens of men?"

He almost laughed at the obvious trap she'd laid before him. "I'd wonder where you found the time to raise a kid, put in fifteen years on what sounds like a demanding government job, and still manage a fairly long-term marriage that left you a single parent. Then, I'd say that it doesn't sound anything like what I know of you. *Anybody,* man or woman, who'd been with 'dozens' of lovers is far less than discriminating—no matter what they have to offer." He waited a beat, maybe thinking over his next words. "Not to mention a little stupid and a lot careless, what with all the stuff floating around out in the world today. Honestly though"—his voice slowed—"I don't think you've had a great deal of experience."

She swallowed a lump of very hard air. "How do you know that?"

"Call it a hunch, Boo. Am I right?"

The heavy sigh escaped her with the blunt force of a belch, and gave far less relief. Davida covered her lips with the back of her hand.

"Am I right?" he insisted.

"Okay. You're right, but I'm not volunteering any numbers." Not that she had that many numbers to volunteer—Skip had been the first, and the other two, one a coworker, didn't even matter. He was right, and what the heck, this time she couldn't hold back the silliness. This man had the most uncanny ability to make her feel better—about a lot of things.

Her eyes strayed to Des's door, then back to her own reflection in the window. "Actually, I haven't had a lot of luck with romance. Something always seems to be off, something always goes wrong, and someone always winds up being hurt. It's very difficult to find balance."

"You think it could be an intimacy issue?"

"Sounds like somebody at your house has been watching *Oprah*."

"What's an Oprah?"

Davida giggled. "I'm not out there looking to have a wild affair, just to raise my batting average."

"You sound like you need a hug, Boo. If you want to fly on down to Hotlanta, I'd like to volunteer to help you out with a couple."

The unsubtle teasing behind his words salved the roughness unearthed by her heartfelt revelation and Davida smiled. "That's very generous of you, but I think not. I kind of like our relationship the way it is—it really does give us a special kind of freedom, don't you think?"

"You mean not even knowing each other's names?"

"Yes, that and maybe a little bit more." She held her breath.

"A freedom from commitment? A freedom from some of that romantic stuff you said never works for you?"

"You're teasing me?"

"Sure I am," he said. "Is it working?"

"Pretty much." Here she was smiling at this man again. She marveled. "I guess you're right, though."

"Good. Then, maybe this is the kind of accommodation more men and women need."

"A meeting of the minds" she suggested, "like we have."

"Exactly. We've become friends without ever seeing each other, just 'cause we enjoy talking and have a few things, like a brother and a sister, in common."

His voice, mellow and clear, was comforting in her ear, like something she'd waited a long time to hear. Davida tucked one leg beneath her, swinging her foot like a little kid, she clicked the remote a final time leaving the channel set on BET, with a smoldering view of Toni Braxton singing, complete with all too vivid lyrical pledges.

"Okay," she said softly into the phone. "But, there are just as many things that we don't have in common."

"Like what?"

"Well, like age. You're thirty-three, thirty-four? And I'm not." At his age, she was already married. Her "swinging single" days were pretty much gone for good, and he was still out there "sowing wild oats."

"Almost thirty-five, and age is just a number . . ."

"Easy for you to say, you don't have a fortieth birthday looming on the horizon."

"But consider the challenge, Boo. Life is a challenge, and you've just begun to face yours."

"Right. From where I sit, life is a road, and forty is a hairpin curve!" His laugh was infectious and Davida joined him in spite of herself.

"Okay," he finally admitted, "anything else?"

"I have a child to consider, and you don't. And even if you did, I doubt you'd have the same considerations I do."

"Why do you say that?"

Renee was right. Her brother really did seem to be part cat—the curious part. "I guess I forgot to mention it, but Des has sickle-cell disease."

"Ooh, I see. Sickle cell, huh? Not the trait, but the full-blown disease?"

Unintentionally and almost unconsciously, she stiffened. Her skin felt cold, rankled by goosebumps. This was where he got real quiet, and eased off the phone, and she'd never hear from him again. What if he asked the same question that stupid nurse had?

During her pregnancy, Davida, newly promoted and struggling to rise to the challenge, experienced one highly stress filled month of training and reorganization that left her reeling. The nausea and dizziness that drove her from her home that cold and rainy Wednesday night were accompanied by unaccountable sharp joint pain and endless cramping that sent her to straight to the emergency room. Odd lengths of paperwork completed, Davida and Skip sat through endless hours of blood tests and a hurried ultrasound, while she swallowed tears and tried to be brave enough for the two of them and their unborn child.

"Buddy is a little girl," Davida whispered, watching the fetal monitor.

Skip's hand tightened on hers. "Don't worry, babe. Buddy just gave me the 'high' sign." He winked a red-rimmed eye and held on tighter. Davida promised herself to hold on, too.

She'd barely cleaned the clear jelly from her rounded belly when they asked for Skip's blood. Watching the needle slide beneath his skin, Davida's poise had almost given way. Whatever was happening, nobody was telling her anything. They simply nodded and whispered professionally, glancing at her from the corners of untouchable eyes.

Davida folded defensive hands over her full twenty-two and one third weeks of pregnancy and prayed for her child. She made impossible deals with God and begged for intervention from every saint she'd ever heard of and even invented a few along the way.

The white-coated doctor with the grave, tired face finally folded his large knuckled hands on the steel table between them and explained the source of her pain. He attributed the problems to sickle-cell anemia—not that she had the disease, or was in any immediate danger. Davida heard herself gasp, and tried to recall ever being tested for the disease before. Her memory ratchetted through her childhood, further wracking her nerves in the process, finding nothing.

The doctor's eyelids drooped heavily as he refused to meet her eyes. It was, he said, the immediate joint stresses of her job change and the pregnancy that caused her red blood cells to "sickle" for the first time in her life.

Davida shredded tissues into the lap of her bright red maternity jumper. "But I can fly. Changes in temperature don't bother me. I've never . . . why didn't it affect Skip?" She hated the hysteria, so evident that even she heard it in her voice.

In the face of her near panic, the doctor was very clear. There was no threat to either her or her baby. Bed rest, proper nutrition, and plenty of fluids would, in fact, remedy most of her pain. The true problems lay ahead for the child Skip had already nicknamed Buddy.

"Buddy is still our baby," Skip said, almost to himself.

Tests proved both Skip and Davida carried the sickle-cell trait, and Buddy had inherited the disease.

Davida, two years later, sometimes caught in the throes of a nightmare, still heard the doctor's proper northern voice, just before she awakened to Destiny's tears and pain. "Your pregnancy is too far advanced to consider abortion, but amniocentisis will give you a better idea of what you and your husband may be facing."

"No," Davida and Skip said jointly. "We'll take whatever comes."

A bright, yellow-skinned, white-uniformed nurse hovered at the doctor's elbow, shaking her head. Davida didn't know the woman personally, and in her heart of hearts, she was glad she never would. The well-meaning, or perhaps intentionally sadistic, nurse patted her shoulder when she collapsed in tears. With hands on both Skip and Davida's shoulders, the woman in white whispered, "Why didn't you abort when you could? It would have saved you all a lot of heartache. Umph, the things that child's going to have to endure. Gonna go through all the tortures of hell, you just watch." Then, she disappeared.

The challenges Buddy would face throughout her life might be many, but facing each other, her parents were horrified by the implications of the woman's suggestion.

On her couch tonight, with her child sleeping safely in her own bed, over the space of more than eight years, Davida found she was able to feel a little more charitable toward that nurse. Just a little more . . . but this man on the telephone . . . If he asked, then she would just hang up. She didn't know him, and she didn't have to tell him anything she didn't want to. She'd only known him a little while, how much could she miss him?

"Yes," she said into the phone, "Des has full-blown sickle cell."

"I understand it can be very painful."

Davida licked her lips, and noticed Toni Braxton still on the television screen, now working a skin tight white catsuit for all it was worth. "Yeah. If my little girl had a choice, my guess is that she'd have picked another lottery to get lucky in. You know, one in about every five hundred African-American children is affected by the disease, and she's the one in her group."

"Mmm. I've read that sickle-cell anemia is the most common genetic blood disorder in the United States."

"Yes. Des started reading early—she was four."

"Bright kid." He sounded impressed.

"My pride and joy," Davida replied. "I've always suspected it was because she was hoping to find something in the newspaper— something about a cure, maybe. Anyway, can we change the subject? I guess I've just got sickle cell on the brain tonight—I was afraid Des might be going into a crisis. She didn't, but it gave me a little scare."

What a woman! Was there nothing she didn't handle with dignity and grace? His chair creaked again as he sat forward. "I'm glad Des . . . Destiny, right? I'm glad she's alright." He smiled and it poured through the telephone line. "Her name is pretty, how'd you and . . . where did it come from?"

The memory of naming her child came through with the sweet clarity of a chiming bell. "Right around the time Skip and I had just about given up on having children, she came along. And when she was born, she was perfect. Even with the sickle cell, she was perfect. We thought she was a gift of fate, of destiny, and what else could we call her?" Her gaze returned to her daughter's closed door.

"That's a nice story." His voice smiled even across all the miles that separated them.

At least he likes kids. So many men didn't, and made no excuses for dismissing the responsibility. Her own father had resented being tied down to a wife and two children; finally he'd walked out when Davida was still a baby. She was glad to have found a man like Skip who, once Des made her grand appearance, was as much in love with his child as he was with his wife. Having had one man like that in her life had been a blessing. Could any woman rightfully and fairly expect two?

"Still there?"

"What?" His question made her jump.

"You were so quiet, I thought you'd gone to sleep on me."

"Sleep? No, I was thinking."

He seemed to grin and again it carried over the phone line. "About me?"

Davida felt her throat tighten. "About Des," she lied.

"I'd like to meet her sometime. What do you say?"

"What? Me . . . no! How would we meet you?"

"Well, you know"—back-pedaling now, the man spoke quickly—"maybe sometime when I'm up in St. Louis visiting my sister and brother-in-law, we could get together for a drink or something. Do a day at Busch Gardens or Six Flags, or something, and include Destiny. I have a nephew . . ."

"Oh, I don't think . . ."

"I don't have any plans for a visit anytime soon," he said, "but sometime, maybe . . ."

"Mommy!"

The sleepy, dream-confused child's cry brought Davida to her feet. "I've got to go."

"Wait!" The man on the phone was confused and startled. "Was it something I said?"

Des coughed and then her voice changed to a ragged sob as the door to her room opened slowly.

"I really have to go," Davida explained hastily. "Good night."

"Good night."

She was gone before he got the words out.

"Destiny? Where are you, darlin'?" Davida's eyes pressed against the dark. Aided by a spill of light from the two corner windows that left a shadowed pattern across the comforter covering the child's bed, she finally located her. Going closer, she lowered herself to the bed. Feeling through the dark, she found a small, cool foot and shook it lightly. "What's up, sweet pea?"

Des shifted and repossessed her foot, tucking it beneath her gingham nightgown. She was a small movement among dark shadows that rustled lightly against her sheets and pillows. "Nothin'."

"You're sitting in the dark, baby. You're all bunched up, up here, and you called me. All of that is for nothing?" Davida, holding her breath, touched the sentimental velvet of her daughter's cheek. It was cool and she was grateful. "Was it a bad dream?"

Silent, Des moved again. Davida sensed a nod. "Why don't we turn on a light and talk about it?"

"In your lap?" Des sniffed loudly.

"Of course." The words were hardly past her lips before the child dumped herself against the comforting flesh and cloth of her mother. Davida slid a little closer to the bedside lamp, turning it on and collecting her child.

Small and dainty, with a creamy white ruffled shade, the lamp base was made from a cedar knee. Davida looked at it tonight, and the charming, cunningly curved, sleek, natural wood of the base looked nothing like what it really was. It looked like art—smooth, fluid, and seamless. Completely and simply beautiful, it looked like an exquisite gift from a compassionate, loving God. For whatever reason, Des had been instantly and completely enthralled with the shape of the golden, above-the-water root.

Jewell Morrison bartered with an impossibly old man on the side of a dusty Florida backroad for the souvenir. He'd scratched his balding head with gnarled hands, blacker than their own skin, and grinned at Jewell. She got the knee for a kiss on his grizzled cheek and a couple of dollars. That was the spring they'd journeyed to Florida. They'd gone to Eatonton for the Zora Neale Hurston festival. "Three generations of Morrison women all together" Aunt Wesie called them. Then six-year-old Destiny loved the idea of being a woman. She also loved the cedar knee.

Jewell drilled the base and wired the lamp herself.

Davida tugged the blue and white ruffle of her daughter's gown from beneath her legs. Des sat still enough to let her do it. The light from her lamp was warm and comforting, but Destiny was preoccupied. She toyed with her mother's hands, then pulled them close. Her heart banged in her little chest with a pace like a running rabbit. Davida held her tightly, and used the other hand to smooth the child's brow.

"Was it a very bad dream?" she asked in her daughter's ear, not moving her face. Des nodded solemnly, the ends of her braids brushing the corners of Davida's mouth and heart. "Can you tell me about it?"

Des twisted, locking her arms tightly about her mother's neck. "Mommy, sometimes people die."

Was that the dream? Had she dreamt she was dead?

Des pulled back. Her face in the light of her special lamp reminded her mother of something sweet and melting—a tootsie roll. "Mommy, if I die, will it hurt?"

Pressing the dearest little face in the world closer to her own, Davida listened to the sound of their joined heartbeats. It was a sound she remembered from before Des was born. It touched her then, and bound her even more tightly now. "Why are we talking about dying, Des?" Davida hoped she sounded normal.

Des scooted around between her mother's legs, resting her back against Davida's breasts. She moved her legs slightly when her mother rearranged the fabric of her nightgown again. "Sometimes, people with sickle cell die." She looked up. "You know."

"Oh, Destiny." Davida shook her head. "Baby, you're not going to die. Not for many, many years."

"Promise?"

"Oh, baby, yes. I promise."

Looking at her hands in the mellow yellow glow from her lamp, Des seemed to come to a decision. "If anything happened to me, you would be all alone. You know?" She pressed her lips together and extended her decision. "Mommy?"

"I'll never be alone, I'll always have you." Davida dropped her cheek to the top of her daughter's head and hummed a response. "I'll always have you," she whispered, touching the child's head. The soft black hair, braided into long plaits hung just below the child's shoulders. Stray hairs, maybe the ones dislodged by her nightmare, tickled the mother's skin and reminded her of just how precious this little person was to her.

"Mommy, everybody has to die, right?"

Davida bit her lip and elected not to lie. Des looked up at the hesitation. "Yes, Des."

"And I'm your 'loved one,' right?"

Davida nuzzled the soft brown cheek beneath her own. "Yes, for ever and always, you are my loved one."

Des twisted again, slipping out of her mother's lap, to sit beside her. "Then, Mommy, when we die, can we do it together?"

The room was suddenly devoid of air. Davida wondered if she would faint from oxygen deprivation. The brown eyes, so like her own, watched her patiently. *Oh, Destiny. There is nothing in this world or the next I wouldn't fight for you,* she thought. *There is no other person, man, woman, or child, who will ever be more important to me than you. You are my loved one.* Her thumb stroked the tender cheek. Des caught the thumb and squeezed. She smiled and her mother returned it with the same slow curve of her full lips. "Why do you ask me that, Des?"

"If we die together, Mommy, I won't have to worry about you being by yourself. Like you were tonight."

But she wasn't alone. She was on the telephone with a man—a man who almost made her forget that she and Des were the most important couple in her life.

"Can we, Mommy? Can we die together?" Des looked directly into Davida's face.

Davida's fingers caught the child's chin, and she brought her face close enough to drop a kiss on her nose. "Listen, my loved one, you don't ever have to worry about us dying together, 'cause that really isn't going to happen anytime soon. Besides, do you know, I'll kill a rock before I let anything happen to my baby?''

Des giggled. "A dead rock, Mommy?"

"A dead rock," she promised.

Des smiled, then stretched and yawned. Turning again, she found her way under the covers, pulling her favorite comforter with her. She sighed and looked at her mother.

"We're going to be together for a very long time, Des. Nothing will ever replace you in my life," Davida vowed, leaning suddenly forward to sweep the child into her arms, burying her face in the clean, giggling, little-girl-ready-for-bed smell of her.

If the telephone had rung at that very second, Davida knew there was nothing that could have made her answer it. That man on the phone? He was a momentary dalliance, a fantasy, nothing more. Destiny was real. Destiny was hers. Davida held on tighter and whispered into her daughter's ear. "Nothing, and nobody will ever replace you, my loved one."

CHAPTER FIVE

Marc stood over the phone frowning. What made her hang up so abruptly? Couldn't have been him—everything he said was perfectly innocent. Well, maybe not perfectly, but close enough. Maybe the problem was his suggesting they might meet somewhere, sometime. If that's what it was, then she'd taken this "secret pal" thing way past extreme. What did she expect, anyway? Men and women, mature men and women—they had social needs that went far beyond the telephone system's capabilities—didn't they?

Besides, everybody in the world knew the urge to mate was one of the strongest for any animal. Shoot, ask any of the fellas he'd gone to school with, and they'd guarantee they'd rather mate than eat. But, that wasn't how he approached her. All he asked about was meeting. What was wrong with that?

To meet, it made perfect sense, if you looked at it. Every few months or so, he was in St. Louis on business, or to see Renee and her family, or to return J.B. after a vacation visit—why shouldn't he get together with a friend? No reason not to see what's-her-name for maybe dinner and drinks; something casual in the West End, or someplace like Talanya's over on Skinker. And if anything came of it . . . like maybe a fancier dinner, some dancing . . . slow, really close, cheek-to-cheek dancing . . . His frown deepened—what would be wrong with that?

See? He shook a mental finger at himself. Every time he let Boo into his head, he started making impossible plans. He started thinking about what moonlight looks like when it's reflected in a beautiful woman's eyes. He started thinking about how warm she'd feel pressed against him when they danced, her body molded against his own. He started thinking about the tiny slip of movement rippling her skin there at the tender base of her throat where her pulse beats. He started thinking about how she'd smell when . . . Boo had already told him no, so which of those two letters did he not understand? Not only that, he didn't have a clue as to what she looked like.

And the plans he wanted to make were completely impossible, as long as he was more than four hundred miles south of her. It was real hard to hold a woman in your arms when she was in St. Louis and you were down in Atlanta.

"Besides, what kind of plans do you want to make?" he asked himself in a whisper. Looking around, he wondered why he was bothering to lower his voice. He was home alone, who was there to hear? And, what did he care if they did? Cocking his head, he put up his palms to stop himself. What he really needed was a real flesh-and-blood woman in his life, not a sexy smoke and sound phantom on the phone. So, the thing for him to do was to figure out a real good reason to go see about Renee.

See about Renee, and J.B., and George, too. See about them and meet this seductive woman with the rich telephone voice and enticing intellect. Her voice was like music; music in a tuneless world, Marc thought. And her words taught him more than he'd ever imagined about himself. Every time she spoke, it was like little symphonies, and anytime he closed his eyes, the music played again.

Seeing her, having a face to put with the voice, would be like the words that made a song complete in your head. Knowing the words, and the music together, her song—that was what he wanted now.

"No." Common sense intervened. He knew it was common sense because it was still shaking that finger in his face. "Leave this woman where you found her. You talk to her on the phone and that's enough. It's all she wants, and it's all you need for right now. You've got enough on your plate with your work."

Yeah. Work. It should have been enough that he'd dreamed of almost nothing but the cartoon man all through his teen years, then worked endlessly on Bro'Man for the first eight years of his career. It should have been enough that Bro'Man had been a "guest" superhero in several other internationally famous print and animated cartoon series, but it wasn't. In his heart, Marc had always known there was more to come.

Now, Milt had found the deal of a lifetime for Marcus Benton and Bro'Man. He'd found the break, the deal, the magic, courtesy of his daughter Tannie.

Tannie and her crew loved MC Feng Shui. They quoted him, they dressed like him, and they thought his videos were the best thing in the world. Milt just thought he was too loud, but as a favor to his daughter, who learned of her idol's troubles from Marissa Kaufman on the six o'clock news, he made a trip down to the Fulton County jail when the performer got pulled in for traffic tickets—several thousand dollars worth of unpaid tickets. Milt got him off for a cash settlement— and tickets to his sold-out concert for Tannie and company.

Milt also learned that Feng Shui was a major entertainer, a rapper with school-age children of his own, and he hated the reputation he'd gotten, was even embarrassed by his traffic tickets. He hated the reputation even more than he hated his real name—Herbert Ormond Jenkins.

Settled in the Ritz Carlton suite, sipping sweetened ice tea from one of the hotel's trademark blue crystal glasses, Milt began to assess his newest client. Herbert, alias Feng Shui, wasn't a bad guy at all.

"I'm thinkin' I wanna do business wit'chu," the big man decided. "I want to leave a legacy." His voice was thick with hints of his native South Carolina. "I got the money, but no where to put it. I got no, how do you say . . ." He snapped his fingers, searching for the word.

"Diversity?" Milt supplied.

"Diversity." Feng Shui nodded. "I want to be more like Puffy, like Will," he said, propping his feet up on the cocktail table. "I'm gonna do that, I gotta have diversity. I gotta invest." He picked up a much-read comic book, rolled it into a tube and slapped at his meaty thigh, and Milt got his great idea.

"You like comic books," he asked.

The man across from him nodded. "Yeah. That's where I got some of my best first ideas from, back when I was a kid. Other guys, they was out tryin' to repeat all the words to 'Rapper's Delight,' and I was pickin' up the real from my boys, like Spider Man with a touch of Ice T, and learnin' what it felt like to be appreciated for bein' original."

"Then, have I got a proposition for you," Milt grinned. When he finished the impromptu presentation, Feng Shui not only wanted to invest in Bro'Man, he was willing to guarantee his support with interest.

MC Feng Shui, Herbert Ormand Jenkins, a big black man of African, Cuban, Hatian, Vietnamese, Chinese, and American descent saw himself as Bro'Man. He saw Bro'Man as a way to prove to his children that Daddy was not a part of the big bad world of "East Coast-West Coast" conflict that the television and magazines said he was. Bro'Man, the way Milt painted him, was the way to a legacy for Feng

Shui, with Marcus Benton as his personal messiah—and he was ready to sign checks. Big ones.

"Creative freedom?" Marcus demanded while Milt giddily boogied around his living room humming Feng Shui's latest hit. "Do I get autonomy?"

"As much as you need. As much as you could conceivably want." Milt flipped pages, then boogied some more. "It's right here. This clause covers it," he pointed and hummed louder.

Marcus's eyes followed Milt's slightly jigging finger, and when he read it, there it was spelled out in words so clear that even a layperson could understand. All Marc had to do was sign, and draw.

And, therein lay the problem. Marcus Benton had to concentrate to do the work, and all he could think of lately was Boo. He shoved his hands into his pockets and started away from the telephone. His path was circular and brought him directly back to where he started. She was right. He rocked back and forth from his heels to his toes pretending this dilemma belonged to anyone but him. *We agreed on that "don't ask, don't tell" policy, and I'm sticking to it.*

Marc took three steps away from the phone, then stopped and looked back over his shoulder. No. He shook his head, clear and definite resolution crossed his face. No way he was calling her again, and he was certainly not getting on a plane to try to find her. The least he could do was to have a little dignity. There was no need to go running behind a woman he'd never seen—never would see—with his tongue hanging out.

The resolution lasted a week.

Rolling the last of the series he'd completed for DC Comics into a mailing tube, Marcus had the peculiar sensation of being watched, or maybe it was more like being summoned. The feeling had nothing to do with the MC Feng Shui deal, though Marc had developed a creatively gifted, rapping sidekick for Bro'Man.

Looking around the bedroom, the large bright one he used as a home studio, he knew he was alone in his loft. Thirty-three hundred square feet of space, and he knew not another living soul was around. Still the siren sensation was undeniable and seemed to be coming from the cordless phone he'd tossed on the futon earlier.

Laying the sketches aside, Marc swiveled on his stool to face the instrument. His hands rested on his thighs, and he leaned slightly forward. Not even straining, he seemed to still hear—something. He didn't know quite what it was, only that it was persistent and demanding, and kept whispering her name. When his fingers strayed to his opposite wrist, straightening the heavy gold links of his watchband, he noticed the time. Ten o'clock—just about the time he usually called her.

Why did the damned thing keep whispering?

He looked at the phone again, and was almost ready to swear the damned the thing was vibrating and glowing, maybe even doing a little side-to-side jig, demanding his attention. If he'd been illustrating this scene for one of his comics, he'd have drawn a tiny voice balloon above the telephone, then he'd have lettered in the words, "call her."

"That's stupid," he growled to himself. Sighing with disgust, he glared at the phone. It was daring him not to call her. He could call her if he wanted to, and it wouldn't mean anything other than that— just a phone call to a friend, like any other. *Oh, yes it would mean something else,* his mind told him, *'cause you're addicted to the sound of her voice and the lure of her innocent words. You can't even say you're attracted by the beauty of her face or the grace of her figure. Addicted, that's what you are.*

"Right," he agreed dryly. He'd read it in *Psychology Today.* One of the classic signs of addiction was the constant promise of walking away from the source of the addiction, and never quite making it.

"Uh-huh, walk away. Turn your back, and walk away. Just like I'm doing right now," he said, walking over to the futon to pick up the phone. The hard black plastic felt warm in his hand, and he punched in her number from memory. "I ought to just put her on speed-dial."

"Hello?"

Funny how familiar her voice had become. Maybe it was that music thing again, or simply the overall effect of his rapidly growing obsession. "Hi," he said. "It's me."

"Well, hey, you. How are you?"

Dropping to the futon, giddy with the relief her voice brought, Marc grinned at his knees, then settled back more comfortably for a conversation with the woman whose name he didn't know. "I'm losing my sanity."

"Really?" she teased. "Are you bragging about it?"

"Nope. Just plain ol' lost my mind."

"How can you tell?"

His grin broadened. Okay, she made him laugh. That was a good reason for calling, she made him laugh. "What are you trying to say?"

"What are *you* trying to say?"

"I've been talking to my phone."

"That's what phones are for." A light chuckle crossed between them. "And your problem is . . . what, exactly?"

"I'm a tad bit humiliated to confess, but there was no one at the other end of the line when I was doing all this talking."

She paused, looking for the right words. "No one on the line. Yeah, you're right. We may have a problem here."

"Didn't I say so?" He laughed. "You think celibacy could be a factor?"

"Celibacy? Who's making you celibate?"

"I am, I guess," he answered after a moment's thought. "Told you before, I've never been much interested in sleeping around, and I don't know many people I feel like being intimate with, right now."

Including that woman who broke his heart? Davida hummed with sympathy. "That is a problem. What are you going to do about it?"

"I'm kind of considering checking out the airlines, flying up to St. Louis."

He pronounced it "St. Louie," like a native, and Davida smiled. "What would you do in St. Louis?" she asked.

"I'm considering coming up, hanging out, eating some good food, listening to some good music, and maybe seducing you," he murmured the last so lowly the woman on the other end nearly missed the words. "What do you think?"

"I think you were right earlier," she snapped, though she still sounded almost amused. "You *have* lost your sanity."

That's another thing to like about her, Marc grinned. She knows how to take a joke.

Or, had it been a joke? Refusing to inspect the question, he pressed what he hoped was a conversational advantage. "Just in case I ever *do* try to seduce you, is there anything special I need to know?"

"Know about what?" Incredulity and laughter threaded through her voice.

"What it takes to seduce you. I was always a good student, and I know the only way to do well is to study and understand what you're doing, so tell me, what do I need to know about you?"

"I'm not quite sure what you're asking me."

"Oh, yes. I think you are."

"I mean, what do you mean, 'how would you seduce me'? I mean, you sound like you've got more than a little seduction experience in your past. Like maybe you ought to know what you're doing when you ... and then, to ask me? Why would I be any different? A seduction's a seduction—isn't it?"

Marc pulled the receiver from his ear and studied it. Was she really that naive? "Man," he said when he brought the phone back to his ear.

She murmured something he didn't quite catch, and he didn't ask her to repeat it. Instead, he closed his eyes, tried to imagine her face and spoke to her, as he knew her to be. "A seduction is *not just a seduction.* It's different for everyone, Boo. What is intimately erotic and special for one woman, one couple, may be a complete turnoff for another.''

Embarrassed, Davida giggled softly. "I suppose that's true. I don't think I'd care much for whips and chains, and such.''

"No?" Laughing, he raised his hand to massage the back of his neck. "So, what would rate high on your list?'' he asked, trying to believe he was only teasing and not making real notes for future reference.

"I can't believe we're having this conversation."

"Call it a fantasy, because we *are* having this conversation.'' Marc tried to ignore his body's response to the suggestions of their conversation. It was all too easy to imagine himself seducing this particular woman—and he'd never even seen her! "What would be your idea of the ultimate seduction?''

She hesitated for so long that he began to think she wouldn't answer.

"I guess I'm pretty traditional,'' she said at last, wondering if she should continue. The last man she'd made this confession to had laughed at her. Jeff Watson was a coworker she'd thought to find comfort in, and he'd hurt her feelings badly when he said she suffered from, "typical black women's too-much-televisionitis.'' His lips curled derisively when he declared, "that stuff you want, it ain't real.''

Davida walked away from him, from the experience, wondering if what she wanted wasn't real at all, or if it wasn't real because Jeff feared and believed he could never live up to what she wanted, which led to a lot of maybes.

Maybe he blamed his uncommitted fears and failures on black women in general. Maybe it wasn't real to him because it was more work than he thought he had to do to get and keep a woman. Maybe it wasn't real because he'd never considered all the things there were to value in another person, a person who made you more than what you could ever be alone.

Her stomach curled in on itself, and Davida had another memory of Jeff Watson—extreme relief when he was transferred to Dallas two months later.

"Then, tell me what a traditionalist needs.'' The male voice questioning her needs made Davida breathe a little deeper, the oxygen going straight to her head, making her a little drunk on him.

A traditionalist needs for it to be real—the hearts, the flowers, all of it. She'd listened to the stories Anne Laird and Mel and her other women friends told and she knew they couldn't *all* be made up. There were women out there who had feelings and experiences she'd only dreamed of. Deep in her heart, Davida refused to believe what she wanted to give and receive was anything less than real. Shyly, she smiled at the unseen man and said, "I guess I really am pretty traditional. Flowers, candles, soft music, a crackling fire."

Marc nodded. "A really good bottle of wine?"

"No, I'm not much for drinking," she said. "But, I do eat."

He'd pretty much expected that from her. It was part of what delighted him about her. "What would you like?"

"Something really good, and fairly exotic. Or at least a wonderful appetizer or dessert—something I've only heard of, but could remember the taste of forever."

"Would chocolate be a factor here?"

"Is chocolate a known aphrodisiac?" The question was innocent, he heard it in her voice.

"Mmm, there've been rumors." She made his mouth water. "How about a bearskin rug?"

"Ugh! No, no, no, no! No dead animals, please!"

He choked on his laughter. "Uh, o-kay. So, you've described a setting. Now, what about the man? Tall, dark, and handsome—traditional to go with your traditional setting—or could he be something else? A pro basketball player, maybe?" Marc grimaced as he asked the question, hoping she wouldn't describe Jordan or Barkley, though it might be alright if she started with Spudd Webb.

"We've been here before, remember? You already asked me what I was looking for in a man," she said.

"And you answered. . . ?"

"That I didn't know. That people tend to be too superficial—fixing on things like height and weight, and eye and skin color, instead of things like character and integrity and humor. I think I might have told you that the right person should be . . . um . . . special. It would be nice if he was intelligent, loving, caring, unselfish . . . those are things that would attract any woman. Or maybe I should say, any person."

Marc wondered if she realized how much she'd just revealed about her relationship with Skip, and if she realized how much she would expect from another man. Skip must've been a helluva guy. He must have shared a lot with her in the time they had together. He wondered if he could measure up? Marc was suddenly aware that he was jealous. "Should I, er, *he* bone up on poetry?" he asked. "Something like *Phenomenal Woman,* maybe?"

"Oh, yeah. Right. I'd feel really stupid if some guy grabbed my hand, stroked it gently as he looked deep into my eyes and started sighing pretty words at me." She laughed a good long while, long enough to make Marc wonder how much of it was real, and how much of it covered need for the alleged source of her mirth. "Maybe

I'd believe it by the time he got to the part about, 'the curve of my back.' "

"So, does that mean the poetry's out, then?"

"Actually," she replied slowly, "a little rhymed romance might be nice, but only if it were sincere." She paused, and he heard her draw a slow, wistfully deep breath. "Sincerity is important, and I would know in a heartbeat if it was a game."

"How?"

She smiled. "The way women always know these things—when we admit them to ourselves. There would be an edge, a bitter little edge to the way he read or said the words. They, the words, would be directed at me, not to me—trust me, there's a difference."

Her words made Marc recall their first conversation. "Like the difference between love and lust?"

"Exactly."

Her answer made Marc squirm restlessly, crossing then recrossing his legs, as he tried to regain comfort on his futon. Her single word hit too close to home, and suddenly the phone felt unnaturally sweaty against his palm. Realizing the strength of his grip, he consciously loosened his hand on the telephone. Clearing his throat, he reversed his legs again. "Okay, then that means we have flowers, candles, music, a fire, exotic food, and soft, heartfelt words. Anything else?"

"Like what"

Her soft voice seemed to have picked up a sensual vibration that tipped Marc's equilibrium. "Like the actual lovemaking?"

Her low moan of embarrassment brought him back to himself. "Oh, I can't do this."

"Sure you can. We've talked about almost everything else. Tell me what you like—slow and easy? Hot and rough? Taking the initiative and the whole night to please . . ."

"Oh, stop." She drew the words out almost the way he would have expected her to in a moment of passion.

"Turning you on?" He crossed his legs again, and realized the conversation had definitely done its job on him.

"No. That's enough," she ordered firmly.

"Okay," he conceded. "I didn't mean to embarrass you."

"Yes, you did."

He laughed. "Okay, you're right, I did. It's cute when you blush."

"I thought you were the man who hated 'cute,' and how did you know I was blushing?"

"Your voice was blushing."

"Maybe my voice needs a cold shower."

"It's getting late," he said. "Maybe that cold shower's not a bad idea." For both of us.

"I'd better go, then . . . um . . ."

Marc's forehead furrowed at the unasked question. "Yes?"

"*All* night?" The question was tentative, *but she did ask.*

Recalling his question, he grinned. "It has been known to happen."

"All night." There was wonder in her voice. "Have you ever . . . ?" She let the question dangle between them.

"Oh, Lord. Now, you've got *me* blushing!"

". . . but, what . . . how do you even begin . . . ?"

"Boo, sometimes it can start with words. Sweet, soft, gentle, but emphatically meant words. Words that touch you. . ."

". . . like a lover's hand," she finished for him. Where had that come from?

"Seems you have more experience than you gave yourself credit for."

"No, it was just a good guess. Maybe," she said softly, "maybe it was the mood."

"Oh, Boo." Marc smiled. "This is getting a little deep. I gotta go, good night."

"Good night."

Marc thumbed the button to disconnect the call only because he knew she was already gone. "Why the heck did I start this?" he groaned. Standing, pushing his fingers into the small of his back, he pulled himself tall and stretched. Without thinking, he moved through his studio and down the hall, turning out lights as he went. Finally reaching his bathroom, he pulled his shirt from his pants and unbuttoned it as he faced himself in the mirror.

"I don't *even* know why I went there with her. A woman I don't have a name or a face for, and I had to go playing his 'n' hers matching fantasies." He could still hear the sultry echo of her soft words playing in his ear. "*All night?*"

"Yeah, Boo," he answered, tossing the shirt aside, not caring that he spoke to the memory of a phantom woman. "With the right person, and the right circumstances, all night."

He reached into the shower stall considered for a moment, then turned the water on full blast. Icy darts, drops of breathlessly cold water splashed his bare chest and arms—exactly what he was looking for. Better to make this a cold shower—the colder, the better.

Davida shook the pillow again, feeling the heavy feathers slide to the side and clump, then settle more evenly. She pushed her face into the pillow, then jerked herself up to a sitting position. "There'll be no sleeping in this camp," she whispered to herself, "not tonight." She thumped the pillow again, then dropped her head into its mounded center. Rolling onto her right side, she pulled her knees to her chest and closed her eyes. The backs of her closed eyelids were like a movie screen where her earlier words insisted on playing themselves out in Technicolor.

Picturing herself, her crackling fire, complete with flowers and candle-scented air, and a faceless man, Davida sighed so helplessly and needed so tremendously that she grabbed at the cotton sheets on her real bed. Her eyes popped open, and she stared out at the shapes of her darkened, familiar room. This was all her own colonial furniture, not the rustic wood of her dream. The lights moving across her walls came from the vague headlights of neighborhood traffic curving past her corner lot, not the reflection of firelight on crystal.

Moving her arm across the cool bedding, across from the warm spot where she lay, she knew she was alone—not with the man in her dream. Alone. Not with the man in her mind who caressed her nude body with skillful hands. Not with the man who murmured soft, alluring words that promised to fulfill, in the deeply seductive voice of her telephone caller.

All night?

Turning her face into the pillow, Davida groaned and swallowed quickly. This fantasy was exciting, and way too good. Pushing up on one elbow, she glanced at the little brass and china clock. It was now missing one of its pink china roses thanks to Destiny's gymnastic skills, but it still worked, and right now it said one forty-five.

Davida flopped onto her back and threw an arm across her face. She had to be up at six, and all she could think of was him. The fantasy was exciting, but now it was costing her a night's sleep.

All night? Davida blushed in the darkness and wondered what it would be like to do anything, let alone make love, all night long.

All night? And he said it was possible.

"Oh, Lord," Davida breathed, and twisted the knot of sheets tighter. "What must that be like?" She couldn't help herself as she bit the sheet, and squeezed her eyes closed. So, this was the desire all those romantic movies and love songs told about? Maybe it felt better if you shared it with someone.

All night?

She groaned again, and tried to disown the sound she knew was her own. The room seemed unbearably hot, though she knew it wasn't. Parts of her body that she publicly denied knowing about, seemed to demand full and immediate attention from the hands of a man more solid than the one in her dreams. Throwing the covers back, she pulled her long legs free, and headed for her bathroom. Standing over the sink, letting the water run cold, she passed her hands beneath the faucet, bringing double scoops of cool water to her heated face. Fingering stray hairs back from the moisture, Davida held her hands to her cheeks and wondered at the sensations triggered by a telephone call from a stranger.

Finally, she raised her head and caught sight of her own large dark eyes in the bamboo-framed mirror above the sink. Part of her could hear Aunt Wesie's warning, a leftover from childhood, "Be careful what you ask for, you just might get it."

For right now, though, Davida didn't care. She knew what she wanted, what her body told her she wanted more than almost anything else she could think of.

All night?

"I don't know what it's like," she told the mirror, "but I sure would like to. I surely would like to."

CHAPTER SIX

"Until it's done, can I at least get a lick? You know, to hold me over?" Destiny raised her eyebrows and leered hungrily at her mother.

Davida looked up from the mixing bowl she was carefully scraping and turning into the greased and floured cake pan. Destiny wrapped her legs around the tall stool where she sat. For all her little girl awkwardness and sugar cravings, she was surely her mother's child. The dark eyes and strongly defined features all leading to a small and pouting mouth were her true inheritance.

But, like her father, she was not above a little side-betting. "I could wash that for you if you wanted me to." She fluttered her eyelashes and smiled, showing off the gap where she'd lost the tooth earlier in the week. Davida had to move fast to bat aside the little finger that swooped into the batter and landed in her daughter's mouth.

"It's not ready to eat yet, Des." She laughed. "You keep doing that, and I'll have just enough here for a birthday cookie."

"But you'll share it with me, 'cause I'm your loved one. Right?" Des laughed at her mother's smirk, and stole another fingerful of batter. "This is good, but I wish it was the yellow kind instead. I like it better."

"But, it's *my* birthday, babe, and I decided I wanted chocolate cake with milk chocolate frosting. So, chocolate it is, take it or leave it."

"Oh, I'll take it. I was just saying . . ." Des looked up at her mother and squinted her eyes.

"What?" Davida laughed. "Why are you looking at me like that?

And what were you going to say?" Setting the empty bowl aside, Davida wiped her hands on her apron and punched the eject button on the mixer, releasing two beaters loaded with chocolate cake batter. Her daughter bounced with leg-swinging excitement as she eagerly accepted one.

"I was just wondering. Do you want chocolate 'cause it's that 'time of the month'?"

Watching, poking her tongue through the metal gap to catch the sweet batter on her own tongue Davida blinked. Moving the beater slowly, she tried to neutralize her face. "Honey," she crooned, swallowing hard and enunciating clearly, "what did you say?" When Des wiggled her brows, Davida fought to keep her own still. She didn't trust herself to move.

"I ast you if . . ."

"Asked. You 'asked' me, with a d."

"Right. I asked you, with a d, if this was 'that time of the month'. And you didn't answer me yet," Des responded.

Davida bought a few seconds by licking the almost clean beater again. "No, Des. This is not, 'that time of the month' unless you mean my date of birth, and this month, in particular. Do you know what that means, 'time of the month'?"

"Sure." Des claimed the empty bowl when her mother turned to put the cake pans into the already hot oven. "Tawanna told me."

There ought to be a special school for kids like that one. Davida hoped her smile was warm as she turned to face Des. Not that hers was a whole lot better. "What did she tell you, Des?"

"Oh. That's when you eat a lot of chocolate an' stuff. An' you know, she said that 'that time of the month' is when ladies can make babies—if they want to." Raising her eyebrows, Des shot her mother a questioning look, then, "Do you?"

"Do I what?"

"Want to make babies."

This was almost as bad as the, "You need a man in your life" conversation they'd had in the car last Saturday on the way back from Des's tap class. That conversation, too, had been precipitated by a comment from Tawanna Mallory. Gotta keep her away from my kid, Davida thought. Clearly, it was the only way to preserve Destiny's childhood.

Leaning across the central island in their spacious blue and white kitchen, Davida was tempted to try to change the conversation—maybe talk about the copper pots twinkling overhead—past experience had proven it wouldn't work. Instead, she looked into the dark brown eyes that matched her own, and tried to read a few minutes into their future. "Sweetie, it doesn't exactly work that way."

"Oh, I know. You have to have a man, too." Her snaggle-toothed smile was bright with suggestion.

Du-uh! Tawanna Mallory talked too much. Davida leaned her chin into her palms and waited for more from her *wunderkind*.

"You know, it would be okay with me if you had a man *and* a baby. 'Course it would change our family some, but it would be alright." She looked at her mother's face, and continued on the wings of childish insight. "Oh. Mmmm, this is one of those things I'm not supposed to know until I'm older, isn't it?" Destiny let her lips curl to the left, the way she always did when she was thinking. "Well, that's okay, we can just forget it for now, if you want to, because whatever happens will happen anyway."

More pearls from the lips of Tawanna Mallory, Davida supposed. The clear chimes of the front doorbell saved her from making any response.

"I'll get it!" Destiny scrambled down from her high bentwood stool and raced for the front door.

"No! Des, wait, don't open that door," Davida warned. Following her daughter, wiping her hands on her apron as she went, Davida half wondered who she was afraid might be on the other side of her door. *At least I know who it's not.* She was glad that there was no way that it could be her Atlanta caller—Des would only try to clarify his presence through Tawanna Mallory.

Though it might have been nice to have a special gentleman caller on the other side of her door. A man with flowers, candy, and a big smile—all to celebrate her. That and her birthday—of course. Trying not to think of those fantasies now, Davida looked out the small window of her front door before opening it. The tall man in the brown leather jacket stood, head down, with his shoulder and back to her, and the morning's *Post-Dispatch* lightly tapping his leg.

Pulling hard at the door, using her foot to block its further progress, Davida looked out. "Yes?"

The man held up the newspaper and turned slowly. Davida stepped back, only to feel her smile widen and her pulse quicken with pleasure as he faced her. "Glenn!"

Bending from the waist, brushing his bearded cheek against hers, and smelling of soap, her brother tossed the paper aside and his arms closed around her almost before she could shut the door behind him. "Hey, Cookie."

"Aw, Butch. It's so good to see you." She lifted her face for his kiss without loosening her grip on his neck, and still managed to hold on, dangling above the floor. Inches above six feet, Glenn Morrison stood well above Davida's five feet nine inches. "Are you going to stay with us?"

He shook his head. "All of forty, and you're still doing that." He patted her back and swung her in a small circle, much to Des's laughing delight.

"But, are you going to stay with us? Or are you going home—to her?"

"You have no tact, girl." He shook his head. "LaDonna's a little more than I can take right now. I need some rest, and relaxation, but I didn't want to tear up your weekend. So . . ."

"Come on, Butch."

"It's your birthday, don't you have any special plans? Something to do with that crew of wild women you like to hang out with?"

"No, and they're not wild women."

He raised an eyebrow and stared. "Really. I seem to recall your friend Mel . . ."

She hugged him tighter. "She was all of sixteen, and didn't know any better."

"As I recall, Anne Laird has a little thing for the boys . . ."

Slopping a wet kiss against his cheek, Davida rolled her eyes. "He was sooo lonely."

"Uh-huh, then there's crazy Quita Walton . . ."

"Dropped on her head as an infant." Davida giggled. "So, will you stay with us?"

"Maybe if I'd had a chance to call before I barged in on you like this," he said slowly.

"You know you don't have to make reservations with us, Butch. Stay."

"So, I can bring my suitcase in from the car?"

"Boy!" Davida punched her brother's shoulder. "You made me beg like that!"

"It seemed like the right thing to do. Anyway, happy birthday." His dark, lean face softened with the half-smile he gave his sister— his version of a grin. His eyes, dark brown and thick lashed, a perfect match for Davida's and Destiny's, showed tiny lines at their corners. The lines, earned by hours of reading and writing the legal briefs that had gained him the respect of lawyers and judges throughout the country, made him look serious and highly deserving of his conservative reputation. "You don't look half bad for forty."

She let herself be lowered to the floor, propped her hands on her hips and pursed her lips in mock asperity as she looked back at him. "I'll have you know, I not only don't look bad, I am *phat.*"

Glenn hooted with unanticipated laughter. "*Phat?* Now where did you pick up a term like that?"

Davida let her head and shoulders swing, as her finger waved up at her brother. "I have it on very good authority that I am officially, pretty, hot, and temptin'—even at forty. Shoot, especially at forty, thank you very much.''

Looking down at Destiny from his great height advantage, Glenn passed a hand over his shaved head. Mellow morning sun gleamed and shaped itself against his skull, turning his skin a rich and brassy shade of brown. "Your mother is *phat*. What am I supposed to say to that?"

When Des crooked her finger, he knelt, folding himself down and closer to her height. Reaching for him, she swung her arm around his neck, brought her face closer, and whispered. "Uncle Glenn, nothing else to do, you just gotta love her."

He stared at his niece, then glanced between her and her mother. "I guess you're right." He nodded.

The little girl knew approval and unlimited love when she saw them, and flung both arms around his neck. She planted a very wet sounding kiss on his cheek. Her index finger traced the high, definitive bones of his cheek, stopping at the corner of his mouth. "I know it's my mom's birthday, but did you . . . ?"

"Des . . ."

"You'd better believe I brought you something special," Glenn said, digging into the pockets of his denim jacket. "How could I not? Matter of fact, I brought you both something." He slanted a look at Davida. "I smell something, something good."

"It's cake. Chocolate." Destiny offered, still watching her uncle's pockets.

Patting his jacket, Glenn stood and reached for his niece's hand. Des frowned and looked up at him. "Where's my present? You said . . ."

With a husky chuckle, he looked at his sister. "You're teaching her really well."

Davida held her palms defensively. "Not me. I don't know where she gets it, but I try and try . . ." The sound of her child noisily clearing her throat made Davida look down in surprise.

When Destiny ducked behind her uncle's leg, out of scowling range, Glenn frowned to hold in his laughter. "It's in my suitcase, little girl. I didn't forget you, and you're going to like it. I promise."

"Cool," she chirped, and did a happily impromptu head and hip shaking version of the macarena.

Davida laughed at the quizzical look Glenn gave her. "I call it the Tawanna Mallory effect."

"Tawanna? Mallory?"

"One of her friends from school," Davida explained.

Glenn nodded as if that made all the sense in the world. He tucked one of Destiny's dancing hands in his own and walked out to his car to get his bag.

* * *

Glenn Morrison was sprawled lazily on the couch in the great room clasping a cold, long-necked Corona in one hand. He offered his sister his half smile, and closed his eyes. Sitting together, they enjoyed the quiet now that Destiny had finally managed to fall asleep—it felt like old times. "There were an awful lot of candles on my little sister's birthday cake."

"Means *you're* getting old," Davida returned, nudging him with her toes, and grinned companionably when he nudged back.

"All those candles, what'd you wish for? he asked.

"I can't tell you—you know it won't come true if I say it out loud."

"You sound like Des." Glenn tilted the bottle to his lips, his eyes still on Davida. Moving the bottle slightly, he let his half-smile grow and dangle. "I'll tell you what I hope you wished for." He bent his long arm back and settled his head against his hand. "I hope you wished for a man, a real good man to keep you company."

How did he know? When she'd drawn breath to blow out those forty candles Des insisted on, Davida had closed her eyes and thought—just for an instant—of hearing the telephone ring. Of hearing the voice of a man she'd begun, too easily, to care about.

"A man?" she said now. "I don't need a man. I have you and Des. What do I need a man for?"

"See? That proves it. It's been so long since you shared your life with anybody else, you can't remember what it's like, or why it's worth doing."

"Oh? You're a fine one to talk," she retorted. "Out in the world, slamming your legal weight around, no time for a private life, acting like the original lone wolf." Davida's eyes narrowed and glowed with challenge. "Or are you still involved with that she-wolf, even though you told me . . . ?"

"Over and done with, Cookie," Glenn muttered into his beer.

Davida reached for her Diet Coke and let it spill from the can, foaming over melting ice. "I can't say I'm sorry."

He shrugged. "Neither can I. She's moving out this weekend."

"Oh." Now it made sense, perfect sense that he would spend this time with her and Des.

"I guess part of me knew that it would eventually come to this," he continued. "We all make mistakes."

"And LaDonna was one of yours?" The grimace crossing his face made her wish she'd kept the comment to herself. Almost ashamed, Davida crossed her legs, and pulled her feet under her. "Are you seeing anyone new?"

"What do you think I am?" He shook his head "Truth is, I haven't had much time for socializing lately. How about you?"

She'd known this was coming. She cleared her throat, sorry she'd opened herself up to this question. "No," she said, "not, really."

"You're going to say you don't need a man again, aren't you?" When she nodded, he looked to the ceiling. "Stubborn as anything— must be your Taurus birthdate."

Davida wrinkled her nose. "Being born in May has nothing to do with anything."

"Says you." Glenn scowled. "When are you going to start living for you again, Cookie? How long are you going to sit around defining yourself by your child and your job?"

"My self-esteem is fully intact, thank you very much. I rather like my job, and my child is going to have special needs for the rest of her life."

"You say that like she's physically or mentally disabled and needs you to help her breathe. Des is a perfectly normal child, and you should know that better than anybody. You didn't elect her genes, and you shouldn't spend the rest of your life doing penance." He sucked at the beer again, finishing it in one long draught. He set the bottle down with a solid thump. "Dammit, Cookie, you're a young, beautiful woman. You shouldn't be so alone."

"Come on, Butch." He frowned at her use of his nickname. "I'm not all that alone . . ."

"Why? Because you got over being 'the widow' and made some progress at work?" He shrugged. "A lot of good that does. You turn down every promotion or change that might send you and Des anywhere but right here in St. Louis."

"I couldn't just uproot Des, not after she lost . . ."

"And what did you lose when Skip died, Cookie? How much of you did you lose?"

Davida allowed her lips to pull into a childish pout, and she crossed her arms tightly across her chest. "It's my birthday, and I don't want to talk . . ."

The sharp ring of the telephone cut off whatever else she might have said. Davida closed her eyes and tried to remember how to breathe. *Oh, Lord! It was him!* She knew it instinctively. Not tonight. She knew she wished . . . but not tonight . . . It could be Mel, but she had a feeling . . . *Lord, let me be wrong . . .*

"Aren't you going to get that?"

Davida's eyes flew open when she felt her brother's weight shift on the sofa as he reached for the telephone. She wished she'd accepted the MemoryCall service when the telephone company last offered it to her. She wished she'd purchased a new answering machine back when she bought the Caller ID unit. She wished she'd turned the blasted phone off. She wished she'd told the man . . .

"Kind of slow aren't you?" Her brother reached for the receiver. Her lunge was too late. "Yes?" Glenn Morrison narrowed his eyes suspiciously. "Yes, this is 555-3857. Who do you want to speak to?"

It's him. I know it's him. Davida bit at the inside of her lip and did a mental flip-flop. He didn't know who to ask for, she suddenly realized. He didn't know her name and he sure couldn't ask for "Boo."

"Who are you, and where are you calling from?"

She imagined him, stranded there on the other end of the line, stumbling for an answer to Glenn's less-than-gracious questions. Finally able to move, she held out her hand. "It's for me," she said. "Give me the phone."

His features took on a sharp craftiness as Glenn angled his body slightly away from his sister. "Who you wanna talk to, man?"

"Butch, give me my phone. Now!" Davida hissed.

Reluctantly, Glenn placed the phone in her hand.

"Thank you." She closed her fingers around the receiver, and lifted it to her ear. "Hello?" Her voice sounded thin and nervous to her own ears. Her palms were damp, and Davida wondered if she only imagined the relief that flooded the phone line.

"I didn't know you had company, and I didn't know who to ask for."

Even with Glenn listening, Davida was warmed by the rich, deepness of her caller's voice. "It's all right," she assured him, refusing to look over her shoulder. "You've just had the pleasure of meeting my charming older brother."

"Glenn." His voice lightened. "I thought he was, maybe a likely prospect for that affair you were aiming for."

"I keep telling you, I'm *not* looking to have a . . ."—she turned her back to her brother, who made no effort or pretense of giving her privacy—". . . well, you know what. Don't you ever think about anything else?" She jumped when her brother's beard touched her cheek. Covering the phone with one hand, she fended him off with her elbow. "Get a life, and leave mine alone?"

Glenn huffed and flopped into his corner of the sofa.

"That really is your brother, isn't it." The caller laughed in her ear.

"Oh, yes."

"Does he know about me?"

"No."

"Why not?"

"Because . . ."

" 'Because' is not an answer."

A quick look over her shoulder dictated her next remark. "This really isn't a good time to talk."

"Then tell me your name, so I'll know who to ask for next time— when I call back."

Her eyes widened, and she looked at the floor so that her brother wouldn't continue trying to read her face. "No."

"It would make things a lot less complicated. Besides, who am I going to tell?"

"No," she said flatly.

"You mean, you really have no intention of ever telling me?" he asked incredulously.

"Look, we agreed." She fought to remain calm, even as her caller cursed under his breath. When he was silent for what seemed like hours, Davida whispered, "Hello?"

"I'm still here." His words were terse and she could hear his breathing—it sounded angry. "We agreed not to meet, and given the distance . . . I can understand that. But, I thought the name thing . . . I thought that was just a game, something we'd get tired of after a while and stop playing. I got tired, but you, you're not playing, are you? You don't intend to tell me even your name, not now, not ever, do you?"

"Uhm, n-no," she stuttered.

"So what does that mean? I'm some kind of long-distance therapist? You've just been using me like some kind of, what? Cheap thrill?" His voice slowed as he swallowed hard, almost choking into the phone. "You know, if I'd known that was what you were looking for, I could have made some really raw, raunchy calls—if I'd known that was what you were looking for."

Davida's fingers tightened on the receiver until they went numb. "Are you kidding?" Her voice sounded shaky and she bit her lip when Glenn turned to look at her. She closed her eyes and switched hands. No good, both palms where clammy.

"Kidding? No. I'm not kidding."

His voice was hard, and she wondered how to beg him not to do this, without alarming her already too-curious brother.

"Look," he hesitated, "I don't know what you were looking for, but obviously, it's not me. I must have been crazy to think I could really be friends with someone on the telephone. If there's ever another phone call, you'll have to make it. Try 557-1212 in Atlanta, but only if you have a name. Have a nice life, mystery lady."

"No! Hey! Wait, please!" The words tore from her. "Don't hang up . . ." And she stumbled, but she had no name for him—besides, he'd already slammed his phone down.

"Who was that?"

"Damn," Davida muttered, hanging up her own phone. She'd known Butch wouldn't give her much time, and he didn't disappoint her. She kept her back to her brother, holding off the inevitable.

"Look, Cookie, this is too weird. I want to know what's going on here." He looked at the phone then back at her. "Who was that?"

Maybe her caller was right, but it wasn't just him. Maybe they'd both lost their minds. Suddenly the relationship they'd built over the last month really did seem strange. Backing defensively into her corner of the couch, Davida looked at her brother—her big brother who'd always taken care of her, and who always knew the answers. Her big brother would never get this involved with someone over the phone.

"I, uh . . . it was, uh . . ." She dropped her eyes and her voice simultaneously. "To tell you the truth, I don't know who it was."

Glenn Morrison rose deliberately to his feet, towering above his sister. "You *what?*" His narrowed eyes and sharp features tightened as he made his face into a fist. Davida made herself small against the sofa. He was nothing if not one angry looking man.

She pulled one of the matching kente pillows, one of Des's craft projects, from behind her and hugged it to her chest. "You know, I'm grown, and I don't have to tell you anything—don't you?"

Glenn's eyes widened, the whites clear and intimidating, and his mouth tightened, and he waited, in spite of her bluff.

Wishing that the authority of her fortieth birthday would kick in, Davida bit at her lip. "I don't know who he is," she finally repeated. "I've never met him.

Glenn blinked, then opened and closed his mouth. "Come again?"

"Sit down, and I'll tell you about it."

Five minutes later, Glenn was on his feet again, pacing and shaking his head "Have you lost your mind? Do you have any idea what kind of trouble you've let yourself in for?" He stopped in front of her, hands on his lean hips, and a look of astonished anger on his face. "Long-distance conversations with a stranger. Someone whose name you don't even know? What kind of things have you been telling him?"

"Nothing." Except things she'd never told anyone else . . . "Really."

"Does he know who you are? Where you live? What about Destiny?" Both sets of eyes moved in the direction of the child's room.

"Butch, it's not like we're having phone sex. You know I would never put Destiny in any danger." Davida exhaled impatiently. "I know you mean well, Butch, but I already told you, I'm grown." The words seemed too harsh, and she tried to soften them. "Butch, Glenn, it's like I already told you—in a closed room with three people in it, neither of us would recognize the other. All he knows is my phone number.''

''And you don't know his?'' She shook her head. ''If you trusted him so much, then why didn't you tell him who you were?''

If he knew her name, all of this would be too real, and she needed for it to not be a part of what had become her reality. In the beginning, she didn't tell him because she needed something, and she didn't know what it was. She needed a fantasy and he fit the part like he was heaven-sent. She didn't tell him her name because . . . maybe her brother was right. She was lonely and a little afraid of losing something to age, and it had been such a long time since there was any other man in her life but Butch. She needed to feel sexy and vital again, and . . . maybe a little mysterious, too. Maybe she never realized how much she needed it until he came into her life. And besides that, maybe she just wanted a little risk in her life because she was tired of always having to be so responsible and mature and stuffy.

''Because,'' she said, and her eyes dropped to her hands and refused to lift. Her lips moved as she tried to find the right words to explain her actions, and there were none.

''This is wrong. You need a real solid man you can lay your hands on in your life, not some imaginary lover.''

Did he think she hadn't thought of that? Blinking at her brother, Davida held her tongue.

''We're having your number changed tomorrow,'' Glenn announced grimly. ''I can't believe you don't know his number, but never mind. I have a friend at the phone company—we'll trace him back through . . .''

''No. No, you won't.'' Davida pushed up from the sofa, and planted herself firmly in front of her brother.

''Yes, we will. You can't keep hiding from life, so afraid to take chances that when you finally do, you do something like this.'' Frustrated, he waved his hands in the air between them. ''Substituting a nameless, faceless voice for a shoulder to lay your head on?''

''Butch, this is not an argument.'' Stabbing two fingers into the banded neck of his shirt, Davida reached up to pull his face closer. ''I don't need a shoulder,'' she insisted. ''I don't need anyone. Except you. I need you to accept me as an adult and to accept my ability to take care of myself. This is not the kind of problem you're trying to make it into. I'm not changing my number, and you're not tracing anybody's anything. If I talked too much to a stranger because I was lonely, then I'm responsible for that. Me, and only me. You're going to stay out of it, you hear me? Stay out of it!''

Folding his hand over hers, Glenn Morrison gently detached Davida's hand from his shirt. He wouldn't have looked more surprised if she'd drawn back and punched him in the stomach. They stood staring at each other for what seemed like a very long time. Cookie, this is crazy!'' Glenn exploded.

"But it's *my* crazy," she shouted back. "I'm entitled!"

Staring, they each waited for the other to crack first. Always, in the past, Davida's resolve had crumbled beneath Glenn's more forceful personality. Not this time. He seemed to slowly realize she wasn't going to give in.

"Entitled?" He blinked. "Stubborn, that's what you are." His slow grin haunted his eyes and the corners of his lips. "Always have been. Just plain stubborn—it's that Taurus thing working again."

Davida silently cocked her head and propped her lips in that way that always made her mother admonish her with, "you'd better fix your face, girl." The only difference was, tonight Davida wasn't about to fix anything—it was clear she meant what she said.

"Okay. Have it your way, for now. On one condition," Glenn said slowly, determined to be as difficult as possible right to the end.

"What?"

He stood in front of her with his hands pushed into the pockets of his worn jeans, his hard, usually unreadable face as soft as she'd ever seen it. His dark gaze was unusually warm as it rested in her face. "Now you know I don't like this telephone game of yours, don't you?" He waited for her nod, then nodded his own head in response. "But you're right, you're grown, and you do handle a lot of things responsibly. Just know that if this or anything else blows up on you, I'm here."

He opened his arms and Davida stepped into the loving space he offered. "I'm here for you, Cookie. I'm here."

Leaning her cheek against his shoulder, she nodded again. "I know, Butch. Just trust me. I know what I'm doing." *I hope!*

CHAPTER SEVEN

"What did you think of the movies?"

"I, uh . . ." Cayce Andrews twisted the straight auburn ends of her shoulder-length hair around her finger and pulled. Judging from the tense expression she wore, that hair was the only relaxed thing about her. She'd been doing it all night, that twisting thing, and Marc was beginning to think the habit annoyed even her. "I thought, uh . . ." She flashed teeth and worked the ends of her hair again. "What did you think?"

Boo had warned him about women like her, and he should've listened to her—that's what he thought! Marc tugged viciously at the buttons of his vest, then his shirt, as he relived the scene from his disastrous date. He'd known she wasn't a rocket scientist long before he'd asked her out, but she was attractive and friendly, and he'd been hoping for a little more than air between her ears.

His hope was in vain as Cayce spent the evening molding herself against him, clinging to his arm as they walked, curling against him like a kitten in the movie. She even managed to remove one shoe and work her foot under the cloth of his pants and up along his leg. He shivered at the memory of her bare, crawling toes—it had felt creepy against his flesh. When he asked her about it, she giggled and said she'd seen Jennifer Beals do it in *Flashdance,* and it looked like fun. Marc had moved his leg.

"Flashdance." He would never look at that movie in quite the same way, ever again. The shirt and vest dropped as one unit onto

the back of the nearest chair. Bare chested, he headed for the bathroom. "If Cayce ever had an original thought, I'd lay odds that it died of loneliness," he muttered. Life was hard enough, but to willingly deprive oneself of original thought, to be willing to surrender one's independent thought and opinions just to have a date? Just to find someone to spend the rest of your life with? It made him shudder.

Rubbing a hand across his chin and cheek as he stood over the sink, Marc decided he'd shaved for nothing. Too bad Cayce wasn't more like somebody else. Boo, up there in St. Louis, not only had ideas of her own, but she didn't mind sharing them. Marc caught himself and flinched.

And how long do you plan to do this? his mind demanded. *She doesn't want you, and yet you compare every woman you meet to a woman you've never met? A woman you can't reach out and touch? A woman who won't even give you her name and is so ashamed of how you met that she won't even tell her brother? A woman who, for all intents and purposes, won't let you tell her your name for fear of . . . what?*

"It ain't natural, man," Milt kept saying as they nursed beers and Buffalo wings at Dugan's bar over on Ponce. Marc felt like a fool for getting involved with someone who refused to even exchange names, and he couldn't keep his secret anymore. Of all his friends, Milt seemed like the only one who might understand—after all, he met his wife through a personals ad in a local newspaper.

"Man, it ain't natural. You choose celibacy after talking to this chick on the phone?"

Marc was amazed at the ease with which his ire rose. "She's no chick, man. Besides, you got a wife, a daughter, a mother, and sisters. Not to mention grandmothers and aunts and cousins—heck, you're related to half of Atlanta, and most of them are women. You oughta know what a chick is by now."

"Aw, man. You know what I mean."

"Yeah, Milt. That's just it, I do. Somehow, you think it'll help me out if I can make her smaller, less important." He bumped his fist twice against his chest, hard enough to make an audible and resounding double thump, then pumped the fist solidly in the air between them. "It's a man thing, right?"

Confused by the lack of enthusiasm for his show of solidarity, Milt made a fist of his own hand, and it hovered between them while he tried to decide between pounding Marc's fist or his own chest. He settled for his chest. "Hey" was all he said.

Pushing the basket of fries farther back on the table, Marc fisted his hand again. Passing his other hand over the fist, Marc pantomimed petting. "Milt, chicks are fuzzy, little yellow biddies. And calling women chicks, it's just a cheap, slanderous reference. You can do better than that." He opened the fisted hand and laid it flat on the table, then drummed his fingers. "Besides, this woman is no chick."

"Well, what is she?" the big man asked, rearing back in his chair.

"She's an enigma, that's what she is," Marc told his reflection. "She's a puzzle that I'll never solve, even though all the clues are there. She doesn't want me to know anymore, and I won't try to." He shook his head in denial. "I made my last call, I'm not calling her again, and she doesn't think enough of me to call me, so it's settled."

In his bathroom, Marc threw both hands in the air then brought them down to grip the sink, hard. "Why am I even doing this to myself? You don't fall in love with a voice on the phone," he told himself sternly. So, why couldn't he stop thinking of her? Two weeks later, why was he still finding her in the narrow twists and small corners of his mind? "Because I miss her." He sighed heavily, the answer was too easily attained. This phantom woman got to him like no one else he'd ever met, and he couldn't get her out of his head.

Since that first accidental call, how many nights had he lain in bed, trying to change the course of his thoughts by enumerating all the words he knew for insanity? That's certainly what this was. Even now, he could think of half a dozen really descriptive terms that would work for what he was feeling. Amok had always been his favorite—maybe because it felt so foreign on his tongue. Then there was deranged, accompanied by demented and frenzied and raving, all of them descriptive of how he felt trying to build a life around a phantom.

Looking at his watch, the time made him shake his head. Ten thirty. He hadn't been home from a date at this hour since those first ones, way back in junior high, when everybody had curfews. But, thanks to Cayce's willing acquiescence, they'd given up on the dead date and here he was. Alone.

Ten thirty. That's the time he used to catch her with his phone calls. Marcus remembered.

He almost cringed when the phone rang. "God," he prayed, "let it not be Cayce. But it would be just my luck ..." He hoped she hadn't dropped an earring or left her scarf or purse on the floor of his Saab. "No, it can't be her," he tried to reassure himself, though he was afraid it was. Maybe she warmed up that one original thought, reviewed it, and wanted to apologize, or worse, demand an apology. "Oh, yeah, that would be a great way to finish off the night." He leaned against the sink and made a decision—let the machine get it.

On the fourth ring, the answering machine kicked in, and without moving, he listened to the spiel he already knew by heart. "Hello, this is Marcus Benton, and I'm currently unavailable. While I apologize for my absence, your call is very important to me. If you'll leave your name, number, and a brief message at the tone, I will be happy to return your call," he recited the words with the machine. The tone sounded, and he closed his eyes.

"Marcus? So, that's your name." The woman's voice was throaty but tentative, and unbelievably familiar. It roused him to immediate attention. Hurrying down the hall in stocking feet, Marc skidded to a stop next to the machine while the woman continued.

"I'm . . . not exactly sure of what to say. That is, I know what to say, but I'm not sure how to say . . . uhm. Maybe I'd better start at the beginning . . . my name is Davida Lawrence, and I'm calling from St. Louis, Missouri. We've been talking to each other . . . that is . . . I hope I've dialed the right number." She took a deep breath before saying more. "I'm sorry about the other night on the phone, I didn't mean to . . . that is, I . . . What I really want to say is, I'm sorry I hurt you when I . . . Marcus, I know I'm babbling, and I know that I'm probably asking a lot, but could you please call me?"

He had the receiver to his ear before she finished speaking, surprised to note that his hand was shaking. "Don't hang up," he said. "I'm here, Boo."

Surprise and the breath she took collided in her throat, and threatened to choke her. "I . . . I . . ."

"Davida? Are you still there, Boo?"

"I'm here, Marcus." His name felt strange in her mouth, the way it slipped so easily between her lips. Marcus. Marcus Benton. She finally had a name for the man who had somehow become her friend— her confidante.

"My friend's call me Marc, with a c, and I'm assuming you're a friend."

"Okay. Marc, with a c." Davida shook herself on the other end of the line. Speak up! she told herself. *You called to apologize: you wanted to talk to him again, and now you can't seem to string more than two words together.* He was saying something, and she mentally hurried to catch up. "I'm sorry I missed that."

Davida Lawrence. Such a beautiful name, lyrical and almost poetic. "I just repeated your name," he said. "Davida."

"Davida Lawrence," she confirmed, wondering why they were so awkward together now. It had never been like that before.

"It's an unusual name, Davida. Is it a family name?"

"You could say that." It was the same voice, a little higher, a little nervous, but definitely her. "I was named after my father, with an "a" on the end," she giggled.

"I see. Why did you decide to call me, Davida Lawrence, to suddenly tell me your name?"

Suspicion curved his words so that she knew he hadn't forgotten their last conversation. "I did some thinking," she said, "and I owe you an apology. I realized you were right—to some extent, anyway. I guess I was using you—like you said. You were a kind of emotional outlet for me. I guess I felt safe, and distanced from commitment with you as a no-risk fantasy friend."

"Is that really how you see me? As involving no risks?"

She swallowed hard and her mind locked, forbidding her to disclose truth. Their new found contact was too fragile for the word no. "Marc, I see you as a very kind man, who's been kind enough to listen, and sensitive enough to share," she said carefully.

He was silent, and she began to fear he'd hung up. "Marc?"

"I've missed you, Davida."

His simple statement made her limp with relief, and brought a lump to her throat. "I've missed you, too. Can you forgive me?"

"What's to forgive? I understand your caution, and then there's the fact that our friendship hasn't exactly been conventional, has it?"

"No, not exactly," she agreed with a small laugh.

"So, what have you been up to since the last time we talked?"

Missing you. Davida smiled, and kept the thought to herself. "Just working, doing a little skating, hanging out with Des . . . stuff like that. And you?"

The conversation was still stiff, stilted and awkward, but it was enough to make Marc squat on his heels in his hallway, preparing for a long comfortable talk. "Pretty much the same ol', same ol'."

"No dates," she teased.

"Oh, yeah. I've had dates, like I said, the same ol', same ol'. The lady I was out with tonight?" He let a shiver creep into his voice. "She was nothing like you. She tempered every word, censored every thought, and did the kind of 'girly' things an insecure woman does to . . . well, you know. She did the kind of things that make a woman look desperate—to a man."

"Sounds scary."

"It was. I told you, she was nothing like you." *Nothing at all like you.* Marc let his legs lever him lower against the wall, then dropped himself to the floor. Crossing his legs, he ran his tongue along the plumpness of his lower lip.

"Well, she wasn't me. What did you expect? We've had a few months to get to know each other."

"That's true," he agreed, wishing he knew more, "but this was different. I consider you a friend, Boo, and I enjoy talking with you. I think we could talk just about anywhere; dinner, on a beach, over drinks, and thoroughly enjoy each other. You make me laugh and think. You read, you observe, you challenge me. You're a great listener, an even better sounding board. You never seem bored, and you have yet to manage to bore me—unlike my charming companion of this evening.'' And the only way to make this complete was to meet— face to face.

His sigh was deep and touching, and Davida was warmed by his words in spite of the lonely sound. ''Your date tonight? Not a successful one by the sound of it.''

''Boo? You have no idea.'' He launched into an exaggerated account of his miserable evening, making her laugh again and again, as he recounted the hair twirling terror he'd spent way too much time with.

''Where, did you meet her?''

''Fuddrucker's. It's a high-toned burger place, here in Atlanta. She forgot her money, so I chivalrously stepped up and bought her lunch, then I asked her out.''

''No money for lunch? Maybe that should have been a clue.''

''You got that right.'' His sigh was overdone and intentionally melodramatic. ''Lunch was around ten dollars, and the date was a bust. I guess that just proves, you really do get what you pay for.''

''Hmn, . . . or maybe, . . . a fool and his money . . .''

''Please, Boo.''

''I really am sorry about your date,'' Davida commiserated. ''Sounds miserable.''

''It was,'' he agreed. ''I don't suppose that big ol' mean, hairy brother of yours is still hanging around?''

''Glenn? No, he's got a case somewhere in Puerto Rico, and Des and I threw him on a plane out of here yesterday.''

''Ah, good,'' he said, and Davida got an instant mental flash of a faceless, but grinning man, wolfishly rubbing his hands in glee. The picture popped like a soap bubble when he continued to speak. ''You know I'm a desperate man here, don't you? Nobody suitable on the foreseeable horizon, Boo. I just may yet have to make my way to St. Louis, complete with flowers and flattery for you.''

Take the bait, he prayed. Holding his breath, Marc wondered how she would react. After he got over being angry, he'd come up with a plan—not a good one, but at least it was a plan. If she would just say the word . . .

''Sure, sure, sure,'' she said, ''and I would just have to pile the flowers and you up in the corner with all my other admirers.''

''How many other admirers are there?''

The comment sounded a little too sincere. She quickly changed the subject. ''Have you heard from Renee?'' Not exactly a smooth transition, Davida realized as she waited for him to speak.

Marc decided to let her get away with it. ''Talked to her last night.''

''Have you ever told her about me?''

The soft voice was gently probing, but Marc felt the definite sting of accusation in the question. Turnabout, he'd heard, was fair play. "Yes."

Silence, then, "She knows about me?"

Straightening his shoulders against the supporting wall, he winced. "She does, now."

And boy, what a conversation that had been. Marc got the bright idea while working J.B.'s suggestion into Bro'Man's latest adventure. The little boy seemed to think Bro'Man needed the ability to mentally calculate numbers and random equations at the speed of light. "That would go along with his other stuff. He needs superstrength, and x-ray vision, too."

"That'd make real superpowers, Unc, not like some phony magic, or a Batman belt. Right? See, if he was like this human computer, sort of, he could use math to predict how a space ship was going to move, or how a crook's bullets would go, or even if somebody fell off a building? I mean, that'd be like something people could use for real, and he's like a math teacher in real life, so that's like something he could really use. Right?"

J.B. was truly a child of his times. He wanted a fantastic but practical hero, and the powers he suggested made a lot of sense, besides Marc liked the idea of collaborating with his nephew. When J.B. handed the telephone over to his mother, Marc was struck by an almost physically stinging bolt of inspiration. Sitting down with J.B., getting some real feedback when the little boy looked at the colored panels and read some of the planned dialogue, was a good idea.

But, there was more. If Marc was *already* in St. Louis, then it would just be natural to call the woman he talked to so often—just to say hello. He already knew her telephone number. How far from a telephone call would dinner be? The only problem was, how to get Renee to play along—how to get her to make his idea palatable to a woman who might never believe it otherwise. Marc was almost, but not quite, ashamed to admit he felt a need for his little sister's collusion. Somehow, though, having her available to back up his visit made his plan feasible. How to get Renee to agree, though—that was a problem. He already knew he couldn't just come right out and tell her he was flying in and what he wanted to do—and she was certain to ask.

Sensing something in his voice, Davida frowned on her end. "Renee doesn't approve of me—of what we've done?"

"Oh, not of you. Remember, I didn't even know your name when I mentioned meeting you on the telephone. It's just that she . . . she tends to be a bit overprotective," Marc explained carefully. "I don't think she fully understands the way things are between us." Didn't understand? Went ballistic was more like it.

When he tried his carefully constructed tale of flying in, "just to touch base" with his nephew, he felt her antennae go up. "When do you want to do this base touching?" Renee asked craftily.

"I thought I'd fly in next week, maybe Tuesday night. Or I could drive up on the weekend."

"And how long do you plan to stay?"

"I hadn't given it any thought, Renee. If it's inconvenient, I can always go to a hotel."

"Hotel? Uh-uh, no you won't! Mama would get on me like white on rice if I let you go to a hotel, and you know it. No way, my brother. You're in St. Louis, you'll be staying with us, and that's all there is to it." She paused barely long enough to gather breath. "Why do you want to talk to J.B. again, and why does it have to be face to face? He was so excited, I didn't get the reason straight, so you tell me."

Marc ran his story past her again, a little more smoothly this time—he thought.

"Well, bring your sketch pad, and maybe some samples of your work when you come. This trip, you'll have to earn your keep."

"I'm not looking for a job Cookie, I just want to look up a friend . . . uh . . . run this stuff past J.B."

"Aha! I knew there was a 'friend' involved. I know you, Butch. I know you." Marc heard the sticky sound of the plastic receiver against her skin as she nodded, congratulating herself on ferreting out the truth. "Trying to use my baby to get next to some woman. Who is she? Do I know her? No, I don't know her, 'cause if I did, you wouldn't be trying to sneak in here to get close to her. Where did you meet her? Does she live in St. Louis or Atlanta? What's her name? Who. . . ?"

Coming clean, confessing fully was the only way to save himself from the barrage of questions. Marc told her everything.

"You won't let me fix you up with a real person"—Renee sniffed—"but you can go and attach yourself to a perfect stranger on the phone—and for all you know, she's not that perfect. If you want my help in this little charade, and I don't know why you would . . . but you're my brother so I guess I'm stuck . . ." She suddenly brightened. "You can stay with us, and we'll be your alibi, on one condition."

"What?" Marc was leery.

"Like I said, bring your stuff. You'll have to come speak at my school. Career Day."

"Aw, Renee." That was just what he needed; to spend a delightful afternoon with a couple hundred bored teenagers torn between catcalls, throwing spitballs, and falling asleep. "They don't want to see me. I'm not a movie actor or a really cool musician, or anything like that. I promise you they don't want to see me. It would be different if I was some kind of top gun or undercover cop, or something, but I'm not."

"You're my brother, you're good at what you do, and that's good enough for me. Bring samples."

"Hey, look, Fort Leonard Wood is not that far from you. You could get somebody with a uniform and lots of shiny medals. Kids love uniforms and medals."

"Already got that covered. You want to come to St. Louis, fine. You're welcome to come, you'll stay with us, and you'll be at Career Day. That's the deal, take it or leave it."

He took it.

"You didn't really tell her—did you?" Davida's voice broke his reverie.

"Would it make you feel better if I hadn't?"

"Yes."

"I could lie," he offered.

Davida sighed. "No, don't lie."

"She thought it was strange, but who I see and certainly who I enjoy on the telephone are not my sister's business."

"She would think it was strange, though. I guess I can see her point," Davida said. "I'd feel funny if I found out Glenn had some kind of ongoing dialog with a stranger, and you already know how he felt."

"Yes, he was very clear on that, but you're blushing again. I can hear it in your voice."

It was uncanny. He knew her too well. She changed the subject abruptly, for the second time. "What movie did you see tonight?" His chuckle was light, and she almost missed it. She had done exactly what he thought she would do—he knew her too well.

"We saw two. *Cabin in the Sky, and Green Mansions.*"

"Oh, gosh. Two old black films. *Cabin in the Sky,* with . . ." She strained for a name, "Is it Ethel Waters? And *Green Mansions?* I don't remember who's in it, but isn't that the one with the fish frys up in heaven?"

"Very good." He sounded impressed and Davida smiled. "I'd heard about them, but never seen them before."

"What did you think?"

"I thought they were both interesting, in light of when they were done, and that song she sang . . ."

"The one about how, '. . . heaven is like Little Joe'?"

"Yeah," he agreed. "I thought it was great. The whole time, though, I kept thinking what a shame it was to be sharing it with a woman who didn't have a clue, and who didn't interest me in the least."

The unplanned frown that crossed her face hundreds of miles away, was heartfelt. Davida didn't like thinking of him on a date with another woman any more than he apparently cared for the thought of her with another man. *Have to examine that later*—the thought lodged almost subconsciously in her mind. "It must be nice to feel that way—the way she looked when she sang that song. To look in someone's face, know you were home, and feel your heart lodged there—it must be nice."

"You really are a sucker for romance, aren't you?"

Her short laugh touched his ear like a courting fingertip. "I suppose I am, but I warned you that I was very traditional," she said slowly. "Maybe because I've never really known the kind of romance that you read about. I mean, what I had with Skip . . . , what we had was different. It was solid and definite. I always knew he was there for me, and that I would always be there for him."

Marc grimaced in spite of his resolve, and Davida heard the brush of his breath against the telephone. "He wasn't the love letter type," she said. "I mean, he was romantic, but not the kind where you're left with love letters tied in satin ribbons and smelling of sachet. I'll never have those kinds of things to smile about when I'm an old woman."

"Is that what you really want, Davida? Faded corsages and musty love letters?"

"No," she said too quickly. "That kind of stuff probably doesn't exist anyway. Real people don't hang onto junk like that even though it does make for a pretty wonderful fantasy."

"Would you believe me if I told you real people do hang onto things like that? That that kind of romance does exist, Boo?" His voice was low and husky, and tilting her head, she found herself thinking of things that went on all night, and wanting to believe him. "You just haven't found the right man to share it with yet."

"Do you write love letters, Marc?"

"I've written my share, Boo."

And what did they say? Did they promise that special woman that he would always be there stand by her side through good times and bad, or did they only promise temporary flirtation, fleeting fascination? Did those letters of his tempt a woman who'd never really listened to those kinds of pretty words before? And how did he learn to write those letters? Back when she was in school, they didn't teach such things in English 101 . . . "Really," she said, "tell me about them."

"I think I wrote the first one when I was six. To my first grade teacher, Miss Keller, and I used a bright red crayon."

"Six, Marc?"

"I was a prodigy." He laughed, and in spite of herself, Davida found herself joining him. "To tell you the truth, some of my letters were probably tossed as soon as they were received. But, you know what, Boo?"

"What, Marc?"

"I'll always want to believe that they were all read, and that every woman I've ever loved was touched, and knew, if only for the moment, that she was the most important thing in my life and that I would never forget her."

"Spoken like a true romantic." She made her voice light, hoping not to betray what his words stirred in her heart.

"I didn't think I was a romantic until fairly recently. Now I'm beginning to believe I really am."

Disturbed by the new infusion of intensity in his voice, Davida asked without thinking, "When did you come to this amazing conclusion?"

"Right around the time I found myself falling for a voice on the telephone," he answered.

The words had the effect of ice water on hot skin. They wracked her heart, left her gasping for breath, and wanting more. Davida found herself looking over her shoulder in her own bedroom, afraid to share the suggested intimacy of his words with another living soul. "Uhm," she was trembling and nearly mute. Swallowing hard, her fingers tightened on both the telephone receiver and the post of her Rice bed. "It's getting late, isn't it?" she commented lamely.

"Yes, I guess it is." He sounded patient. Understanding. Maybe he understood the full effect he'd had on her composure.

"I think I'd better go now."

"We'll talk again, Davida Lawrence. Soon."

That it was no question was a very good thing. Davida knew she couldn't have answered one—not even if her very life depended on it.

CHAPTER EIGHT

"And, girl, you know he really likes kids." Quita turned the Styrofoam cup between her palms as if warming them, then leaned farther back in her chair. Crossing her legs, she let a black patent leather slingback pump dangle from her toes. "Some men don't care for children, but not Calvin. He's got four, so you know he's already used to them."

Davida tapped the bridge of her nose with one finger, then used it to push her reading glasses higher. Looking up from the telephone logs and her notes, she blinked absently, then seemed to realize she wasn't alone in her office. "Quita." She blinked before removing her glasses. "I'm sorry, what did you say?"

The half-empty cup sloshed violently as Quita dropped her foot to the floor. "I don't know why I bother trying to help you out! You weren't even listening!" The tiny-waisted Help Desk supervisor stood and perched a fist on her wide hip. "Here I am, just about giving you a wonderful, completely available, totally straight man on a silver platter, and you're not even listening!" She looked around to make sure no one overheard, then touched her finger to her Fashion Fair blushed cheek. "Now look, Dee, I'm trying to tell you, my cousin Calvin? He's a BMW, girl—a black man, working. All right? Like I said, he's available, and I could fix you up . . ."

"Fix me up?" The wire frames left Davida's fingers, and her nose wrinkled. "A date?"

"Why? Would that be so bad?" Quita planted her hands and leaned over the desk to stare. "Honestly, Dee, sometimes I worry about you. What could be wrong with a date? A little dinner, a movie? It hasn't been that long—if you can't remember, then surely you've read about how it's done—maybe seen it on TV?"

"Quita." Davida shook her head and tried not to laugh at the other woman's disgusted face. "Yes, I remember the custom—but just vaguely."

"Okay, so that means all you need is a refresher course. We should plan for, what . . . this Saturday? I could have him call you . . . at home, or here?"

"No way."

"Yes, way! You've gotta do this." Quita grabbed her cup and took a desperate swallow of now cold coffee. "Girl, I already told him about you, and he's a 'hearts and flowers' kind of guy, really sweet. He's expecting to . . . What are you afraid of, anyway?"

"Nothing. I'm not afraid of anything." Yes she was. She was afraid he wouldn't be her ideal man. She was afraid to invest the time it took to find out that she was wasting her time. She was afraid he wouldn't say the right things at the right time, that he wouldn't make her think and feel . . . Shaking her head, Davida smiled, trying to soften her words. "This Calvin is . . . he's your cousin, and probably a really nice guy, but I'm not interested." *Because he's not Marcus Benton?* Davida concentrated on squaring the edges of the pages on her desk in an effort to avoid looking into Quita Walton's narrowed eyes.

"You would like him if you gave him half a chance. He's a gentleman."

"So you say."

Quita sucked her teeth and tossed her head in disbelief. The lacquered curls atop her head didn't move. "I don't know what it is, but something's going on with you. You're so intense lately . . . You couldn't even laugh at the stripper we sent you for your birthday . . . I don't know."

"He wasn't funny." Davida gathered her papers and headed for her office door. Angling her navy pump against the door to hold it open, she waited as Quita squeezed past. "A grown man in a diaper?"

"But he was *built,* girl," Quita let a hot little quiver run through her voice as she rolled her eyes in mock passion. "He was too fine. Besides, when a man can dance like that . . . Doesn't it make you wonder what else he does well?" She licked her lips, blew a small wet-sounding kiss into the air, then remembered where she was, and put a little hustle in her step to draw even with her quarry. "Look, Dee, don't change the subject. I don't understand—why are you, a drop-dead-gorgeous woman, single, and smart as you want to be . . .

Why are you so determined to live like some musty old nun? Have you got an answer for that?"

Stopping, Davida let her tongue play along the straight ridge of her teeth. It gave her a few seconds to marshal her thoughts and avoid a childish, "none y'a" as in "none of your business" defense. "Let's just say I have looked at the available dating stock, and decided to quit while I was ahead."

Quita did an amazing trick with her lips. She pouted and pooched them, then gave them a defiant twist. "Quit before you get started, is more like it. When are you going to figure it out? Everybody is not like Jeff Watson. He's gone and forgotten. Why won't you give another brother a chance?"

"I had a wonderful marriage to a wonderful man, and now I've got Destiny. She's enough to keep me occupied, and I'm happy. Can we leave it at that?"

"And what will you have when Des grows up and leaves home? 'Cause she will grow up, you know."

"Why does that line sound so familiar? Have you been talking to my brother, again?"

Caught, Quita had the grace to look mildly embarrassed. "I can talk to an old classmate if I want to. But you didn't answer my question. An empty house is what you'll get, that's what. An empty house, and an even emptier life." Quita answered before Davida could open her mouth. "Are you still going to be happy when you're spending the rest of your life waiting on a phone call from someone you never get to see?"

Davida felt like a refugee from an old cartoon show, one of the ones where the character gets smacked in the back of the head with a brick and its feet fly up in the air because of the shock. She willed her head not to turn and her feet to keep moving, and was moderately successful in the effort. She blinked quickly to prevent her eyes from staring and giving her thoughts away. How did Quita know about the phone calls? *She can't know,* logic intervened, *she's got to be talking about Des.* Whatever else he might have said, Butch would never tell her about Marcus. Davida closed her mouth and swallowed hard before the words spilled out. "Quita, I'm not ruling out all future relationships," she finally said. "I'm just not interested in going out on blind dates."

"So, if you don't date, where are you going to find this Mr. Perfect?"

"I'm not looking for Mr. Perfect."

"Then just keep in mind, that there's nothing wrong with Mr. Right Now, while you're waiting for Mr. Right to come along—even if he is a blind date."

"I'll keep that in mind." Narrowed brown eyes studied her face, and Davida was half tempted to tell Quita about her regular blind date. And what in the world would she say? Davida imagined dropping a cavalier little bomb. *Oh, I don't need blind dates, I've got a man in my life. Where did I meet him? On the telephone. What does he look like? I don't know, I've never seen him, but he's all mine every time the phone rings.* Certainly that would stop Quita's rant, *for about thirty seconds.* It would take that long for the madness to register.

If she opened her mouth to Quita, she'd have her committed, and her business blasted all over the free world in about thirty more minutes. As good a friend as she could be, Quita could spread news faster than CNN. Davida willed her smile to be enigmatic.

"Okay," Quita conceded reluctantly. "No blind dates, but how about if I give a party sometime soon?" She raised her hands defensively. "Not a setup, a party with a lot of other people. I could invite you and Calvin both, not like a date or anything. Would you come, then?"

Davida leaned against the wall, and pressed the taxpayer requests closer to her chest. "Maybe. I don't know. But, if I promise to think about it, will you quit following me?"

Quita shook the empty Styrofoam cup at her. "You just think about it." She turned on her heel, then turned back. "You promised, and I'm going to hold you to it."

"I know you." Davida nodded. "And, I know you will."

"Just so you know." Quita backed a few steps farther down the hall before turning and heading to her own office. Davida could hear her chuckling to herself as she walked on.

Why she let Quita's good intentions crowd her, she didn't know. Davida sighed. Shifting the stack of paperwork, she remembered what she'd been about to do before having to run away from her personal matchmaker. "Quita, Quita, Quita. People want their problems resolved, and that's my real—"

"Davida!" Papers went everywhere.

Her head rang with the sharp sound of her name and the sudden collision of her head with another. The floor seemed to rush upward as the wall met her back, and Davida felt herself sliding down. Belatedly clapping a hand over the now sore spot on her forehead, she struggled to find dignity and gain control of her rising skirt and escaping paperwork. The effort was in vain. Surrendering to the more immediate pain, she closed her eyes. "Essie," she said.

"Yes," the almost cheerful voice replied. The division administrator had a well-earned reputation for clumsiness. Gingerly examining her own temple with questing fingers, Esme Cofing blinked and offered a weak smile. "I was just coming to see you," she said. Pulling her knees demurely close, she managed to rise with some grace, and offered her hand to Davida. When they were both standing, she thoughtfully brushed at a dusty spot on the gabardine sleeve of Davida's jacket.

"You said you were looking for me," Davida prompted, brushing at her own jacket. Every time she had one of these little encounters with Essie, she seemed to get the worst of it.

"Yes," Essie cooed. Her eyes were bright, and her round brown cheeks were infused with an artificially inspired blush. From a distance, she reminded one of a small brown bird. Up close, one was able to identify the bird. A sparrow, Davida thought.

"I've been looking for you because I need a little favor." Her head tilted and she blinked quickly, then tipped her head to the other side, smiled and shifted it back.

"Okay."

"Oh, don't agree so easily." Essie tittered, pleased with her little joke. "Actually"—her hands fluttered lightly between them, glancing off Davida's—"it's a sizable favor."

"Essie," Davida said slowly, "what's the favor?"

"My daughter. Actually, it's Beaumont High School, my daughter's school. They're having a Career Day, and I was supposed to go in and do a little something for them." She looked down at her still fluttering fingers, seemed to be surprised to find them moving, and folded them neatly before her. "I'll be in D.C. for training that week, and I can't back out. I'd like you to take my place."

" 'Career Day'? Oh, Essie, I don't know." Davida wrinkled her nose, and looked down, intent on organizing the paperwork she'd retrieved. "I don't think I have anything interesting to share; not with high school students. You know how specialized our work can be. I'd only bore them."

"Ah, Davida, you underestimate yourself," Essie sang. "You're a very entertaining woman."

Right . . . I'll only be entertaining if I wear a clown suit, learn to juggle, and make balloon animals. Davida's face testified to her unspoken words.

"C'mon. It'll be fun, and it's for the children."

So much fun, Essie couldn't wait to dump it on her, and get on to Washington. "Essie, I don't want to go to Career Day. I blew off my own kid's Career Day. Do you know, I baked six dozen cupcakes instead of showing up to talk about my job?"

"That was different, Dee. Little Des is second grade . . ."

"Third," Davida said curtly. "She's in third grade." She hated it when Essie called her Dee.

"And she's as cute as a button and as sharp as a little tack! But I'm talking about high school," Essie continued unfazed. "I'm talking about teenagers about to step into the adult world. Why, you'll have an effect on the shaping of their whole adult lives. Besides, the effort will look good on your next personnel review.''

She pursed her lips and patted at Davida's hand. "You have one coming up, don't you? In about a month?" She blinked brightly while she waited for her words to sink in. "I'll have to sign off on it, so don't forget to add a line or two about this—under 'activities.' '' Davida thought of the sparrow again; a mean little sparrow with promotional leverage. "You'll enjoy this little speaking engagement. I already know you can clear your schedule."

"What date?" Davida hoped her voice sounded as put upon as she felt—not that it mattered. Essie had claimed victory and was already as good as cruising the Beltway.

"The fifteenth. That's next Tuesday at two. Take along a few visuals. Some 1040s, and instruction books, have them fill them out. Oh''—Essie looked inspired, and Davida wondered what kind of cat might get rid of this particular bird. "Talk to them about the new TAXI program. Kids love all that interactive stuff." She probed a molar with her tongue as she thought. "I think it's under 'www.irs.gov/taxi.' Pretend they're getting refunds; they'll love it!''

Yeah, right! Every good American teenager loved to fill out tax forms, especially electronically, and they did it every chance they get. Davida was tempted to stick out her tongue at the bird woman's departing square-shaped figure. Tongue at the ready, she parted her lips, then snapped them closed as Essie turned back to her. "Oh, and Dee, your contact person is Mrs. Renee Johnson."

"Beaumont High School. Tuesday, the fifteenth, two o'clock. Mrs. Johnson. Got it.'' Turning in the opposite direction, Davida didn't even pretend to smile.

Swinging the red Accord off the street and in the direction of the narrow parking lot was not the easiest thing Davida had ever done. Rain sheeted across her windshield in direct defiance of the swinging wiper blades, and she hoped she'd remembered to replace the battered umbrella she usually kept under the passenger seat. One hand off the wheel, her fingers crawled through the mess of books, forgotten schoolwork, and lost Happy Meal prizes Des had left behind.

"I don't have an idea in the world what I'm going to say to these students," she said, withdrawing her hand and glancing at her dirty fingers. "Ugh!" She scratched under the seat for a tissue or napkin, and came up dry. "Ugh!" She wiped her fingers on the side of the box containing the 1040s. Squinting through her window, she shook her head. It was like trying to see through Vaseline. The box slid sideways as she reached for the radio, and Davida warned herself about trying to do too many things at the same time.

A man, a very young man in a bright yellow Camero, who simply had to be a student cut in front of her, and she jammed her foot on the brake. Head rocking to a thundering beat, the boy never noticed the near miss. The girl at his side made a face and tossed several pounds of braided hair over her shoulder as the engine gunned, and the car sped off.

"One more escaping taxpayer," Davida muttered and drove on. On the muddy outskirts of the lot, she finally located a spot. Using her sleeve to clear the windshield, she sent up a silent thank you, and headed for it.

The dark brown Saab swooped out of nowhere and directly in front of her like a low-flying bat, and Davida swore without thinking. Determined to wrest some small degree of satisfaction out of defeat, she rolled down the passenger window and glared at what she could see of the offending driver. He seemed to feel her eyes, and turned his head to face her. Lifting a hand in acknowledgment, he shifted and backed out of the spot she'd prayed for.

"Well, well, what do you know," Davida whispered, "a gentleman." Impressed, she drove forward to park.

The Saab backed farther along the row of cars, finally settling at the end. Davida watched the stranger's shadowy form move out and around his sleek vehicle, then down the row toward her. She busied herself looking for the missing umbrella. Failing to find it, she settled for a plastic raincoat from the back seat.

Backing out of the car, towing the box of forms, the last thing she expected was to find the courteous stranger at her door.

"Can I help with that?"

Trying to see, stand, turn, and pull proved too great an effort. The only thing Davida succeeded in doing was bumping her head and snagging her plastic raincoat on the car door. A gust of wind caught the hood of her raincoat and snatched it straight back, dumping cold spring rain in her face and down her chest. The stranger watched her crawl back into her car, where she sat with her feet and legs exposed to the elemental onslaught.

"You look like you're having a hard time."

"Me? No. I'm not having a hard time. I like rain." She pulled the wet plastic from beneath her. Her fingers tested the wet spot on the back of her skirt. It didn't feel natural, and realizing what people—especially teenagers—would think when they saw it, her heart sank.

"I like it, too, but it looks like mother nature's taking unfair advantage of you."

"And, she's winning." From where she sat, the stranger looked like an attractive collection of features gathered beneath a dripping brown fedora. Dimples on a clean shaven caramel colored face, framed a sensuously full mouth. Perfectly even, white teeth touched his lower lip as he smiled. *He smiles like he knows me,* she thought, knowing that he couldn't possibly. *He couldn't possibly know me, because him, I would remember.*

He shifted the strap of the large black portfolio he carried on his shoulder. "Here for the Career Day festivities?" Davida nodded. Another gust of wind threw itself against them, making her car rock lightly. "Me, too," the stranger said, looking up at the steel gray sky. "Why don't I take that box in, and it'll give you a little time to get yourself together? I'll meet you inside?"

"Thanks." Davida folded the flaps over Essie's precious 1040 forms and handed the box to the man. Watching him navigate the muddy puddles, she kind of liked the way he moved. His rolling gait was spatially possessive without being presumptive. He walked like he was in exactly the right place at precisely the right time, like he knew where he was going. His trench coat flared on the wind, then settled neatly around him as he made his way to the building.

What a nice man, she thought, then caught herself. She didn't know that man. Presumption. That was how she got into the mess with Marcus Benton, because he was a nice man. *That's the one thing I don't need in my life right now,* she told herself, pulling the wet plastic straight, and close to her body, *the major complications of another nice man.*

Gravel slid beneath her foot as she tried to avoid the worst of the potholes and mud in the parking lot. Guest speakers shouldn't look like they wallowed in mud. Guest speakers should also have a topic! Pulling the heavy door open, she groaned inwardly.

Colorfully bright, slightly awkward, and some amazingly professionally hand-lettered signs hung from almost every vertical surface. Crepe paper streamers rattled on the breeze that accompanied Davida's entrance. She was really here. Now she had to come up with a valid topic—or at least fake it 'til she made it. She took a deep breath and tried to convince herself that it was really too late to run back to her car.

"Hi, can I help you?" Startled, Davida took a step backward. Her shoes made an embarrassing squishing sound against the tiled floor. The attractive woman's oval face took on a look of mild concern as she walked toward Davida.

Hoping to look more like she was in the right place, Davida tried to shrug neatly free of her raincoat. The darned thing wrapped itself around her and clung like glue. Getting her arms free was a contortionist's nightmare—it stuck to every exposed part of her body. Still approaching, the other woman tilted her head curiously and raised her eyebrows. *Oh, no. She thinks I'm homeless.* Finally free, Davida adjusted her purse, then used both hands to flatten the plastic raincoat against her already damp suit.

"I'm Davida Lawrence. I'm here for Career Day. From the IRS. Essie Cofing was supposed to be here today, but she's been called out of town for a meeting, and I'm covering for her. I'm supposed to see Mrs. Johnson." She paused for a breath and tried for a bit of poise while she was at it. "I'm sure that was enough to confuse anyone. Should I repeat any of it?" She smiled.

To her relief, the pretty woman returned the smile and offered her hand. "I'm Mrs. Johnson, Renee Johnson, and I'm glad to see anyone who would brave weather like this for our kids." Leaning close, she spoke softly. "I don't know if I would have done it, but I'm glad you did." She smiled again. "You've got about thirty minutes before we start," she said, looking at her soggy guest speaker. "I think I can help you out with a blow-dryer, if you'll follow me."

"I'll follow you anywhere," Davida said, catching at the hem of her skirt and flipping it away from her leg. It *would* be nice to be dry again. Inspecting her hose, she was glad to find them in one piece, and without the series of rips and runs she'd feared.

Feeling the presence of watching eyes, she looked up, and from six feet away, caught the glance of the stranger from the parking lot. Whether he was watching her legs or her face didn't matter. What pretty eyes he had, and he was watching her. Her hands went instantly to her hair. *Lord, please don't let my hair do what we both know it can do. Don't let him see me looking bad, with my hair standing all over my head.* The thought was there and gone in the space of a heartbeat, hardly recognized, except for the intimate haunting of his stolen glimpse. She smiled and was rewarded with his smile in return. Davida held the man's eyes a second longer, then followed Mrs. Johnson.

Easing into her onstage seat, Davida blessed the makers of blow-dryers, hairspray, and cosmetics everywhere. Her deep breath and inspiration surged through her body at the same time. *I've got a topic,* she thought. She'd had it all along. She'd talk to them about all the things she'd done to get from where they were to where she was, and what it took to go even farther. And she was going to start by doing a little damage to some of the papers she'd brought along.

She could already see it in her mind; her telling them that she'd come to deliver one message, but would share something more personal instead. She knew just how to do it, too. It would feel good to tear up some of that paper, and it might even get their attention.

Smiling, she pressed her knees together, and looked at the table of props behind her. Not seeing the cardboard box containing Essie's recommended 1040 forms, she swiveled in her seat and bent slightly, trying to see under the table.

"You look pretty good for a woman who had to swim the last two hundred yards from the parking lot."

Unexpected, but familiar, the voice made her jump, and Davida looked up into the eyes of the stranger from the parking lot. They were nice eyes, every bit as nice as she thought she'd remembered, and she smiled into them. "Thanks for your help," she said, straightening. "It's hard to swim carrying boxes."

He smiled and offered his hand, then winked with both eyes when she shook it. "Glad to help." He looked around the auditorium. "Seems like we're on the spot up here." He sat, shielding his eyes with his hand and looked out into the restless sea of assembling students. "I used to hear people say that you couldn't see individual faces from up here on stage, I guess because of the lights, but you can. You can see a lot of little details." Reaching for the large black portfolio he'd carried through the rain, he peered at the crowd, appearing to memorize individual faces.

"Really." Davida lowered her lashes and hoped it passed for blinking in an interested conversation. Starting at his feet, she let her eyes tell her all a woman really wanted to know about a man. His shoes, good quality and well heeled, were dark and casual. Not bound by convention, and completely unlike the sober black-suited mortician in the high-water pants on her left, the stranger wore khaki slacks and an olive-colored jacket of raw silk. His vest, a rusty-toned African mud cloth, both matched and complimented the salmon-colored cotton shirt. His posture, like his stride, was relaxed but fully possessive of the space he occupied.

She liked that. Davida let her lids flutter again. He had a well-developed sense of style and color. The clothes looked good, and he wore them well, but underneath it all, she found a much more interesting, well-muscled, compact body. Not as tall as she would like, but a little taller than she was, she thought. Not that he was her type. Davida had always preferred her men bigger, like Skip. Well over six feet and in the two hundred twenty to two forty pound range. This man was smaller, maybe twenty to thirty pounds heavier than her own one sixty—if that.

That he was fit was obvious, but his hands were clean and uncalloused, the nails neatly trimmed. She immediately ruled out construction. His thighs looked strong, lean definition lining the fabric of his

pants, and she found her eyes straying higher, her thoughts wandering.
She wondered if he worked out . . . She watched him cross his leg to
stabilize his sketch pad against a very flat stomach. "Rock-hard abs,"
she remembered the words from an ad on a late-night cable television
infomercial. Legendary abs. She sighed and pulled her own stomach
tighter. *I'm as bad as Quita,* Davida thought, blinking faster, shifting
her vision higher.

His chest appeared broad, not wide and hard like Skip's had been,
but strong and well muscled, like where a woman might place her
hand, and it would fit just right if . . . Davida cleared her throat and
shifted in her seat. A hairy chest? From where she sat, Davida saw
enough at the open throat of his casual shirt to think it was entirely
possible. She crossed her legs and sat straighter, then she blinked
again.

She wondered what he did for a living.

"I'm an illustrator," he said, moving his pencil across the page.

He must also be psychic. Davida narrowed her eyes and focused
her thoughts on the man's curly head—at a spot just above his ear.
So, what's your name, Cutie? she thought.

"My name is Marc."

He was psychic! How ironic though, to be attracted to two strangers,
both named Mar—Could this one be Marc with a c?

"That's Marc, with a . . . ."

". . . c," she finished for him.

"That's right," he said slowly. Laying his pencil in his lap, Marc
with a c looked fully into her face. Pausing, his mouth open, then
closed, and he shook his head. "You know, you remind me of someone
. . . someone, and I can't quite put my finger on who." Dropping his
foot to the floor, he balanced his pad flat on his lap and studied her
face again.

"Now that you mention it, you remind me of someone, too." Davida
tapped her lips with her forefinger and concentrated. "Something about
you is so familiar to me. It's like . . . uhm." The words drifted away
in search of memory. She looked into his beautiful eyes and shook
her head. She would always remember, never forget, those eyes.

The screech of a maladjusted microphone barged between them,
and made everyone onstage clap hands over their ears. Looking toward
the offender, Davida and Marc faced Renee Johnson as she outlined
the days' program for her young audience and indicated the speakers.
She closed her remarks by introducing, ". . . ladies first." She smiled
and beckoned the only other woman on the stage. Davida stood, glad
her shoes had dried and confident of her new topic.

"I would like to introduce Mrs. Davida Lawrence of the Internal
Revenue Service."

Davida Lawrence? IRS? Marc's pad hit the floor immediately followed by his pencil which bounced merrily across the stage, teetered on the edge, then plunged to the floor, where it bounced from eraser to tip before rolling to a stop under the seat of the vice principal. Inexplicably on his feet, a blank stare replacing his usual curiosity, Marc's lips formed her name. Davida Lawrence—there couldn't be two.

There couldn't be two women with that name, not in St. Louis or any of the suburbs, he would bet money on it. He'd already checked the Internet and the white pages. Marc knew there weren't even any D. Lawrence's listed. This had to be her. He closed his mouth and stared.

Standing beside Mrs. Johnson, the one and only Davida Lawrence looked over her shoulder, tried not to notice Marc's odd behavior, smiled warily, and lifted her hand to wave at the applauding students. A wolf whistle rose sharply above the sound of creaking chairs and slapping palms, and she smiled at that, too.

Marc, beating his palms together in whatever rhythm the student-faculty audience established, had a hard time bending to fit back onto the folding chair reserved for him. He wanted to run to the stranger at the podium, fling his arms around her and demand her name again, instead he focused on making his hands stop their stupid clapping. The mortician turned to look at him as though he'd just broken into a crazed boogaloo. Marc tried to control the silly grin he knew he wore, but the funeral director continued to look grimly disapproving. Marc gave up on him and turned his face rigidly toward the audience.

Given time, it seemed fate had the darnedest way of dumping surprises smack into his lap. He wanted to laugh out loud. He wanted to share his newly discovered knowledge with anyone in hearing range. He wanted to walk up to the pretty, well-endowed embodiment of his fantasies and kiss her full on the lips. He wanted to see that leg she'd displayed earlier.

So, this is Boo, he marveled from his chair.

She was everything he'd imagined and more. Tall, regal. He'd known she would be tall. He shifted the pad on his knees, and sat straighter. Renee was right. He should have worn a suit. He pulled at his jacket, then changed his mind. Wasn't it Thoreau who said you should beware all enterprises that required new clothes? Marc wondered if that included meeting women you met over the telephone.

Mesmerized, he watched her. Every moment etched itself in his mind with digital clarity, and his artist's eye collected her like a miser collects his gold. He wondered how she saw herself—she'd never told him. Watching her from behind, he smiled as he recalled the time she said she might, *might* believe a man quoting *Phenomenal Woman* by the time he got to the part about "the curve . . ." of her back. His smile grew larger. That really was quite a generous curve shaping the back of her black pin-striped skirt.

Standing so tall and straight, obviously caught up in the story she was telling, she turned a near perfect profile to him, and Marc had an instant vision of a Corinne Simpson cameo he'd once seen. Her short hair glowed under the stage lights and caressed the rounding of her ears and the small gold earrings she wore. It curved along the path of her skull, providing an expressive frame for her unique features. That hair was troubling. Teasing strands led his eye along the path of her cheek, following the delicious chocolaty flow of her skin. What must that skin feel like? He refused to speculate. This was the wrong place for it.

Had she been of any other race, an observer would have said she was, "neat" or "attractive." They might have even referred to her as a handsome woman, in a society that prized its petite princesses. Unconsciously, Marc shook his head narrowly, she was more than that, this was no princess. This woman was a wondrous, full-bodied queen. As far as he was concerned, he had never seen a more perfect face or figure—not on any real woman he'd ever seen. Rubens, with his lust for the lush kind of curves she offered, would have killed for a model like her. *Boo is a babe!* The thought escaped, and he mentally checked himself.

Take it easy, man. She still doesn't know who you are, he warned himself.

But, she was going to find out. His stomach lurched. There was no way to anticipate her reaction when she found out. And she was going to find out. Panic scratched an icy curve along the line of his thoughts. He'd come all the way from Atlanta to meet this woman. He was willing to do whatever it took, and now fate or kismet or the Universe, or angels . . . something had put them this close . . . now she was going to know. Marc barely heard her words, and as she finished, he stood and mechanically applauded.

Davida Lawrence can smile like the sun, Marc concluded as she returned to her seat. She settled neatly on the metal folding chair at his side, and he felt his good intentions grow faint. He plucked at his pants, preparing to resume his own seat. She smiled again, and Marc lost track of his hearing.

Davida Lawrence is like a narcotic, Marc decided, smiling back at her. Looking over at Renee, he was able to recover his hearing and his breath. His sister wrinkled her nose, and lifted a questioning brow. She knew! From childhood, Renee had always been good at puzzles, and she'd put the pieces of this one together in record time.

Okay, he thought, knowing the pep talk wasn't going to work, *I can do this.* His stomach was already flipping like a trained dolphin. Okay, all he had to do was lean over and quietly tell her. "Great speech," he said.

"Thanks." She was a little breathless and the word came out in a whispered rush. The little man in Marc's brain was dumbfounded, and nothing else came out.

Still talking, facing her student audience, Renee Johnson grinned broadly. "I take very special pleasure in introducing our next guest." Still grinning, she looked over her shoulder and winked both eyes. Marc looked down at his hands as she faced her students. "He's an outstanding example of his field, and I can honestly say, 'I knew him when.' You see, he's my older brother, Marcus Benton."

Davida's lips parted and her eyes widened. "You? You're . . ."

Nodding, he stood and headed for the podium because there was nothing else to do and nowhere else to go.

CHAPTER NINE

"I can explain!"

"No, you can't."

"I vote with her."

"Renee, you keep out of this. You're enjoying it way too much."

A nonchalant shrug and barely concealed smile proved Renee Johnson was indeed having fun at her brother's expense. Davida glared at her just long enough to make her shift her eyes uncomfortably, then turned back to Marcus. "You could have told me who you were." Her hand went to her hip, fingers beating a tattoo on the rounded firmness barely concealed by her staid, businesslike suit. "As a matter of fact, you should have told me, and told me right away. Instead, you sneak into my life like . . . like . . ."

"The Thief of Hearts?" Renee Johnson folded her hands demurely in front of her body.

"No!" Davida's eyes lasered twin daggers at her. "Like . . ."

"A thief in the night, just creepin' an' crawlin' through all the little nooks an' crannies . . ."

Davida's brows rose emphatically.

"A sneak thief?"

"Renee . . ." Though there was question in his voice, the pleading in Marc's eyes was unmistakable. Of all the sisters in the world, why couldn't this one seem to help a brother out?

"Look, Davida," he said, "I'm not some kind of wayward stalker. I didn't come creeping up here from Atlanta just to sneak into your life. I didn't even write your telephone number down to bring with me.'' Not that he would need to. Marc would have sworn hers was one number he would never forget, though this didn't seem like the right time to share that tidbit. "I'm here in St. Louis on legitimate business."

"Legitimate business that brought you to Beaumont High School? Where I just conveniently happened to be? What were you going to do, transfer yourself into a new school district?"

"Oh, now, she's got you there, Butch."

"I don't need a scorekeeper, Renee' " Marc said miserably as he shifted from foot to foot, refusing to look at his sister. He had the distinct feeling that if he moved his eyes Davida might try to scalp him. "Come on, Boo. I didn't get Renee to plan this Career Day thing just to lure you over here today. You've got to realize that." Sexy and self-possessed, Davida Lawrence wasn't buying it. Lifting her head a little higher, she met him eye to eye, daring him to say whatever came next.

"Renee, my sister, teaches here. You already know that—I told you that." Marc's raised hand indicated his sister, who still hovered on the outskirts of their conversation. Hearing her name, the pretty woman raised a languid hand and twinkled her fingers at them. "She was responsible for setting up this Career Day—for her students."

He looked into her eyes and found himself smiling at the intelligence he found there, flaring around her anger. "You know, Boo, I didn't know who you were, and you didn't tell me your name either."

"I was going to, just out of politeness, and then she introduced me, and I didn't have a chance to . . ." *Now why am I getting so defensive?* she thought. She hadn't done anything wrong. She wasn't the one trekking all over the southeast trying to track down somebody she'd met on the telephone. Davida took a step back, crossed her arms tightly, and fought the urge to look at him the way she really wanted to. This man, Marcus Benton, handsome and clever as he was, had a lazy, too easy, "get over" kind of attractiveness—far too charming for his own good, that's what he was. He looked like he was very used to women bending over backward to assuage his every wish. Davida had no intention of being one of those women. "Besides, you didn't ask," she finished, refusing to surrender easily.

"And strange men always come to your aid?"

"Yes. As a matter of fact, they do."

Renee's low snicker crackled in his ear. "Ask a silly question, get a silly answer." Her words were hidden beneath her smile. Marc wished for a ledge, a really high one, and about three seconds—that's all it would take to push her off, he was sure of it.

"Oh, there you are Mrs. Johnson." The thin woman in the obviously homemade, grass-colored suit bore down on them with singular determination. "I need you in the cafeteria," she called hastily, fingering the ruffled collar of her white blouse. "I need you right now. We don't have enough cookies, and the punch is running low." She threw her hands into the air, and shook her head at the futility of mere need.

"Merlie Walker," Renee whispered. "Teaches Home Ec, and she's just as nervous as she can be about the world in general." Turning, she pasted a concerned and helpful look on her own face.

"Mrs. Johnson? You *know* how these people are about sugar." There was a tearful edge to the words.

"Okay, Merlie, honey, let's go. I'm pretty sure I know where we can find more cookies, and we'll give them Kool-Aid if we have to." Merlie's face wrinkled nervously. "They won't mind, sweetie." Renee placed her hand firmly on the other teacher's elbow, gave Marc a significant look, then guided a still complaining Merlie back down the hall.

Marc said a quick silent prayer of thanks. "You know that gave her almost physical pain, don't you? To have to leave us on our own like this?" He turned back to face Davida, and grinned boldly. "I told you she likes to get her I-told-you-so in every chance she gets."

"I-told-you . . ." Unable to stop herself, Davida threw a hand over her face, then peeked at him from around her fingers. "She knows?" Davida closed her eyes and took a deep breath, still hiding "No, you couldn't have?" She opened her eyes. "You really did tell her all about us, how we sort of met—the phone—everything?" She dropped her head, half turned, then pivoted to look him directly in the eyes. "This is the singular most embarrassing thing that has ever happened to me."

"No, it's not."

"What?"

Marc grinned. "You remember telling me about your first pair of pantyhose?"

Davida's mouth dropped open, and her eyes darted along the empty corridor. "Ssh!"

His grin widened and he leaned closer, his voice low. "You told me about getting all dressed up to go with your brother and the other big kids, that Easter when you were twelve. How, when you got on the bus, trying to look grown-up and cute, and right there in front of everybody the darned things slid right down your legs and puddled at your feet." He nodded. "Yep, I'd say that ranks way up there, pretty high on the Most Embarrassing Things list."

She let her hand fall from her face, and her lips imitated his infectious grin. *He really does know how to make me smile,* she thought.

He knows me too well. "Okay, I'll give you that one, but only if you promise not to dredge up anything else."

"You've got it." He winked.

She extended a hand, and he took it immediately. "It's been nice meeting you Marc, but I need to go." Taking her hand back, she made a show of looking down at her watch.

He repossessed her hand. "This is not going to be that easy, Boo. Besides, now that she's met you, and obviously approves of you, Renee will never approve of my not following up on this chance meeting. Let me buy you a late lunch, or an early dinner, whichever you choose."

"As enticing as that offer is, I can't. It's Tuesday, and I have to pick Des up . . ."

". . . from her scout meeting by four," he finished for her. "But, your mother usually gets her, and takes her to the library for the children's reading hour, then out for dinner, and home to you by seven, so you can get her in bed by eight thirty." He looked at his own watch. "Unless you're an inordinately slow eater, that gives us plenty of time."

He knew her too well. Something told her that no matter what excuse she came up with, he'd find a way to counter it. Davida tilted her head, and pressed her lips together. "You're determined to turn this accidental meeting into something it's not, aren't you?"

"No, not at all. What I am, is determined to know you better, Boo. I owe it to fate; I owe it to the universe." His arm circled her waist, and he turned her purposefully toward the nearest exit. Walking slowly beside her, he looked into her curious face.

Her mouth, her lush, full lips parted in wonder as she pondered the possibilities of his words. Their eyes clung while a delicate thread of intimate promise spun itself between them. Marcus was unable to drop his eyes before her steady gaze, even though he feared she could hear the loud thunder of his heart, feel the heat of his attraction. He had already noticed the rapid rise and fall of the swell of her breast beneath her genteel and somber suit jacket. Her brown eyes so dark and intense as to appear bottomless watched him, and he felt pinned to her side.

"Uh-huh, right," she finally replied. "The universe?"

"Absolutely." Spreading his hands, Marc tried to look convincing. "Do you know how many millions of phones there are in the state of Missouri alone? Now what are the chances that I would dial the wrong one and find you on the other end? What do you think the chances are of finding that number, finding you, and then meeting you like this? Do you think it's all just happenstance, or could it be fate taking a hand in our lives?"

"Now you're implying we might somehow be 'meant' for each other?"

"I didn't take it that far, but . . ." He held the door for her and she stepped through. The rain had slowed to a small, sullen drizzle, and Davida unfolded her plastic raincoat in preparation. He held it for her. "What do you think, Boo?"

She slipped her arms into the raincoat, then used her hand to slick dripping water from it. "I think you're not going to leave me alone unless I agree."

"How perceptive of you—even if you do go out of your way to misunderstand the question."

Davida found herself suppressing a smile. *He's got me doing it again,* she marveled, *I'm flirting with him.* "All right. Dinner."

"Good. Your town, you name the place."

Name the place? That was a heck of a question to ask a woman who's chief restaurant experience was mostly limited to McDonald's and Chinese take-out, these days. She tried to think of places she could remember Quita or Melanie talking about. Some place they talked about, but weren't likely to show up at this afternoon. "Uhm, how about Culpepper's? The one over in the West End?" That was far enough from her office downtown on Spruce Street. Culpepper's wicker, glass, and fern decor was also a far cry from a romantic hide away—that ought to be safe enough.

"Buffalo wings?" He nodded appreciatively.

"You know the place?"

"Know it? Renee and George and I have eaten so many pounds of wings there, they ought to charge us rent." He laughed. "It's a good place. Should we take your car or mine?"

Davida remembered the sleek, chocolate brown Saab he'd arrived in, and wondered how it would feel to be swaddled in that leather interior, riding with a man who . . . Who—what? "I'll drive my own, and you should, too." she decided.

"I did the right thing," she reassured herself as she pulled the Accord's steering wheel hard to the right for her turn on Natural Bridge.

If I did the right thing, why am I still trying to talk myself into it? she wondered twenty minutes later as she parked her car down the street from the already crowded restaurant. She didn't have time to search for an answer, as Marc tapped lightly at her window.

He was cavalier, every bit as much the gentleman here as he'd been in the school parking lot. Solicitously opening doors, helping her escape her clinging raincoat, seating her—it was nice to have a man's attention centered on her solely as a woman and not as a mother, though she denied a small inner yearning for more of the same.

Suddenly dropping his elbows to the table top, Marcus Benton leaned forward and grinned at her.

He was looking at her as if she was something good to eat. Davida leaned back in her chair, succeeding in almost putting some distance between them. "What?" Her fingers plucked nervously at the narrow lapels of her blouse, then found the thin gold chain she wore at her throat.

"Oh, I was just thinking of how different you look from what I pictured."

She blinked at him, unsure of how to respond.

"I thought you'd be taller, like around six feet. And thin, like a model, almost ethereal."

Self-consciously, Davida pulled her stomach in and sat straighter. She fought the urge to suck in her cheeks. "That's one of the funny things about voices," she said. "We don't always look like we sound."

"But, that's just it, you do. In a way, you're exactly what I expected. Obviously intelligent, strikingly beautiful, but not at all typical." He sighed. "And exactly what I'd ask for if I still believed in Santa Claus." His eyes seemed to drink her in, collecting and categorizing each feature and every movement.

He called me beautiful. Davida refused to look around to see if anyone else heard the words her body insisted on singing. She busied herself with realigning her silver, and was more than grateful when the waitress approached them.

"Am I different from what you expected?"

"Uhm." She was at a loss for words. "The curly hair, and the dimples are . . ." Nice. "You look really young, but older than I thought you would . . ." And she was grateful—at least people didn't think she was out with her son. "When we talked, you told me you were in your thirties . . ." And lately, that sounded so young to her.

"I guess that's a compliment." He lifted his beer and tilted the glass to her in salute. "At least, I hope so. You don't look forty either."

Did he have to remember everything? "Could we change the subject? At the school, I heard you say that you've begun to work on a special project?"

"Bro'Man, yeah." Marc's face lit up and he smiled like a small boy. "Did you ever read Superman comics, when you were a kid?" She nodded. "Well, I'm the guy, or at least one of the guys who helps to make him real."

"Real?"

"Yeah, as an artist, it's important to avoid the small but jarring inaccuracies that have occurred in comics in the past."

"Really?" She raised her brows.

"Sure. You know, back in the fifties and sixties, they used to have Superman flying through space?" His dimples flashed at the absurdity, and Davida wondered what it would take to make it happen again. "Can you imagine a humanoid—a being that has to breathe, and this one breathes the same kind of air we do—can you imagine him flying in an environment where there is no air?"

Davida shook her head and hoped for the dimples again.

" 'Course, if your creation lasts as long as Superman, you've got a little time to correct a few minor errors. But"—he clapped his hands and grinned—"I want my creation, Bro'Man tight, right out of the box." He leaned his face against his fist, and the smile broadened. "Now, imagine a black man, an African-American man, born of the mud at the foot of the Kenyan hills, and brought to this country by two struggling black anthropologists. 'Course, they're married, and they adopt this child, who grows into Bro'Man."

"Okay," Davida countered, "but isn't that a bit of a ripoff of the Superman legend?"

"Not really. See . . ." He launched into an intricate and well-worn character sketch. Bro'Man never failed to thrill him. An hour later, Marcus was still detailing story lines, sketches, and animation techniques, and Davida was captivated.

Watching him like this, with his dark eyes shining, his face so totally animated, and his expressive, long-fingered hands cleaving the air between them, she wanted to know him better. She wanted to reach out, grasp those hands that looked so definitively masculine, and press them hard against her body. She wanted to place her face close, her hand on his chest, and hear his voice move through her skin. This was the kind of man, sharing, spontaneous, and giving, that she'd hoped Skip would grow into when she'd married.

Well, not exactly "grow into", she corrected herself. If Marcus Benton was anything, he was absolutely the wrong man. This man wasn't likely to grow into anything remotely right for Davida Lawrence. He was too short, too young, too cute, too flighty, too prone to hearing the thoughts behind her words, too . . . good to be true. His vivacity and dimpled smile were contagious, and she found herself sitting closer to him at the small round table—closer than a friend, but not close enough for a lover. His khakied knee brushed her Hanes Silk Reflections the first time and made her blink. The second time, all she could think of was how to get out of them.

"I—I'll be right back," she stuttered, standing suddenly. "I need to check on Des. She'll be worried if I don't call." Her napkin barely made it onto the chair as she stumbled away to the ladies room. Inside, she rushed past the pay telephone stand and hid in the first stall she came to. Close to hyperventilation, she pressed both hands over her nose and mouth, and crossed her legs tightly to still the throb he'd caused, all the while willing herself to breathe normally.

She was forty years old, and he was still pretty much a kid. She didn't have any business thinking about him as anything other than a nice young man. He was only thirty-four or so, and just getting ready for long-term commitment to a project that was obviously his heart's desire. In no way was he ready for the kind of commitment a relationship with someone like her would require. He'd never even been married. By his own admission, he had trouble getting dates, and as cute as he was, she didn't know why. She closed her eyes, and tried to keep her thoughts in a straight line.

Don't think about how cute he is, she warned herself.

She had been married and was raising a child ... Besides, they didn't even live in the same state. She brushed her hands over her skirt, then straightened her blouse. So, why was she so attracted to him? This had to be what they called a "dalliance." There was no future in it. In a year, five years, he'd have gotten on with his real life and forgotten all about her."

"And he's reading way too much into this 'coincidental' meeting. I don't care what he says, that man came all the way from Atlanta to meet me," she whispered to herself, "and as flattering as that is, he shouldn't have. I'll just have to convince him that it was a mistake, that he should go on back to Atlanta and dial some other woman's number. Preferably a younger, less involved, single woman's—I have too much responsibility to play games with either of our lives."

But, to watch his eyes as he'd looked into hers had been more than nice. For just a little while, she hadn't been Davida Lawrence. She hadn't been mother or sister or daughter, or even "the IRS lady." For just a little while, in his eyes, she had been someone altogether different. In his eyes, she was a creature of passion, a woman conceived in fantasy, covered in fascination, and nurtured by love. What he saw in her wasn't real. It couldn't exist in daylight. But, those moments on the telephone, in the dark with his voice wrapping around her mind and smoking through her soul ...

Washing her hands didn't seem to help ease her conscience. "I just have to find the words to tell him, this can't continue," Davida told the vanity mirror. "I have to set him straight, ask him not to call again, and ..."

"Him who, girl?"

Davida's voice put on brakes in her throat and the skid nearly choked her. "How long have you been standing there?"

"Obviously not long enough." Quita walked closer. "Who's got you talking to yourself? Are you alright?" Her face in the mirror peered anxiously over Davida's shoulder. When Davida nodded, Quita drew closer, turning faucet handles in search of hot water, then splashing liquid soap and cold water over her own hands. "What happened, you decided to come out this afternoon? That's not like you. Did you come with some people from that Career Day thing you did?"

"Something like that." Davida tried to look pleasant as she nodded. Edging toward the door, she kept the smile in place.

"Wait a minute," Quita called as the door opened. "I came in alone, I was just going to get something to go, but I might as well join your group." Davida's heart seemed to pop like a balloon, and she was amazed that her legs still worked.

Marc stood as they reached the table, and without looking, Davida knew Quita was smiling for all she was worth. Unable to sink through the floor, though she tried with all her might, Davida made polite, obligatory introductions.

"So this is your party," Quita whispered, bending close to Davida's ear. "Sooky, sooky, now."

Behave yourself, Davida prayed, as Quita went to work. Quita loved doing what she did so well, and her joy showed as she probed the very affable Marcus Benton for every available detail of his life. In fifteen minutes, even allowing time to order food and a Long Island iced tea, she knew as much about Marcus than Davida had learned in more than three months of telephone conversations.

"Atlanta's a nice city to visit." Quita ran her tongue along her teeth in an economically feral sweep. "Speaking of visits, how long do you plan to be here for this visit?"

Marc's eyes shone with merriment, and Davida refused to believe he could possibly enjoy the grilling he was getting. "About a week," he answered, "but I could be convinced to stay longer."

"So, are you going to try to convince him?"

Davida wondered why the room was suddenly so hot.

Moving her eyes easily between them, Quita looked back to Marc. Casually sipping her drink, her eyes lowered demurely, Quita unleashed a calculated, but innocent sounding bomb. "So, Marcus Benton, how does it happen that our little Davida has found such an obviously successful, talented, and unattached gentleman, such as yourself?"

Davida cringed and tried not sink lower in her seat. Quita had no problems with sliding out onto thin conversational ice.

Marc grinned. "You make me sound like a lost puppy."

"She's my friend, and I'm just wondering about your intentions . . ."

"Quita!"

"And where she's been hiding you?"

"Quita!"

"And for exactly how long?"

Marc's hand moved quickly, covering Davida's on the table, then folding his fingers through hers—establishing firm contact, and stating possession. She didn't move. He leaned forward, and she thought she detected a slight and subtle change in his face. Resolution and privacy hardened his mellow voice. "You're a good friend to worry about her, but you don't have to. I've got this."

Surprised, Quita sat back in her upholstered chair and blinked. She set her drink carefully in the center of the small white cocktail napkin beside her plate and licked her lips, then blinked again. "Uhmm. I guess you told me, didn't you?" She looked at their joined hands, brightened perceptively, and began to collect her jacket and purse. "I guess you do have this," she said to Marc. "So, I'm going to leave you to it. And you"—she winked at Davida—"I'll talk to later."

They watched her pause at the entrance, pull dollar bills from her purse, then move through the door of the now crowded restaurant.

"I am so sorry . . . She's . . ."

"Your friend." Marc trapped her hand between both of his. His eyes, long-lashed and clear bore into hers, and Davida wouldn't have had it any other way, not even on a bet. "So, what do we do now?"

"I can't . . . " Davida stole a glance at her watch. "It's six thirty, and I need to . . ."

He leaned forward and pressed his lips to her cheek, kissing her as gently as he'd ever kissed anyone. When her head tilted in silent acceptance, Marc followed the urgings of barely concealed desire.

His lips closed over hers, and effectively sealed off further protest. Barely opened, his warm mouth was firm and slightly moist. Promising, and offering no reason for resistance, he held her in place with her lashes fluttering, and her resolution breaking. Her free hand, her right, came forward to cup his cheek and to hold him close. Letting him go would be a mortal sin. Their kiss, finally coming to a close, her own lips meeting and parting from his, she drew a shaking breath, then remembered where she was.

Marc's eyes, tender and demanding, met hers. "I wish I could say I was sorry for that," he said quietly.

Me, too, Davida thought, *but I'm not. Not even a little bit.* They looked into each other's eyes, and it was as if they were alone in the hectic and crowded restaurant. Davida could feel an undeniably strong and steadily growing attraction to the man she already knew was the wrong one.

Watching him, Davida was conscious of something happening in her body, the unsettling motions of desire. For a moment she had the uncomfortable feeling that she was betraying Skip, betraying a sacred memory. Hoping for invisibility and knowing it was impossible, she sat motionless. It had been a long time since her body had reacted like this to a man. She was suddenly, stunningly aware of how deprived she was, how hungry she'd become.

Pulling her hand free, she sat back in her seat—debating and knowing the issue was already decided. Could it be that he was right, that their meeting was fated, and neither of them had any choice but to be swept along a course of Kismet? That was too easy. Folding her hands together, she strove for dignified options. *I am . . . , I was a married woman, and I was not going to let this go any further,* her thoughts tumbled. For all intents and purposes, this man was a stranger, and a younger stranger at that. She didn't know enough about love or sex to teach anybody anything, and God knew, she was too old to learn how to swing from the chandeliers at this late date . . .

She had absolutely no business sitting up in a restaurant, a public place, accepting even one little kiss on the cheek from him. Instead, here she was exchanging a full-blown lip-lock, and part of her gave less than half a damn about who saw it! What kind of magician was he . . . what was she letting him do to her?

She looked over at him, at all his special features, including the sweet curve of the full lips she'd just kissed. Like small perfect pillows, his lips were generous and firm, curling with just the right blend of arrogance and appeal, so animated and human against her own. Those lips presaged the kind of memories she wanted to die with. Her forefinger pressed at the corner of her own mouth, then followed her lip, trying to correct and straighten no longer existing lipstick.

"So, what do we do now?" he repeated softly.

Unable to meet his eyes, she looked into the blushing remnants of her wine. The crystal bounced softly lit images through the liquid and along its curves, but it didn't work. There were no answers. As hard as she stared, Davida found no clues to what the future might hold residing in the bottom of the glass.

She wished she could find the courage to chuckle. Here she was with so many of the elements she'd counted important to seduction, and she was half—no, more like three quarters—afraid to be seduced. But that other quarter—it was in there kicking and screaming to be set free—in there rattling bars and banging walls, begging to discover all the passion she'd so pristinely avoided for so very long.

"Boo?" He sounded like he needed an answer. "What do we do now?"

She took a deep breath and made a decision. "I take a walk on faith, and you put your face a little closer to mine, and ask me that question again in exactly the same way."

Marc hesitated for the first time since they'd actually met. His eyes telegraphed dual messages. *Do you really mean it? Are you really ready for this, Boo?* Following the guiding hands that cupped his chin so confidently, he leaned closer, letting her lead him to her waiting lips.

"Ask me," she whispered.

"What do we do now, Boo?"

"We kiss and make this whatever-it-is we've stepped into the very best it can be, for as long as it lasts." Her lips met his with more acceptance and commitment than he'd ever dreamed possible.

Two passing waitresses exchanged a glance, smiled, then looked away. It was always so nice to see people falling in love—whether they wanted to or not.

CHAPTER TEN

Irritated, Davida's finger tapped at the earpiece of her headset again. The darned thing was making odd sounds and toying with her hearing this morning, and she'd had just about enough of it.

Beep. The sharply metallic sound scraped at her nerves for the last time, and she tossed the errant headset across the desk. She would have been lying if she'd said she didn't feel a strong degree of satisfaction when it slid from the corner of her desk to land in the trash basket. She wouldn't have said it, but it felt like divine intervention and she was glad for it.

Not to be denied, her telephone rang again.

"Good morning, Davida Lawrence. How may I help you?"

"Morning, Cookie. You're sounding chipper—want to talk about it?"

"Butch." Davida dropped her professional poise and settled back in her chair. "What's up with you?" She grinned.

"Nothing much, I've just got to make a quick trip to Maui for one of my cases, so lunch is out this week."

"But we were going to Famous-Barr," she whined, making a conscious effort to sound pitiful. If he was going to Hawaii, he should at least feel guilty.

"I know, but you can still go," Glenn said, making an effort to placate his sister. "Take Quita, enjoy the French onion soup, and charge it to me."

"It won't be the same." Davida knew that if she did as he suggested, and she fully intended to, there was going to be a pair of Aigner shoes and a matching bag in the deal.

"You can shop a little, and we'll do lunch when I get back."

"Promise?"

"Promise."

"And you'll bring me a souvenir?"

"That's where Des gets it from, but yes. I'll bring something for both of you."

"Good." Satisfied, Davida grinned again. Glenn Morrison would no more break his promise to his younger sister now then he would have when they were little kids, and she knew that, too. She crossed her legs and smoothed her skirt over her thighs. "I did want to tell you something though. Over lunch."

"Yeah?"

Butch always seemed to take her news better over food, Davida reflected. Her top leg began a lazy pendulum swing, and she watched it. Her circling ankle provided a focal counterpoint and she wondered if sharing her news with her brother was the right thing to do, but who else was she going to tell? "Yeah," she said.

"Well, come on, Cookie. What is it?" She could almost see him looking at his watch.

Davida opened her mouth. Nothing came out. She took a deep breath, worked herself into a different spot in her chair, and opened her mouth, again. Nothing came out—again.

"Cookie?" He waited. "Oh, you're taking too long." Davida heard his chair squeak as he sat down. "This can't be good."

"I met him," she blurted without further preamble. "The man from the phone."

"You . . . how . . . when?" The chair squeaked again, and she imagined him up, pacing like a caged tiger. "No. Just tell me why. That's all I want to know. You said you weren't going to . . . why, Cookie?"

"Look Glenn, it was an accident, pure and simple." And he called her Boo. Her stomach lurched happily.

"Uh-huh."

"Butch, it turns out he's really a nice guy. A talented and upstanding citizen, and if you'd like to wait, I can run down the hall and check to see if he pays his taxes on time, but I'll bet he does." She rushed through the story of the Career Day meeting, trying to ignore the still spreading ripples in her stomach.

"Cookie . . ." She could almost see him shaking his head. "I don't know . . . it just seems like . . . You really like him, don't you?"

"He's nice." And, when he kissed her, she felt like a Boo—his Boo. She sighed, and switched the phone to her other ear. Pressing the telephone between her chin and shoulder, she began to idly finger her way through a stack of telephone inquiries, as though faking work would help her explain her feelings. "I'm not sure where this . . . thing . . . is going, but it's nice."

"I told you, you spend too much time alone."

She bristled. "And, I told you . . ." The light tap at her office door brought her eyes up. Quita Walton's head followed by her stylish lemon-colored linen suit clad body eased into the room. She pressed a finger to her lips, nodded, then waved her fingers at Davida, while lowering herself into the opposite chair.

"Butch"—Quita's brows rose—"I have about as much company as I can stand," Davida countered.

"Tell him I said, 'hi,'" Quita whispered sweetly.

"Quita says, 'hi,'" Davida repeated.

"Tell her I said . . ."

"Look, you two," Davida interrupted, "I don't work for Western Union. You two want to pass messages, do it on your own time."

Quita smiled.

"I might just do that," Glenn said, surprising his sister. "When I get back, I just might."

"Well, alright then. Have a good trip?"

"You bet."

The receiver had barely left her hand when Quita leaned forward, her hand covering Davida's. "What did he say? What did he say about me that made you look like that?"

Looking down, pretending to ignore the question, Davida seized her black plastic government issue ballpoint pen and made quick notes. Quita fidgeted, making loud noises in her throat. "I asked you a question."

"Testy, aren't we?" Davida concealed her smile.

"Don't look at me like that," Quita wailed impotently, "what did he say? Tell me what he said about me."

Swinging up from her chair, Davida bent over her desk, pretended to check her calendar, then straightened her jacket. "That he might call you when he gets back in town," she said, folding her hands in front of her, tucking her tongue into her cheek.

Delight made Quita's eyes and cheeks glow with a sudden flush of anticipation. "Really? When?"

"I can't stand this." Davida giggled. "I shouldn't have said anything."

Pausing, Quita seemed nailed in place by a random thought. "What if he forgets?" She turned her stricken face to Davida. "What if he forgets to call? Or . . . or if he can't find my number?" She tilted her head, suddenly cagey. "You know, you could hook a sister up."

"Mmm, where have I heard that before?" Davida shook her head in denial. "Please. Girl, if you even *think* you want to get closer to *my* brother, you need to drop LaDonna Crane's old tricks—they don't work anymore."

"Well then"—Quita, resting her elbow on the chair arm, thoughtfully dropped her chin into her hand—"I guess I'll have to wait for him to call me. And if he doesn't, then I can always call him."

"You could do that."

"I really came by to follow up on something else," Quita said, primly.

Caught off guard, Davida stopped and propped her hip on the corner of her desk.

"I've been patient, and I've waited." Quita leaned forward. "Now I want to know what's going on."

"With?" Davida gathered a group of folders from her desk, tapped them against her knee to align them, then clutched them tightly to her chest.

"With you and that man!"

"What ma—?" Davida's lids lowered over her rapidly moving eyes. Her lower lip was already tucked between her teeth. "Oh," she said, "him."

"Yes, him!"

"He's just a nice young man I met when I did the Career Day for Essie."

"And that's why, when I looked back, you were kissing him?"

Davida closed her eyes and wished for the earth to open and swallow her whole. "There's nothing to tell—nothing going on between us."

"Girl, please." Quita's finger stabbed the air between them, punctuating her every word. "You couldn't go out with my cousin, but you can sit up in a public restaurant, in front of God and everybody, and kiss a stranger? Then you have the nerve to tell me there's nothing going on? And, I'm supposed to believe that, right?"

Davida looked up miserably. "Quita, he's not really a stranger, I've met him before."

"Really?" The interest was more than casual, and Davida felt the other woman's curiosity charge the molecules of air in the room.

"We've, uh . . . we've talked . . . on the phone."

"And whatever you talked about, on the phone, precipitated the not-so-little kiss I witnessed?" Quita tapped her foot and tossed her head. "I don't think so," she said.

"Quita." Davida caught and held a deep breath. "I don't know why I'm going to tell you . . ." she let the breath go in a sharp blast. "Yes, I do. I'm going to tell you to get you off my back." The red-labeled folders made a slapping sound as they hit her desk.

"His name is Marcus Benton, and he's a cartoonist. He lives in Atlanta, Georgia, and he was here because his sister was responsible for the Career Day I did."

"So you kissed him. Oh, yes, that explains everything." Quita leaned farther back in her chair and, elbow still propped, moved her cheek to her fist. "Stuff like that never happens to me. But, you said you met him on the phone."

Scooting farther back on the corner of her desk, Davida's eyes found the floor and remained lowered. "He was trying to call his sister, and he got me by mistake."

"Stuff like that *never* happens to me." Quita's voice was filled with wonder. "You obviously like him, so you kept talking to him." She nodded to herself. "He's cute, too. I guess that explains why you were less than impressed with the stripper we got you."

"Quita? He was a stripper!"

"Hmmm." She nodded. "I see your point. The stripper goes home when he finishes, and you get to hang on to that little cutie I saw you with. I do see your point."

Davida used both hands to fend off the notion that Quita was even close to right. "No, you don't. Marcus is a nice young man, but he's not the man I plan to . . ."

"Oh! So, he's a diversion!"

"No, but he's . . . he's . . . so short."

"Girl," Quita moaned, "you pick the worst reasons to close a man out of your life." She turned up her nose. "How long have you been keeping this short man a secret?"

"Obviously, not long enough."

Quita rolled her eyes. "He didn't look that short to me."

"You're so short," Davida countered, "that's easy for you to say."

"You're a snob, you know that?" Quita sucked her teeth and leaned back to cross her arms tightly beneath her bosom.

"I am not! Why would you say that?"

"You are, too." Quita shook her head in disgust. "I could understand if he picked his nose in public or had a religious thing against taking baths or something." She frowned for maximum emphasis. "Putting down a perfectly nice, completely eligible man because he's short—I don't get it."

"I told you, it's because you're so short. I can look right into the man's face—if I put on heels, I'll look down on the top of his head. I'll bet you anything we're the same height, and I probably outweigh him by at least ten pounds." Davida looked up, then dropped her eyes abruptly. "You know, I was used to Skip. He was so much bigger than me. He made me feel . . ." Her eyes rose and she sucked air, then pressed her lips together. Releasing the air, she pressed a hand to her chest. "He made me feel delicate, fragile, protected." She shivered slightly. "Somehow, it made me feel the way all the movies and books tell us a woman is always supposed to feel when she's with a man."

"And you figure a short man can't give you that?"

Davida shrugged. She closed her eyes, and Quita assumed it was because she was remembering Skip. What Davida was recalling was the delicious thrill of Marcus Benton's strong, long fingers on her hand, the glide of his palm against her own, and the unmitigated hypnotism of his beautiful walnut brown eyes—that made her feel like a woman, too.

Clearing her throat, she felt a sudden need to throw Quita off the scent, somehow make her believe that nothing was going on, to keep the magic for herself. "He's young, too." Blinking, Davida wondered why she'd chosen to throw that precious little tid-bit out.

Quita nodded, and she started a little dance in her seat. "Oh, I see." She pointed one gold lacquered nail. "I see. You're trying to get your *Stella* on." She grinned and crossed her arms beneath her breasts. "Go on, girl. Terri McMillan has nothing on you."

Davida eased herself from the desktop and pouted. She paced her office then turned on the other woman. "Quita, it's not like that at all."

"How young is he?" she challenged.

"Thirty-four, thirty-five . . . I don't know!"

"Okay, 'Old School,' I see where this is going. You see yourself as a cradle robber now, and you don't understand the attraction."

"What I have with Marc is not . . ."

"So, you admit you have something with him?" Davida threw her a dark look, and Quita smiled. "It's okay, sweetie, you don't have to admit it out loud, you don't even have to admit it to me, but be fair and admit it to yourself. It shows all over your face when you talk about him. In fact, I knew something was going on when I saw the two of you together for the first time—even before that kiss. Does he know about Des?"

"You know I wouldn't hide or deny my child, of course he does. He went to Six Flags with us, and he brought along his nephew. Des likes him, them."

"Good. That's a really good start." Quita sucked at her teeth and wiggled her eyebrows up and down. "Spending time together is a very good thing. Besides, you needed to get out." She winked. "You look like you're really impressed by him, in spite of his . . . shortcomings, if you'll pardon the pun. From what I saw at Culpepper's, he was totally captivated by you. The only thing left now is to get you two in the same place at the same time. How are we going to do that?'' She snapped her fingers and looked brightly inspired. ''I could give a party, and we . . .''

''No, Quita. *We* are not going to do anything.''

''Then you give it, just remember to invite me and your adorable brother.''

Davida threw up her hands. ''I don't know why I tell you anything.''

Quita rose and patted the sleeve of Davida's silk jacket. ''Because I understand, girlfriend, I understand. Just don't you forget *my* hookup.''

Dugan's, on Ponce De Leone Avenue in midtown Atlanta was their place. It had been their place for, ''sitting back and talking smack'' since their sophomore year, and both men liked it that way. As restaurants went, Dugan's would never rank high on any gastronome's list because of the simple burger, fries, wings, and anything-with-cheese menu. But, it was a neighborhood bar where nobody bothered you if you needed to think, and where everybody bought you a drink on your birthday. It seemed like the right place for talking this particular Saturday afternoon.

A big white MARTA bus roared past, leaving the building and the chairs where they sat vibrating in its wake and the two men nearly missed Yvonne's call of recognition because of the noise. Yvonne Collins always waited on them. She had worked at Dugan's for as long as either Marcus or Milt could recall, and she didn't feel any real need to alter her situation. Her job and her friends, she was quick to say, suited her just fine.

What Yvonne didn't always say was that her tips and Georgia HOPE Scholarships put three kids through Georgia State University, and paid the mortgage on her neat little triplex around the corner— and that was also fine with her. Long since divorced, and twice abandoned, petite and sassy Yvonne enjoyed her biweekly excursions to the dog tracks in Alabama, and hitting the local lottery every now and then. She claimed she never put up with a man she didn't like.

Now she worked at Dugan's because she liked the company, and it always did her heart good to see men eat. Of all the Dugan's men she loved so dearly, Milt Thomas was almost her very favorite customer. He ate a lot and tipped well, but mostly he ate a lot.

''What'll it be, baby?'' Yvonne purred at Milt with all the eloquence of Eartha Kitt, then she winked at Marc while she copied the substantial order. Once complete, she tapped the pad with her pen and glanced at Marc, again. ''When you get over your health craze, Slim, maybe you'll be more like your buddy, here.'' She patted Milt's shoulder. ''See, he don't order a meal when he come here, he order groceries!'' Leaving both men laughing, Yvonne made her way back to the kitchen.

"Heiniken all right?" Marcus asked as he stood to head for the broad oak bar that was the huge room's centerpiece. Milt nodded and seemed more than content when Marc returned, setting the cold green bottles between them.

Settling back in his battered wooden captain's chair, Milt made a tube of his big fist and air-tootled a near-silent tune while he waited. He pretended to watch the Braves lineup on the color set over the bar, but what he was really watching was the man sharing his table. Marcus Benton sat across from him with the battered Braves cap pulled low over his eyes, looking every inch the college frat-rat he'd been when they met at Morehouse College fifteen years earlier. *Even the damned grin is the same,* Milt thought, watching his friend. When he could stand it no longer, Milt broke their companionable silence. "When are you going to get rid of that raggedy hat?"

The once-red bill of the cap tipped slightly, just enough for a marginal field of vision. "You ask me that every year," Marc said.

"An' you keep wearin' that durned cap. It's been over seven years," Milt muttered.

"And they've been winning for over seven years." Two fingers tapped the cap. "This cap is a bona fide good luck charm."

"You don't think it's the pitching staff?"

"Nope. It's the cap, man. It's definitely the cap." Slumped deep in his chair, Marc crossed one foot over the other and waited. There had to be more to this meeting than questions about his much favored, sun- and sweat-faded headgear.

Milt nodded at the television, approving the pregame commentary. "You playing ball next Sunday?"

"Yep." Marc nodded back. "My bat's in the trunk. I was figuring on getting out to the cage, getting some practice in, later on. Are you playing this week?"

The aging outfielder grinned and patted the table. "Damn, Skippy. When's the last time I missed out on a game?"

"Or the free beer afterward." Marc laughed.

"Okay. All right." Milt chuckled. "You got me. You know me." He took a long draught from his Heiniken. "How was St. Louis?"

Marc almost laughed out loud. He'd known this was coming. In fact, he had a little bet going with himself as to how long it would take Milt to get around to asking. He looked at his watch—sixteen minutes and counting. The man was a model of restraint.

"It was a good trip," Marcus replied lazily. "Had a chance to get some feedback from a couple of kids, got some work done, did that Career Day for Renee . . ." Nodding absently, he let his voice drift away to almost nothing. "And I met her while I was there."

"Her, who?" Nothing wrong with Milt's hearing.

The cap tipped just enough to reveal Marc's big smile.

"Really? *Her?*"

The Braves cap rose and fell with Marc's nod. Milt's chair scraped sharply against the bare wooden floor as he pulled closer to the table, primed for this conversational bear. "So, you finally met her. What's the mystery lady like—no, wait. Before you tell me what she's like, tell me what she looks like."

"Man"—Marcus chuckled—"you are so shallow."

"I know, but I'm consistent. Consistency is just one of my many charms." Milt managed to keep a straight face. "What did she look like?"

Elbows on the table, eyes drifting on a memory, Marc's face became mobile and dreamy. Milt was more than a little surprised at how close to the surface this almost visceral response lurked. "She's an angel; soft, sweet, pretty. She's an Amazon; strong, intelligent, and formidable. She's all that, man. All that and more."

Impatient, Milt pointed a finger, and shook it vigorously at the Braves cap. Noboby he knew was interested in the romanticized version. Besides, he'd waited almost two solid weeks for the information. "Now, see there," he said, "that is not what I asked you."

"I know." Marc sat up and finally removed his cap. Folding his hand across his face, he let his fingers massage the Saturday growth of beard. "She's a full-sized woman. I guess you'd call her 'big boned.' "

Milt, always sensitive about his handling and occasional mangling of the English language, started, determined to defend the term. "Nothing wrong with being 'big boned.' Deb is 'big boned,' and you don't hear me complaining."

"Deb is five four, and weighs two hundred pounds."

"An' you don't hear me complaining," Milt repeated stubbornly. "There's nothing wrong with stating the facts."

"Unless you're the woman being referred to, and it is almost always a woman—then it's demeaning. It's like that other term the fellas like to use." Marc snapped his fingers, trying to get the word right. "Oh, yeah. 'Thick.' You call a woman 'thick'—now what is that supposed to mean?"

"It means . . ." Milt used his hands to describe impossibly voluptuous curves in the air. "It means . . . don't change the subject. Tell me about her."

Marc's hands imitated his friend's. "That's not what it means, and you're a lawyer, sometimes known as a literate man, so I know you know better."

Chastened, Milt muttered something that sounded like, "muzza muzza muzza foomf."

"Anyway"—Marc smirked—"in terms you can understand, Boo is a babe. She's tall, about the same height as me, long legged, got the softest looking skin—beautiful black, chocolate skin, beautifully shaped eyes, and her little mouth is like . . . like made for kissing." He shook his head.

"And you just happened to meet her at Renee's school thing."

"Sure did." Marc chuckled at the memory of her response to that chance meeting. "She 'bout went up in smoke when she found out who I was."

"Mmm," Milt hummed appreciatively. "Nothing like a fiery woman, with a passionate temper." He shook his head, and muttered something about "mysterious ways."

"No, my brother." Marc shook his head again. "Ain't no mystery here. Her name is Davida Lawrence, and she's got a voice that could scrape a man's soul raw, and a mind that can dissect anything you throw at her. She's one of the sexiest, most complex women I've ever met."

"And you know all this based on one accidental meeting at a high school Career Day?" Milt's rounded face was shadowed by doubt, and his voice demanded the details he hoped lurked behind Marc's comments.

"Our initial meeting may have been accidental, but we had a chance to spend a little time together."

"Doin' what?" Milt leaned forward eager not to miss a shred of what he anticipated to be the real meat of this conversation.

Marc ignored him. "I don't mind tellin' you, it felt good."

"What? What felt good?"

"Come on, fool—not what you're thinking. Being with her—having a chance to talk to a woman who I could feel listening, a woman with a mind and emotions and opinions of her own." Marc toyed with the salt and pepper shakers. He looked up at the television and studied it as though the score might mean something important.

"And, it didn't hurt that all that good stuff came wrapped up in a pretty good-looking package, right?" Milt wiggled his thick black eyebrows.

"I'm not just talking about sexuality, here."

"Right. You're talking about a woman who touches your soul, and makes you dream in poetry." Milt shook his big head.

"You know how awesome that is? A woman who's not afraid to stand on her own two feet and be independent, be who she is? To think for herself?" Marc's eyes caught and held his friend's.

"You know," Milt said slowly, "I once read somewhere that the mind is the sexiest part of the human anatomy."

"That's what she's like," Marc said. The flat of his palm pressed his chest, and his eyes shifted. "Physically, she's got it going on, but when you talk to her . . . there's this connection. That's what she's like, man, a connection. And it feels like she's the answer to a lot of the questions I've been asking lately. So much about her is right for me. So much about her fits me so perfectly. This is meant to be," he said remembering the press of her lips on his.

"Uh-huh. You keep saying stuff like that, and you're going to fool around and convince yourself."

"Look, Milt, I'm not saying that I plan to snatch this woman up and incorporate her instantly into my life or anything like that." Marc raised a hand, and Milt, waiting, slowly closed his mouth to listen. "This woman, Davida, well she has a lot of responsibility, and anything we decide to do will take time—I can understand and respect that. I have to. She's got a career and a child to manage. She's mature and she's not looking for kicks, and neither am I."

"I'm not liking what I'm seeing and hearing here. You're sounding suspiciously like a man in love."

"Am I?"

"You are, and I think you know it." Milt leaned closer. "Not to beat a dead horse here, but do you remember what you said about Kenya Witherspoon the first time you laid eyes on her?"

Marc shrugged. "So? I was wrong?"

"I hope you put a capital "W" on that word. To refresh your memory, you said things like, 'love' and 'marriage', and she didn't."

The derisive little snort escaped him before Marcus knew it was coming. He leaned his elbows on the table, studying the scraped, white-ringed, cigarette-scarred wooden surface. Kenya, the aspiring model-slash-actress-slash-singer-slash-dancer from Valdosta, Georgia. It was almost funny, but Kenya Witherspoon had a way of turning up in his life and his conversations just like a bad penny.

Marc wondered what it would take to permanently exorcise her pretty face and shapely body from his world. If Boo had been there, right there by his side, right then, he knew what she would have said, and she would have been right. He cleared his throat. "Yes, well, Milt, ol' buddy, when it comes to Kenya, the only two words for what we had are *wrong* and *over*. I didn't know what I was getting into back then, and I didn't know that every promise she made wasn't meant to be kept."

Mark sighed lightly. "It's too bad there's not a vaccine or some kind of congenital immunity to women like Kenya. You know, women who have all the right looks, all the right moves, and make all the right sounds." He looked up and grinned. "Unfortunately, Kenya seems to think men are like the charms on her little gold bracelet."

"No, man. Women save those little charms to show off like little collectibles, and they hang onto them because the more you like 'em, the greater their value. Kenya though, that woman wanted to use you as a place holder, just like you use a zero in multiplication. She was hangin' on to you until you hit big-time, or she found somethin' better—whichever came first.''

"Hey! That's a touch bitter, don't you think?"

Milt leaned back in his chair and scratched indelicately at his well-rounded stomach. "The truth is the light, and long may it shine, my brother." Stretching, his arms held wide and high above the bronze dome of his balding head, he looked around. "How long's it going to take to get a Philly cheese steak, around here?"

"Quit your moaning, dude. You could live on body fat for a week," Marc teased.

"I'm going to ignore that," Milt said with a sniff. "You said this lady in St. Louis was mature. What's that mean?"

"Like I said. She has a lot of responsibility—serious government job, young child. She just turned forty, and . . ."

"Forty?" Milt closed his eyes and huffed in mock pain, then shook his head. "Whoa! Hormone alert, man. That's when they start to get all emotional about that 'biological clock' stuff, and then there's all that other menopausal stuff." He wrinkled his nose distastefully.

"Man, buy a book and get a clue." Marcus looked at the ceiling in disgust. "This is not an 'us versus them' situation." Dropping his eyes to the table, Marc turned the Braves cap a quarter-turn to the right, then back again. "Did you think about stuff like that when you married Deb?"

"No. I guess I didn't." Milt brought his lips together tightly, obviously thinking of his dred-locked wife of thirteen years. Debra Thomas was about as willful as they came, a street lawyer who spent her days defending abused kids and their sometimes deliberately misunderstanding parents, she was also four years older than her husband. "I didn't think about any of that, though some days I wish I had."

"Would it make a difference?"

"Not a bit," Milt said immediately. He reached for the Heiniken in front of him, then tilted it to touch the bottle Marc held. "In praise of older women," he said as the bottles clinked between them. He drained his bottle easily and set it aside. "You thinking about marrying this woman you mostly only know from the phone?"

Turning his own nearly empty bottle in a small controlled circle, Marc tried to clarify his thoughts. Exactly what was he planning to do with this woman he mostly knew from the phone? For a long moment the only thing he was sure of was that he had no intention of letting her out of his life.

He looked at Milt, who cocked his head and lifted an eyebrow in question. "She's forty years old, man. You said she'd been married before, she's got a kid. You know it's got to be an issue."

"I'm thinking about commitment."

"Commitment? That's a young, single man's word. Forty-year-old woman, you've got to think long term. You got to think permanent. You got to . . ."

"I get it, big man, I get it. Okay—yeah, she makes me think about where I would be in five, ten, twenty years, with a woman like her. Probably married." Marcus nodded. "Definitely married." The words fit what was in his heart and in his mind. "But before I get to any of that, I'm going back to St. Louis again—and again, if I have to."

"You feel like that and you've only seen her once?"

"You forget we were on the phone for the better part of three months?" Marc's warm smile filled in a lot of blanks. "You talk enough, you learn a lot about someone. But while I was up there, we had a couple of dinners, a lunch, and a well-chaperoned trip to Six Flags. J.B. and Destiny kept a close eye on us."

"Destiny? That's her daughter?"

"Yeah, and she's quite a little lady." Poking his tongue into his cheek, Marc remembered pretty Des with her dancing feet, quick questions, and her little silver Medic-Alert bracelet. She was quick to show it off and explain its existence. She was even able to identify the medical terms listed on the bracelet. The sickle cell, she assured him conversationally, was a mere inconvenience. What was more important, was that you had to see and do and feel as much as you could while you could, then she grinned, and Marc knew he was in love.

"You are thinking about marriage, aren't you?"

"Milt, all I can tell you is we'll see, because I'm going to give all of us—me and her, and her daughter—all three of us, every possible chance I can."

"You with a kid?" Milt chuckled at the implausibility.

Gripping the worn arms of his chair, Marc tipped himself back until the chair touched the wall behind him. Balancing with his toes, he held his pose a second longer before asking, "What's funny about that? Me with a kid?"

"That little Saab Turbo you drive is not exactly a family car, you know."

"So? I could buy another car—a station wagon."

"And I know about those little jaunts you like to take on the spur of the moment. Weekends in Nassau, excursions to Curacau, that Wine Country tour last year . . . Maybe they'd work for Mom, but you can't just haul a kid along—even if she does have a passport. There's all the little needs to consider, like school and braces and Little League.

Girls play in Little League now, you know. Plus, homework's gotta be checked, and library books have to get back on time. It's a full-time job, brother.''

A moan went around the room, and Milt's eyes shifted back to the television just in time to see the New York runner cross home. He joined the general moaning chorus.

Turning back to Marc, he grinned as though uninterrupted. ''I ever tell you about the time Tannie walked in on Deb and me while we were gettin' . . . you know.'' Raised brows and a fixed frown implied exactly what Milt's adopted daughter had walked in on.

''Get outta here! Really? And what did you do?''

''Duck and cover, man. Duck and cover.'' He laughed. ''On the serious side though, when kids are around, it changes a lot of things. Man, stuff you wouldn't even imagine. And if you get involved with this woman . . .'' Milt shook his head. ''You'll be getting yourself in real deep from the very beginning—a woman with expectations, a ready-made family—that's a lot.''

''And that's all I thought about on the drive back down from St. Louis.'' Marc's chair thumped hard against the wooden floor as he leaned forward, his intensity made his eyes shine like gemstones.

Milt's eyes wandered back to the television, but he really didn't see a thing Tom Glavin or any of the other Braves did. He just nodded and remembered that nothing in the world could have dissuaded him from Deb's side—not then, and not now. He heard the same conviction in Marcus Benton's voice. *This lady had better be worth it, because for better or for worse, whether they know it or not, they're both in this for the long haul,* he thought. Milt had a feeling that forever with someone you didn't know or didn't love could be an awfully long time.

The door at the back of the long barroom swung several times before fully opening, catching the attention of both men. They watched Yvonne emerge from the kitchen with a loaded tray and ease her way past a patron stumbling from the bar.

''That's gotta be ours.'' Milt grinned, happily clutching and arranging his fork and knife.

'' 'Course it is, baby boy,'' Yvonne teased. ''You know I wouldn't leave you hungry, sugar.''

''That's why I love you, Yvonne,'' Milt said with sincerity.

''I know you do, baby. Lemme get those dead soldiers out your way.'' Expertly replacing empty beer bottles with fresh cold ones, Yvonne also magically moved food from the tray to the table. Milt clapped his hands in gleeful appreciation of her expertise

Shaking his head, Marc tried not to laugh at his friend. ''Look at you, Milt. You know what they say about gluttons, don't you?''

Almost bouncing with joy, pulling himself closer to the table, Milt grinned at his steaming plate and liberally doused everything with ketchup. "What? That we're good at sex?"

Marc's laughter rang out as the other man attacked his food.

CHAPTER ELEVEN

The tiny figure in the blue denim shorts, bright pink T-shirt, and matching high-topped Reeboks looked exactly like so many of the other summer-free kids playing on the hot sidewalk. Then she rose from her place on the steps of the narrow town house and capered on her toes, as the Accord rolled down the tree-lined, red brick street. "That can only be my baby," Davida noted, pulling her car to a stop at the curb.

Watching her child move to the music only she seemed to hear, Davida felt her heart wrench with the love she would never have enough words to express. Small, neat, and graceful, Destiny was like a pixie or an elf. No, she was more like a fairy—a little brown-skinned fairy from one of the story books she loved to read. Her optimism and supple elegance seemed boundless, the way only a child's can be, and she never hesitated to find an opportunity to express her personal brand of joy through movement.

Davida sometimes wondered what it took to be that happy, that free, to move that easily. What would it be like to master something as consuming and potentially life threatening as the disease Des dared with every school day, every dance class, and every movement she made? Davida watched her child and thought of all the millions of other diseases and complications that might have affected Destiny, and knew that for all it was worth, they were among the lucky ones. Destiny was right to celebrate her life every chance she got.

In spite of her intentional avoidance of the thought, Davida wondered at the hours and occasional days of fatigue and breathlessness Destiny sometimes experienced, and always managed to recover from. How she managed to be so optimistic, to rebound from each terrifying episode, in spite of the joint and bone pain was far beyond her mother's understanding. A special child, Des always seemed able to rise above it, even when denied the kinds of treats other kids her age offered to clean their rooms for.

But, that didn't necessarily make things any less painful.

What wouldn't she give for Des not to have to deal with sickle cell, to promise her a completely happy and normal life? Davida couldn't think of a single thing she would hesitate to trade for her child's health, including her own right arm, or years of her life.

Holding her hands behind her, Des danced forward from the steps, lingered near a sapling and waited *en pointe* for her mother. "Wanna see what I've got?" she giggled and tipped from toe to toe. "It came in the mail today, and Mama Lou let me bring it with me."

"Destiny! Child, if you don't get back up here!" Mama Lou called from the top step. Anxious, as always, about her granddaughter's susceptibility to the St. Louis summer heat and proximity to city streets, she shook her head at the little girl's protests. "I don't want to hear that noise, just come on back up here." Des walked to her on leaden feet. Protectively, cradling the child's head, Mama Lou pressed her against her hip, and walked her into the cool dimness of her living room.

"Come on in, Davida, sit yourself down, and have a glass of this lemonade. I made it fresh this morning while the cookies were baking." She smoothed her hands over her white cotton Bermuda shorts, then sat and poured tall glasses full of the pale sweet drink and passed them around, along with a warning to Des to sit still. The little girl whispered a "yes ma'am" and managed not to swing her legs for all of thirty seconds.

"Mama Lou, you know you are a wonder. I don't know a single soul who still bakes, let alone bakes ginger snaps, and you spent all day at the zoo with Des and the scouts." Davida inhaled the pungently sweet aroma, and quickly made short work of three of her mother-in-law's specialty cookies.

"I'm just doing what satisfies me and makes me happy. That's what I promised myself I would do every day that I was able. I made that promise to myself after Papa Carter passed."

"But, Mama Lou, these cookies are so good, they're sinful." Davida bit into another. "I don't know anybody who does these better than you."

"Me neither," Des said around her own cookie, then, "guess."

She reached across the small space separating them to wring at her mother's fingers. "Guess, Mom."

"What, Des?" Davida repossessed her bruised fingers and directed her full attention to her daughter. "What is it you want me to guess?"

"You already forgot." Frustrated, the little girl collected all eight of her shoulder-length plaits and pulled them to the top of her head, where she let them fall back into place. Multicolored barrettes clicked and swung frantically as her head moved in sync with her words. "I want you to guess what came in the mail for me today."

"Ooh, Davida." Mama Lou slapped at her forehead with an elegantly beringed hand. "I completely forgot myself, but it was addressed to her, and I didn't think you would mind if . . ."

"But, I want to tell it!" Des shouted. When both women looked at her sharply, the little girl remembered who and where she was. "May I please tell you what came for me in the mail today?" She smiled meekly.

Unable to resist, Mama Lou smiled back. "Go on, baby. You tell it."

Standing, Des walked importantly to the center of the carpeted floor and turned her back. Spinning to face her mother, she pulled a rolled sheet from the mailing tube she now held. Grinning, she slowly unrolled the nine- by twelve-inch manila sheet. The drawing was a charcoal sketch of a little girl dressed in top hat and tails, a spangled vest, and tap shoes. The features were regular and familiar, and when Davida tilted her head just a little bit more, the resemblance was obvious.

"It's me," Des crowed, dancing with delight. "I axed, and he drawed it. He told me he could do it, and he did it. He drawed it just like I axed him to!"

"Asked," Davida corrected automatically. "You asked, and he drew, not drawed." Then it hit her, and she was afraid to ask. "He, who, Des?"

"Marc." Obviously pleased, she turned the drawing around to face her. "I ax—, asked him to do it when we went to Six Flags with J.B. and him. He said he would, and here it is." Holding the sketch in front of her, she leaned over her grandmother's chair and looked up at her. "Looks just like me, doesn't it, Mama Lou?"

"Why, baby, it surely does." Curious eyes turned to Davida.

"Marc draw . . . drew." Des glanced at her mother as she corrected herself. "Marc drew it for me. I can't wait to show it to Tawanna Mallory." She began to tuck the rolled drawing into its tube. "I'mma put it . . ."

"I'm going to," her mother corrected.

"I'm going to put it on the wall in my bedroom, right next to my

TLC and my T-Boz posters. Okay?'' Her mother nodded and the child gave herself a shake not unlike that of a happy puppy. "You'll keep it for me?"

"Of course." Davida accepted the tube, watching her daughter dance toward the kitchen and out the back door.

Mama Lou watched Des, then tipped her head thoughtfully. "You think she'll ever grow?"

"Yes, I'm sure she will," Davida said slowly, waiting for the other shoe to drop. "Dr. Saylor says not to worry, that children with SCD are often a little slow to grow, that they have little growth spurts, just a little slower than other kids their age."

"She's eight. Do you ever think about puberty?"

Davida tried not to shudder. "No," she answered honestly. "I don't want to think about the things I have to prepare her for any sooner than I have to."

"I guess it's hard, knowing the statistics for children with sickle cell." Louise nodded, not wanting to pursue the possibilities either.

"But, you know, Des has always been a blessed child. She always seems to overcome the odds and outlast the obstacles."

Louise Lawrence nodded, then sat in her chair and waited. Waiting seemed easy and natural for the lovely sixty-two-year-old, and she did it well. Her white shorts and navy tank top folded neatly about her trim figure as she toyed with the slender gold chain at her throat. She crossed her ankles, white leather sandals passing deliberately, one over the other. Davida looked at the woman's flawless features, surrounded by the smart salt-and-pepper hair and thought Skip's mother looked an awful lot like a tall version of Lena Horne.

Davida also thought she was the most formidable figure she'd ever encountered.

"I guess I should explain."

"Why?" Mama Lou smiled sweetly, and said nothing more.

Davida set the mailing tube on the floor at her feet, then looked at her hands. She sighed deeply. "Mama Lou, I met a man," she said simply.

"Really?" Hands on the arms of her chair, the older woman leaned forward. "What's he like? Where did you meet him? When did you meet him?" Then she sat back in the chair. "Why didn't you tell me about him sooner?"

Davida tried to smile at her hands, and it didn't work. "I didn't tell you because . . . well . . . because. . ."

"Because I'm your deceased husband's mother."

Davida nodded.

"And you thought I'd blame you for being unfaithful?"

Unable to lift her eyes, Davida's nod was small and tight.

"But most of all, you were afraid I would resent you for trying to replace my son in your life?"

Davida felt a tightening around her throat. It was a sense of the unfairness and the anger she still felt for the heart attack that ended Skip's life, and it crowded her uncomfortably now.

Mama Lou's hand rose and stopped sharply. She made a "bvrrpp" sound that forced Davida's eyes from her lap. "Davida! Girl, please. Don't you know, with you or without you, life goes on? I'm telling you exactly the same thing I would tell Skip if he were sitting there instead of you. Davida, you were a good wife, the best I could have asked for for my son."

Davida had trouble meeting her mother-in-law's eyes. Would Mama Lou still say that if she told her she'd barely known Marcus when they exchanged their first kiss? And, what if she told her that though the first one was a kiss between strangers, almost a mistake, a kiss she wasn't even sure she knew the meaning of, there was a second kiss. But, the second was different, it was a gift from her to him. It was the kiss of a woman left on her own for too long—and she enjoyed it, too. What would Mama Lou say then?

Louise Lawrence looked at the younger woman with wise eyes, and for the space of seconds, Davida had the feeling that her mother-in-law could see right through her. It felt like she was seeing and somehow sharing all the intimate little thoughts that Davida had yet to find words for, the intimate little thoughts that spoke of things that men and women can only share in the most personal of circumstances.

"I trust you the way you're going to have to learn to trust yourself. Trust yourself to know what you need, and then fill the need." Louise sighed as though reading the younger woman's mind.

She stood and crossed the room. Stopping at the rose marble fireplace and mantel, her fingers lightly touched the frames of her son's and husband's photos. "Carter and I had no way of knowing that we would have Skip for such a short time, and you made him very happy and gave him no reason for anything but pride. You made his life complete, helped him be the man we hoped he could be. I'll always be grateful to you for that." She suddenly turned and smiled. Then she began to laugh softly. "You and Destiny more than make up for any loss I could imagine—and I thank you both.

"It really is time for you to live a little of your life for yourself, though. I suppose, if you're looking for my blessing"—she smiled—"this is it. You'd better go on for yours, 'cause if you don't, who will?" Louise returned to her chair, perched daintily on the edge and grinned like a teenager. "So? What's he like? How did you meet him?"

"He's real cute Mama Lou, a little short, though."

Mama Lou giggled. "You ought to know every man is not going to be as tall and heavy as Skip. My baby was a big ol' boy, wasn't he? Six four, two hundred forty pounds, and all muscle." She looked proud.

"Yes." Davida nodded. "But Marcus is different, he's not nearly that tall, or that big. He's right around my height."

"But, you like him, so what does it matter? Sweetie, I'll bet you can find Cinderella's slipper in a variety of sizes these days, and if worse comes to worst, you can always carry him over the threshold. What really matters is that you get the right man. Besides, you know what they say . . ."

Davida lifted an eyebrow in question. "What?"

"They're all the same height when they lie down." Louise laughed comfortably.

Davida gasped, then had to remind herself to close her mouth. Her mother-in-law's bawdy side had a way of turning up when she least expected it, and it always caught Davida off guard. "I don't know anything about that, Mama Lou, but he is awfully cute, and you would never believe how we met." She bit into another cookie and wondered if anybody else would ever believe in the power of a wrong number.

"Child, try me. I love a good romance."

"Keep smiling like that, Mama Lou, and you're going to make me think you're keeping a few secrets of your own."

"I don't know what you mean." Louise Lawrence's smile was one of serene beauty that belied her words.

"Would one of those secrets be that tall, good-looking man, Dr. Randall? The man who escorted you to the Homer G. Phillips Memorial banquet last month?"

"Mind your manners, dear."

"Yes, ma'am." Contrite, lowering her eyes to the hands she clasped in her lap, Davida reminded herself to be respectful of her elders. *Mama Lou is a grown woman, and fully entitled to a life of her own,* she thought. *She's at least as entitled as I am.* And certainly a woman as vitally attractive as Louise Lawrence was bound to draw her share of equally attractive men.

"Come on, child, we've talked about my business, now let's get back to yours. Dish it up, baby. Don't leave me hanging like this," Louise urged, interrupting. "Tell me everything. Start at the beginning, and don't leave anything out."

"It was a dark and stormy night . . ."

"Very funny," Louise pouted.

"No, Mama Lou, it really was. Remember all those storms we had back at the end of April and the first part of May . . ." Davida told the story, from its stormy, wrong number beginning to hand holding on a Ferris wheel at Six Flags. Mama Lou hung on every word. Sitting on the edge of her overstuffed chair, in the middle of her neatly elegant parlor, she looked younger than Davida could have ever imagined. Creamy, café skin, bright and clear in the late afternoon light, and shining eyes belied her years and evidenced the youth in her heart.

She's exactly what I want to be when I grow up, Davida thought lightly.

Mama Lou pulled her shoulders high and hugged her knee to her chest. "I just have one question, Davida, and you can tell me if I'm out of line . . ."

"Okay. What's the question?"

"How did you manage to hold that man's hand wearing that ring of Skip's? Didn't it feel funny?"

The cookie went south in a big way. Davida bent almost double choking and coughing, and Mama Lou rushed forward to pound her back relentlessly. Davida wasn't sure if the pounding was meant to dislodge the cookie or punish her for handholding with another man. She kept coughing.

"That ought to be better now," Mama Lou said finally, rubbing and patting Davida's back.

So, the pounding wasn't punishment. "I'm fine," Davida said, and cleared her throat. Sipping at her lemonade, she tried to find words to answer the question she still felt hanging so heavily between them.

"Well?"

Davida's eyes crawled away from her mother-in-law to actively examine her skirt, and then the carpet at her feet.

Mama Lou sat down in her chair, her brow furrowed, and she pulled her knee close again. "All I want to know is when you're going to take that ring off and get back to being a woman, instead of a widow." She raised a hand to ward off any protests. "I know it's not my business, and certainly, it's not my call. Like I said before, I'm not saying anything to you I wouldn't say to Skip, but the boy's been gone for going on almost five years now."

"Mama Lou, I know, but . . . it just seemed wrong to take it off."

"Why?"

"Because," she wet her lips. It was a good question, but unfortunately Davida had no ready answer. Looking at the shining band didn't help. This little ring, this little symbol of fidelity and undying love—was it really meant to bind her to a man whose arms she would never feel again in this life? Or was it a justifiable and safe place to hide? A part of the habit of not being in places where your heart and your feelings got hurt? Though she wanted to ask, Davda already knew the answer, and she wondered when it first began to filter across the barrier of her consciousness. Maybe it was around the same time she exchanged names with Marcus Benton.

Davida twisted her wedding band, and bit at her lip. "It feels like I—I've worn this ring so long, I'd feel naked without it."

"Naked, like with no clothes, or naked like fully exposed, with no hiding places?"

"Mama Lou, I don't know. What do you think I should do?"

"Oh, no you don't!" The older woman dropped her knee and crossed her ankles, again. "This is in no way a decision for me to make. You know who you are, and what you want—and if you don't, well then, it's high time you found out for yourself."

Twisting the slender band, Davida tried to remember all the reasons she'd wanted *this* ring, from *that* man. At first glance, the ring wasn't at all impressive. As wedding rings went, she had to admit, this one was a bit on the cheap side. It was something a very young man would buy; something a very young hardworking man could afford. A simple white gold band circled with tiny, perfect white stones—it was the innocent declaration of faith with which it was inscribed that made it priceless, and held her yet in thrall.

My Destiny, My Life, My Eternity, My Wife.

The words and the man were indelibly imprinted on her life and her heart. She had no need of this tiny band to prove that to anyone, and especially not to herself. Davida had a list longer than her arm, a list of the reasons she could count her marriage to Skip Lawrence as a good one—one good enough that it could be called a part of her history, but not her reason for living now. She didn't need the ring to remind her—maybe once upon a time she had, but not anymore. "You've got a point," she said, sliding the ring from her finger.

"No," Mama Lou insisted, *"you've* got a point. You have to decide how to get on, just like I did after Carter passed." She shrugged.

Davida looked steadily ahead, both seeing and not seeing the older woman. "How did you do it?" she asked softly.

"I looked at the simple little fact that I loved Carter. I looked at all the good things we'd shared, and all the love he'd had a chance to experience while we were together—everything from getting his medical degree to being able to practice at Homer G. Phillips, a black hospital in his own home town. He was as proud of our marriage as he was of anything else—right down to being able to deliver his only son's first child—and that was enough. For both of us—that was enough, and I could let him go." She smiled.

Holding the ring in her closed fist, Davida wondered what she would do with it, now that it was off her finger—where she would put it because it deserved keeping, what she would replace it with because she already missed its slight familiar weight. The wall safe in her bedroom, though hidden behind the Synthia St. James print, seemed inadequate, and a safe deposit box seemed ridiculous. Selling it was out of the question.

I loved Skip, will always love him, but it is time to move on, and the idea struck her so suddenly, that she had to squint at the impact of its brilliance. "Mama Lou"—Davida's face was suddenly radiant—"I know what to do, exactly what to do. I'm not going to wear it, not on my hand anymore, but I'm going to keep it. The ring will go to Destiny when she's twenty-one. It will be a reminder of the love that brought her into the world, and a celebration of her life, since so many kids with SCD don't make it to adulthood. It'll be a gift from her father and me, and always acknowledge that Skip and I did have something special in her and in each other." She raised her brows and waited.

"Perfect," Mama Lou breathed.

CHAPTER TWELVE

Outside, the hard running edge of an electrical storm whipped the sky. From his studio window, Marc could see the moving skirl of dramatic wind-ripped black clouds. He stared out at the gathering storm and felt overwhelmed by a curious loneliness. The loneliness was only compounded by the fact that he was unable to focus on his work, even though Bro'Man stared determinedly over at him from his place on the easel across the room.

Early silver drops of rain slapped at his window, slanting predecessors of the storm. The drops looked like tears tracking the pane, and he could hardly stand the melancholy poetry that stabbed his thoughts. Folding his arms across the firmness of his chest, Marcus turned away from his drawing board. It was at times like this that he missed her most. Davida Lawrence. A woman he'd met on a storm-directed wrong number call. A woman he had yet to hold in his arms exactly the way he wanted to. A woman who'd marked him forever without ever knowing it.

There ought to be a name for the kind of feeling she roused in him—a name for the challenge and stimulation excited by thinking her name. Nobody he'd met before or since was as good at making him feel whole—nobody else seemed able to make him laugh at himself the way she did. No other woman had ever seemed able to show him the places in his soul where the light shone through. Only her, and though the part of him that openly declared itself a "rugged individualist" resisted, he liked it that way.

Refusing to dilute the stormy darkness with the intrusive glare of even a single electric bulb, Marc left his place at the drawing board. He needed no light to find his way to the telephone. Glowing buttons and muted beeps encouraged him and he dialed her number from memory. Listening to the tone, accompanied by his own shaky, shallow breaths, he waited. She picked up on the fourth ring.

"Hello?"

Relief flooded his body and made his knees unsteady. Her voice went through Marc like an IV filled with something sweet, buttery, and too totally satisfying for any words he knew. For a minute, just one, he'd thought she might not be there—that he might get a machine, that she might be somewhere else, with someone else—then there she was. His voice caught in his throat. What did he call her? Boo had seemed fully appropriate when he'd had no other name for her, but now . . . He licked his lips and almost tasted her kiss. "Hello, Davida."

"Marc."

"Davida." The name tasted good in his mouth, but not quite comfortable. She was, would always be Boo, and Marcus already knew he would always prefer it that way. He cleared his throat and dropped onto the futon. Stretching his legs, he crossed his ankles and leaned back comfortably. "You know, we sound like one of those old-time radio soap operas."

"Well, you started it." She smiled and he felt it through the telephone lines.

"I guess I did, at that. You were on my mind, and I thought I'd call. How are you?"

Pulling her feet under her in St. Louis, Davida had to move Addie, Destiny's favorite doll, before she could curl into the corner of her couch. Pushing the African-American, "American Girl" doll to the other side of her, she gripped the phone with both hands and held it close to her cheek. The hard plastic receiver was a poor substitute for the touch of his hand or the whisper of his breath against her skin, but for now, it was good—very good. "It's been a long day," she said, "but I'm fine now." *Now that I hear your voice,* she thought.

"A long day in the IRS salt mines." It was what she'd said the first time he talked to her. It was what she said before he knew he was going to fall into whatever the state was that made humans crave the sound of one another's voices. Whatever that state was, it was definitely where Marc was with her.

"Not today," she said. "Today was . . . different." Her throaty voice did sound different, the husky edge pitched a little lower than usual, her words slower than normal.

"You sound a little tired."

"Gee thanks. That's a compliment I've always wished for."

"Give me a break." Marc grinned. "I'm new at this infatuation stuff. You know I don't have a lot of good practical experiences to fall back on. What happened?"

"We started out normally. I got Des to her campsite, and went on to work. A couple of hours later, they pulled me out of a meeting." She stopped, stricken by the memory of the telephone call. Even as the camp supervisor tried to explain what happened, Davida heard her child's sobs. "Des had a sickle-ing."

"Sickle-ing?" Marc frowned on his end. "Is that like when the, uh, is it when the red blood cells kind of like bend? And, don't they like, clog up arteries or something like that?" He was struggling to recall something he'd slept through in freshman biology classes.

"Yes, that's pretty much what happens." She seemed impressed with his recall. "Seems that while she was playing today, she had a minor sickle-ing."

"Just like that?"

"Yes. I guess maybe part of it is that it's been so hot lately, and Des hates to drink water. Dehydration is a big factor for children." Sensing his unasked question, Davida drew a deep breath. "I'm not sure how to explain the kind of pain you feel during one of these incidents. It's not like a toothache or being struck. It's more like a sudden, intense ... I don't know ..." She was disappointed that words failed her.

Marc waited, and when she didn't continue, he called her name softly, "Davida? Was she alone?"

"No." She brightened perceptibly. "That's the good part. Des has this smart little friend, Tawanna Mallory, and under ordinary circumstances, she's a lot more than I can take—but she really came through today. Tawanna knows about Des and she knows enough about sickle cell to recognize a problem. She had the good sense to sit Des down and run to get help. Though Tawanna is not one of my favorite little people, she is attentive, calm, and clever, and she truly cares about Des as a friend."

"But, that's not the worst of it?" Marcus knew before he asked.

"The camp counselor said she was short-handed, so that meant I had to get to Des on my own. Then, I got there, and Tawanna fell out on me, I guess a child can only take so much. She screamed and cried and refused to let Des go without her. What could I do? I grabbed both girls and threw them into my car, I called Tawanna's mom on my cell phone. Fortunately, she's one of those folks who thinks life is one big field trip, so it was okay. And there I was, trying to contend with two frightened children and a hospital emergency room, alone."

Hollow, desperate, disappointment lumbered drunkenly through Marc's heart. *She shouldn't have been alone. Never alone.* It was a moment of caring unlike anything he'd ever experienced, and it made his chest sore, somewhere in the vicinity of his heart. He pressed his hand to his chest, found the palm damp against his cotton shirt, and rubbed it against his jeans. "It must have been very hard to deal with that on your own."

"But, it had to be done Marc, and there was no one else for her, only me."

The truth of her words burned his ears and raised a welt on his soul. Someone should have been there—for both of them. Someone who cared, someone whose presence would have made a difference. Maybe me?

Maybe me? That was a heck of a question to start with, and even echoing through his mind it felt like childish bravado. What real good might his presence have done? A child in pain needed someone around that she was familiar with, someone she trusted implicitly, not a man who was trying to get next to her mommy. And what about Mommy? Didn't she need and deserve someone who knew more about the problem than what he half-remembered from a passing article? Didn't she need and deserve someone who really understood some of what she was feeling? Marc held the phone, even as he hung his head— she did deserve more, and he knew it.

Am I really up to that kind of challenge? he asked himself, and heard Milt's voice in response. "There's a lot more to falling in love," the big man had said, "when there's a child involved." And damned if he wasn't right.

Somehow, Marc knew that already. He knew it in the back of his mind, even as he was fashioning all those romantically lusty dreams on his way back from St. Louis. He knew it as he sang her name into all the old Motown tapes he traveled with. He knew it as he fantasized about the curve of her hip, and all the other intriguing physical turns of her body. From the very beginning, he'd known that a large part of her was already taken: obligated to her child.

And that's as it should be, Marc lectured himself. She wouldn't be the kind of woman he wanted in his life if she cared any less, but was there room for him, if she cared anymore?

You're being Paranoid, man, he told himself. Of course it was paranoia. If anything, she needed his support. Marc sighed heavily, seeing a vivid picture in his mind. He saw himself, sitting close to Davida, a supporting arm around her shoulders, cradling her tense shoulders—being there for her.

"Marc? Are you still there?"

Oh great! He'd been sitting there dreaming solutions to her solitude, plotting sensitivity. She was still talking, and he hadn't heard a word she'd said. "I'm sorry," he blurted, "I missed that. What did you say?"

"Nothing much. I was just sort of thinking out loud." She sighed. "You're good for me that way, you know. You make me feel like it's alright to let some of my private thoughts and feelings out."

"I'm glad." Marc was pleased that his voice sounded calm. "I like it when you talk to me."

She sighed again, relaxing into the intimacy of his words and his voice. "If this had to happen, I'm glad she was out of school, because kids can be awfully cruel. Do you know, last year, one of the older children—not even one in Des's class, started a rumor that sickle-cell disease was like AIDS; that it was contagious and fatal?"

"But, it's not—is it? I mean, everything I've ever seen or read—"

Suddenly angry, she cut him off. "Exactly, but unfortunately, the other children and a lot of their parents believed the rumor . . . they're kids, for heaven's sake! But the parents . . . they should know better . . . and Destiny had to deal with it. It was all so stupid and mean! Then when the PTA and the Health Department finally stepped in, we spent the rest of the school year trying to clear up the mystery and misunderstanding. I'm still not sure everyone got it, but on the positive side, two teachers did register for the bone marrow project."

"The bone, what?" Marc wanted to know.

"The bone marrow project."

"That's what I thought you said. How does the bone marrow project work?" He blinked in confusion, and from across the room, Bro'Man just stared. "What good would bone marrow do a kid like Destiny?"

"A kid like Destiny might make it to a normal kind of adulthood without organ damage," she said quietly. "There's a . . . a national registry for potential donors."

"I hate to sound like a coward, but what's the process like? Does it hurt? Do you know?"

Davida smiled at the questions. He was the most special man. She could almost see his face crunched with tension as she listened to his voice. "No, you don't sound like a coward, and if you wanted to get registered, you'd start out with the local Red Cross. They take and type your blood, and if you're called for donation, it takes a few hours at a local hospital for the actual marrow collection." Marcus drew a tightly hissing breath, and Davida imagined his face again. Wishing she could press that face between her palms and hold it close, she said nothing, just sat and waited for him to speak again.

Finally, "Can anybody register or can it only be relatives?"

"Family is considered the best bet . . . but you never know, Marc . . . there are a lot of genetic traits that are unique within specific racial groups."

"So, in the meantime, what do you do for her?"

"Make sure she's properly rested and stays fully hydrated, which is sometimes a challenge, because she hates water and as you already know, keeping her still is just this side of impossible."

"I'm glad Des is feeling better, but I've got to admit you were my main concern."

"Me?" Flattered Davida hugged herself again. "Marc, where have you been all my life? Thank you for caring, but honestly, I'm fine."

"Really?"

"I promise I am." Why was it so amazing to feel so good because he cared how she was? Davida raked her fingers through her hair, pressing the strands back into place as though he might catch a glimpse of her.

"Then, I guess this is a good time to confess, I'm not."

"Not?" she echoed.

"It's you, Boo. You've plagued my thoughts since the last time we were together " Her giggle chimed in his ear and he wanted to hold it there. "Is that corny? 'Cause see, I know that such admissions are not considered cool."

"Corny or not Marc, it was very sweet." She hesitated, and Marc sensed a coy reluctance. "Since we're doing corny things tonight, I guess it's my turn. Would it be forward of me to ask when you're coming back to St. Louis?"

It would break my heart if she didn't, he admitted to himself. "Missing me already?"

"Yes no, . . . that is, I was just wondering," she stuttered.

"I'll be there anytime you want." *Just try and keep me away.* "Actually, I've got a batch of 'use or lose' frequent flyer miles, so sure—next weekend?"

"Oh, Marc. That would be . . . would you, I mean, you don't have to . . . but I'd like you to . . ." Why was she choking on it? She'd rehearsed these words at home, at her desk, and in her car every day for the last week. She knew what she wanted, why couldn't she get the words out? Davida looked at the phone, then took a deep breath, and blurted, ". . . come to meet my family? Saturday? It wouldn't be a big deal," she emphasized the words, maybe a little too much. "Maybe a cookout or brunch, something simple, and I would love to have Renee and her husband, and J.B, as well. And if you stay for the weekend, we might get to do something else." She was out of breath.

"Something else?" he echoed.

"Maybe dinner over near Soulard Market," she suggested.

"That would be nice." Marc's voice was light and casual, but his mind went into overdrive. Moonlight, soft sheets, soft music, and softer skin overwhelmed his thoughts and left him pulling at the top buttons on his shirt. "We might get to do something else," she said. *If only . . .* Marc thought, his mind still conjuring endless pleasantries. "Wouldn't that be a bit much, entertaining with Des being sick and all?"

"Actually, it's more like what we both need. Something down to earth, you know, something normal and reassuring. Besides, Destiny is a real champ when it comes to handling her SCD. So, will you come?"

"Your big ol' mean, hairy, overprotective brother coming, too?"

"Glenn's not that hairy' " Davida promised, "besides if he brings a date, my mother and aunt will keep him contained and on his best behavior."

"So, that means your mother and the infamous Aunt Wesie will be in attendance?"

"Oh, you can bet on it. They wouldn't miss a chance to meet any man who'd struck my fancy."

"Have I done that, Boo? Struck your fancy, I mean."

Davida sighed, enjoying the quick heat of the blush he caused. It was almost funny. Here he was, this cute little young man, so different from rangy, six foot-four inch Skip, and he made her feel like this. *Yeah buddy,* she wished she dared reply, *you strike a whole lot more than my "fancy," and maybe someday soon, I'll get to return the favor.* "You could say that," she said.

Marc would have slapped himself a high five if he could have.

"While we're on the topic of this little get together, I guess I should tell you that Louise Lawrence always joins us."

"Louise Lawrence?" he asked, searching his memory. He drew a blank. "Should I know the name?"

"She's Destiny's paternal grandmother. My mother-in-law."

Marc scrambled to hold his heart in place. Her husband had been gone almost five years, and Davida still referred to his mother in the present tense. She claimed the woman like they had an ongoing relationship, and it immediately troubled him. He looked across the room, staring at Bro'Man as if he knew the answer. It didn't help. The drawing offered no suggestions, and it took all Marc's will power, trying not to jump to any conclusions—but the obvious one jumped at him. Whatever the etiquette, Davida was still holding on to that part of her past. What did that mean for the two of them? For any future they might have? It was jealousy talking again, and he knew it. The picture in his head, the one with him comforting her, "being there" for her, grew hazy, like an overwashed water color. *Shake it off man, shake it off,* he told himself. He tried, but it didn't quite work.

The lump in his throat prohibited swallowing. "You still have a relationship with your mother-in-law?'' Though it was meant to be a politely probing question, the words sounded flat, even to his own ears.

"Of course I do. She's Destiny's grandmother, and I want Des to know all of her family—not just me."

"I see."

"Oh, come on Marc. Are you jealous or something?"

Yes! "No. Why would I be jealous?"

She ignored the pettiness she heard in his tone. "I guess I don't want Des to wake up someday and realize that there are generations of people she has no knowledge of, when she might have learned so much from my mother or Mama Lou. I don't want her to feel like . . . like a lot of us felt when *Roots* first came to our attention, back in . . . was it '76?'' She seemed to think about what she'd just said. "Are you old enough to remember *Roots?*"

"They show it in reruns," he said drily.

"Oh, yeah. So, you've seen it. Well, I don't want Des to have to make desperate efforts to reconnect herself to a past that is so accessible through the words and memories of women she can touch today. That's one of the big reasons why Mama Lou and I will always be close, she knows so much and shares so willingly. Besides, she's a wonderful person."

Chastened, Marc grunted.

"Mama Lou is a hoot, especially when she gets together with my mom and Aunt Wesie—you'll see. Anyway, she and Aunt Wesie were best friends growing up, and my mom is three, no four, years younger. They thought it was providence when Skip and I got together." She laughed shortly, then grew sober. "After he died, she was my rock."

"I, uh . . . I'd like to meet your mother-in-law." *Nice recovery,* he congratulated himself. "Let me ask you something, though. While I don't mind meeting your family, including your mother-in-law, doesn't that do something to our relationship?"

"Something?" She sounded cautious. "Something, like what?"

"Like move it up another level? Increase the emotional investment? Remember, you were the one who was so insistent on the 'don't ask, don't tell' phase of our relationship." He waited in the dark, wondering if she'd back off. "I figure this is the first step to a real commitment. Do you really want to do that?

"Well, Marc, uhm . . ."

She was hedging, and saying nothing, Marc pressed his lips together and willed her to say what he knew was the right thing.

Like Marcus, Davida pressed her lips together, and willed herself to say the right words. "I've kissed you in public, and introduced you to my child—it doesn't get a whole lot more invested than that," she

said, trying to remember what had come before that kiss. As for commitment, she looked at the now bare third finger of her left hand. The pale mark of the slender band was still there, though she was convinced it faded slightly more day by day—just like the hold Skip'd had on her heart all these years.

Marc swallowed hard, remembering the soft touch of her hand against his face, and the warm nearness of her body when she kissed him. And, the lady certainly did kiss nicely! Closing his eyes, he could still see the thick, sensual lips that invited a man's touch, still feel the heat that radiated through her demure cream-colored blouse. Against his wishes, his mind took a quick turn to anticipation, quickening at the juncture of his thighs. A first time was always the best, and always unrecoverable, and part of him wanted to reach right through the phone to grasp her and hold her closer than his own skin.

Opening his eyes, knowing he'd never wanted to be this close to another woman, Marc wanted to argue. He wanted to make a point that she would never forget. "Oh, yes, Boo," he countered, "it can get a whole lot more invested than that." it was a simple but eloquent argument, and the best that he could muster.

"Then, I guess it's like Aunt Wesie says, "in for a penny, in for a pound."

Thinking of what it would be like to touch her for the first time and any other times they might be blessed with, Marc felt his heart bang hard against his ribs in response. "Aunt Wesie's got a way with words."

"I'll tell her you said so."

"I'll tell her myself, when I get there." He shifted the phone and glanced at Bro'Man again. "You know," he said, lowering his voice, "there's a little weekly paper down here. It's called *Creative Loafing*, and they've got all these personals ads."

"Are you placing ads, Marc?"

"No." He grinned. The thought had occurred to him after Kenya, but he'd never had the nerve—in spite of what Milt said. "There's all these ads from people looking to meet people, all these ads that end with 'LTR desired . . .' "

"What's 'LTR' stand for?"

"Long-term relationship. All those years, I looked at those ads, and never really understood what those people thought they wanted, or why, but now I do. Because of you, Davida."

"Oh, Marc," she interrupted, playing her fingers against her leg, "you sound so old and wise. I'm not so sure that's a good thing." *And,* she thought, *I don't know why I ever thought you might not understand, why I thought you might be too young for me, or why it even mattered.*

"I just want you to think about it, okay?"

"Why? Is there a quiz later?" She bit her tongue and silently cursed her glib defensiveness.

"Just keep it in mind, okay? Think about what 'LTR' could mean for us, Boo." He held the phone between his palms, realizing for the first time that she hadn't thought that far ahead, that she was maybe even a little afraid to—but that's okay, he promised himself, one step at a time makes a journey.

"So, about this weekend? Promise me—you'll come?"

He liked the hint of hope, with its intimate swirl of seduction flavoring her invitation. "Wild horses couldn't keep me away, Boo."

CHAPTER THIRTEEN

Marc squirmed in his coach seat on the Delta jet, and wished he'd chosen first class as his elbow bumped the elderly woman at his side for the fourth time. He could feel her breathing, watching him work, and it made him nervous. Sketching rapidly from memory, he completed his work and started to close the sketchbook. The woman's finger, tapping the page stopped him.

"Your daughter?" the woman asked. Marc looked over at her. She blinked at him. Her disarmingly charming southern accent and gentle movements made him think of Jessica Tandy as Miss Daisy in the Morgan Freeman movie. Light blue hair, and pale myopically blue eyes magnified by bifocals greeted him, but her smile was sweet and he returned it reflexively.

"Actually . . ." he closed the pad and folded his hands possessively over it on the tray table attached to the seat in front of him. "Actually, she's the daughter of a friend."

"She's pretty, does she look much like her mother?"

"Yes, she does. A lot."

The sweet mouth turned down at the corners. "And the mother is your 'friend'? Is she married?"

"Well, no, ma'am, not any more. She's a widow."

The narrow, slit lips turned sweet again. "And you've set your cap for her, haven't you?"

"Well, yes, ma'am. I guess I have at that."

The woman flashed the sweet smile and extended her hand. "You'll be seeing her in St. Louis, I trust," she said with direct certainty. "That is where you're going, isn't it?" Delight played across her features when Marc nodded eagerly. "Oh, I do like you. I didn't get your name, young man."

"I'm Marcus Benton, of Atlanta." He gently held her pale blue-veined arthritic fingers in his grasp. "And, you are . . ."

"Miss Aurelia Ross of Newnan, Georgia." She lowered her lids behind the thick glasses, then inclined her head with the slight, but highly effective air of the coquette. "Tell me," she drawled, "are you nervous about seein' her again?"

"Miss Ross"—Marc's index finger pulled at the crew neck of his black T-shirt—"to tell you the truth, I'm 'bout as nervous as a long-tailed cat in a room full of rocking chairs."

"Oh, you darlin' boy." Miss Ross laughed, clapping her hands. "Tha's the way it's supposed to be. None of this nineties, 'I'm so brave' stuff." Her lashes fluttered. "Din't your mama warn you? A special woman, your special woman, should always make your heart pound and your temperature rise, don't care how long you've been together. If she don't, you're dead—an' you don't look dead to me, young man."

Marc felt himself blush, and mumbled something along the line of, "thank you, ma'am."

"I have an idea." She folded the magazine she'd tried to read earlier in the flight, and tucked it into the seatback in front of her. "Why don't you practice on me. Tell me what you're nervous about."

"Miss Ross, that's kind of you, but I couldn't impose."

"Ohh," she cooed, "I have always admired a courtly gentleman, but you mustn't be silly, my dear. Manners be damned, do share."

Silly? Marc looked at the elderly white woman with her bifocals, blue rinse, and neat floral silk dress. She looked like she was ready to teach Sunday school or entertain in her parlor, sitting there with her hand resting beside his bent arm and her slightly swollen ankles crossed daintily, just above her neat Cobbie Cuddlers. This was about as far from Davida Lawrence as he might ever hope to get. He cleared his throat and looked out the window, then back at Miss Aurelia Ross of Newnan, Georgia.

"My dear, Marcus—May I call you Marcus?" She waited for his assent. "My dear, Marcus, though I never married, I have known many men in my eighty years, and still more women. One thing I have learned is that we are not so very different when it comes to matters of the heart. P'haps if you were to share your story, I might be able to offer you a little insight into your lady's heart."

Dropping his eyes, Marcus drummed his fingers atop the sketch pad, took a deep breath, and made a decision. "You might at that, Miss Ross."

She smiled brightly as he told of the storm that brought him to Davida Lawrence. She chuckled, and admitted having been an elementary school teacher when he told her about Destiny. A small sympathetic moue and a whispered belief that, "faith moves mountains," graced them both when he told of the child's challenges with sickle-cell anemia.

Miss Ross leaned forward, bringing her thin, narrow shoulders high with excitement when he told of his accidental first meeting with Davida. "And what did you think when you knew her for who she really was?"

"That I'd always known her, in my heart, and I should have known her in the flesh. I should have known her the second I laid eyes on her."

Raising her hand, Aurelia Ross touched her lips, then patted Marc's cheek.

"And now," Marc concluded, "I feel that meeting Davida's family and friends, even with my own sister and her family there . . ." He shrugged.

"Makes you a little nervous. It's like a defining moment in your courtship of this woman," she finished for him.

How succinct! Marc blinked. "You know I'm courting her?"

She smiled and tapped her lips with one demure, mildly arthritic finger. "Course, I do. Don't you?"

Marc nodded slowly, leaning back to rest his head against his seat. Davida dawned there, in his head, like some kind of incredible genie. Her smile emerged against his closed lids almost as easily as that of the Cheshire cat in *Alice in Wonderland,* but meaning so much more.

"Moments," he finally said, opening his eyes. "There don't ever seem to be enough of them. I feel like I have to grab and hold on to every second we have together. In fact, I wish I'd agreed to let her pick me up from Lambert Field. It would have been nice to look into her face when I leave this plane and see expectation. To look into her eyes and see trust and acceptance—that alone would be worth the trip." It would be even nicer to kiss her lips and feel awakening passion when he finally held her in his arms. That made him draw his breath and hold it.

"Darlin' Marc, how you feel, it's completely understandable." The older woman patted his hand and Marc found himself staring down at the contrast—her milky, almost blue skin against the heartily aggressive bronzed sheen of his own.

"Sounds to me like you've got the strongest ally in the world, Marc. You've got this woman. This Davida of yours is a woman who, even if she can't admit it to herself, is a woman well on her way to falling in love. When you love someone, you don't much have to worry about anyone else's opinions. And, as far as defining your relationship, well it sounds to me like you have a pretty clear idea of what you want, and your Davida is learning to work with it. All y'all need is some time, and you're young, so you've got that." She patted his hand again.

The small sound of chimes echoing within the confines of the cabin brought Marc to attention. He looked around to see cabin attendants settling passengers for landing. "We're here already?"

"Don't look so surprised, dear boy, we've been talkin' for 'most over an hour." She pulled her small handbag from somewhere in the depths of her seat. The pert look on her face was enough to make Marc wonder what she had in her purse. "I'm wonderin', sir. If I give you my address, will you let me know how all this comes out? Will you send me an invitation so that I can dance at your weddin'?" She flipped the hem of her flowered silk gaily. "I do still kick up my heels from time to time, when the right occasion surfaces."

"You may count on it, Miss Ross." Marc accepted the small engraved card she offered.

Touching down, the plane seemed to accelerate then slowed, and holding her breath, she closed her eyes. "I do hate these landin's," she whispered. "Might I hold your hand?"

"You might, indeed," Marc offered, closing both her hands in his.

Safely on the ground, Miss Aurelia Ross of Newnan, Georgia, took back her hands. She stood to allow him to step free of the narrow row of seats. "Now, Marcus Benton, I'm continuing on to Cleveland, Ohio, my sister, Eunice, lives in Euclid, but you remember your promise. I am to dance at your weddin'—and you'd better hurry up. I did tell you I was eighty, didn' I?"

Marc shifted his sketchbook and patted his pocket. "I'll remember that, Miss Ross, and thank you." He leaned forward to place a small kiss on her cheek, then turned away.

Watching from her seat, the tip of her finger tapping her chin, the older woman smiled to herself. "If I'd have been forty—no, maybe thirty years younger, I'd have kissed him back," she whispered to no one in particular, "and he'd of remembered it, too." Miss Aurelia Ross of Newnan, Georgia, raised a hand to pat her cottony soft blue hair and smiled at the young man's back as he made his way off the plane. "He did have the prettiest eyes." She sighed.

Standing in Lambert's terminal, Marc shifted from foot to foot and tried not to glare at his watch. Making fast mental notes, he shook his head when the watch won, and he had to look down at it. Time never seemed to be on his side lately. By the time he picked up his rental car and dropped off his bag at Renee's . . . *No, I'm leaving my stuff in the trunk,* he decided, *if I stop to drop off the bag, Renee will try to climb in the car with me. She'll jump right in the front seat, and that's all I don't need.*

It was enough that Davida had invited Renee, George, and J.B. to join them, but to have to ride with his sister—it was a thought too horrible for contemplation. His small bag took its time completing the short run around the luggage carousel, and Marc snagged the zippered, brown leather barrel-shaped tote as soon as it was within arm's reach.

Shouldering the bag, he wished again that he'd accepted Davida's offer to meet him. *I'm going to see her in less than two hours.* The thought made him smile, and Marc hoped that just seeing Davida again would be enough, though he already knew that just laying eyes on her would never be enough again. He ignored the itch in his palms that seemed to warm up in direct response to her proximity.

Following signs, heading for the car rental counter, Marcus couldn't help noticing the frequent reunions of couples as he walked through the terminal. Women rushing into the arms of much loved men, men hurrying back to where they rightfully belonged, surrendering to the kisses of beloved women; the simple acts of commitment made Marcus stop and stare. Apart for days or weeks every one of those people seemed to need their mate. From a distance, he watched as lovers embraced and kissed, renewing whatever they held for one another. Marc felt empty, missing Davida, the woman he was rushing to. He wanted to be reunited, too—right here, right now. He wanted desperately to be more than just the single man he was right then. He wanted to be part of a couple, too.

The tall, full-hipped woman in the flowing, tangerine-colored, ankle-length summer dress nearly walked straight into him, and Marc had a moment of near delirium. It seemed somebody, somewhere had somehow magically heard his prayer and made his wish come true. For the briefest space of time, she looked just like Davida. In a saner moment, Marc would have accused himself of unforgivable chauvinism, but at first brush, when he touched her bare arm, she felt just like Davida, too.

Unbelievably pleased, he looked again, anticipating the sweetest smile he'd ever known, and was bitterly disappointed. It wasn't her. His palms stopped itching.

"Excuse me," he immediately apologized. As much as he wanted her to be, this wasn't Davida. This woman's hair was longer, curling just beneath her chin; and it had a bold red tint and complicated styling

that Davida would never have considered. Her makeup was heavier
than Davida's and far more deliberate, applied with a calculating hand.
The woman smiled and Marc bared his own teeth in polite response,
nothing more. The woman's long-nailed hand on his arm felt like a
crawling, impolite grope and made him want to draw away.

"Well, hi, good-looking," the woman said, not moving her hand,
even when Marc moved back a step. She looked down at the bag in
his hand, then back into his eyes. Her gaze was frank and appraising.
Her eyes moved stealthily through him, touching buttons of sensual
orientation that Marc had never guessed he possessed, or that a stranger
might find—and on the first try, too.

"I see you've got your grip." Her words reminded Marc of gloating.
"Visiting?" Her face was mobile and suggestion danced across her
pretty features.

"Visiting," Marc repeated stupidly. "Yes, I'm visiting a very good
friend for a few days," he said. Her smile magnified and he saw
hunger bleed into her eyes.

"Then, you'll want to take my name and number, 'cause I could
show you things." She pouted, leaving one hand on Marc's arm and
propping the other on her well rounded hip; her heat never ebbed.
"I'm Sierra Lee." She held the hungry smile in place and turned up
her personal heat, even as she spoke. "My mama had a fixation on
the mountains, I don't know why, but then, I don't worry 'bout things
like that. I'm available as a local tour guide—if you need one. I
could show you wonderful things," she promised, licking her lips and
pressing closer. Her breasts were impossibly rounded and threatened
to summarily free themselves from the low-cut bodice of her dress,
and she noticed that the man in front of her couldn't help noticing
them.

Marc sighed, made an earnest effort to avert his eyes, and shook
his head in denial. He was sure they would have been things he would
have loved to have seen, under other circumstances. Looking at the
woman again, he wondered how he could have ever thought she looked
anything like Davida. First of all, she was too short. Then there was
her mouth—wide and mobile, it had a cruel touch at the corners where
her lips tipped downward. Davida's lips, her mouth so warm and
welcoming, tipped up like a smile lurked there just for you. This
woman's eyes were not so deep and chocolaty brown as Davida's.
Rather, the stranger's eyes were tight and calculating, casting no
reflection, like the centers of burned raisins. The woman's bosom
thrust itself at him again as she heaved a sigh.

"Last chance," she offered.

"I'll pass," he rejected.

She tilted her head and gave him a smile that made two other passing male travelers turn and gaze at her with barely suppressed hope. "You sure?"

Marc opened his mouth, then hesitated. "On second thought, you did say you could guide me . . ."

She grinned. "I knew you'd change your mind. What can I show you first?" Her chest lifted and the suggestion was more than obvious.

Marc looked over her shoulder, then over his own, and back at her. "How about the Hertz counter?"

He ignored the name she called him.

Accepting the keys from the smiling, gold-jacketed rental agent, Marc found his car and eased into traffic. Fiddling with the radio he found a station he could tolerate. First, Gerald Levert then James Ingram assured him he'd done the right thing by walking away from the woman in the airport. Sierra Lee, wasn't that what she'd said her name was? His eyes touched the rear- and sideview mirrors, and he wondered what got into parents when they named their children. Who knew?

Turning through streets with vaguely familiar names, he wended his way through St. Louis City and into the County. Davida's house was the one on the corner lot, and it looked exactly as he'd pictured it. He pulled to the curb three houses before he reached hers, the white one with the red trim, right? He pulled the scrap of paper with her address on it from his pocket and glanced at it—right address. Pulling in a hard, deep breath, he wondered why it didn't go down. Nerves? What was there to be nervous about—here in a lovely residential neighborhood, on a beautiful late summer day, on the way to see a woman who meant more to him than he'd ever imagined possible?

What was there to be nervous about?

Marcus turned the keys, shutting off the rented Saab's engine. Two little boys, wearing bright striped shirts, on ten-speed bikes waved at him as they pedaled by. Watching them, he had time to think of the things that brought people together. Sierra Lee, back there at the airport, obviously thought it had a lot to do with breasts and availability, and there was a time when he might have agreed with her.

But not any more. Not since he'd dialed a wrong number on a dark and stormy night.

Pushing back into his seat, Marc tried to make himself more comfortable. It didn't work. The butterflies in his stomach were frantic, and he gripped the steering wheel, wishing them back into whatever fragile little cocoons they'd escaped from. Davida Lawrence was the reason for the butterflies. Marc knew he was going to invite her to Atlanta for a weekend, a week, a month, a lifetime—whatever he could get. Miss Aurelia Ross had helped him make up his mind. He and Davida needed time—together. And she had to come. She had to see him, to be with him. She had to know him in his own environment—away from the telephone.

Do you even know what you're saying? he asked himself, and himself sounded suspiciously like Milt. *Yeah, I do know*. He knew that he wanted to do more than talk to this woman on the telephone for the rest of his natural life.

His fingers toyed with the Hertz tag on his keys, and part of him heard the boys' laughter as they rode the wind and the asphalt curves of the street on their bikes. *Life is too easy when you're that young,* he thought, squinting through the window.

What if I can't make her understand how important this is, that talking on the phone was the easy part. If I don't do this . . . When does passion, all that I feel for this woman, when does that get to be an active part of this relationship? he wondered, thinking of all the wonderfully intriguing things he wanted to do with and for Davida.

The sudden shift of his thoughts brought him up short. Suddenly, in his mind's eye, he saw them together in the grocery store arguing over pasta and salad fixings. He saw himself with Davida at K-Mart trying to figure out what to buy in the "Easy Living" department. He imagined them paying bills together. He even had a quick flash of what it would be like to clean out an attic cluttered with twenty years of life debris. "I could do that," he said aloud.

His mind shifted again, and Marcus wondered what Davida saw when she looked into her future. Destiny would be there, and her job with the IRS, of course, but what else? Something very near panic ridged his spine when he wondered if and how he figured in her version of the future. *Of course I do,* he postulated, and refused to think otherwise, but the fact that he even had to touch on the idea was enough to raise other questions. He wanted a family, and she was forty. Then, too, she already had Destiny. That was eighteen years of parenting for him, and . . . Counting, he ticked the years off on his fingers, twenty-six for her. How would she feel about that? Marc brought his hands to his ears and wished he could shut off his thoughts. No matter how he turned it, things between them were never going to come out equally.

But, they never do, not in a family, and that's what you'll have with her. A family means compromise. Now, where had he heard that before . . . his mother? Marc's quick snort of laughter punctuated the irony of the thought. Joyce Benton, enjoying her tour of the Holy Land was light years away from her puzzled son, but her words still haunted him. And, dammit, she was right.

He was going to have to take his chances.

Whatever happened between them was a direct result of that first fateful long-distance call, and now was not the time to become faint of heart. He had to convince her to come to Atlanta, that's all there was to it. Once she's there, he could work on convincing her of his sincerity and the rightness of them together. They could work on the rest of it, the compromise part of it, later.

He thought hard. The mental strategy was an exercise in futility. As far as he could see, she would logically counter every suggestion he made. He already knew it. Just thinking—alright, plotting—it was more torture than a sane man was supposed to willingly endure, but if they had no time to get to know each other . . . Marc shrugged in the empty, Saturday morning silence of his rented car. He knew he was not supposed to just jump on her and expect her to throw her dress up over her head, but he was not a monk, either.

Miss Aurelia Ross of Newnan, Georgia, was right, they needed time together. Three or four months on the telephone wasn't enough to predicate a lifetime on, and a lifetime was exactly what he knew he was hoping for. Now she had him hoping.

Marc slung a hand through the steering wheel to the steering column. She had to come. She had to be willing to step out of her safe life and see what he had to offer. He looked out the window again, the boys were coming back. Hands in the air, pedaling faster, they were daring their balance to fail them, and they were winning as they passed him.

Balance. Maybe that was the word, among other things, that had stopped him from taking Sierra Lee up on her generous offer this morning. Balance. In a word, it was everything he imagined having with Davida Lawrence. *What if she can't balance what she had with her husband with what she can have with me?* Marcus wondered.

When this trip came up, she'd sheepishly suggested he stay in a hotel. When he'd echoed her "hotel?" maybe he *did* sound a little disappointed. Before he could explain that he would stay with his sister and her family, that he always stayed with his sister and her family because Renee wouldn't have it any other way, Davida hurried to explain that she couldn't have him waking up at her house, with Destiny wondering where he'd slept the night. Not yet.

She was off balance.

He huffed another breath. At least the idea of "not yet" left hope for the future, but how long could a man live on hope—especially hoped relegated to some nebulous "not yet"? Marc looked around him, how long could a man live in a car? *They said, "a coward dies a thousand deaths, a brave man, only one." Time for my one,* Marc decided, gathering his sketch pad, overpriced airport flowers, and the book he'd brought for Des. She could only say no, once. This time. Stepping out into the street, Marc looked down and judged himself presentable.

He stood at her door and rehearsed his first words. He was going to tell her that he missed her, and she'd smile. He was going to tell her how he'd felt all the way here, and she'd get that look in her eyes. He was going to tell her about Miss Aurelia Ross of Newnan, Georgia, and they'd laugh. He was going to tell her . . .

His mind was still a jumble when she pulled the door open. Then she stood there wearing a long, strappy, denim sundress that molded itself to her body and flared near her ankles. The cool looking garment, cut low across her chest and under her arms, accentuated all the generous curves he'd admired from their first meeting. Marc felt the smile spread hopelessly across his face as he slipped painlessly, helplessly into love. He couldn't remember a single word of his planned greeting.

"You're here." She smiled, opening her arms to him.

She looks better than I remember, Marcus marveled, *and I remember her looking real good.*

Pushing the small bouquet of wildflowers forward, he watched her accept them with the grace of a queen before a commoner. Her arms opened again, and Marc stepped into the place she offered, and let his own already encumbered arms enfold her. Her fingers touched the back of his neck lightly, and Marc closed his eyes and tried to convince himself that she was no fantasy. Holding her close, breathing in the vanilla fragrance she wore, he believed his arms would never open again—that he would stand there with her, just like this, until the day after the world ended. When Davida stirred in his embrace, Marcus fought the urge to protest, squeezed her tightly before polite release. Stepping back, he looked at her long enough and hard enough to reassure himself that she was real, and not a lust inspired dream.

Davida felt her cheeks warm beneath the man's intense inspection. She'd had other men stare at her, attracted by whatever it was that men found so appealing about a woman, but with Marc, it was different. There was something in his smiling, golden-brown eyes that she couldn't define—something new. It was something that made her want to preen and pose, and be generally perfect for his approval.

She took a moment to study him in response before stepping back into her home. He looked young to her eyes, much younger than her forty years, and she questioned her sanity in inviting him into her life. She looked at his skin, golden brown like the hot caramel toppings she'd loved as a child, and unlined in the morning light. People might think . . . she bit at her lip and refused to even contemplate how any other human in this world might view what she felt when she looked at this man.

"Come on in," Davida invited again, not sure quite what she was doing as she extended her hands to him. Marc shifted his packages and reached for her again, and she went willingly. Sunlight through the high window in the front staircase fell across the two of them, and he smiled up at it. His short curling hair, dark brown and thick, glinted with tiny red highlights in the late morning sun, and Davida surrendered her fingers to its softness.

Trailing fingers drifted across his features, and he closed his eyes, letting her read them like braille. His nose, square and upturned, wrinkled slightly when she touched it, making her smile. His cheeks, tightly firm, slashed by disarming dimples, fit neatly against her palms. Unwilling to stop herself, Davida stepped closer fitting herself against him, and forgetting that he wasn't particularly tall.

"Marc!" The sound of her daughter's excited voice and thudding tennis shoes reminded Davida of where and who she was. Pelting heavily down the stairs, Destiny threw her arms wide and flew at them. Stepping away from the man who'd only held her like that in her dreams, Davida greeted her daughter.

Clapping her hands, Destiny danced a complete circle around her mother and Marc. Stopping suddenly, balancing on one foot, she grinned and stretched her arms overhead. "I'm so glad you came. We're gonna have such a good time!" She lunged for his hand and gripped it tightly in both of hers. "I was lookin' for your car, but I didn't see it." She bounced on her toes. "I din' even see you drive up. What kind is it?" Looking around his leg, then up at his face, Des frowned. "You don't have no . . ."

"You don't have any . . ." Davida automatically corrected.

The little girl frowned. "You don't have *any* clothes with you."

Her mother cringed. "Destiny . . ."

"You're not gonna stay?" the child finished.

Marc grinned and winked at the embarrassed mother. "I'll be around for a while, but I'm gonna hang out at J.B.'s house," he said.

Crushed, the little girl moaned, then immediately recovered. "J.B.'s comin' over here today. Are you gonna . . . ?"

"So many questions," Davida intervened brightly, ushering them deeper into the house. "Why don't we at least let Marc have a seat and catch his breath, Des?"

"In the kitchen?" Without waiting for an answer, Des grabbed for Marc's hand. Letting his fingers swing with hers, she led him forward.

Marc stood in the middle of the large bright kitchen, admiring the sheen of light on gleaming copper pots and shining ceramic counters. In his heart, without ever having seen her home, he'd known Davida would crave light and space as much as he did in the depths of his artist's soul. He turned slowly, taking in the details.

"Sit here," Des ordered. Marc obediently climbed atop one of the cane-bottomed stools at the center island. When Davida raised an eyebrow and offered a tall glass of lemonade, he shrugged and looking unreasonably attractive in a wholesome, guy next door way, accepted the glass.

His eyes dropped to the glass as he lifted it to his lips, and Davida watched him sip. The parting of his lips, their press against the glass seemed well worth watching. "You're the first one here," she said, suddenly shy.

"Good. That means I have time to give you something." Marc separated a slender package from his sketchbook, and handed it to Destiny.

"For me?" Des wiggled on her seat and ripped the Disney wrapping paper to shreds. "It's a book, Mom." She held it aloft, then turned it to face her. *"Puzzles,"* she read, tracing her finger over the cover. "A lady wrote it. A lady named Dava? Walker?" Her eyes found her mother's, "that's almost like your name, huh? Dava." Flipping the book open, Destiny turned pages slowly, then looked up puzzled. "Is it about a little girl?" Her head went low as she studied the pages intently. "A little girl like me? A little girl with sickle-cell disease, like me?"

Marc nodded, then had to move quickly to capture Destiny as she rushed into his arms, hugging his neck tightly.

"It is! It's a book about somebody just like me!" One armed, Destiny swung the book around to face her mother. "Marc," she said turning and planting a kiss on his cheek, "this is the bestest gift ever." Her voice dropped to a whisper, "thank you." And she was gone.

The one-sided grin creased Marc's cheek, and he self-consciously slid his hand over the spot Destiny kissed.

"Marc, that was so . . . that was so thoughtful of you. Where ever did you find it?"

He wondered when she'd crossed the narrow distance between them to stand so close. Davida's hands moved to touch him, one folding over his, the other touching his shoulder from behind as she drew nearer. Moving around to face him, her eyes holding him with a tenderness Marcus knew only from his dreams, she sat on the stool Des had vacated. Her knees barely touched his. He could smell her vanilla scent again, and it took a deep swallow of lemonade to clear his head.

"It was . . . I found it on the Internet. I found it in the Emory Hospital pediatric website the night you told me about her crisis at camp."

"You did that for Des." Her hands folded gracefully and rose to her lips.

"It was important."

"Thank you," she said.

"She's been alright since?"

"Yes"—Davida nodded—"she has."

"That's good. I was a little worried when you told me."

"That's . . . thank you for worrying."

"Davida"—Marcus set the glass down, and leaned forward to place his hands over hers in her lap—"why are we trying to make small talk? We've been here and done this part before. If we're going to talk, can we talk about us?" His eyes gripped Davida like a pair of strong hands.

"I . . . what about 'us'?" She struggled to look away, and unsuccessfully found herself dropping her face, only to lift her eyes to his.

"Come on, Davida," he urged, squeezing their joined hands. "Think about it, Boo—I have. I pretty much did nothing else from the time you suggested this little get-together. Shoot, even before that, the little times I've had a chance to spend an hour or two with you between flights and meetings and work and stuff. I think maybe it was that first phone call that got me started. I want more. I need more time with you, and we deserve it."

"I'm not sure what you mean, Marc." *Lord, forgive me,* Davida prayed, *I am such a liar!*

Marcus looked like he'd heard her thought. He smiled and studied her face, committing her to memory, just as she was sitting there in her pretty blue and white kitchen. "We can't go forward if we insist on going backward, Davida."

She knew that; why did he think she kept backing up as fast as she could? Davida sat blinking. Saying nothing, she turned his hands over, laying her open palms against his. *Marc,* she confessed only to herself, not trusting her voice, *I don't know where to go with this.* This was completely foreign to her, and he'd already caused her far too many sleepless nights. She didn't know what that first phone call started, but he kept her tossing and turning enough as it was, and he was four hundred miles away with her still dreaming of all the things that can be done when you have all night to be together with someone you care about. *And, I,* she swallowed hard, looked away, then back at him, *I am beginning to care about you, Marc. I care a lot.* "Maybe . . ."

"No." He shook his head the way Des would if you tried to convince her that candy wasn't sweet. "No, maybe about it, Davida. When I handed you those flowers, when I held you in my arms out there, all I could think of was kissing you at Culpepper's and wondering how soon I'd get to do it again." His hands closed, holding hers securely. He watched her lips curve, forming a lush and rounded "o" as she exhaled. Marc distinctly felt something tighten inside his chest as he denied the urge to meet and hold her lips. "I've been thinking

that we need some time to get to know each other better, Boo. No
pressure, just get to know each other better.''

No pressure? Her body shook slightly with her exhalation. No
pressure, he said, and he sat here looking at her like this, with those
eyes. ''Marc, we know so much about each other already. We've
spent so much time on the telephone . . .''

He leaned closer, sliding from his perch, and taking possession of
her space. As he stood so close, nearly capturing her tightly pressed
knees between his thighs, Davida offered a prayer against hot flashes.
His eyes, a rich brown reminiscent of walnuts, thickly fringed with
dark lashes, worked hard to sweep the words of doubt from her lips
and her mind. No pressure, and he had the advantage of eyes like
those. She felt her resolution slip another notch.

''You know something Davida? There's life beyond the telephone.
I want you to think about coming down to Atlanta . . .''

''Oh, I can't.''

''. . . so that we can spend some time together, getting to know . . .''

''Marc, I really can't. See, I'm already committed to . . .''

His index finger touched her lips and froze her words. ''Your own
life,'' he finished for her. ''Davida, . . .''

Brushing his finger aside, she slapped a hand over his mouth, halting
his words. ''No, Marc.'' His eyes sparked above her hand as he ran
the tip of his tongue over her fingers. She pulled her hand away as if
burned.

Crossing her lips again with his finger, he flashed his dimples.
''Don't answer now, think about it.''

His lips drew closer by inches, finally pressing hers, replacing the
finger that silenced her only seconds earlier, and Davida tried to
remember exactly what it was that she was so committed to. There
was Destiny, her job, and for the life of her, desperate as she was for
enumeration, she couldn't recall another thing. She felt him draw on
something vital that smoldered and melted at her core. The puckering
suction of his lips pulled at the woman she'd sought to submerge. She
could think about it, but . . . ''Atlanta?''

Marc pulled back and looked at her, searching her eyes for an
answer he wanted to find. ''Atlanta.'' Pressing forward, he kissed her
again. ''I'm going to ask you again, you know. Soon.''

''I missed you, Marcus Benton.''

He smiled against her lips.

CHAPTER FOURTEEN

"Well, I was tired." Destiny shoved the Gameboy with her elbow, and seemed satisfied when it skidded to the edge of the card table.

The little boy in the Reebok cap placed his hand over the plastic box and frowned. He liked Destiny Lawrence a lot, thought she might even be a friend, but she *was* a girl, and frankly, he wasn't sure how trustworthy a girl could be. "You didn't act tired when we were at the . . ."

"If you really want to know, J.B., I was tired. I just got tired all of a sudden, and that happens a lot when you have sickle cell."

"You've got sickle cell? For real?"

"Yes, for real." Des twitched the Medic Alert bracelet defiantly. She looked up when she felt her mother's hand tap the top of her head. "Tell him, Mom, tell him it's true. Tell him I do get tired, sometimes when . . ."

"It's true, J.B." Davida nodded, debating about saying any more. Part of her wanted to leave this little battle entirely up to Destiny, to allow her to find her own way. She would need to fight it over and over throughout her life, and not just with little boys. Destiny would have to learn to defend herself and her illness from the speculation and ignorance of others, enlighten and teach where she could. The other part of Davida's heart wanted to do all she could to shore up her daughter's growing independence.

"Why don't I take that." It wasn't a question and Marcus, appearing at Davida's side, didn't wait for an answer. Fitting an arm comfortably about her waist, he lifted the fruit bearing tray from the hands of his hostess and turned them, tray and all, toward the heavily laden buffet table.

Tempted to refuse the help, Davida opened her mouth to protest.

"It's okay, I've got it." He shifted the tray just enough to bring his lips close to her ear. "Bet you a dollar she can take him," he whispered. "He's my nephew, I ought to know." Davida looked into his face, studying his eyes, touched again by the closeness of their height. Marcus brushed his shoulder subtly against her bare one, and Davida opened her mouth again. She had no idea what she'd intended to say, how she'd intended to address the gesture. It seemed immediately wrong to tell him how much she liked it. Instead she backed away, followed him, and let Des handle her business.

"There's a lot you don't know, J.B.," Des said, "and, if we're gonna be friends, I'll just have to teach you, but you have to be willing to learn."

"J.B.? Son?" Renee stirred on her chaise, dropped her feet to the grass and looked around for her pride and joy.

"We just talkin', Mom."

" 'We *are* just talking.' There's a verb in that sentence, son," Renee corrected tersely, "present indicative plural."

The little boy skinned the Reebok cap from his head, nodded. Destiny patted his hand. "It's okay," she whispered.

"My wife teaches English," George stage-whispered to no one in particular from his seat near Renee.

"And you make a valiant effort to support our child's learning process, don't you, darling?" A lifted brow emphasized her point.

George nodded and inclined his head toward his son. J.B., having gotten the message, looked back at Destiny, who nodded again. Across the yard, Davida smiled when she caught Renee's eye. It was good to know she wasn't the only mother fighting the grammar battle. The doorbell rang, preventing Davida's comment, then there was a tapping at the side door, offering the perfect excuse to move away.

Gathering the full skirt of her dress in one hand, Davida took fleet-footed, near running steps across her backyard. Marc's eyes followed her until she reached the house and held her as she paused to look back at him over her shoulder. He continued to watch her as she disappeared behind the glint of screening.

Moving through the house, Davida wondered at her wasted motion. "I could have just as easily opened the gate and walked down the drive as through the house," she muttered to herself. But if she'd walked down the drive, she would have missed the tiny thrill of having him watch her move, of having him touch her like that, even across the intervening distance. "That's positively hormonal," she scolded herself. "I sound like Quita."

Unsnapping the lock at the side door, Davida forced a quick smile into the faces of Yvonne and Tawanna Mallory.

"Yo, neighbor. Here's my girl!" Yvonne yelled, waving through the glass upper portion of the door. Yvonne had an obviously misplaced sense of the ethnic and it showed, but she was a neighbor—Davida waved back. Tawanna pulled at her short overalls, pushed her backward Cardinals baseball cap lower on her plaits, and tried not to notice her mother.

Here's teen angst in the making, Davida thought as she smiled and nodded at Tawanna Mallory and her mother in their matching "home-girl" outfits. A black woman, one generation away from her inner-city roots, and Yvonne couldn't seem to buy a clue. Point of fact, she didn't seem to want one either. Yvonne really should have thought twice about that tied-on jacket effect . . . definitely a fashion "don't" for women with hips. Davida reluctantly opened the door wider to let them in.

"How do you like me, now?" Yvonne turned in a prissy little circle, modeling her trendy gear. "I'm not going to stay, but it was so nice of you to invite Tawanna over today. She gets such a kick out of being with Destiny, don't you, dear?"

Tawanna looked at her mother and sighed painfully. Looking back at Davida, she pasted a put-upon smile on her round face and stood looking for all the world like a Cabbage Patch Kid. "Is Des okay?" she asked. "I mean, I was hopin' we could play some today, if she's okay. I brought a new game." She held out the electronic cartridge.

Remembering the little girl's bravery, it was hard not to love her, in spite of her overwhelming precocity. "Destiny is fine today, Tawanna, and she's waiting for you in the backyard." The child passed her like a shot, and Davida had to call after her, "tell Des to introduce you to J.B.!"

"I, personally, plan to hang out." Yvonne ran her thumbs along the straps of her faded overalls. "I might as well be comfortable and look cool while I hang out, don't you think?"

Thankfully, the front doorbell rang again and Davida was spared the need to comment.

Jewel pressed harder.

"Wesie, I'm telling you, this is more than just a little flirtation or a crush." Louise Lawrence faced the big front door and refused to look at her lifelong friend. "I saw the girl's face when she first met him, and I know what I saw."

"All I know, is that I didn't have to pry it out of my nephew like you apparently did with my niece." Wesie plucked at the pleats in the front of her teal slacks, then slid the navy alligator belt into a more comfortable place at her waist. "If this is the same man she was carrying on with on the telephone, well then my little niece ought to have a little more talking to do this morning."

Jewell turned her face up to the sky, looking for all the world like she was hoping for divine intervention. She pressed the doorbell again.

Louise shifted the sweater she carried over her arm to glance at her watch. "It's after twelve. It's afternoon—and it's about a man."

Wesie flipped an impatient hand. "So, you really think that's what this little command performance is really all about? A man?"

"I'm telling you . . ."

"Wesie? Louise? You two old crows need to just close your beaks and be glad for my daughter," Jewell Morrison whispered, desperately pressing the doorbell. "Whatever or whoever the surprise is, she promised we'd like it, so hush up and get ready to look surprised."

"Oh, looka here, looka here! The Supremes have reunited!"

Recognizing the voice, the three women turned and smiled as a unit. Jewell's head lifted, and her hand went to her hip. "Miss Diana Ross wishes she looked this good," she promised, smiling up at her son.

"You're probably right," Glenn Morrison offered, bending to accept a round of kisses from the three women. The door creaked and he straightened to look into his sister's face.

"Y'all know I don't allow such carrying on out in front of my house." Davida grinned from the doorway. "Butch, you and your harem had better get inside before the neighbors see you." She laughed, pressing her lips to gently blushed cheeks.

"Is he here?" Mama Lou, walking through the door, was bent at the waist, peering around corners.

"I just want you to know, Cookie, I still don't think this is such a good idea," Butch whispered, in passing.

"I thought we agreed to let me live my own life," his sister replied in a low sing-song voice.

"I thought we agreed to leave him on the telephone." The pleasant expression of moments earlier, was almost completely gone from Glenn Morrison's lean, dark face. "He's in your damned house, Cookie!" The harsh whisper threatened to become an outraged shout.

"So are you, for now."

Glenn's eyes tightened. "Cookie," he warned.

His mother slapped at his hip. "Be nice son," Jewell cautioned, "this is a family gathering." Turning to her daughter, she offered a quick hug. "Where's my granddaughter?"

"Backyard."

Jewell fluttered her fingers in farewell, and pushing her sister ahead, towed her son behind. Mama Lou followed of her own accord.

Davida turned to press her back to closing the front door, only to be stopped by the short woman forcing her way through the door. "Quita."

"Just thought I'd run by." She grinned and slipped through the opening. "Did I see Glenn come through here?" Quita tugged at her jean shorts, bobbed on her toes, and indicated the door with a nod of her head. "That is his car in front of your house, isn't it?"

Sudden casual strains of gentle jazz, Najee by the sound of it, drifted through the house from the back yard. *Butch must have found the tape deck,* Davida thought.

"Oh." Quita tried to look surprised at the sound of music. "You have more company."

"Like you don't already know."

"Whatever do you mean?" Davida crossed her arms and stared. Quita blithely ignored the expression and looked toward the kitchen, then back at her friend. "I could just run out, say hi, and be on my way—is that okay? Just say hi to Glenn, be friendly, you know."

"Oh, this is way too much. Trying to fake nonchalance and man chasing on a Saturday morning . . . Quita Walton, you have no shame. None, and I guess I'm just lucky you didn't bring Melanie along to back you up." Davida pressed her lips together and followed Quita back through the house.

"Backup? I don't need any . . . Oh, my goodness!" Both Quita's hands flew to her chest and fluttered there. Genuine surprise stitched through Quita's lowered voice. She turned, with parted lips and stared.

"What?" Hands on hips, Davida stared back.

"Is that the 'Culpepper Cutie,' out there?" She turned, shielded her eyes with one hand, and squinted. "What's he doing here?" Turning back to Davida, hands on her rounded hips, she blew a kiss into the air. "You should have told me! What's going on?"

"I invited him, er, since he was visiting his sister here."

Davida's brown eyes grew bright, and Quita grew instantly suspicious. "Which one is his sister?" she demanded.

"The one in the green shorts set." Davida pointed through the screen. "She's on the chaise. See her?"

"What's her name?"

"Renee."

Quita peered through the screen again. "Okay. So, she's real, she's got a name, and he's here." She shrugged and lifted her palms in question.

Davida tucked her lips in, and let her eyes drift away.

"You're too quiet, Dee. What's up?"

Backing against the kitchen counter, Davida leaned back, crossing her ankles, and drummed her fingertips against the tile. "I asked him to come by today, and he asked me to come to Atlanta—to visit."

"Atlanta? Go, girl! You'll never get to know the man long dist . . . in spite of the phone thing, you know what I mean."

"I've already told him I can't do it."

"You told him, what?" Quita's foot tapped impatiently. "Like you're so important." She frowned up at the ceiling. "And you can't go to Atlanta because . . . remind me . . . why?"

Without moving her head, Davida let her eyes state her obligations.

"Let's see, Des would love the time with either of her grandmothers, both of whom have years of experience in taking care of children. And"—Quita ticked off another finger—"it couldn't be your job, could it? You do have an assistant, or didn't Essie tell you? Besides"— she ticked off another accusing finger—"it's not like you have pets or anything to worry about, and I'll water your plants, if need be. Go."

Determined to hear no more, Davida crossed her kitchen. "I'll think about it, you go see my brother. Make sure he doesn't attack Marc."

"I can do that."

"I knew you could." Davida held the screen door open.

"Well, good morning, good morning all," Quita called gaily as she stepped out of the house. Homing in on Glenn Morrison, she put a SAC missile to shame. Finding him quickly, even in sandals, she barely came to his shoulder, but that didn't stop her from showing him all of her lovely dental work. Encouraged by Glenn's return smile, she posed against the low wall surrounding Davida's garden, and looked gratified when he joined her.

"Looks like our Davida is not the only one around here interested in a man," Aunt Wesie whispered, turning her face up to the sun and into the casual, summery breeze. She fanned herself lightly with a folded copy of *Ebony,* and tried to look as though she hadn't noticed the woman moving so deliberately toward her nephew. "What do you think, Louise?"

At the redwood picnic table, Mama Lou languidly shuffled a deck of cards she'd found there. The cards passed fluidly through her hands, and she appeared fully involved with their motion. She didn't really know how to play any card games, only how to shuffle, and she thought it made her look more removed than fanning with an old *Ebony,* so she shuffled. "I wasn't really paying Butch a lot of attention, to tell you the truth." She riffled the cards again. "But that little guy of Davida's, he's sure cute!" She drew the final word out like a stricken teenybopper, and shuffled some more.

"Did you notice how, when Davida and that young man look at each other, it's like"—Wesie gave an almost imperceptible shiver and her words sizzled through clenched teeth—"it's like gears meshing. Like something between them just locks into place."

"No, Wesie, I did not notice that, and furthermore, I am not listening to you two, even if I would like more grandchildren," Jewell hissed, sliding her shades lower on her eyes, and appearing to admire the silver maple tree above them. She too refused to turn.

"Well, it's not like we know a lot about him. Davida's being unusually closemouthed, where he's concerned."

"How much can you tell about a man you met on the telephone?"

"Wesie, she's an adult, and she doesn't need our permission," Jewell defended, turning slightly, waving at Destiny and the other two children. "Besides, didn't he come through here on some business a week or so, ago?"

"Well, yes, but an hour or two can't give you much of what a man and a woman need . . ."

"Not unless his first name is Oatmeal." Mama Lou giggled. "You know, 'three minutes, and you're done.' "

"Lou, you're just bad." Wesie smirked trying not to laugh. Her sister hid her smile behind a demure hand.

"Is this a private conversation, or can anyone with an opinion just hop in?" The three older women jumped and beringed hands went to rapidly thumping bosoms. Renee, always an advocate of surprise, grinned at them. "I'm Marcus's sister," she announced.

"Renee, right?"

"Oh, you've got a good memory." Renee beamed. "I brought cake." She offered a plate of sliced golden homemade pound cake, then juggled dessert plates, forks, and napkins onto the table. "Is this an adequate bribe? If not, I could swipe some of that hand-cranked ice cream . . ."

"We haven't had lunch yet . . ."

"Is she always like that?" Renee asked, grinning broadly at Jewell. "Cake is good for you."

"What flavor is the ice cream?"

Renee turned lightly on her toes. "Want me to go see?"

"Sit down, child, before you make us all fat." Mama Lou laughed.

"You didn't have to try to bribe us with cake." Jewell accepted a plate and pinched delicately at the evenly browned crust. Letting the bits of cake melt in her mouth, she closed her eyes, savoring the taste.

"But, it worked." Wesie touched her lips with the yellow paper napkin. "Sit down, and tell us all about your brother."

Eager, Renee climbed onto the plank seat, wriggling her legs through the opening like a little girl. A heavy lock of hair fell forward as she looked to see where her feet were, and she pushed it back quickly. She folded her hands and leaned forward. "Where do you want me to start?" she demanded.

Jewell tipped her face to the sky, and sunlight fell through the silver maple to cross the dark chocolate of her skin as she thought. "Where's *your* mother today?"

Renee was quick to answer. "Holy Land tour with her church." She smiled beatifically. "Daddy went with her." The smile flashed and disappeared as she became businesslike. "I know a good bit about Davida, because as you can see"—she indicated her brother and son with a tilt of her chin—"the men in my family are quite taken with the ladies in yours. Wouldn't you like to know a little more about my brother?"

"So, tell," Mama Lou demanded impatiently.

"Marc wants her to come visit—down in Atlanta."

Jewell's mouth opened slowly. "He . . . what? He . . . he really doesn't know her . . . that well . . . does he?"

"But he wants to."

"That's important," Wesie offered. The three women looked at each other, then back to Renee, waiting for more. Glad to have received implicit permission, she began. "His real name is Marcus James Benton, but he likes it when you call him Marc. Davida is such an unusual name. How did she get it?"

Jewell's forehead wrinkled. "She was named after her father. His name was David, but you were talking about Marc."

"Oh, yeah." Renee, elbows on the table, leaned forward. "He's an artist—a real one. Marc's art, until he met your daughter, was his passion. He's big on passion. His birthday is October twenty-eighth, eleven months to the day, before mine."

"October twenty-eighth? What is that, Lou? That's not Libra, is it?"

"No, Wesie, that's Scorpio. They're supposed to be exciting, very artistic, very passionate, and very good at everything they do." Mama Lou raised her eyebrows deliberately. "From what I hear, none of them are named, Oatmeal."

"Oh. Ooooh!" Wesie and Jewell caught the innuendo at the same time. Louise Lawrence found the cards and shuffled vigorously.

"He's going to be thirty-five, this year." Renee snapped her fingers and straightened perceptibly. "He's got this project, Bro'Man. Do you know about that?"

Jewell slowly moved her sunglasses. "Tell us about it, dear."
So, Renee did.

Marc looked guilty, caught in the act of serving peach cobbler to
three happy children.

"You may have dessert when you've finished your meal," Renee
cautioned J.B.

"Sounds about like you, Cookie," Glenn added sullenly, rubbing
at his arm.

"It does." Quita nodded, then returned her attention to the man
sharing her table in the shade.

"Well, Butch, that's a mother's job."

"Does a mother have anything available for mosquitoes?" He
rubbed at his arm and waved away a suspected flying insect.

"You're such a baby." Davida smiled. "Let me see." She moved
closer. Quita looked at her pointedly. Glenn pushed the sleeve of his
T-shirt higher and offered his arm.

"See? Right there." He pointed. "I think a 'no-see-'em' got me."
He tapped his bicep. "Right there." Quita made a sorrowful, sympathetic face, and lightly fingered his skin.

"Hey, man." George Johnson, short and dark, arrogant mustache
bristling over his oddly pink lips, materialized at his side. Glenn looked
surprised to see him. "Is that a brand?" George's finger tapped the
mark barely visible beneath the white sleeve of Glenn's T-shirt.

"Brand? Yeah." Glenn pushed the shirt sleeve higher displaying
the diamond framed Greek letters burned into his skin. "It's my frat,
Kappa Alpha . . ."

"Psi!" George exploded with laughter and pushed his own sleeve
high, exposing his matching brand. The two men clasped hands and
formalized their bond with a complicated handshake that left Quita
gaping. He dropped into one of the two remaining chairs at the table.
"Where'd you pledge?"

"Lincoln, up in Pennsylvania. You?"

"Harris-Stowe State." He turned, motioning over his shoulder.
"Marc! Come here, got something to show you!"

Marcus wiped his fingers on a paper napkin, and dropped it into a
nearby trash basket. Strolling closer, his eyes finding and holding
Davida's, he came to stand by the table. "Whatcha got?"

Glenn's face closed and darkened immediately, distrusting the new
arrival.

"You are not going to believe this." Undaunted, George was apparently immune to the cold front that proceeded Marcus to the table.

"Look at this." He pushed at Glenn's shirt sleeve, laughing when Marc's jaw dropped.

"I don't believe it."

"What?" Glenn groused.

"There's way too much synchronicity, here." Marcus folded back his own T-shirt, the higher the sleeve went, the more of his Kappa brand lay exposed.

"I don't believe it." Glenn looked at his sister. "You didn't tell me."

"I didn't know," Davida laughed. "All I knew was that you both had a sister you called 'Cookie,' and you shared the nickname 'Butch.' "

"Well, put it up here, Butch." Glenn stood and gripped Marc's hands fraternally. "It's a small, small black world, brother. Where'd you pledge?"

"Morehouse," George and Marcus answered jointly.

"That's Pi chapter, right?"

"You got it." Marc laughed.

"Nupe!" The men's fisted hands, all bearing the ruby and diamond fraternity rings, touched like toasting glasses. "Is there anything else I ought to know?" Glenn dropped his hands to the table top.

Marc relaxed against the arm of Davida's chair, draping an arm across the back, and Davida was pleasantly surprised to find she didn't mind—at all. "I'm eleven months older than Renee, you?"

"Aw, man—us, too. To the day." Glenn pointed between his sister and himself. "Anything else?"

The hand that cupped her shoulder was warm and welcome. Davida relaxed against Marc's hip and felt more secure and wanted than she had since . . . since . . . she couldn't recall ever feeling quite this way with a man. Even Skip.

"I like your sister—a lot." Marc grinned. "Sorry man, mine's already taken." Nodding, George chuckled and folded his arms across his barrel chest.

Closing her eyes, content that the two men in her life had found common ground, Davida barely heard or registered Marc's next words. "I've invited her to Atlanta. I want her to come down, plan for a week, but I'll take whatever she'll give me."

Glenn leaned forward. "Cookie?"

"Thought you didn't like him," Davida returned. "Thought you didn't trust him?"

Behind her, Marc appeared stricken. "You didn't like me?" he asked in a faked but tearful voice.

"Didn't want me to like you, either." Davida tattled.

"That was before I knew you." Glenn's lean face split with his slow smile. "That was before I knew what kind of man you had to be, I mean, you being frat and all." Davida looked to Quita as the men agreed and pounded fists all around. Quita looked cuddly and scooted her chair closer to Glenn's.

Recovering, Marcus shifted his hip on the arm of her chair, and Davida refused to sigh as the rough cloth of his pants rubbed against the soft skin her shoulder with agonizing slowness. She rested her hand against her shoulder.

"Well, your brother likes me now, and my intentions are honorable, so"—he extended an inquiring hand before them—"how about it, Boo?"

"Oh, did you hear that," Mama Lou whispered. "He called her Boo."

Renee and Jewell shushed her and strained to hear more.

"When will you come to Atlanta?" Marc asked again.

"Oh, why, did you have to ask me that?"

"Because, Boo, I want you to know I mean it. I want to spend time with you. I want us both to see where this is going." His hand moved easily along the silk of her summer-warmed skin. "I'm still waiting for an answer."

"Sounds to me like he's going to keep asking 'til he gets an answer." Quita tipped her head slightly.

When Marc lifted her hand to hold it between both of his, Davida looked up wishing she could deny or somehow refute what she was feeling. Instead, appreciating the unnamed emotion swirling through his long-lashed brown eyes, she accepted his touch. "I have a feeling," she said softly, watching the eyes she knew she would die remembering, "he's going to keep asking until he gets the answer he wants to hear."

The smile he gave her was like the sun after a long, dark storm. "You know me too well," he said, pulling her to her feet. "You'll excuse us, won't you?"

Glenn and George nodded affably, and Glenn rested a hand on Quita's knee when she started to rise, causing her to drop demurely back into her seat. "Des can always stay with me," Jewell whispered deliberately, as the screen door closed behind her daughter and the young man Jewell was convinced was quite extraordinary.

Waiting only long enough for the screen door to close behind them, Davida repossessed her hand. Holding it tightly against her body, almost hiding behind it, she looked squarely at Marcus Benton. Refusing to buy in to his dimpled charm, or the stirring look in his eye, she swallowed hard and went straight to the point. "Marc, I've worked really hard to put Skip's death behind me. I've tried to take all the best of what we had together and put it in place for Destiny. I've dealt with all the racism, sexism, and any other random 'isms' associated with my job.''

He looked confused, utterly, endearingly, totally, confused.

"I mean, I've got things together now, financially. Destiny's health is mostly stable. Things are working just right. I mean . . .''

He stood looking at her, blinking. Blink, blink, blink-blink.

Her hand slapped the blue and white tiled counter and her eyes swept the ceiling. Her tongue crossed her teeth, and she knew she could never take back any of the words she was about to say. "What do you want from me, Marc? Why is it so important to get me to Atlanta?''

He blinked innocently, and she could have screamed—but she didn't.

"Marc, I'm about as whole as I can get, right now, and I don't want to jeopardize that. I have to control my life and you, you want to . . . to what, Marc? What do you want from me?''

He gave her that clean, firm-chinned, all-American look, then side-swiped her with a blinding smile. "I want to be sure, Davida. That's all. I want to be sure, and I want you to be sure, too.''

When he opened his arms, she planted her palm in his chest, stiff-arming him. Forcing him to keep his distance had to be a crime against nature, but she needed to think, she needed air, and she would never find that in his embrace. "Sure of what?''

"Sure that I want to see you every day for the rest of my life, sure that the music I hear every time you speak is real. I want to be sure that we think enough alike, so that the next time there's a crisis, yours, mine, or Destiny's—we'll be there together.'' He gave her that innocent look again. "Don't you want to be sure, Boo?''

Her knees teased her, pretending to be supportive, then they deserted her and Davida had to grab for a nearby stool.

"Don't you want to be sure?''

Why does he keep asking me that when he knows the only real answer is yes? she thought. *Yes, I want to be sure. Yes I need to be sure.* His hands closed over hers and she was sure he felt the heat rising beneath her denim dress. "Marc, our lives, the timing . . . this is all meant to be so different from what you say you want.''

He frowned, then looked confused. "How, Davida?''

She closed her eyes and sighed tiredly. "This is like a conversation with Des, and that's the problem.''

"Des is a pretty sharp kid, was that supposed to be a compliment?''

Opening her eyes, Davida was surprised at how close his face was to hers. He was so close, everything about him seemed intensified—the fine caramel color of his skin, the bright whiteness of his teeth, and the bowed fullness of his lips. When had he moved so close, and why did he smell so damned good? *Breathe, Davida, just keep breathing, and you'll get through this.* "Marc, honey, I'm five years older than you. You've got to go where I've already been. I have a child, this house. I have ..." She started to move her hand in an inclusive motion, but he held her in place. "Marc, I can't play 'the girlfriend' for you, and God knows I'm not about to shack up and play house with you. I could never disrespect my child or myself like that."

"I would never ask that of you, Davida, and that's not what I'm asking now. Can you just be what and who you are? That's all I'm asking. Come to Atlanta, we'll get you a separate hotel room. I'll show you the city, we'll spend some time together, and just get to know each other. If there's anything else, we'll find it together, and in our own time. Would that be so bad?"

"Marc, see"—she shook her head—"I've heard a lot of those, 'no pressure' speeches over the years. You say one thing now, I get to Atlanta and it becomes a totally different song."

"I thought you knew me better than that. Davida, I know that trust comes to you by inches. I know it takes you a while to build trust, I've learned that in all that talking we've done. All I'm asking of you now is to take a step based on the trust you already have in me. Atlanta's a good place, and I promise not to take unfair advantage of you."

"Nice speech, Marc."

"But you won't come?" He looked crestfallen.

"Yes, I will."

"Yes?" He brightened instantly. "You will come?"

Breathe! she reminded herself. She really could use a vacation. She tried to think of how long ago it had been since she'd actually taken time for herself. She had time, lots of accrued vacation time. *Breathe!* Still thinking, she pressed her lips together. A vacation would be a good excuse for the serious shopping she'd promised herself. "Is it still hot in Atlanta?"

Marc, sensing victory, used his eyes the way old-time burlesque strippers used their fans. "It's always hot in Atlanta," he promised.

Breathe! "A week?" She was almost afraid to look into those eyes again. "I guess I could get away for a week."

It was almost magic worthy of David Copperfield, the way his dimples came one at a time then made a dancing frame for his lips. *Breathe!* "In two weeks, is that alright?" she asked tentatively.

"I get a whole week?" His breath against her skin as he exhaled made her want to moan, but not as much as when her lashes brushed his cheek when she received his kiss. "Two weeks from now, is fine, Boo."

CHAPTER FIFTEEN

"You are so good, I swear, you wear a man out." Marcus was still breathing hard. The exertion, simple and natural as it was, was still far more than he'd bargained for.

"Hey." Davida smiled down at him. "I'm just good at what I do." When his face moved upward, hovering closer, she tapped his chin with her forefinger. "Besides, I've been at it longer."

"You're not going to pull rank on me, again—are you? That 'older woman' stuff?"

"No, I'm not. It just takes practice is all . . . that and maybe you ought to pick your battles more carefully in the future. Only challenge me at things you know you're good at." She winked and gave him a smile he wanted to memorize.

"Hey." He beat at his chest with a fisted hand.

"Really." Her finger traced a lazy, curving line along his cheek, losing its way, and surfacing near his mouth before she withdrew it.

Marc knew a sane man would ignore the finger and the woman attached to it, and he usually tried to be sane. Even if she hadn't been tall and elegant, her flawlessly dark skin and generationally defined profile would have demanded his attention. Turning away from her, he reluctantly shifted the high-booted inline skates to his other shoulder and fitted his key into the lock. "When you offered to teach me how to skate," he huffed, "I had no idea you meant all afternoon or all over Piedmont Park."

"That park was a great place for your first lesson, it has those great inclines, and the curves . . ." She let her hand swoop through the air between them. "Des would have enjoyed . . ." She took a deep breath and began again. "You said it was the sight for the what exposition?"

Marc tsk'd lightly and shook his head. "Gotta bring you up to speed on your history. Piedmont Park was the sight of the Cotton States Exposition in eighteen—"

"I don't remember the date, Marc. I do remember the part about it being the sight of Booker T. Washington's 'five fingers' speech," she interrupted. "It was the one where he said that blacks and whites could live together but as separate as five fingers on a hand." She wrinkled her nose and grinned boldly.

"Okay, smartie, you get points on that one. Meantime, welcome to my humble abode." He pushed hard, swinging the heavy door open wide and was pleased by her stunned gasp.

"Marc." Davida turned in a small stunned circle. "This is incredible." The huge, Pantheon-like foyer was one of the reasons he'd bought the Anthony Ames designed co-op apartment with the first really big money he'd earned.

"Oh, Marc." She didn't know where to look first, her hands tracing, but not touching the walls and woodwork, her eyes overwhelmed by the amount of space before her. "I've never been in a house, or an anything, like this before." Davida turned, trying to see it all, trying to understand the minimalist revelation surrounding her.

"This building," she said, her voice hushed. "On the outside, it was so barren and austere, like something from a science fiction movie."

"Yeah," Marc agreed sheepishly. Kenya Witherspoon always said it looked like a place where you went to buy used plumbing parts.

"But it's not, not on the inside." Davida turned again, facing the walls, her mouth open in awed delight.

"At least you got to see the Freedom Parkway and the Carter Library on the way over, and we're close to downtown." Marc shoved his hands into his pockets and tried to see his home through her eyes.

The dining room, an elegant open space with a vaulted ceiling and skylight, was unbound by walls and opened into his living room. Comfortable furniture, from where Davida stood, appeared to be at a minimum. Marcus preferred art to upholstery, and it showed. The openness of what appeared to be his primary living area was arresting, and he wondered if it wasn't almost suspiciously haunting to a woman who'd probably grown up with comfortable overstuffed cushions on everything. Along the western wall, the twelve-foot-high windows of what had once been a functional warehouse were haphazardly shaded with yards of artfully thrown muslin, turning the twilit urban twinkle of downtown lights into a neo-realist study.

Nearly every square inch of the walls, both the red brick and the hi-tech, high-gloss, steel-gray lacquered surfaces, was covered by a sketch, a canvas, a drawing, an eclectic framed print, a watercolor, an oil, all done by Marcus Benton. "These are all yours." Davida opened her arms to embrace as much of the loft as she could. "How long did it take you?"

"To paint or to hang them all?"

Davida dropped her hands to her hips and cocked her head in response.

"Years." Marc grinned. Pointing to a small yellowed crayon drawing, something vaguely impressionist from the looks of it, he looked up at her. "This is my earliest. My mom saved it from kindergarten."

Davida pouted, pushing out her lower lip, making him think of succulent summer plums. "That is so special."

"No, she really did. That was my 'primitive' period. There are others, like this one of Renee. It's from junior high school."

He set his skates down by the door, and the tour began in earnest. Waning light beyond his windows draped the room in long shadows, and he was tempted to reach for a switch, but bringing electric light into the same space as Davida Lawrence seemed like a desecration, the wrong thing to do. Instead, Marc followed his instincts, liking the frequent touch of her hand on his bare arms as individual pieces caught her eye.

A series of small studies and miniature portraits adorned one of the two brick walls in his kitchen, and she stood before them transfixed.

"Marcus, this is incredible."

She turned back to him, and he thought she was the most incredible sight he'd ever seen. Even in the black shorts and red Cardinals T-shirt she'd worn skating, Marc saw, in her face, all the dignity and tenderness he'd detected in their first telephone calls.

Early evening light caught in her short, tousled hair and spilled along her dark cheek, loving her so much, it refused to leave her. She seemed to absorb the light, leaving shades of ochre and umber to catch in the underlying firmness of her profile and enchant Marc's artist's eye. *One day,* he promised himself, *one day very soon, when I paint her, I'm going to emphasize the sweetness of her lower lip, and the long graceful column of her throat.* That she might not want to be painted never entered his mind.

"Oh, God!" Davida clutched at Marc's arm and seemed unsure as to whether she should run away fast or go closer. "What *is* that?" She pointed across the room. *"Who* is that?"

Marcus patted her hand and walked across the room to stand beside the six-foot cardboard figure. "This is Bro'Man." He patted the cartoon man's shoulder. "He's the project I told you about."

Crossing the room to stand beside Marc and his product, Davida studied the cartoon man. Well over six feet, with muscles enough for two men, and skin like midnight, the cardboard figure was formidable, even if he couldn't stand up without a stick stuck to his back. "You did a great job on him, but there's something about his face." She tilted her head and studied him. "When you described him and showed me your sketches, I pictured him differently."

"This one is different from the sketches you saw." Marc patted Bro'Man's shoulder and grinned. "This guy was a gift from MC Feng Shui. He's wearing Feng Shui's face."

"Is that good?" Davida looked unsure.

Marc shrugged.

"I thought you said he was going to stay out of the production end of this project, kind of like a silent partner."

"He is. He's contractually obligated to do so, Milt saw to that, but Feng Shui thought this was a nice gesture, and he sent this guy over to celebrate our association."

Davida looked at him, her lips lifting at the corner. "And you believe that?"

"So far, he's been a man of his word. You want to see the rest of the place, or you want to argue about cartoons?"

"What else is there to see?"

"My studio, a couple of bedrooms." He let his voice trail off when she stood unmoving, holding her skates firmly, protectively in front of her body. The air around them was suddenly quiet, and her smile died a lingering and shy death. Was it the idea of bedrooms that put her into this quiet state?

"We can look at the rest later, if you like. Are you hungry?" he asked, for lack of a better topic. He took the skates from her and set them aside.

Feeling twelve years old and completely exposed, Davida found herself folding her hands into the hem of her T-shirt. "I could eat," she said, not looking at him.

"Good." He caught her hand and headed for the kitchen. "You sit here," he indicated the plain pine table. "I'm going to fix us right up."

"You always wash your hands in the kitchen sink?"

He looked over his shoulder and nodded. "They tell me washing hands is a good thing, no matter where you do it." He snapped a couple of towels from the roll over the sink, dried his hands, then tossed the used wad of paper into the bright yellow wastebasket.

"Two points," Davida admired.

He lifted his brow and winked. "What can I say? I've got skills."

He leaned against the slate counter, looking too cute for any of the words Davida knew. "Anything you want, in particular?"

She turned her palms up and shrugged. "I'm open. You decide."

"Then, let's see what we've got."

Bending to unload the refrigerator, he looked deep inside, moving things around. *Look at him. Wonder what he does to make his . . .* Davida thought and quickly looked away from Marcus at his work. Wondering why a man looked so good from behind was right up there with checking out his bedroom. *And I'm not quite ready to know the answer to either,* she admitted to herself.

Marcus banged a skillet onto the gas burner and made interesting motions with yellow, green, and red peppers. When sizzling sounds and good smells became the reward for his efforts he looked at his guest. "I make this look easy, don't I?"

"You said you had skills."

"And so I do," he said, chopping chorizo sausage into the skillet.

"Can I do something?" Davida asked, standing. "I'm not used to sitting around waiting for someone to do things for me." She moved toward his cabinets. "Since you're doing the cooking, I can at least set the table." She hesitated, one hand in the air. "Which cabinet?"

Marc moved his skillet from the flame. The easygoing grin he gave her was like a skilled thief, slipping under all her defenses and pulling the resistance from her intent. He moved across the tiled floor like a dancer, finally standing behind her, breath catching the small hairs at the base of her neck. One hand found her shoulder, the other her extended arm, giving it every reason to fall slowly to her side.

"Come on, Boo, this is a vacation, time for you to relax."

Her fingers touched his where they still rested on her arm. "I can do this, besides when you come to my house, I'm going to put you to work." She resisted the urge to rest her cheek against his. "Aside from that, don't you know, too much relaxation isn't good for anyone?" But how bad could it be when a man slipped his arms around your waist and held you like this?

Turning slowly, chest to breast, deliberately not finding his eyes, Davida spoke into the space between them. "Marc, this is not right for me. I didn't just come to Atlanta to do things I couldn't do in St. Louis. This is just a visit between friends. I'm not here to . . ." Words failed her, and she had to try again.

He only shrugged. "I didn't ask you to come all the way down here for sex. Is that what you're afraid of?"

She couldn't put her qualms into words—not even for herself. Feeling exposed, she crossed her arms at her waist, and turned from him, concentrating on the dark silence in the room. "It's getting late."

Marc reached for the light switch, a rheostat, and allowed muted light into the kitchen. "We've talked on the phone much later than this, Boo."

She felt him moving closer, then felt him stop only inches behind her. "Do I make you nervous, Davida?"

Hell yes! He was making her have to think to remember who she was. With him, here, right now, she was not quite sure who he wanted her to be—and worse, who she wanted herself to be. She didn't want to deny his fantasy, but this was not the telephone. Her fingers tightened on her forearms leaving barely visible marks in the dark chocolate of her skin. "Nervous? No, of course not," she lied, hoping he wouldn't notice she was trembling like a leaf. On second thought, nervous didn't convey half of what she was feeling right now.

Hands landed gently on her shoulders and she managed not to jump. "Davida?" She closed her eyes, too vividly aware of how close he stood to her, of how minimal a barrier two cotton T-shirts made, of the warmth of his palms on her skin, and the whisper of his words in her ear.

"Would you look at me?"

She moistened her lips, but her eyes remained closed.

His lips touched the back of her neck, then the pads of his fingers touched the same spot, pressing like unforgotten memory. "Look at me, Boo."

Very slowly, she turned. He was smiling, his golden-brown eyes crinkling at the corners, dimples curving deeply into his cheeks. He cupped her face in his hands, still gazing into her eyes, and it frightened her to think this was all it took to hold her in place. "Come on, Davida. It's only me, the same ol' Marc you've been on the phone with for the nearly five months. Same ol' Marc."

The same ol' Marc, who'd entered her life so unexpectedly and become so important to her before she'd realized it. He was the same ol' Marc who made her tremble with a smile. The same ol' Marc who made her want things her mind and body thought were long ago put behind her. That, she already knew, was the problem. He was the same ol' Marc who no longer haunted only her sleeping dreams, but her daydreams as well.

"I have a confession to make."

"You do?" She cleared her throat trying to make her voice less husky. "You do? What is it?"

"I'm glad you're not wearing heels right now."

Heels? For the first time, it occurred to Davida that they were both in socks, having removed their skates downstairs. Her shoes were somewhere on the floor of the Saab. "What?"

"It's kind of nice to be eye-to-eye with you. I'm not normally intimidated by women who are taller than me, but just for now, just for tonight, I'm glad you're not towering above me.''

She couldn't help smiling. "Why tonight?''

''Well, I guess I'm a little nervous, too. It just makes it easier that we're kind of on the same level.''

''Why? What do you have to be nervous about?'' Davida asked, half-skeptical.

His smile deepened, and his eyes reduced her willpower to something with the consistency of warm candle wax. "Don't you feel it?''

Hardly breathing, she felt the fine tremors rattling the fingers that cupped her face. Marcus was trembling, too! "Why?'' she whispered. His lips crossed hers, startling her with something she would only think of as the brush of a butterfly's wing, too brief for response.

''I've never wanted anyone like this, Boo. I've never needed anyone this much. And I promised not to rush you. Davida, I swear I meant it when I made you that promise. I mean it now, but I'm so afraid of doing something wrong, something stupid that might make you push me away.''

His admission of uncertainty twisted her heart, further weakening her already shaky resistance. Davida lifted her hands, tentatively resting her palms against his chest. She felt his heart beating rapidly, forcefully. At her touch, he drew a deep, slightly ragged breath. His smile remained, but she saw the strain at the corners of his mouth. ''Are you pushing me away, Boo?''

I should. The thought stood militantly forward in her mind. Somewhere at her responsible core, she knew that the right thing to do was to push Marcus Benton and his beautiful eyes and promising smile away. She knew she should. But, oh, how she wanted to kiss him, to be swept again into that swirl of pure sensation he generated within her. She remembered his kisses in her kitchen, and the feelings he generated—feelings of being more than mother, sister, or daughter. Was it memory that exaggerated her response to his earlier kiss—the kiss that lured her from the security of her St. Louis home? Would she react the same way here in Atlanta? What would it cost to try again?

She looked at him, willing him to take the decision and the responsibility—just this one time—take the decision out of her hands.

His gaze was still locked with hers, when his mouth brushed hers again. Longer this time, by just a bit; harder this time, by just a bit, but still not nearly enough, and Davida nearly moaned in frustration. He wasn't going to make this easy for her, she realized abruptly. He wasn't going to make her decisions for her, and be guilty of pushing her later. She would have to make the first move.

Her fingers gripped the sturdy cotton of his shirt. Very slowly, she leaned toward him, and he met her halfway. His lips curved upward in a satisfied smile when they touched hers. And then the smile was gone, and he was kissing her with the same greedy hunger she'd sensed in him in her kitchen. Davida lost herself in his need and her own. Her arms went around his neck even as his locked behind her. They strained together, mouths and tongues expressing everything they hadn't been able to say with mere words.

Davida couldn't remember ever wanting like this, ever needing like this. She wasn't certain she'd survive if she acted on those needs, wasn't sure she'd want to if she didn't. She didn't know that she really had a choice.

In her mind, Davida termed what she felt as madness when she returned his kiss. Unrestrained, uncontrollable madness that claimed them both, sweeping away doubts, reservations and inhibitions, leaving only aching need in its wake. "So long," Marc whispered, clasping her fiercely against him. "I've wanted you for so long."

"Ah, Marc," she whispered. "I want you, too." She pressed her lips together and wished for the words that would clearly express her feelings. There were none.

When her lips parted, he waited. Marc watched her lids lower, closing him from the vivid luster of her eyes. Wanting more, not daring to demand it, he pulled back only enough to allow him to see her face. His eyes were dark, turbulent, his hands possessive and healing as he continued to hold her. "You don't have to go back to the hotel tonight, Davida."

She stiffened slightly, and caught her lower lip between her teeth; he held her anyway.

Protectively, Marc brushed wisps of hair off her forehead and cheeks. Sweet heat emanated from her body, and warmed his soul. Her heart thumped madly against his in perfect counterpoint. "Let me love you tonight, Davida."

Torn, feeling the desire, fear, hunger, and uncertainty that had forbidden her connection to this man for so many wasted months, her gaze went to the tiled floor.

Following the look, Marcus seemed to understand. "If I'm wrong for asking, Davida, I'm sorry. But please, don't go away. Not yet."

Through half-lowered lashes, she studied the face that had already become so familiar to her. Standing close enough to touch, yet far enough apart to run, she no longer felt they were so new to each other. *I feel lured, drawn to him,* Davida thought. *I feel charmed and seduced.* The thought was dizzying.

Truth be told, he'd seduced her long before this night, before this trip. He'd seduced her in intimate, candid conversations, shared laughter, hazy dreams. He'd seduced her with words that soothed and connected to her remote and lonely soul. Seduction of the mind, she realized, was just as powerful as flowers and poems in a conventional courtship. He'd made her want him long before she'd ever laid eyes on him. Now she could touch him, taste him, feast on the physical attraction of his coppery skin, and golden-brown eyes. And she wanted him even more.

She released a sigh of complete acceptance mingled with anticipation. "I don't want to go, Marc. Not yet."

The words were lower than a whisper, almost a thought, but he heard them. Standing close, Marc released his hold on her, offering her his hand. She placed her hand in his, an instinctive gesture of trust. They rocked slightly, slow dancing to the music of their beating hearts, both waiting for a sign.

"Is this that 'walk on faith' you mentioned the first time we met?" Marc asked against her cheek.

"I suppose it is," she replied, then began to pull away from him. When he held her closer, and pressed her hand against his chest, Davida shook her head. "Marc, we've been in the park all afternoon, I . . ."

His hand moved against her body, curving along her spine and lower, then moving back to her hip and supporting her back. "Let's just take this as it comes, okay, Boo?" His tongue touched the corner of her lips, and Davida felt her head fall back to better accommodate him. From the corner of her mouth, he traced the soft wet inside of her lips and allowed her tongue the joy of both parry and thrust as he met her equally.

Lifting her shirt, his hands explored the softness of her torso. Davida automatically pulled her stomach in and mourned the almost forgotten bikini days of her past. Marcus Benton couldn't have cared less. He seemed delighted with every cushioned inch of flesh he uncovered.

His fingers lightly traced her spine from shoulder to hip, and her body, hot and ready, responded immediately. They both caught their breaths in ragged unison at the sensation. Molding his hands against her flesh, he pulled her even closer until their bodies were pressed together from breast to knee—and it wasn't enough. They both knew they needed more.

Marc found a spot Davida would have sworn didn't exist. When his tongue found and probed the tiny spot, a marginal area, just beneath and below her ear, Davida cried out and lurched against him. His head moved, her hand held him in place, urging compliance, and he repeated his touch. Her body rocked again, and she put out her hand for balance. It was only with the aid of the kitchen table, sturdy enough to bear their weight, that she remained upright and in his arms.

Paying slow, loving homage to her full firm breasts, easing her

shirt over her head, Marc teased and cajoled, using his tongue to
overcome her mild protests. Thoughts of lost muscle tone were
drowned in the heated moisture of his suckling.

The look in his eyes as he undressed her excited her, and she
barely registered the thought as her hip grazed the tabletop. His
hands blazed knowingly across her skin, pulling at emotions and
sparking the kinds of flares she'd been hoping for. "Oh, Marc."
She heard herself sigh, clinging to his head and shoulders, feeding
him more. "Oh, Marc, I . . ."

Omigod! Panting, blinking, and suddenly grounded, Davida was
aware of clutching this man to her nearly naked body. She was suddenly, critically aware of being ready to make love to this man with
every cell of her being, *and she was climbing up on a kitchen table
to do it!* "Marc, wait . . ."

"Davida?" He looked confused.

"Marcus . . . this is your kitchen table."

"Yes?" He still looked confused.

She wanted to cover herself, but the Cardinal shirt lay out of reach.
Sliding back to the end of the table, her hand resting just low enough
at her breast to ensure modesty, Davida placed her other hand on
Marc's cheek. "Marcus, this is your kitchen table, and I don't think
I can make love on it tonight and have breakfast on it in the morning.
Could you please show me your bedroom, now?"

Marcus fought not to laugh out loud, at least she was planning on
sticking around until breakfast. His lips twitched and he managed to
keep his smile discreet. "I can do that, Boo."

Following him along the long, painting-lined hall in near darkness,
Davida had time to reflect. Marc had once called her a traditionalist,
and he was apparently right. It was funny how very well he knew
her, and if she admitted it, how much he taught her about herself.
Turning her thoughts carefully, inspecting them for incidents of suspicion, or regret, or loss, she found none. Marcus Benton was the right
man, and his bed, instead of the kitchen table was the right place for
them to be—together.

Passing through clean, perfect spaces, Marcus led her through an
open niche between the hall and the master bedroom. "I'm going to
show you all of this in the morning, in daylight, just before I fix you
breakfast, and serve it on that table—in the kitchen," he promised,
leading her past a dramatic glasswork shaped like a morning glory
blossom.

"Oh, Marc," Davida breathed as they entered the master bedroom.
"I seem to keep saying that, but this is so . . ." different from the
kind of home you share with a child.

"You like it?" The stark-white bedroom suite, with porthole doors leading into closet and bathroom, had the feel of a commodious, compartmentalized luxury liner.

"I do, Marc." The room had no real external view, so Marcus had painted two murals in his rounded, surrealistic, near cartoon style. They were rustic Jamaican scenes, inspired he told her, by the view from his favorite villa on a beach near Negril.

Delighted, she turned back to him, placing a slow, lazy, deep kiss on his surprised mouth. When he lifted his hands to her, she gently pressed them away, and using his T-shirt, pulled him closer. His hands lifted again, and she again pressed them away, then pulled the T-shirt over his head. Still kissing him, wanting to hold the moment for a lifetime, she caught his hands when they lifted again, pressing them behind his back and holding them there.

Eagerly, Davida pulled at his shirt, glad she could remove it on her own. She exposed the warm glistening skin beneath the T-shirt he'd worn. His bronze chest was marked by a line of curling hair that Davida knew she would willingly follow to its ultimate destination. His chest and shoulders rippled with an unsubtle musculature that she would never have attributed to an artist. Drawing her palms slowly down from his shoulders to his waist gave her a pleasure so intense as to be indescribable. Marcus held his breath, his long-lashed eyes grew heavy lidded, watching her. Davida hoped her pleasure with his body was as obvious to him as his had been to her.

He surprised her by taking a step back and sitting on the huge bed, spilling her into his lap. Freeing his hands, catching and holding her, he aggressively assumed control of the still lingering kisses.

"Oh, Marc." She squirmed beneath his hands. "I'm too heavy for this." She moved her hips, and if he'd been speaking, Marc would have stuttered. "I'm afraid I'll hurt you."

"No you won't," he countered, lowering his face. "I'm just grateful to an abundant God for all your gifts."

The look in his eyes as he finished undressing her excited her. Her body seemed to delight him more with each inch he uncovered. Marc took his time exploring her with his eyes and hands. His murmured praises rippled through her, washing away the remainder of her inhibitions. Beneath his hands, she let her head fall back and her eyes close as he brushed her bare shoulders on his downward path. His open mouth trailed a moist path as he gathered the taste of her salty skin from breast to navel.

Pausing there for only a moment, then dropping lower, his journey forced Davida to bite at her lip to hold back a cry of pleasure and anguish, her hands convulsing at his shoulders. *Lord, how do you do this when there are children in the house?* she wondered vaguely, as his name crossed her lips for the tenth time in as many seconds.

Craving the feel of him against her, praying not to incinerate before she saw his face again, she tugged at him, urging him higher. No longer doubting her physical needs, knowing that Marcus Benton was what she wanted, Davida opened her arms to him and laughed at her own foolishness.

He's too young, he's too short, he's not anything like the man who preceded him through my life. Why had any of that ever mattered? she wondered.

Marc tore at the foil packet and rolled the latex sheath into place, while she waited patiently. Her fingers drifted over the flow of his back, and she marveled at the formation of his spine. It was so amazing how nature knew exactly what to do to make a man.

His task completed, Marc turned to cover her, his tongue filling her eager mouth in bold imitation of the more intimate joining to come. Davida welcomed his weight, and moist silky flesh weighed the heavy, throbbing evidence of arousal, with satisfaction gained only when two shudderingly became one. Their limbs became fluid, their bodies sinuous as they moved together, hands skimming, caressing, their mouths seeking and sampling. Urgent whispers and harsh, ragged breaths testified to their pleasure—pleasure that burned along the boundaries of pain.

Rigid with the effort of restraint, he groaned and flexed, his mouth covering hers when she would have cried out in pleasure so complete that she'd forgotten her need for discretion. Her heart beating against his, her body entwined with his, Davida opened her eyes to find Marcus looking back at her, his eyes penetrating the shadows surrounding them, and holding her more tenderly than the most precious jewel. Abruptly she realized that what she felt was more, much more, than desire.

Oh, no. This can't be love. Freeing her hand to stroke his sweaty brow and shoulders, she watched his eyes. His eyes beseeched her, begged her to recognize what it was she felt, and she had to remind herself to breathe. Afraid to name the volcanic emotion swelling within her chest, Davida squeezed her eyes shut, concentrating on the physical, the definable. Willingly surrendering to the trust Marc's whispers called for, she clung to him in breathless anticipation. Anticipation was nothing compared to the reality.

Her toes clenched, her breath locked in her throat, and her face was flooded by heat. She tried to cry out, but her voice was gone and she could do nothing more than gasp. His muffled groan signaled his own release, and then he was shuddering in her arms. Hot tears blinded her to everything but Marcus Benton, and she wanted to share everything with him. Holding him tightly, her heart aching and defining emotions she'd tried to deny, Davida pressed her lips tightly and found she couldn't speak.

For no reason she would ever be able to name, Davida suddenly heard Mama Lou's voice run through her head. Clearly and distinctly. *"They're all the same size when they lie down."* Mama Lou was a very wise woman, but she hadn't told Davida anything about what it would feel like to fall in love with this little man who was so very different from anything and everything she'd ever expected.

Slowly recovering, with Marc's heart beating beneath her cheek, Davida closed her eyes and savored Marcus Benton in full. How could she have known it would be like this? How could she have anticipated something she'd never experienced—even in her dreams? How could she regret knowing such intimate and consuming ecstasy, even if only for now? She couldn't.

"Davida?"

She stirred lazily, stretching with feline grace. "Mmm?"

He reached out to snap on the small lamp on the nightstand, making both of them blink in its glow. "Are you, um, okay."

She shifted, her cheek moving from his chest to the pillow at his side. Adjusting her head to see better, she smiled slowly. "I'm fine, Marc." His lips captured the fingertip that traced his lips. He sucked at it gently, finally closing his hand on her wrist to turn the palm up, where he planted another kiss.

"See, Marc," she said softly, her words riding the crest of a sigh. "You're trying to start things, again, and that's what I wanted to talk to you about." She rose on one elbow to look at him. A study in ebony and gold, her skin a timeless flow of satin perfection, she coiled closer, her legs folding over his to bind him to her. Ivory sheets wrapped around them, slid low, revealing the deep crevasse separating the fullness of her breasts, which rose and fell with her breathing. "You once told me that this could go on . . . all night long . . ."

"Are you asking for proof?" Marc lay on his back looking up into the face he'd once compared to an African queen, pleased by her nodding assent.

"But this time," Davida said, "can we leave the light on? I want to see everything, maybe take a few notes. You know"—she smiled, her tongue trying her lips and tasting him—"for later."

CHAPTER SIXTEEN

The office suite on the fifteenth floor of the Robert A. Young building wasn't all that different from any other business office designed and built during the late twentieth century—unless you happened to be Davida Lawrence. If you were Davida Lawrence, nice carpeting, recessed lighting, and carefully filtered heating and air-conditioning systems meant nothing to you. The new I.R.S. computer and telephone systems, along with a slew of serious and hyperefficient employees meant even less.

The Robert A. Young building had felt an awful lot like a prison since her return from Atlanta. Removing her gold-rimmed reading glasses, Davida closed her eyes and tried to ground herself, but it didn't work. She didn't want to be grounded. In fact, if you'd asked her right then, she wanted to be anywhere except where she was. *No,* she thought, bringing the glasses to her lips and carefully tapping her front teeth together on their tips. That wasn't exactly true. The one place she wanted to be more than anything was in the arms of a certain artist down in Atlanta.

Fingering the side piece of her glasses, she tried applying common sense to her predicament.

She was at work. She was supposed to be working—not remembering. From where she sat, common sense was going down in flames.

A short sigh caught her twirling her glasses in a slow circle on the desktop, and she closed her eyes only to see Marc's face, all golden skin, bottomless brown eyes, and touchingly sculptured undeniably male planes and angles beneath the sweetness of his beautifully curving lips, as he leaned closer to kiss her over a cup of coffee and the *Atlanta Journal-Constitution.* It was a tender, long-lasting kiss distinguished by the soft brush of his long lashes against her intensely sensitized skin. That was Marc, completely inscribed with a palpable maleness so instinctively inborn and natural that she could still feel and smell, and almost taste, though he was hundreds of miles away.

Opening her eyes, Davida caught her lip between her teeth and knew she couldn't pretend to work any longer. The engulfing surge of heat that she tried to dissipate with a fanning hand wasn't going anywhere, and the urge to talk to him was almost overwhelming. She needed to hear his voice, just his regular speaking voice. He could talk to her, in his resonant and warm voice, about anything, and she still wanted to hear it. Heck, the man could read the phone book right now, and Davida knew she would sit and listen to him do it.

They'd talked for hours in Atlanta, and it wasn't enough. They'd talked face to face about so much of what had only been shared over the phone in the past, and it was nowhere near enough. They'd talked in bed, whispering and giggling together and murmuring in timeless agreement, and Davida knew it wouldn't be enough to last her life-time—but it would have to do. She had to return to her daughter and her real life. That's what you did when you had responsibilities, she knew it then, just as well as she knew it now. But, that didn't make it any easier, or cure her from longing to hear his voice. Reaching for the telephone, she stopped, her hand hovering above it.

It's not like we spend all our time talking dirty, or anything, Davida thought defensively. And, all that talk certainly must have done some good. The first thing Davida heard on her return to work was all about how good she looked, how relaxed she looked. Quita had followed her everywhere, begging for details.

"So? Talk to me." Quita was close enough to whisper this morning, as they stood near the copier. Tell me how it went, how things were between you? You've been back all this time, and you haven't said a word. Was it as good as you thought it would be?" Feeling obviously deserving of details, she did everything but sit up and beg.

"Quita, stop asking me questions," Davida finally demanded. "When I have something to tell you, I will. Until then, don't ask." She shook a warning finger to drive home the admonishment. Quita backed off—for the moment.

The fight for privacy was difficult. Quita had managed to get both Glenn and Melanie to pick up where she left off. Glenn called last night, checking up, he said, on his frat brother, and the doings of his Crimson and Cream brothers. When she'd been slow to answer, he'd begun the slow methodical probing that worked so well in legal arenas.

Finally, reaching her badgering limits, Davida had cut him off. "Butch," she said wearily, "this is no *voir dire*. I have nothing else to tell you. G'nite." She hung up on his retort.

Mel was even less successful. Leaving the shampoo bowl at Phillipe's Friday afternoon, she'd used one hand to hold her towel wrapped hair in place and the other to tap Davida's arm. "So, how was your trip?"

"Really good, actually." Davida seated herself at a dryer, and smiled, pointedly opening an issue of *Black Hair*.

"Well, girl, we all need time away." She took a deep breath and sighed. "Just coming back to the day to day grind"—she winked—"it takes a minute to reacclimate yourself."

"You understand exactly." Davida winked back, and lowered the dryer hood. Burying her eyes in her magazine, she was glad she could claim not to hear her friend over the roar of the hot black dryer.

As much as Davida wanted to tell, to share her feelings, she wanted to hold them in—to savor and relive them all on her own. She wanted to take her feelings out and examine them one at a time at her leisure. Aside from that, if she was going to talk to anyone about how she felt, it was to the man who'd raised all these roiling and sometimes conflicting feelings in her soul. Her eyes wandered to the phone, remembering the Caller ID unit that still sat on the table beside her bed, and she smiled at the deep sense of déjà vu washing over her.

Her nails tapped at the telephone casing. She couldn't call him from here. She was at work, and she'd talked to him every night for the last two weeks. She knew he was not even at the loft right now. He was handling storyboards today. The best she could do was leave a message. A message saying . . . *I love you Marcus James Benton. I love you and I miss you. and I can't seem to do my job without taking this time to just say the words for you.* "I sound like a Stevie Wonder song," she moaned.

I love you. she could have said it, but she didn't. *Why?* She wished she'd said the words at Hartsfield Airport, before boarding her flight to St. Louis. She wished she'd said the words to him standing there with her fingers linked with his, her arm curved through his, close enough to smell the expensive, citrus magic of his cologne, and feeling the mild stubble of his unshaven cheek against hers.

"Seven A.M. is too early for saying goodbye," he'd whispered, his breath lightly touching the tiny diamond stud in her ear. "Seven A.M. is too early for wearing these clothes." His fingers traced the curving neckline of her coral colored blouse. "These are traveling clothes, going away from me clothes. It's not too late to change them."

Without moving, they both watched the airline crew prepare for boarding passengers, and part of her longed to agree with him. Part of her wanted to run away with him and be wherever fate would allow.

But I have responsibilities. Those were the words she'd said to him.

The responsible, logical part of her heart and mind backed away from anything but her planned and known itinerary. Torn and reluctant to say anything, squeezing his fingers tightly, wanting to stay so badly it hurt, Davida knew she would get on the plane. She knew she would leave him. *Maybe if I'd said it then,* she thought, *told him what I really thought and felt, maybe then I could stop saying it now.*

But, at least they'd had goodbye. Davida turned her chair to the wall to hide her face. Anyone looking at her right now would know exactly what she was thinking. Her fingertips pressed her lips. If she'd been standing, Davida knew her knees would be as buttery soft now as they were in Atlanta. When final boarding was called for her flight, Davida'd stepped closer, her hand going to his cheek and resting there. Her light, fluttery kiss brushed his lips lightly. It was meant to be a kiss of closure, of farewell to a fantasy interlude.

But a low sigh from Marc's lips put an end to softness and a lie to farewell. His hands at her elbows pulled her closer. "That's no way to say goodbye to someone you're going to see again," he whispered against her lips, taking full control of the kiss.

At the first touch of his lips on hers, she moved her hands up, over his shoulders, touching first the skin at the nape of his neck, then holding on for dear life. Pulling her closer, barely on the side of public decency, Marcus molded her lips to fit his, holding the swell of her bottom lip until the full of her mouth opened to him.

Assuming permission, his tongue, probing and molten, sent shocked waves of passion rocketing through Davida's body, and everything in her soul declared him real and not a fantasy at all. Davida knew her life could never be the same.

Almost as quickly as the kiss began, it was over. When Marc stepped away, Davida held on, startled by her own small whimper. Reaching forward, stripped of subtle impulses, she traced the moistness of his bottom lip with the pad of her thumb. Watching his eyes, she questioned the wisdom of leaving him behind.

His gaze was filled with unquestionable desire. Stepping back completely, his arms at his sides, his eyes still embraced her. "That was a proper goodbye," he said.

And now, here she sat at her desk in St. Louis anticipating what to say to him; trying to find the words that best fit between goodbye and hello.

Davida looked at the phone again and made another move toward the receiver, then paused. She lowered her hand back to the hard wooden surface of her desk, knowing that such a call wasn't going to happen. Not this morning, it was the wrong thing for a hardworking single mother to do on her good government job. *Besides,* she scolded herself, *what do I sound like, going out of town, sleeping with a man I met on the telephone, and then talking myself into an infatuation?*

She could do better than this. She stood and ran her fingers around the band of her skirt, adjusting her blouse. She was at work, she was going to work—in a minute.

Walking toward the door, thinking coffee, or at least a cup of tea, might clear her head, Davida stopped, bringing two fingers to the bridge of her nose. Wondering at the sudden stuffiness she felt, she turned back to her desk. If she remembered correctly, she'd left a couple of decongestant tablets there the last time she'd had a sinus attack. Sliding into her chair, she smiled at the long red pleated skirt she wore. It was one of her Atlanta purchases. Before Marc, she'd never worn red. It never felt like her before. She smoothed her hand over the twill fabric and was glad she'd met the talented man who made her feel like wearing red.

Folding the foil tab back on her decongestants, Davida flicked it with her thumb. It was funny, but Marcus also made her want to wear regal gold and sassy orange, dramatic shades of purple, and flighty, flamboyant silver. Being with Marcus made her want to wear romantic lace and small silky things not necessarily designed to be seen in any but the most intimate of circumstances. Davida smiled down at her fingers. Deb Thomas noticed it when they went shopping in Atlanta.

"Girl"—Deb lifted a sheer leopard print bra, and made a face—"you keep this up, and you're going to own most of Victoria's little secrets. It looks to me like you're shopping to please a man."

"Maybe, or maybe I just think they're pretty," Davida replied modestly, taking the bra and looking at her fingers through the sheer fabric.

"They'll look good with these," Deb drawled, using her index fingers to dance a matching leopard thong panty under Davida's nose. Davida wrinkled her nose, then lifted the thong from the teasing fingers. "Funny how we lose our minds when we turn forty, isn't it, girl?"

Davida looked away to hide her face. "I haven't lost my mind," she said evenly. "It's a matching set, and I intend to put it on my forty-year-old body."

"And you always wear those matching sets . . . at home, right?"

Looking down at Milton Thomas's short wife, the woman she'd instantly bonded with, Davida tapped her teeth with her tongue. "And your point is?"

"Smell this." Deb spritzed them both with pear nectar body spray.

"I think he's good for you, and I know you're what he's been waiting for."

"Oh, I don't know what you mean," Davida returned, smoothing a scent-matched lotion onto her hands, then sniffing.

"Sure you do. You already told me how you floundered around, mourning Skip all those years, and after that, you sank yourself into your daughter and your work. In less than five days, you look and act like an entirely different woman." Deb made a face. "Besides, you forget, I know Marc, and now I've met you. You know, you said yourself—"

"I talk too much," Davida interrupted, crossing the store and growing interested in a midnight-colored satin and lace peignoir.

"Been there. Done that." Deb turned the price tag on the peignoir and shook her head. "Don't buy that—overpriced." She made a face. "ee cummings once said, 'don't worry about life, you'll never live through it.' "

"What he meant"—Deb shook back a wave of locks that fell toward her eye—"what he meant was, there's good news and there's bad news." Davida looked at her and waited. "The good news is that, as long as you're alive, you have endless opportunities to exploit your life. The bad news is that when it's over, it really is over." She put her hand on her hip and smiled dangerously. "Marc is part of the good news."

"You know, Marc said you were a smart woman." Davida walked back to the table they'd started at and picked up the sheer panties and bra, draped them over her arm along with the black silk teddy and the red lace nightgown, then headed for the counter. "I think he might be right."

"Oh, he's right, and I oughta know. I'm older than Milt, too."

"You are?"

"Yeah, but you know"—she threw the heavy fall of her dredlocks over her shoulder and ignored the slender eavesdropping sales woman in the short black dress and hot pink shop apron—"there's a lot to be said for the intellectual flexibility of younger men. Besides"—she shrugged—"you don't owe the world an accounting or an apology for your man's age."

"Who said he was 'my man'?"

"Every little move you make, girl."

All the way home, Davida heard Deb's words whispering through her mind, a mantra of possibility.

In her office, Davida crossed her legs, liking the slide of the narrow pleats of her skirt against her sheer hose. The whisper of the cloth sounded feminine and suggested something she didn't think you were supposed to think about in business offices. She sniffed, testing her breathing ability, then yawned. Her ears popped. It was only eleven by her watch, odd that she felt like this at this hour.

Maybe the tea could wait. It was almost lunch time anyway. She reached for the stack of files she'd left on the side of her desk. "MacMillan, MacNamarra," she squinted at the next folder, and had to put her glasses on to read the name. "McLaughlin," she swung her chair around, intent on pulling more records, and had to stop. The sudden motion made her slightly dizzy and she stuck out her tongue. "Yuck, I hate when my sinus act up like this, and it always happens after an airplane flight."

Things could have been worse, though, she already knew. She could have been like Destiny. With her daughter's sickle-cell disease, the air pressure, changes in temperature, and possible dehydration made air travel uncomfortable at best, and near impossible at worst. Davida sniffed again. A little congestion wasn't an awfully high price to pay for the time she'd had with Marc.

"The time I had with Marc," Davida said and hugged herself tightly, realized what she was doing and let her arms fall lower to fold beneath her breasts. She'd been like this for two weeks, ever since she left Atlanta. Waiting by the telephone for his call, the chance to hear his voice again. And his voice got better and better every time she heard it. She even had Des eager for his next visit.

That was a little scary, the idea of having Marc and Des together in their home. Interacting in their home. That was the current "pop" psychological term for having them together, wasn't it? The sterile term didn't do a lot to ease the question she felt undefined at the edges of thought. Marcus Benton was coming to visit her and her daughter, and she still didn't feel right about having him sleeping in her home. Having him there in her bed, with her daughter sleeping across the hall.

"Marc, I know it's unusual, but I'm not sure how I would explain . . ."

And he was wonderful about it. "I understand, Boo. Tell you what, why don't I plan on a hotel for this trip. I don't want to crowd you and Des on such short notice." He was thoughtful, and that was just one more thing to love about him, though in the meantime, she worried. What's the proper etiquette for having a man her child knew was not her father, in her bed? Davida didn't have a clue. And her daughter was so excited about him, she's doing the everlasting dance of joy.

Davida had no words for how uncomfortable that dance made her.

It was normal to have him visit in their home. He was a friend, more than a friend—now. Davida had, up until Marcus Benton, always shied away from bringing men into her home and her life with Destiny, not wanting to confuse the child. Destiny knew her father's name and face, mostly from old photos. She even had a few very early memories of the big man—but she wasn't sure how many of them were real, and how many were figments of her desire for a daddy.

The three of them together in her house, like a family, and Des was looking forward to it. She was already asking questions. Destiny had always asked questions, almost it seemed, from the moment she could speak. But this time, the questions were different—not Tawanna Mallory inspired different, but very different. "Is Marc anything like my daddy?" she asked while watching television. "Do you think Marc would make a good daddy?" popped out a few days later. "If you were looking for a man to marry, do you think you could marry Marc?" erupted over breakfast last Saturday.

When Destiny widened her brown eyes last night, and fixed them on her mother, Davida knew she was in trouble. "What is it, honey?" she asked with some trepidation.

"I was wondering." On her knees, Destiny moved closer to where her mother sat reading. "I was wondering, if we axed . . ." She caught the warning look on her mother's face and corrected herself. "I was wondering if we asked him, would Marc marry us?"

Davida looked at her daughter and tried to pinpoint a place in time where this inspiration had dawned. Destiny, shining skin and brilliant eyes as dark and lustrous as her mother's, brushed her shoulder-length plaits and brightly colored barrettes back from her face and continued. "When you went to Atlanta, did Marc say anything to you about marrying . . . us?"

Hesitant, hoping she wasn't setting her child up for some extreme and unpredictable disappointment, Davida shook her head.

"No? Well, why not? Isn't that what comes next?"

"Next?" Davida hated the helpless feeling engulfing her.

"Yes. He likes you and he likes me, right? An' if he likes you so much . . . ? So, then if he doesn't ask you, or us, or . . . whatever, then do we have to ask him? If we ever want to get married, do we?"

"Des, that's not quite the way it works." Now how did she explain this? Davida knew she had words, somewhere in her vocabulary, words to explain what was going on with her and Marcus.

"Or is it sex? Did I get it backward? Is sex what comes next?" Destiny, her eyes wide and innocent was waiting for an answer.

Helplessness gave way to queasy speechlessness. "Des, sex is a very private thing, between a man and a woman . . ."

"A man and a woman, huh? Well, if Marc marries you, then don't I get to come along?"

Opening her arms to her daughter, Davida found her tongue. "Of course you do, sweetie. We're a package deal."

"Yeah, 'cause I'm your loved one, right?" The little girl hugged her mother's neck tightly. "We're two for the price of one."

Two for the price of one. That sure wasn't something Marc talked about in Atlanta. Davida's chair rocked slightly as her foot tapped the floor beneath her desk. Her arms moved to hug her body again.

And it was bound to come up again, that question about sex and marriage. How was she ever going to explain and make it clear to Des how she felt about Marc and why they'd moved to share themselves without making it sound cavalier and too easy? She'd always promise herself she wasn't going to be one of those "do as I say, not as I do" mothers, and Lord, here she was. Just the thinking was hard. Propping her elbow on her desk, resting her chin in her palm, Davida wondered what she would actually say to Destiny, when the time came. She looked at her telephone again, wishing it would ring.

What in the world am I going to say to her? she worried, because the time was rapidly approaching.

CHAPTER SEVENTEEN

Quickly crossing the greenery-flanked ivory and gold lobby of the Regal Riverfront Hotel, Davida took only a moment to congratulate herself on remembering. Just before leaving the house, she'd paused to reroll the collar of her olive turtlenecked sweater in front of the hall mirror, and it struck her. Turning, she'd run back upstairs to pull the shoe box from her closet. The neat, narrow, low-heeled loafers she chose were casual and comfortable, right with her pant-suit. They were also exactly right for coming face to face with a not-very-tall man who liked looking into your eyes.

Her low heels tapped the gold-veined marble path slicing across the subtly figured carpet. It was difficult forcing air into her tight chest as she tried not to run to him. *You can slow down, you know,* she warned herself just as her elbow brushed a tall, ebony-skinned man in a navy-blue business suit. "Excuse me," she murmured with a slight and apologetic smile.

At the sound of her voice, he turned and looked at her. Hazel eyes, that looked like he'd been born knowing how to use them, swept over her seeking the little internal switch that would turn on the reaction he wanted. Liking what he saw, the man shifted his newspaper and briefcase to his opposite hand. "It's alright." He smiled, touching her elbow. His eyes, smoky and deep, invited her to say more, to tarry longer.

He paused for just a second too long, the extended moment suggesting more than anyone in a hotel lobby needed to know. Davida inclined her brows, and kept moving. Tall and good looking, with a voice like silk and a smile like sin, he wasn't her type and there was no need to waste her time. Davida walked a little faster. Her type was waiting upstairs.

That was a cute way to put it—her type. Davida pressed her lips together, suppressing a smile and drawing appreciative glances from a pair of men sitting in comfortable armchairs, ostensibly reading the daily newspaper. It was funny, but not so long ago, she thought of Marcus Benton as being anything but, her type. He was too young, too short, too lacking in direction, and too . . . too everything. Worst of all, at first, he too definitely wasn't Skip. Now, the smile broke through, and her breath quickened. She had to stop for control. Now, he was all she could think of. She wasn't sure where they were going, and she was not at all sure about that "walk on faith," she'd promised them both—but she cared enough to take that walk with him.

Reaching the bank of elevators, Davida pressed the up button. His room was on the eighth floor. Waiting, she pulled at an odd string on her sleeve. Looking up, watching the numbers slowly descend, she fingered the buttons on her double-breasted jacket and tried to be patient. *This must be how guys feel when they come to pick up that first date,* she thought, tapping her foot against the marble flooring. *It's only lunch, and I'm so nervous I could scream.*

Maybe it was her imagination, but she could have sworn the elevators were no longer moving. A quick glance at her watch, a gift from Jewell on Davida's twenty-first birthday, convinced her she was right. The elevators were not moving. She slapped at her leg with her black leather clutch bag, and watched the lit displays. Why weren't the elevators moving? And, just as suddenly, they were moving again. The brass doors whispered open, spilling their passengers all around her. A small boy, all round cheeks, big eyes, and too much curly hair toddled near and grabbed for her. His mother made a gallant lunge and caught him just before he tumbled into Davida.

"Winston, you've got to watch where you're going," the mother cooed, catching him up in a hug and angling her twisted hair away from the child.

"Gaaa-aaah!" Winston sang and waved chubby fingers at the object of his affection. Davida waved back.

"I'm sorry," the mother said in an almost inaudible voice. "He doesn't usually take to strangers." Winston planted his feet against his mother's body and pushed, definite in his effort to get to Davida. "Winston . . ."

"It's okay," she said. Drawing a finger beneath the child's chin, she was struck by the poignancy of his smile. "I'm a mommy, too," she said. "How old is he?" Davida asked the question without moving her eyes from the little boy's.

"Fourteen months." The mother patted his back.

When Davida widened her eyes and made a face that ended with a softly blown kiss across his chubby fingers, Winston laughed and reached for her. He reminded her of Destiny at that same age.

"He likes you," the mother said, still patting. "How many do you have?"

"Only one. She's eight." Davida touched the wiggly fingertips Winston offered.

"You're good with kids." The mother looked at her across the child's back. "You should have more."

Caught off guard, Davida looked at her and blinked. Oh, she didn't think so, not at forty. She shook her head and unrolled her finger from the little boy's strong grip. "See ya later, Winston," she whispered, then ducked into the elevator.

Alone in the elevator, Davida looked up at the changing numbers. Little Winston with his tenderly moist brown baby skin, curly hair, and gorgeous new-tooth smile, stayed on her mind, but . . . *Another baby at forty?* She shook her head, talk about a major undertaking. My God, she'd be—she did quick mental math—she'd be fifty-eight by the time that child finished high school. Then there'd be college, and . . . what if a second child also carried sickle cell . . . ? She clutched her purse to her breast.

The doors slid open and she stepped into the corridor. Feeling unsteady, thrown off by her encounter with Winston and his mother, Davida fought the urge to walk with her hand flattened against the rose and gray flecked strawcloth walls. A deep breath helped her get her bearings and she turned left, following the numbers to Marcus Benton's suite.

The Regal Riverfront was a beautiful hotel, known for luxurious appointments, and it occurred to her to wonder if Marcus had used the hotel before. And if he had, what had he used it for? After all, he had a sister here, and Renee made it clear that her brother stayed with her whenever he came to St. Louis. The only thing Marcus Benton might need a hotel room for was, something . . . like this? Meeting someone . . . like this? Standing outside his door, clutching her handbag, Davida looked at her feet.

She'd come this far because she thought she knew what kind of man Marc was. She'd shared things with him over the past seven or eight months that she wouldn't share with her closest friends or family. Marc was not a player or a liar. He'd been honest enough not to play games with her, thus far. He was in this hotel because of her. He was in this city because of her. *He's this committed to you, do what you came here for,* she told herself, fisting her hand and raising it to knock.

Before her hand struck the ivory door, it swung inward, and Marc stood there smiling. The delightful, dimple-bracketed smile, and incredibly long-lashed eyes were unmistakable, but this was a different Marcus Benton. Different from the free spirit she enjoyed on the telephone, and from the tender lover she'd known in Atlanta. This Marcus Benton was a suitor. Handsome and intent and all business, he'd even dressed for the occasion. The charcoal Armani suit, slate-blue silk shirt, and geometrically patterned tie looked like formal wear on him. The dimples flashed and her heart clenched. *Those dimples,* she thought, *they make one heck of an accessory.*

Recovering from the immediate surprise of his attire, Davida offered a smile. "I was just about to knock. How did you know I was here?"

"It felt like you on the other side," he said simply. "I would know you anywhere, Davida." Stepping back, he invited her to enter with a sweep of his arm.

The sight that greeted her took her breath away. The suite's sitting room was gorgeous. Crystal and brass, accented with fragrant cut flowers. A pale rose carpet, so deep and soft she could have comfortably slept on it, covered the broad expanse of the room she entered. Overstuffed sofas and chairs, covered in elegant, pale-toned velvet and brocade, rested companionably about the room.

An open doorway gave her a glimpse of a bedroom done in the same elegant theme. In the center of the sitting room was a small, round, white-linen-covered table, beautifully set for two. The dark neck of a heavy glass bottle showed above the curving lip of a silver ice bucket. Flowers and candles were everywhere. From somewhere in the background, she heard music playing softly. Indistinct, but fluid, she wondered at the artist. Fourplay? Marsalis? She couldn't be sure.

"I'm impressed," she admitted. She wished she could close him and all of this into her hands and hold on to it for an eternity. If she'd tried Davida knew she couldn't have dreamed a more perfect setting.

"I couldn't find a room with a fireplace in the city, Boo."

She hadn't realized that her eyes had filled with tears until the room blurred in front of her, and she was forced to blink to clear her vision. He'd remembered her words, every one of her words from the night they'd talked of seduction. He'd remembered, and made it real for her. "Oh, Marc."

The trace of vulnerability that colored his voice wrenched her heart when he asked, "Do you like it?"

The smile she offered trembled at the edges. "I love it, Marc. No one's ever done anything like this for me before." Though she didn't want to think of him, just then, Davida couldn't help thinking that

Skip would never have arranged an afternoon like this. His pleasure in Davida had been in her willingness to invest herself in him, in their family, not in sharing candlelit intimacy for two.

Marc caught her hand and lifted it to his lips. "I wanted to give you your fantasy," he murmured. Turning her hand slowly, he placed a kiss in her palm, then folded her fingers closed over it.

"You have," she whispered, looking at her palm, "more than once." How was it he didn't know? How was it he knew so much about her, and still didn't know *he was her fantasy?*

Marc moved closer, his arm slipping around her waist and his other hand catching the back of her neck to bring her mouth to his. She could feel his radiant body heat enveloping her, as the pad of his thumb crossed her lower lip. If it bothered him that she stood face-to-face, on the same level with him, it never showed in his kiss. When her lips parted for his searing tongue, his breath was a low and ardent hissing sound. He stormed her mouth like a starving man, drawing her deeply and leaving her gasping. The discreet knock on the door made him draw back.

"That would be the waiter. Luncheon is served, madam." He faked a very bad British accent, making "madam" sound like "moddom." Stepping back from him, touching the corners of her mouth with her fingers, Davida smiled back.

There was so much about him to smile about. Slipping free of her wool tweed jacket, allowing him to place it on the back of her chair, Davida enjoyed the renewed thrill of being cherished, something he'd taught her in Atlanta. "Because you're a flower," he'd said over dinner. "I will always cherish and adore you." Then his thumb stroked her wrist, finding the rapid fluttering throb of her pulse. "You know, a man who can't appreciate a flower doesn't deserve a garden." He'd leaned closer. "The life I want with you, Boo, is a garden well worth planting seeds for."

Is that what we're doing here, Marc? Planting seeds? She wanted to ask, but didn't dare. Their times together were too few and too far in between to risk questions. Besides, fantasies were known for their frailty.

They lingered a long time over the exquisite meal he'd ordered, talking quietly, savoring tastes and scents and the pleasures of being together. The champagne bottle was empty, the dessert plates cleared, the waiters gone before Marc rose from the table. The overcast fall day seemed to be cooperating with Davida's fantasy, insulating them, isolating them within the flickering illumination of the dozens of candles arranged on every glossy surface and reflecting in the golden-brown depths of his eyes. When he held out his hand, Davida looked at it then up at him.

"Dance with me," he said.

She placed her hands in his. A seductively slow version of something moody—Lauryn Hill, she thought—began to drift from the hidden speakers. Kicking off her loafers, she stepped into Marc's arms and placed her cheek next to his. The feel of him, firm and lean, and unquestionably male, made her want to close her fingers on him. Closing her eyes, she knew this would forever after be one of her all-time favorite songs, and she would think of this man each time she heard it. Such things were always the remnants of fantasies.

The carpet was too plush for fancy steps, but Davida couldn't have minded less. She was content to sway in Marc's arms, her cheek against his, their bodies pressed so tightly together that not even a breath of air might have passed between them. His hand rested warmly at her waist, slowly moving to the base of her spine, with just enough pressure to mold her hips more intimately to his own. Obviously aroused, sensitized to her nearness, Marcus seemed in no hurry to end their leisurely dance.

His slightly ragged breath ruffled the fine hairs at the nape of her neck. She turned her head, dropping her face to taste the firm line of his jaw, her lips nibbling delicately at his smoothly shaven skin. His responding groan rumbled deep in his chest, vibrating against her. His hand tightened on her back, then slowly slid downward to press against the rounded firmness of her soft hip.

Davida brought her teasing tongue to the tip of his earlobe, before catching it between her teeth, pulling it gently between her lips. Marc swallowed audibly, then released her hand from its dancing position to place it against his chest, and moved his own hand to the thickness of her dark hair.

The weight and curve of her head felt natural, resting in his palm. Her short, curling hair caressed his fingers like an old and welcoming friend. The oval lift of her cheeks, the high royal arch that defined her brow, the libidinous curve of her lips, all shadowed and made mystical by the candlelight, delighted him. Seeing her so close again, knowing her as the sweet creation of a benevolent spirit, Marc indulged his artist's eye in the feast of color and layered shape that made up the face of the woman he would love for however long the fates would allow. It made him smile to know that loving her was not a matter of anything he'd made up his mind to do. It was simply the only thing he could do.

Closing his eyes, Marcus buried his face in her neck, and inhaled deeply. Drawing on her scent, he never tried to resist the seduction of her femininity, and it wouldn't have mattered if he had. He knew it even before she turned her face to his, offering her lips. Like a starving man, he devoured her mouth, hungrily seeking his fill. She returned his kiss with a reckless abandon that shocked and tantalized them both.

Working her fingers between them, Davida tugged at the knot of his silk tie. She left it hanging loose and began to unbutton his shirt, still moving to the strains of the music, brushing her lips across his dimpled cheek. The open shirt spread easily beneath her moving fingers. She felt Marc tug at her sweater and removed it herself. The sheer leopard print Victoria's Secret bra was hardly an obstacle as Marc found the front closure. Her unbound breasts, already swelling from his touch, brushed his bared chest, causing them both to shiver in sensual response. Davida slipped her arms around his neck, beneath the collar of his open shirt, bringing herself more snugly against him.

"I love being alone with you like this," he muttered, his arms holding her as though he feared her escape.

He was warm. So very warm, and strong—pulsingly strong. Davida wondered how she'd lost this memory or allowed it to fade. She felt the ripple of his muscles against her and luxuriated in all the differences between male and female, and how beautifully they meshed in the mating dance. The song ended. Another began. Lauryn Hill sang of being too good to be true, and Davida's heart sang along. Marc, in time to the new song, rocked her against him. Pushing one leg between hers, making her aware for the first time that the front zipper of her slacks had been opened. His hands again found the heated bare skin at the base of her spine and pushed lower on the revealed curve. He inhaled sharply when he discovered the narrow, cleft-dividing string of her thong panties, leaving bare but unseen skin to his touch.

"You did this on purpose?" he asked hoarsely. "Just to drive me straight over the edge?"

"Yes," she answered, then caught his lower lip between her teeth.

Marcus groaned and caught the back of her head, catching her with a kiss that sent the room spinning around her. The leg he'd inserted between hers thrust forward as his fingers moved, knowingly finding their target. The blatantly sexual move made her shudder, and her fingers dug into his shoulders. "Marc!"

His eyes glinted wickedly when he lifted his head to give her a roguish pirate's smile. "I hope you're not in any hurry this afternoon."

Her hips moved now without his guidance. "Not a bit," she replied in a voice thick with hunger.

"Good," he replied, covering her mouth with his.

"I have to get dressed," Davida murmured, expressing sated regret to the end of a perfect interlude. The man at her side used his thumb to smooth strands of tousled hair from her eyes, and enjoying his touch, she let him.

Marc's arm tightened around her bare shoulders. "Don't do that." He lifted the sheet, looked down, then back at her, shaking his head. "Please don't do that."

She smiled and lifted her head to look at him. "I fear I must," she lazily informed him. "I have to pick Destiny up by five, and even if it is a Saturday, I kind of need to do it on time."

Shifting languidly against the pillows, Marcus stroked a hand from her shoulder to her hip, dislodging the covering sheet. "I'd like to keep you here—just like this—forever." He slid a hand into the thickness of her hair, fingered the strands and pulled her mouth to his. "I'd like to be your life, a big part of your life—forever," he whispered against her kiss-swollen lips.

Closing her hands against the soft curl of his hair, Davida held the kiss they exchanged for as long as she dared. Of all the kisses they'd shared, this one was different. This one said things she wasn't entirely ready to hear. This one offered to keep all the promises their bodies had already made. She drew back, shaken, her smile wavering. "I've got to get dressed," she repeated, avoiding his eyes as she scooted toward the side of the bed. "And so do you, if you're coming with me."

She disappeared into the bathroom.

The reflection she saw in the wide bathroom mirror made Davida draw back in horror. Her lips had a swollen, bruised look, while her cheeks bore a tint that no cosmetic manufacturer had ever designed, and her eyes . . . dark and passion glazed was the best she could call them. She looked . . . she looked . . . she looked like she'd just spent hours making mad, passionate, unrestrained, unrepentant love. Which, up until thirty minutes ago, was exactly what she'd been doing.

She showered quickly, her head wrapped in a towel. She scrubbed away her faded makeup and the warm comfortable scent of herself mingled with the man whose bed she'd just left. Toweled dry, she pulled a comb through her hair and did fresh makeup. Pulling her sweater on, she retouched her hair. Studying her image, she thought she looked better. Not her best, but definitely less satiated.

Glancing at her watch, she figured she would just manage to get across town to Aunt Wesie's. And, if she was lucky, Aunt Wesie wouldn't ask any questions—even after she saw Marc.

He returned to the main room just as she did. His hair was damp, and he was wearing jeans and dark socks. Carrying his shirt and belt, he seemed oblivious to her staring. The wide planes of his shoulders and disciplined tapering of his waist called to the hands that had so recently claimed him. He was so erotically stimulating, that Davida stumbled over her own bare feet, catching herself with a hand on the back of the taupe velvet armchair. Her fingers clenched the fabric, and she was suddenly all too aware of the wildly rumpled bed they'd left behind.

Was this the only way to have a fantasy? To let it happen to you, around you, then walk away from it? She looked at Marcus again. It must be. If you could live like this always, it would be called reality, wouldn't it? He dropped his shoes to the floor, like any other normal man. *This has to be reality,* Davida told herself. *Living a fantasy could only kill a real woman, but, man, what a smile it would leave on your face.*

He shoved his feet into his own loafers. "I guess we can go, if you're ready." He pushed his hands into his pockets and looked at the floor. Davida looked out the window.

If I'm ready? She didn't like the sudden awkwardness between them, the uncharacteristic lack of expression in his eyes. It was as if he were deliberately distancing himself from her for some reason. Had he reached the same conclusion she had? That afternoons like this were not meant for people like her? For people who had to remain anchored to the real world?

Casting one last look at the bedroom, Davida turned toward the door. Just reaching it, she felt Marc's hand on her shoulder, turning her to face him. Leaning into her body, pressing her back against the door, he framed her face with his hands and kissed her until they were both gasping for breath.

"Now, we can go," he told her, finally drawing away.

"Yes," she repeated dazedly. Moistening her lips with the tip of her tongue, she looked at him. How had she ever seen his eyes as flat, devoid of emotion. It was there, swirling and pulsing just beneath the surface. Placing her hand in his, she dared look at those long-lashed eyes again. "Now, we can go."

The door to the suite closed behind them, and Davida wondered if anyone ever had the chance to visit paradise twice in one lifetime—even on a short visit. Once a fantasy ended, could it ever be replayed? Or was it destined to remain only in heartrending memories that would haunt her for the rest of her life?

"You're gonna stay for dinner aren't you? We have got somethin' so good," Des, still wearing her little black leotard and pink tights beneath gray sweats, flipped her ballet tote onto her other shoulder, and bobbed up and down with excitement. "You're gonna like it . . ."

Marcus watched as Davida unlocked her door. Destiny leapt through and rushed up the darkened stairs before her mother found the light switch. He watched again as Davida turned to relock the door. *Just watching her,* he marveled. *We had all afternoon together, all those hours of lovemaking, and I'm still responding to her like it was the first time.*

She turned to him as soon as they'd entered her living room. He couldn't stop looking at her. Her dark skin still held the mild flush of passion, and her hair was a little less than perfect—reminders of their time together.

You love her. The lack of novelty involved in the thought was impressive to Marc. He did love her. Really. The afternoon they'd shared only confirmed what he'd already suspected. He loved her as he'd never even dreamed of loving a woman before. Watching her turn on lights as she moved efficiently through the house, he wondered how that love was going to change his life.

"Come on back to the kitchen," Davida invited, draping her jacket on a chairback as they passed through the formal dining room. He already knew the way, but he followed for the sheer pleasure of watching her walk.

Destiny thumped heavily down the stairs, then burst summarily through the kitchen door. "I am so glad you're here," she declared. "Know what we're having? Honor of you, of course." She looked at her mother, then climbed atop the kitchen stool.

Marc took his own stool. "Tell me."

"Sloppy Joe." She grinned happily. "She's gonna make us eat salad with it, but we still get Sloppy Joe, Marc!"

"Obviously the house favorite?" Destiny and her mother nodded together. "With salad?" They nodded again, Des making a face at the mention of greenery. *Boy, has she changed,* he thought, getting a really good look at Des. In less than a month, the tooth she'd lost when he'd seen her last had been replaced with a new one. The little girl was at least an inch taller than before, and even prettier. *She looks like her mother.*

"You two might as well get busy, since you know we're having salad." Pushing the refrigerator door closed with a firm bump of her hip, Davida turned, her hands filled with salad fixings. The head of lettuce rolled away as she set the supplies on the counter between Marc and Des. Marc caught it one handed. Des clapped.

"Maybe salad won't be so bad with you here, Marc."

Davida turned to look at her daughter and her . . . man she'd spent all afternoon in bed with. They looked absolutely comfortable together. Like family.

She wondered if—but only if—if they could ever be a family. It wouldn't be hard. Davida pulled plastic bags from the freezer. She broke enough frozen green pepper and onion free for her cooking.

Head bent to her tasks, Davida stealthily watched Marcus's face. The care in his eyes, it looked so much like love, so much like what she always thought she wanted to see in her own father's eyes.

If she'd been talking, she would have bitten her tongue. Surprised that the thought even surfaced, Davida realized she'd never in her entire life let her musings take her that far before, not with Marc or any other man. She wondered if Destiny ever missed that kind of male approval—psychologists said most girls did, and that it went a long way toward shaping their future relationships with men.

For most of her life, the man who was there to approve of the good things and stand between Destiny and the bad things was Butch. Davida tried to bury her sigh in busyness. It was Butch who put together the Christmas bikes and dollhouses. It was Butch who helped Des build her first science project. It was Butch who braved the roller coaster at Six Flags the time Davida cried because her child, barely tall enough, had begged to ride. It was Butch who went with his sister to the dance recitals and applauded as loudly as any of the daddies in attendance.

But Davida knew in her own heart, all the times she missed having a father. She also knew that Destiny was still actively eyeing Marcus Benton as a likely prospect in the daddy department.

Watching him tease Destiny as they wrangled over their joint salad project, Davida began to do little things—stirring ground beef into the skillet with the peppers and onions, finding the jar of homemade sauce from Aunt Wesie, thawing and buttering buns for toasting.

"Okay, okay, okay." Destiny waved her fingers in giggling surrender. "I got a joke. It's a good one." She smoothed her braids back and sat taller. "Okay, Marc. Knock-knock."

"Not a 'knock-knock' joke," he groaned.

She wiggled her head in mock frustration. "C'mon, Marc. Knock-knock."

He dropped his head to look sideways and up at her. "Who's there?"

"Doris."

"Doris, who?"

"Doris open, come on in." Destiny clapped her hands to her knees and howled with laughter.

Marc shook his head and looked adorably chagrined. Turning his head slightly, he addressed Davida. "I suppose you've heard that one before?"

"I'm just clever that way," she said, pouring sauce over sizzling meat.

"I got another one." Des grinned. "Wanna hear it?"

"I don't know." Looking comically worried, he ran a hand along his clean-shaven cheek. "Alright, give me your best shot."

"Okay. Knock-knock."

"Who's there?"

"Hi."

"I know I'm going to regret this. Hi who?"

"Not 'Hi who.' " She swung her feet, looked at her mother, who sang with her, "Hi ho! Hi ho! It's off to work we go!"

Marc smothered his own grin and pretended to be unimpressed. His eyes caught Davida's over Destiny's head. "Where did she get this nutty sense of humor from? I'll bet you were nothing like this as a kid," he teased.

"Sure, I was," she replied.

"Prove it," he dared.

"Prove it? Just for that, I will. Just because you think I can't, I'm going to show you pictorial proof of what I used to be like. Hang on to this."

Marcus jumped to catch the wooden spoon Davida flipped his way. "Where are you going?" He turned to follow her progress across the kitchen.

"Upstairs, I've got a few vintage photos that ought to prove my point."

Her mother had barely cleared the doorway and begun to climb the stairs, when Des stopped laughing and looked up at Marc with huge, pained eyes.

"What is it?" he asked, half afraid she was serious, hoping she was teasing.

"I don't feel so good," she moaned grabbing at her stomach and grimacing in pain.

"Des, is this a joke?" Marc asked cautiously, " 'cause I don't think it's very funny." He moved to the gas range, cautiously lowering then completely turning off the gas under the steaming meat and sauce mixture Davida'd left behind.

"No joke, Marc." Destiny lowered her head to the counter, still holding herself. "I hurt so bad—real bad."

"Davida!" The child seemed to move in a melt, sliding to the side, nearly off the stool. Reaching, rushing toward her, Marc had a moment of complete and total panic when the child doubled up in pain, curling into his arms.

"I've got you, baby," he crooned, holding her seemingly boneless body, praying that she not lose consciousness. *How did this happen so quickly?*

"Oh, Marc," Des murmured through a rush of quiet tears. She burrowed close against his chest, and looked up with frightened eyes.

"Is this what daddies do when you hurt? Do daddies hold you until you feel better?"

Her tears were hot and fat, they burned his skin as they fell. "Sweetheart, this is what anybody does for someone they love." Was that the right thing to say? He held her close, feeling his heart crack under the burden of her need. It had better be the right thing to say, because it was how he felt. Des gagged pitifully and moaned softly, pressing her face against his shirt.

"If my daddy was here, he could rub my arms, where it hurts."

"Right here?" Her elbows seemed to be bent at odd angles to her small body, and Marc cupped them in his hands and massaged. Looking down, he had the ridiculous thought that his hands had never been so large and awkward before. Not even when he'd held J.B. for the first time as an infant, tiny and fragile, had he felt so completely useless.

Destiny nodded to the rhythm of his massage and half choked around a sob. Her body, so small and frail against his, seemed impossibly hot, and Marcus Benton cursed himself for a fool. He'd taken a first-aid course once. He'd read up on this. How could he be here and not know what to do?

Easing Destiny to the coolness of the cleanly waxed pine floor, Marc sat with her resting against his chest. He brushed her braided hair back from her face and rocked her in his arms.

"Hurts, Marc." Her tiny mouth folded in on itself and her nostrils quivered from the onslaught of pain raised in her small body.

Davida would be back any second, now. He looked at the door she'd disappeared through and prayed for her return. Any second. "Sweetie, your mommy will be here, she's coming now. Just hold on, baby. Hold on." He could hear her footsteps on the stairs beyond the kitchen door. "Your mommy's coming."

"But, you're here now, Marc. Be my daddy for now. I need you to be." Des, her face wet, twisted in momentary agony, found his eyes, holding them with her own. Her eyes were amazingly clear and knowing, startlingly frank for a child's. "Don't let me go, Marc. Hold me like a daddy." And she burst into fresh tears.

Des never heard the slap of the scrapbook on the flooring, but Marc jumped at the sharp sound. Davida's eyes were riveted to her child and she moved with ferocious determination to claim her as she crossed the room. Kneeling, she opened her arms to take her daughter, but Destiny moved like lightening. Snaking away from her mother, she tightened her arms and legs around the man who held her, keening all the while.

"Destiny?"

"No!" The small hand pushed Davida firmly away. "I don't want you, I want my daddy!'' Her face turned away. Davida looked like she'd been slapped.

"She's sick,'' Marc offered—it was meager, mere words, far too insignificant, but all he could muster. Davida's face was colder than anything he'd ever thought of, and he would have given anything, everything he possessed to have changed what he saw there. Anger, fury, really—it rippled restlessly behind her eyes, waiting to find a crack, any small hole through which to vent itself.

"She's my child,'' Davida hissed. "I know she's sick.'' Her breath was coming in harsh rasps as she sought a place to put her hands. Perspiration beaded her nose and her upper lip as she finally succeeded in getting a grip on her child.

"Look, Davida, I didn't mean any harm. I didn't realize how sudden the onset could be. I was here, you weren't. She needed someone, I was here. That's all . . .''

"Mommy, please! I need a daddy!'' Des gagged again.

Torn between her child's need and her own fear-based anger, Davida glared at the man she'd spent the afternoon loving. When Des closed her eyes and moaned, Davida scooped her up in her arms, staggered slightly under the weight as she stood and headed for the kitchen door.

"Where are you going?''

The ice in her eyes burned him with ferocity. One silver tear spilled to track her cheek before she forbade another to follow. "My child is sick. I'm putting her to bed.'' She hugged the child closer and turned from him. Destiny whimpered.

"Davida.'' His tone made her stop and look back at him. "Let me help you,'' he took a step toward her and stopped. "I thought we had something. I thought we had something big enough that Destiny could share it, big enough that she was a part of it.''

"Marc?'' The child's voice was a whisper. Her face turned slightly, just enough so that she could see him. "You'll come, too?''

Marc walked closer. He linked his hand with the little girl's and squeezed gently. "Nothing will keep me from your side, Des.'' His eyes met Davida's over the child's head. "Nothing,'' he repeated.

CHAPTER EIGHTEEN

The Bentwood rocker was an almost nine-year-old shower gift from Quita. She'd had it delivered, fully assembled with a big pink satin bow tied around it. "Only makes sense," she'd teased from the time Davida and Skip showed off their child's first portrait. "You've got to rock a baby, might as well be comfortable doing it."

Quita oohed and aahed over the grayish ultrasound "photo," thrilled to know she'd soon be cuddling a baby girl, then rushed out to buy the chair. She, like Mel and Anne and the other women in their little circle of friends, was a self-proclaimed godmother, but Davida secretly believed Quita bought the chair to enjoy during her own comfortable visits. It was a great chair for cuddling. How many rainy afternoons had she found Des curled into it, sleeping contentedly?

Davida herself loved the comforting mellow curves of the wood and rocked her baby to sleep five or ten million times sitting in it. She'd also sat, first with Skip, then alone, and now with Marc at Destiny's bedside while the little girl struggled to breathe and fought against gut-rending pain.

The little cedar knee lamp glowed ethereally at the bedside, and Davida thought she'd pay serious money not to see her child looking the way she did now in the gentle lamp light. It seemed wrong that the light was so soft and the child so troubled. Destiny plucked at the comforter again. She tossed her head and the barrettes she still wore in her hair, clicked sympathetically. She looked at her mother, her eyes asking questions that Davida refused to guess at.

"How are you feeling, now?" Marcus stood at Davida's elbow. His eyes, like Destiny's asked questions Davida refused to address. Without turning, she lifted a hand and Marc delivered the small basin he'd found under the sink in the child's pink and yellow and blue candy-striped bathroom. Des had already used it twice to empty her stomach.

"Marc?"

'I'm here, baby." Reaching across Davida, Marc lay his hand, large, masculine, and dry against the heat of the little girl's forehead. The caramel over chocolate tones would have delighted him under other circumstances, intriguing him with their similarities and differences. Tonight, he only feared the worst. After the scene in the kitchen, the worst seemed inevitable.

"Bathroom," Des whispered weakly, pushing at the comforter. Davida frowned slightly, thought better of it, and helped her from the bed.

At a loss, on his own while two of the most important women in his life were away from his sight, Marc let his eyes tour the room. T-Boz of the group TLC jammed thumbs into the rolled band of her baggy pants and arched a coy brow at him from her poster on the wall across the room. He remembered Des telling him about the poster during that trip to Six Flags. "She's my favorite," the little girl smiled, poking her tongue into the space her tooth had recently vacated. "She's real special, 'cause she's got it, too."

Not understanding, Marc had inclined his head. Destiny accurately read the curiosity in his eyes. "She has sickle cell, too. Mom heard her say so on TV, so we wrote her a letter, and she wrote me back— a real nice letter, and I've still got it. She sent me a poster, too. Signed to me and everything. It's on my wall, and I love it."

Shelves of dolls, ranked in no particular order, lined most of one wall, while colorful books lined another. Mark lifted one hefty volume. Andrew Lang's *Red Book of Fairy Stories* sat next to a couple of Nancy Drew volumes and three of the *American Girl* Addie stories. *Puzzles,* his own gift to Des was open on a nearby desk. Tracing a finger along the page, he noted that it was the part in the story where the main character talked about her illness.

He wondered if she knew this was coming . . . He looked to the bathroom.

"Marc, could you hit number one on the speed dial?" Davida's voice, too calm, too controlled, came from the bathroom.

"Sure," he said slowly, crossing the room. He held the receiver to his ear, it rang clearly. "Who am I calling?"

"Dr. Saylor." Davida's voice was brittle but clear over rushing water and the urgent sound of Des wailing. "She's . . . Tell him she's

. . . there's blood . . . there's bleeding . . . Tell him we're on our way to the emergency room."

Barely able to hear his own words, Marc repeated Davida's into the telephone. The woman on the other end made a further unheard comment. Something about Children's Hospital. He did recall her using the word "immediately." Dropping the receiver, Marcus turned to find Davida carefully but insistently pulling the gray sweats over Destiny's legs. The clothes looked inordinately small, like doll clothes as she manipulated them over swollen joints. The child's tear-streaked ashen face nearly matched her clothing.

Then, time went into overdrive, and the next thing Marc knew, he was running from the house, carrying Des, wrapped in her comforter. Somewhere along the way, Davida recovered the tweed jacket to her pants suit. She was wearing it with the lining side out. Running, she reached her Honda before him, and began arranging the back seat for Destiny. Marcus slid the child into place. Davida looked up, her eyes wide beneath the faulty overhead light of her car. "You know Children's Hospital?"

Marc nodded grimly.

"Then, drive." She tossed the keys to him, seemed confident he wouldn't drop them, and he didn't. She climbed into the passenger seat.

Marc gunned the engine, remembered he wasn't driving his Saab, and backed carefully from the driveway. He held his hands specifically at "ten and two," the way some long-forgotten driving instructor taught him to, and touched his toe to the accelerator.

"If I'd known you were going to drive like a little old lady, I'd have done it myself," Davida complained. "Marc, my baby can't breathe right now."

Can't breathe. Marcus had a rush of total recall. It was the lack of oxygen that contributed to the bending of the red blood cells that clogged the arteries. That was the prime contributor to the pain Des was enduring. The child cried out, as if to emphasize his thoughts.

"Marc?" Davida nudged his arm sharply.

His eyes met hers with the tenderness of a lover, a man who wanted to understand and support, but was unsure of where to start. Davida watched him as his lashes lowered, and his eyes shifted to the back seat, where Des moaned and let her head hang over the edge. When his eyes touched Davida's again, they were changed. Harder, firmer, more determined, they were the mature eyes of a man who would do anything for his family, a man who would die to save his child.

Marc hit the gas like he meant it.

Three minutes later, the red Accord squealed to a stop outside the emergency entrance of Children's Hospital. The tall man sitting atop the stone table drew the stubby end of a cigarette from his lips, stood, and jogged toward the still rocking vehicle.

Jimmy Dawson had been an orderly with Children's hospital for going on five years now, and he mostly liked his job—except on nights like this when his cigarette break got interrupted by sick little kids, and the one on the back seat of the Honda Accord was one of the sickest he'd seen in a long time. Jimmy let the Salem fall from his fingers, and dropped his lanky body into a pivot that let him sprint back into the hospital with the straight-backed ease and speed of Michael Johnson.

Snatching an emergency response kit from the shelf, Karen Martin nearly collided with Eric Saylor as they ran toward Jimmy Dawson. Dawson, good at his job, had already commandeered a gurney and was running back through the glass doors to the parking lot. Davida and Marcus, working together, were gently maneuvering Destiny from the back seat.

"Doctor?" The nurse took a deep breath and pushed the sleeves of her navy-blue sweater higher on her arm. Her exhalation was a puff of white in the cool night air.

The doctor looked down at his young patient. "Well, hey, Destiny." She frowned tightly. "You don't know Nurse Martin, but she came out here with me tonight, just to see what was happening with you." His hands, efficient and decisive, moved quickly over the child. Des moaned, a lonely sound echoing in the cold night air of the nearly empty parking lot.

"Vomiting?"

Davida nodded, her eyes flicking to Marc's. "And her urine . . ." she hesitated, afraid of alarming Destiny. "Bl . . . bl . . . blood."

"Along with severe dehydration, fever—I call it a sickle-cell crisis, all right," Saylor judged. "Let's get her in and on fluids." A tight, nervous, miniparade, they moved across the asphalt into the hospital.

Karen Martin broke the IV seal, and Jimmy Dawson, in his sky-blue scrub suit, thought of how much he really hated this job sometimes.

"I guess somebody had to park the car," Marc sulked, cramming his hands into his pockets. It was true, somebody did have to park the car, but why did it have to be him? A small selfish part of his heart tried to understand why he'd been the least essential person on the scene. After all, he had a stake in all this, too. He loved Destiny as much as . . . more than any other man in that parking lot tonight. Shoot the only thing that doctor had on him was eight years of medical school and an internship; and what was that compared to having that little girl squeeze into his arms and call him Daddy?

Walking through the glass doors of the emergency entrance, he saw no one. "Hope, that's not a bad sign." He hoped because there was a sick little girl somewhere in this warren of exam rooms, offices, supply closets, and waiting areas, and he needed to find her. She might need a daddy again. He looked around him, and still seeing no one, guessed that children didn't usually get sick at this hour on a Saturday night in St. Louis, Missouri.

He walked on, surprised to suddenly notice the drawings on the wall. He stopped, and first stood blinking, trying to decipher them. They held all the clarity of Egyptian hieroglyphs. But, just as suddenly, they made sense to him. The pink pelican, drawn with an outstretched wing, directed him to the nursery. A giant gray mouse with long whiskers, big ears and a looping twirl of tail offered telephones. A green-spotted, purple hippopotamus suggested turning right for radiology, and the blue elephant with an upraised trunk pointed to emergency. Marc followed the elephant and went left.

Davida's profile, drawn tight and held rigid, caught his eye as he rounded the corner. Approaching quietly, he stood behind her. She still wore the jacket on the wrong side and stood with her hands clasped as if praying.

Not, of course, that praying was a bad idea, Marc reflected. He thought of all the deals he'd tried to make with God as he walked through the halls looking for Davida and Destiny.

God, make her well, and I'll be in church every Sunday for the rest of my natural life.

God, make her well, and I'll go back to doing that volunteer work I got too busy to do when Bro'Man started going places.

God, make her well, and I'll never laugh at Feng Shui's gold chains again. Marc rolled his eyes heavenward. *Come on, God. You know that's a big one . . .*

If the situation hadn't been so immediate and frightening, Marc might have laughed at himself. Here he was trying to make deals with God—as if he had something to bargain with. Instead, he offered a little prayer. *Please, God, she's just a little girl . . .*

"What?" Davida turned, startled to find him behind her. She looked at him, then back at the exam table where Des still lay under the doctor's hands. "What did you say?"

"It was just a little prayer," he whispered against the fine hairs at the base of her neck.

Her fingers touched her neck and she looked at him again. "Aunt Wesie says there are no little prayers," she said finally. "Just say what you mean, and let Him take care of the rest."

"Is that what you do?" he asked.

"It's the only thing I can do." She turned back to watch her child.

Karen Martin, slim and efficient in her colorful scrubs, leaned closer and whispered something in the little girl's ear. Des looked at her and smiled. The nurse moved a tiny, handheld electronic unit closer, touching the child's ear. Then it was her turn to smile.

"We're getting close to normal on that temp, doctor."

"Hear that, Destiny? Hang in there, you're doing great!" Saylor grinned, gave Davida and Marc a quick thumbs up, then went back to work on his patient. Des yawned loudly.

Davida seemed to relax. Her shoulders dropped slightly and her head drooped tiredly as she let her hands fall to her side. For the first time, she noticed her jacket, and started to shrug free of it. Marc reached automatically, holding the collar and a sleeve for her.

"I can do it," she said quietly, taking the jacket from him.

"Mrs. Lawrence." Karen Martin smiled, her teeth a broad band of white against the mahogany of her skin. "If you and your husband . . ."

"He's not my husband," Davida blurted, amazed at herself.

"Well, all-righty then," the nurse corrected, with a quick glance at the doctor, "if the two of you want to wait in the lobby, we'll get Destiny settled for the night."

What the hell . . . ? Taking Davida's elbow, Marc swallowed what could have become anger. *Stress,* he promised himself. *It's the stress of the situation. She's not acting like herself. I know her well enough to know this isn't usual . . .* but he watched her expression all the same as she shrank into a corner of the gold vinyl settee in the waiting room.

Distancing herself from him, drawing her knees up to a near fetal position, Davida turned her face to the wall. Had he not been watching, Marcus might have thought her asleep when she closed her eyes and remained virtually motionless. Only the rise and fall of her breast signaled her breathing. Sympathetically, Marc lowered himself to the arm of the settee. From her back, he placed a hand on her shoulder. "Davida?"

He felt her hold her breath before she turned her head. Her eyes opened slowly and she seemed only vaguely aware of him. "How about some coffee, Boo?" She shook her head and Marc wished she'd done almost anything in the world except that.

Moving carefully, Marcus found himself kneeling in front of her. Placing one hand on her bent knee, he waited for her to flinch or pull away, nodding to himself when she didn't. "I've got a pocket full of change, why don't I make some calls for you?"

"It's late," she said absently.

"But I think they'd like to know about Des."

"Who?"

This must be something like that posttraumatic stress disorder, Marc thought warily. "I could at least let your family know where you are, what's happened . . ."

"You're right." She dropped her face to her bent arm, effectively closing him out of her thoughts.

Hands on his thighs, Marcus pushed himself to his feet. Boo? Her face still rested in the crook of her elbow. Two of Marc's fingers probed the tightness at the back of his neck. This had to be hard for her. She needed to lean a little bit for a change. Why couldn't she see he was here? For the life of him, he couldn't figure it out. He was here, right beside her, and she was acting like she was all alone. Why was he suddenly the "invisible man"? He sighed heavily. "Sure I can't get you anything?" He shoved his hands into his pockets and rocked on his toes.

Davida barely moved her head. "No, thank you."

Marc walked into the hall and followed the directions provided by the long whiskered, big eared mouse. He glanced critically at the painted caricature. *I coulda done better,* he thought and walked to the phone bank. Dumping a handful of change onto the metal counter, he turned the pages of the city directory. Picking through his change he selected and deposited coins.

Jewell Morrison took the news well, once she was assured that Destiny was stable and resting. She promised to call Glenn, her sister, and Mama Lou. *Could you give your daughter a wake-up call, too? Could you tell her I'm here, that I'm waiting?* "That's probably a good idea," he said instead.

This was not working for him. Marcus looked over his shoulder. The corridor, as far as he could see in either direction, remained empty. Feeling numb, totally outside himself, he faced the telephones again. If he felt hungry, he'd know what to do. He'd eat. If he was tired, he would sleep. If he was angry, he'd punch something, but what did you do when someone you love hurts the way she does? What did you do when she won't let you in? He scratched through his change, then dropped more coins in the slot. Renee sounded sleepy when she answered.

"Sorry I woke you."

"S'okay," she said. "We were just watching a little television." Marc pictured his sister rubbing sleep from her eyes, probably wearing one of those plaid, flannel, shirt-things she favored. "Movie's off, what time is it?" She yawned.

He turned the links of his watchband to the face, trying to read the time. "A little after ten. Where's George?"

"Went to pick up ice cream," she said. "After ten?" Mention of the time seemed to rouse her fully. "Where are you? I thought you and Davida would be together . . . What's wrong? Why are you calling me?''

''I—we're at Children's Hospital. Destiny got sick.''

''Oh, Marc, Children's Hospital! Poor thing, how is she now?'' Coming fully awake, Renee sniffed and shifted the phone between her chin and shoulder.

''She's stable.''

''And Davida? How's she taking it?''

Marc sighed. ''She's quiet, not saying very much.''

Renee waited, listening between the lines. ''What is she saying to you, Marc?''

''Not a thing,'' he blurted. ''I don't understand it.''

''Aw, Marc. Come on, Butch.'' Sympathetic, Renee slipped easily into the use of the old nickname. ''I know this whole thing is new to you, and with a child involved, too. I know this is different, and nobody seems to be paying you much attention right now, but, Butch, try to understand . . . Davida is hurt, and scared. She needs some time to think this over, and then she has to figure out how to explain it to Destiny. None of this is about you—not right now.''

''I know.'' Marc didn't bother to try to hide his misery.

''I feel your pain, Butch, but think of it this way—That child has been her whole life for the last four or five years—ever since she lost her husband. You're new, and as much as you mean to her, maybe Davida hasn't completely figured out how to include you, yet. That happens a lot with new families.''

''We're not a family, and at the rate things are going, we never will be.''

''But, it's what you want,'' she said. ''I hear it in your voice.''

You got that right, he thought, *it's exactly what I want.* Renee was making far too much sense for comfort. ''I told Mom not to send you to college. You took all that counseling stuff to heart.'' He folded his arms across his chest and leaned his shoulder against the wall.

''Scoff, if you must,'' she chuckled lightly, ''just don't give up on her, Marc.''

''It's just—I don't understand.''

''Butch, you're just beginning to get used to seeing her when her makeup is not perfect, or first thing in the morning. Now, you're seeing her with every nerve exposed, and that's just human in this kind of situation. Nobody is always perfect, unfortunately.''

''Yeah.'' It was a grudging admission.

''Quiet as it's kept, you're not always a joy to be with either, Butch. We all have to work with what we've got, and sometimes, it's just not easy.''

Spreading his fingers like a visor, Marc squeezed his forehead, wishing he could squeeze out the pain. "You make sense, Cookie, but it's hard."

"My point, exactly. Almost nothing worth having is ever easy."

"So what am I supposed to do?"

"Butch, if it was football, you'd fall back and punt."

"What is that supposed to mean?"

Renee sighed. "Butch, I swear . . . for a creative man . . . but, maybe that's an oxymoron." She giggled, then sighed again. "Anyway, it simply means you reinvent—yourself, your relationship, the way you look at things." She paused. "Let her be what she has to be—strong for Destiny, and a lover for you, when the time is right. For now, though, be what you have to be for her. The strong silent type."

"Reinvent, eh?" Marc looked at the phone and wondered if he had the strength. If nothing else, he had the time. "Are you trying to tell me that's how George survives you?" he finally asked.

"Hey," she offered pragmatically. "Old trees survive because they learn to bend and grow with the wind. Old marriages survive because we learn to bend and grow with each other."

Marc grinned, in spite of himself. "You're starting to sound like Davida's Aunt Wesie."

"You noticed?" Renee sounded pleased. "We had lunch the other day. And you know what? She had some other good sayings . . ."

"Excuse me?"

Marc turned at the abbreviated tap on his shoulder. The woman was petite, her head barely reaching his shoulder. She had the sharply pointed chin and high arched brows of a pixie, but the tag pinned to her fuchsia print scrub suit identified her as Marie Wilson, Head of Pediatric Nursing.

"Hold on, Renee." Marc used a hand to cover the receiver, smothering the sound from his end, and Renee stared at the phone in frustration on her end.

"Des?" he asked. "Is she okay, Destiny Lawrence?"

The pixie twinkled at him. "She's fine, but she's asking for her daddy. She sent me to look for you."

"I'm—I, is that what she said?"

"Why, yes." Nurse Wilson twinkled again, and Marc understood why she worked with children. "She told me what you looked like and what she recalled your wearing." Marie spread her hands. "And I found you right away. She's going to be asleep shortly, so we'd better hurry."

Hurry. Of course. "Renee, I'll talk to you later."

"Marc? Wait! Did I help?" She was still sputtering as he hung up.

* * *

His fingers curved over the edge of the door to her isolated room. Des looked odd, stretched out like a sick kid in a bad movie. Marcus nearly convinced himself he'd made a wrong turn, in spite of his excellent guide. He nearly convinced himself that the small figure in the dimly lit room was somebody else's baby. *Not his Destiny.* He might have backed silently out of the door, maybe down the hall, if she had not turned her head on the white cased pillow.

"Marc." She smiled, and one small hand found a way to wave to him. He came closer. She yawned, her mouth wide and pink.

"Hi, Destiny." He stopped at her side and wished he knew what else to say. He wished he'd had time to find balloons or a stuffed animal. Right then, he would have even settled for *Barney.*

Her lips curved again. That smile, it was the same one he'd seen on her mother's face—was it only a few hours ago? She reached for his hand, and clung to it.

"I told Miss Marie about you." Her voice was small and whispery, kind of a sing-song. Her eyes suddenly widened. "I told her you were my daddy. Is that okay?" She yawned and closed her eyes, seeming to rest before she looked at him again, waiting for his answer.

Marc closed both his hands over hers, surprised for the second time that evening at how tiny she was. "Sure, Des. It's okay. Matter of fact, I like it."

"It's not like I told a real lie, is it?"

"Uhm . . ." Marc hated his hesitation. How in the world was he supposed to answer this? Was he supposed to go all clinical and tell her that he was not her biological father, and that she had therefore told a lie? Or was he supposed to say something like, "No Des, it's not a lie. Especially after what we all went through tonight. When you got sick, it scared me like a daddy. When I didn't know what to do for you, my heart hurt just like a daddy's. Your Mom and I still have to work through some things, but you didn't tell a lie."

"Tha's good," she slurred, fighting sleep. Her eyes drooped, then flashed open. She squeezed his hand as though reminding herself that he was not part of a dream. "I got a joke for you."

"Not another one," Marc groaned.

She gave him her mother's slow smile again. "Knock-knock."

"Who's there?"

"Dishes."

"Dishes, who?"

"Dishes a very bad joke!"

Marc grinned and stroked her forehead with his thumb. "That really was pretty bad, Des."

"Have you got a better one?" she challenged, closing her eyes again.

Marc thought about it. "Okay, knock-knock."

"Who's there?" She opened her eyes halfway.

"Goliath."

"Goliath who?"

"Goliath down, you look tired."

Des closed her eyes again. "That was really bad, Marc."

"Okay, Des. I admit, it was the best I could do on the spur of the moment"

"S'okay, Daddy. You'll do better next time."

"I promise I'll try, baby," he whispered.

As he watched, her breathing became slow and regular, and her head drifted to the side, away from the light. Falling into slumber, her features relaxed, but she still held Marc's hand, almost as tightly as she held his heart, and he was content to let her.

CHAPTER NINETEEN

"Mrs. Lawrence?" Dr. Eric Saylor, still wearing his white coat stood back, holding the door with one hand, ushered Davida into his office with the other. He moved with an ease that would have been better relegated to his home than this place of business. Davida glanced up at him, gave him a nervous smile and looked hastily away—if his ease was related to bad news . . . Whatever it was, she already knew she didn't want to know. Finding her way to one of the upholstered chairs in front of his desk, she sat. He waited until she looked reasonably comfortable, and took an adjacent chair.

Somebody had taken the time to try to make his office look "lived in." They'd chosen peaceful, tasteful watercolors in pastel tints for the walls. A healthy, albeit dusty, diffenbachia stood in one corner, while an umbrella tree swayed near his desk, and though the glass-fronted bookcase held an intimidating array of volumes, he looked capable of handling them. The total effect was lost on Davida.

"Can I get you something to drink? Coffee, juice, water?"

He was too polite, too caring, too solicitous, something was very wrong with Des, and he was trying to keep her calm. "What's wrong with Destiny?"

"Nothing, I didn't mean to alarm you." Leaning forward, setting his stethoscope atop his desk, Saylor let his elbows rest on his knees. "Well, not exactly nothing, but we've been here before, haven't we?" He smiled. Davida tried to smile back, but the quivering of her lips deprived her of the action. Saylor nodded, he understood.

Folding her fingers together, she brought shaking hands to her lips. Her lashes swept the curve of her cheek and her mouth tightened above her hands. "Having been here before doesn't make it any easier, does it?"

"No, I guess it doesn't, at that." He felt better when she lowered her hands. It was the fearful look in her eyes that he didn't like. With her trembling, barely controlled mouth, and tightly knotted fingers, she looked brittle and vulnerable, almost damaged, but her eyes were alarmed and dreading, anticipating the worst. Saylor wished he had better news for her.

Failing that, he pulled out his best bedside manner. "Let's start with this," he said gently, aiming for optimism. "For tonight, Destiny is out of the woods. We've got the temperature down, and we've controlled her dehydration and nausea—for now. She's not complaining so much about the pain. Of course, we've medicated her, but I think just the nutrition and the close monitoring you're doing at home is helping."

"For now," Davida answered, using his words.

Saylor nodded. "I guess I should tell you' I've got good news and bad news. Which do you want first?"

"Which . . . first?" Davida's stomach lurched, and she tried to remember why Des liked this doctor so much. She tried to remember why they'd both felt so comfortable with this tall, slender, coffee-colored man who'd chosen medicine over the NBA while a student at Yale, then returned to his hometown to practice.

"He likes my jokes," Des told her. "He likes my jokes, and he's always got some real funny ones to trade with me." Jokes. A sense of humor. Maybe that was a good reason to like a man. Maybe, it was even a good reason to fall in love with a man, but . . . Her child was this sick, and he had "good news and bad news"? That was as bad as one of Destiny's knock-knock jokes. Her stomach lurched again, and Davida shifted the broadness of her hips beneath her, trying to find a more satisfactory position for her body, if not her mind.

She wanted to stand up and shake a fist at this man. Pound on him until her daughter felt better. Knowing that wouldn't work, she grasped at the filmy gray edges of her reality. "The bad news first," she said.

He clasped his hands between his legs and looked up at Davida. His skin was bronze in the mellow light of his desk lamp, and his lips were distinctly pink. His eyes were bright, like tiny mirrors, reflecting her own face, and the lines of exhaustion beneath them looked like they'd been drawn in with heavy crayon strokes. Davida thought he almost looked like he was wearing stage makeup in preparation for the performance he was about to give for his one-woman audience.

When he spoke, his voice was professionally pleasant, aimed at reducing the steadily increasing tension in the room. "My feeling, at this time, is that Destiny is at risk for stroke. That's based on those changes I've been able to see in her over the last two years."

Stroke? She swallowed hard and gripped the arms of her chair. *Stroke?* Accosted with sudden visions of Destiny, Davida was afraid to breathe. A stroke meant . . . it would affect her ability to move, speak, or learn. That would be hell for a child as bright and active as Des. Davida, her mind moving at the speed of light, found a way to swallow the solid chunk the air in her throat had become. *Hold on,* she cautioned herself, refusing to give in to the urge to run from the pediatrician. *Maybe you heard him wrong. Maybe he really didn't say stroke, and if he did he wasn't talking about Destiny—not my Destiny. Just listen. Hear him out.*

"I want to refer her for further testing."

"Further testing," Davida repeated. Why couldn't she stop doing that? Now, she was echohalic, repeating everything he said.

"Yes. I want her to undergo a transcranial Doppler screening, so that we have a better idea of her risk level."

"Transcranial Doppler . . . her risk level for . . . a stroke? And, this is going to make everything okay for her?" Davida's hands covered the lower half of her face, but her eyes asked him for what she didn't trust her mouth to say.

The doctor opened his hands, turning the palms up and out. "The truth is that we both know there is no cure for Destiny—not yet. The good news, though, is that she may be a good candidate for transfusion therapy. This test will be an indicator."

"What is that? The test, I mean."

"Transfusion therapy?" She nodded slowly. Saylor stood, one hand on the back of his chair. "It would mean a long-term series of blood transfusions."

'Transfusions? You talked about risks before. Aren't there risks with transfusions?"

"Yes," his tone became clinical. "Any invasive procedure, short or long term, will carry risks."

Davida felt her skin crawl. *Risks? Invasive procedure?* How did he manage to stand there and try to make this sound like something a mother could understand or appreciate?

"Doctor, you and I both know I'm not a tiny woman. In a physical fight for my child, I think I could take on any odds, but this . . . how do I fight this? And outside of your medical expertise, I'm out here on my own." Davida's hands moved above her eyebrows, raking through her short hair. Air escaped her body with an audible hiss. "There's no other way?"

"Mrs. Lawrence, I could sit here all night and spin you tales of scientific probability, but it really wouldn't change things." His hands went into the pockets of his lab coat, and he shrugged. "We can stick with standard supportive care for sickle-cell anemia. Watching her diet, her fluids, and her activity levels—the same stabilizing care we've always offered her. The thing is, though, all our present studies show that the transfusion therapy can reduce her risk of stroke by up to ninety percent."

"And if we don't use the transfusions . . . ?"

This was the hard part, the part Saylor dreaded. This very frightened mother was seeing her child as a pincushion, or a guinea pig, not as a successful patient or as a survivor. "And if we don't employ the transfusion therapy, she'll continue to endure the crises, while she can. She'll still have the frequent hospitalizations. Then too, as Destiny matures, her chances of stroke will increase. She'll also continue to have chronic pain."

Davida felt faint.

Saylor angled his long body toward her, leaning to give more weight to his argument. "We can consider making her a candidate for the bone marrow project, but . . ."

"I already know' " Davida told the floor. "You wouldn't hold out much hope for success because the chances of finding a match for her are so slim, millions to one."

"You've already been tested?"

"Yes, me and everyone else on both sides of her family, but none of us match. None of my friends, either."

"Still, we'll get her on the register, you never know."

"You never know," Davida repeated, her eyes heavy with unshed tears. "In the meantime, this transfusion therapy . . . I think I saw something about it on television, and I might have seen, maybe read something else . . ." Her voice wavered, dropped, and she studied her hands as though she might find the answer she needed written in the lines of her palms. "How does the transfusion therapy work?"

Saylor's hopes rose irrationally. Maybe, just maybe, she was hearing everything he was saying. "Transfusion therapy means that if she's accepted, she'll receive a blood transfusion every three to four weeks to keep the amount of abnormal, or sickle hemoglobin, to no more than thirty percent of her total hemoglobin."

"So, you just want to go in and play with my baby's blood?"

Saylor, having no words to make it better, said nothing. In his heart he hoped she would ask no more about the risks of the program. Not tonight. Tonight, the last thing he wanted to tell Davida Lawrence was that on top of everything else, Destiny might require long-term chelation therapy to remove excess amounts of iron from her body, or that the child might even build up antibodies that would make the process even more difficult in the future. The little girl already wore a Medic-Alert bracelet, hopefully they would never have to add anything else to the legend it already bore.

He looked at Davida again. She was just as much his patient as her child, and he knew he didn't want, nor did she need for things to be any harder than they already were. He could tell her the rest of the story tomorrow, or maybe even the next day. He just knew he didn't want to do it, tonight. Not now.

Lord, please don't let my head explode. Massaging her temples, Davida tried to make sense of his words. "Tell me about the transcranial . . . thing . . ." Her nervousness made enunciation difficult.

"The transcranial Doppler screening," Saylor moved closer. "It's an ultrasound technique that measures the velocity of blood flow in the brain."

My child's brain. Davida swallowed audibly.

"The technique has been used for years on adults, and has been adapted for use on children by the Medical College of Georgia." Davida moaned softly, and the doctor, fearing he was about to lose her, spoke faster. "We've learned that high blood flow velocities in one or more major arteries of the brain may indicate a significant narrowing in key blood vessels supplying the brain."

Hearing the words, and making sense of them were two different things, and she knew she was doing neither of them well at this point. Davida lifted her hand, palm out, and the doctor, sensing her emotional overload, stopped. "Can you test her here?"

Saylor nodded. "We'll do it in the morning," he said.

"And if she's eligible for the therapy?"

Saylor rounded the corner of his desk, bringing a prepared folder with him. He handed it to Davida, and she looked more nervous. "You don't have to make any decisions tonight, just know that there are several facilities around the country where the therapy can be done. As long as there's a place for her in the program, you have options—just remember, these slots are available, first come, first serve."

"Around the country?" She ruffled the pages of the bright orange folder with her thumb, then rolled it into a tube that she clenched in both hands. "Not here, in St. Louis?"

He shook his head. "No, the closest facility would be Children's Mercy Hospital in Kansas City, Missouri."

Davida closed her eyes wearily. Kansas City? Traveling back and forth? For how long? Her head spun.

"There are other programs in other cities. We've listed a number of them in this folder." He tapped it lightly with a finger, then leaned back. "There's a children's hospital in Brooklyn, New York. There's Rainbow Babies and Children's in Cleveland, Ohio, and St. Jude's in Memphis. There's one in Augusta, Georgia, and another in Atlanta. You could choose a city where both you and Destiny might be comfortable, just as easily as you can find one close to home."

Watching from across his desk, Saylor straightened his arms and looked down at her. "I'd recommend you talk this over with your family, because you're going to need a lot of support. This isn't going to be easy for you or your daughter."

Her head dropped back, and when Davida stared at the ceiling, the doctor wasn't sure what she was trying to see. "Destiny and I have faced all of our challenges together." She smiled, and it saddened the doctor to see the pain it revealed. "We faced her father's death together, and we've been together for all of the trials brought on by her SCD." Davida straightened and looked at the doctor with clear determination on her face.

"Whatever you decide, I have to be honest with you—there are no guarantees, no 'magic bullets.'"

"I see. I understand." Her eyebrows rose and fell quickly. "That leaves us with prayer and miracles, doesn't it, doctor?"

"Mrs. Lawrence, in this case, there's ample room for both."

The smile she offered was weak, a mere trace of politeness, as Davida stood to walk from the room. "I was reluctant to mention this." The doctor laid a mildly restraining hand on her wrist, forcing her to stop and listen to him.

"Destiny is an only child, isn't she?" Unsure of where this was going, Davida nodded. "Is there a chance you might consider having another child?"

Another child? With who? Marc, with his beautiful eyes and sudden dimples flashed through her mind. The only real candidate she'd had in years, and he was emphatically out of the question. Marc had plans for his life, and right now, children were not his priority.

"No doctor," Davida declared, "there are no plans for another child. I just turned forty, and it's already been eight years, since the last time. Besides, my husband is dead, and statistically, you know the chances of conception after forty, and we had a hard enough time the first time around, and . . ."

He held up his hand. "I know all the rationale, but Mrs. Lawrence, the thing to remember here is that a sibling, even a half-sibling is a good bet for a bone marrow transplant." His hand took an extra beat, emphasizing his point.

"Are you suggesting I have a baby just to harvest bone marrow?" The thought was horrifying and fully repugnant.

"No," the doctor said. "It's simply something to consider—especially when you're thinking in terms of prayer and miracles."

Licking her lips, refusing to speculate, then no longer able to hold the scary thoughts at bay, Davida let them wash over her. "Doctor, you know I carry the trait. Lately, I've been hearing about . . ."

"Kidney cancer?"

Unable to look at him, to let him see how rattled she was, Davida nodded.

"You've been tested?"

She nodded again.

"Then, I wouldn't let that be the fear, right now."

The fearful look in her eyes dropped a notch, but the eyes still jittered nervously. "Any other child, though. Any other child, I mean I'm not having one, I just want to know. But any other child I have might carry the trait—right? And, if Destiny has children?"

"We're getting a little ahead of ourselves. That's a conversation we'll have when the time comes."

Her smile was bitter. "Why buy trouble when so much of it is free, right?"

Saylor watched as Davida stood to leave. "Have a little faith, Mrs. Lawrence, that's all it takes."

She stopped and looked over her shoulder. "It had better be, Doctor Saylor, because a little faith is all I have left." The door closed silently behind her.

Outside, standing with her back to the door' Davida closed her eyes. This was one of those times when it was supposed to be nice to have someone to lean on, but for her, there was no one. Destiny was no one else's responsibility. She had to be here for her.

There was no one who could do anything to make the terms of her daughter's life any more definite or any safer. The tough decisions had to be made, and there was no way to play Scarlett O'Hara, no way to put the decision off, ". . . until tomorrow." Destiny's life would bear no waiting. *Where do I go from here?* A graceful hand covered her mouth, and Davida looked toward the telephone bank. Marc said something about the telephones, but there was no one there.

Destiny. She should go look in on her. Without thinking, Davida turned, automatically walking. Glancing at the admission papers in her hand, she casually noted the room number, stopping only when she reached her daughter's door. Preparing herself for the worst, Davida pressed a hand against the door.

Marc wasn't unsure of the force that seized him as the door swung open. Moved, not to run, but to stand as witness, he released the child's hand and pulled the soft pink blanket over her sheeted form.

He stepped away from her bedside, and into the deep shadows gathered by the privacy curtain pulled into the corner.

Destiny lay in the center of the crisp, white-sheeted bed, the fingers of her right hand curled slightly against the pale pink blanket. As her mother approached, she inhaled deeply, and turned her face into the light. *She looks tired,* Davida thought.

From his corner, Marc watched Davida as her beautiful mouth silently formed her daughter's name. Pausing, her eyes cast down, seeing only the small figure on the bed, she seemed caught in thought, and pinned by indecision. He wondered what she was seeing, what she was remembering. Des as an infant, or maybe even before that. In her place, that was what he'd be thinking.

Feeling every bit the voyeur, afraid to make his presence known, Marc watched her. Pulling a chair close to the bed, she leaned forward to whisper to the sleeping child. Weightless, loving fingers hovered above the child's skin, finally touching the corner of her mouth, then the center of her two lips. Destiny's lips parted, then closed in a sleeping kiss, and Marc's heart nearly broke at the striking tableau they made.

Seeing them together, an elegant flow of ebony and bronze curves and planes, shaded blue and rusty gold in the yellowed electric light, they were a dark study of love. The tall woman, her broad figure replete with courage and maternal passion, was fully devoted to her small tasks. Marc's fingers itched to capture the sadly eloquent, time-less image. More, his arms ached with the need to comfort.

"Sleep well, loved one."

Her whispering reminded Marc of the other times he'd heard the tone and similar words, but never had he heard them uttered with such emphasis on tenderness and compassion. Reminded of Renee's words, her call to empathy, Marc was tempted to step from the shad-ows, tell this woman how much he loved her, and promise her anything. But it felt wrong, selfish, almost sacrilegious to contemplate interrup-tion while Davida, head bent, eyes still bright with unshed tears, continued to whisper to the sleeping child.

"Oh, loved one, you gave me such a scare tonight." Her face came closer, and Destiny's features moved fluidly, as though in response to her mother's voice. "If not you, who would I have to skate with? Who would take me to McDonald's? I love you so much, and I need you more than anything," her breath caught in her throat. "Nothing but death will ever separate us."

And a man foolish enough to try deserved to get his feelings hurt. Marc didn't dare to breathe.

She was still whispering, her words tortured poetry in the empty room. "And that's not going to happen, loved one. Remember what

we promised?'' From her chair in the spare hospital room, Davida
pressed the child's hand between hers. She could almost hear Destiny's
voice, the words brushing her skin and ruffling her hair.

"Mommy," the little girl had asked, "when we die, can we die
together?''

Ignoring tissues and blinking fast, Davida used the back of her
hand, then the sleeve of her jacket to wipe away tears she refused to
claim. "You know, Des," her fingers moved to the child's hand, and
she smiled when the small fingers curled around hers, closing and
holding though she still slept. "You know, neither of us is going to
die until we're both very old women—older than everybody we both
know. We're going to dance at your grandchildren's weddings. We're
going to wear dentures and orthopedic shoes together, little girl.''

Marc watched Davida smooth the covers under Des's chin, and
tried to find his place in her world. What she needs is not necessarily
what I've always wanted to be. *And, what have you always wanted
to be, Marc?* he asked himself. An artist—he'd always wanted to be
the one to make the world sit up and take notice. He'd always thought
he had a story to tell. He'd always wanted to be the one to bring the
story of a brave and heroic modern black man to the world. He'd
always wanted to create something as big and as wonderful as Bro'Man
promised to be.

*I guess I've always wanted to be the father of a new American
icon, but I'd sure as hell give it all up to be her father.* He looked at
the sleeping child who'd called him her daddy, and at the mother who
touched her so lovingly. He'd give it all up to be the last thing Davida
saw at night, and the first one she saw every morning, to have her
look at him with trust and know that it was rightly placed in him. It
was too late to walk away from them, so what did that leave?

"Davida?''

She gasped and started from her chair as he stepped from the
shadows. "Marc?" Her eyes widened and searched the dark corners
of the room. On her feet, her fallen jacket lay in a forgotten heap as
she gripped the back of the chair. "How long have you been here?''
Why are you here? Her voice was a possessive hiss.

"Des asked to see me, before she fell asleep.''

"You?'' She found the jacket, and plucked it from the floor. "Where
was I?'' She backed toward the door and opened it.

"I don't know. You were gone when I passed the lounge.'' Marcus
followed her into the hall.

The door swung shut at his back, leaving Marcus to face Davida
squarely. She moved back as he took a step toward her.

"Where was I?''

"You were back there when I went to the phone.'' His nod indicated the lounge where he'd left her on the gold vinyl couch. "You were kind of out of it."

While I was in with Dr. Saylor. "What business is it of yours . . . why would you . . . you should have come and gotten me . . ." Her eyes flared, her finger flashed in his face, and her bosom heaved. "You had no right . . ."

Helplessly, Marc flung his arms wide. He wrinkled his brow, and it took two tries before he could get the words out. "Davida, why do you think you've got a lock on loving that little girl? Why do you think you're the only one who can love her—or you, for that matter? And why do you think I'm here? I'm here *with* you, I'm not here to take anything from you."

"Is that what this is? You're waiting for me to feel grateful that you saved us? Grateful that you hung around and didn't abandon us?" Like her father did? Like a lot of men would do under stress?

Her eyes narrowed and her breathing grew ragged. "I don't need saving, Marc. I've been taking care of my child and myself for quite a while now, and I've gotten pretty good at it. Des is getting the best care available, right now, and that's all there is to it. Thanks for riding in on your charger, but we don't need you."

"Well, what if I need you, you and Destiny?"

Her lashes moved quickly, and the corners of her mouth quirked. "You don't need us, Marc. You never did. You've got your art, you've got Bro'Man. You've got your own life." She stepped to the side, just enough to make him turn, clearing her path through Destiny's door. He caught her wrist as she moved to open the door.

"Where does that leave us?"

She swallowed hard, closing her eyes. "It leaves you in Atlanta, and me in St. Louis. Go home, Marc."

Squeezing, he held her wrist tighter. "Is that really what you want? After this afternoon, after. . . ?"

"Yes." She pulled her wrist away from him. "Especially after this afternoon. This afternoon was for lovers, not for responsible people. This afternoon was part of that fantasy I wanted to believe in when we talked on the phone, and I had no right to sacrifice anything to a fantasy. This afternoon was . . . it was something else, but it wasn't real. Marc, Des's condition is not occasional or scheduled, it's real. It's not an inconvenience or an interruption. It's a fact of both our lives. I can't ever not be there when she needs me, and I sure can't ever let her depend on somebody who might not be there for her— every time she needs them." Her hand went back to the door. "Go back to Atlanta, Marc. I can't let you play 'Daddy' in my child's life."

Marc felt his muscles clench in anger. "Don't I get a say in this?"

"No," she answered.

He watched the door close behind her. Every nerve in his body urged him to follow, to push his way through the door and bully his way into Davida's consciousness. He wanted desperately to make her understand. He needed to say the words, to clarify his own understanding of what he had to offer. Rational thought intervened. He knew it was rational because he hated the thoughts.

I walk through that door, and we wind up screaming at each other, saying things neither of us means. Des wakes up, hears us has some kind of relapse, and we end up hating each other. I walk away, and maybe there's a chance that somehow, we'll find each other again. His hand on the door, no pressure, Marc closed his eyes. No matter how he tried to see it, there seemed no other solution. Renee said he should learn to bend. She should have told him how to bob and weave.

Turning, he shoved his hands into his pockets and headed for the bank of telephones to call a cab. He would need one to get back to his hotel.

CHAPTER TWENTY

Davida stared at the new photo sitting alone in the corner of her desk. It was a school picture, one of the sort that kids hide and hope no one will ever find once they reach their teens. It was the sort of picture that parents hang on to and continue to show even when their children have children of their own. She'd only had the photo since Monday, but Davida already adored it.

Small and silver-framed, the color photo of her daughter held her eye. Destiny had begged for curls for the class picture, and Jewell Lawrence and Mama Lou had been her willing accomplices. Mama Lou had bravely distracted Davida while Jewell wielded the hot curlers, and though she'd immediately disapproved, Davida did have to admit Des looked pretty in the temporarily disciplined ringlets.

Reaching for the photo, holding the frame in both hands, Davida felt a small stab of warmth in the vicinity of her heart. *That's what love feels like,* she thought. She'd had the sharp little feeling almost from the moment that she'd learned of her pregnancy. She still got it every time she looked at Destiny.

Marc used to give her that feeling, too.

She brought the photo closer, close enough to see the tiny gap in the almost nine-year-old smile. January, she smiled. You'll be nine years old in January. It almost didn't seem possible, but it was. Davida set the photo back on the desk.

Her loved one would be nine years old, not quite a woman yet, but certainly not a baby anymore. Of course, it was hard to remember that she was so grown up when she was in the midst of a crisis, but still . . . For right now, Destiny was fine—she was back at school, back in dancing classes, and begging to spend the night at Tawanna Mallory's house. Tawanna had convinced her mother to allow a new puppy in the house, and both girls were fascinated by it.

My child is doing well, and her future is a little more certain—or at least it will be when we get the final results on her testing and placement details for the transfusion therapy. By all accounts, things should be fine in my world. The problem, she thought, bringing her lips together in a pout, *the problem is that the telephone isn't ringing for me anymore. And, why should it be?*

Suddenly caught off guard, Davida turned her head to the side and sneezed, catching at a tissue on her desk, and just managing to cover her mouth. "My goodness," she started, caught by a double repeat of the reflex action. Clapping both hands over her mouth, she refused to sneeze again, choking off the next one.

Sipping at her tea, trying to taste the lemon, hoping it would quell the vague nausea swirling through her stomach, Davida wondered why her sinus cavities were so annoying. She brought her fingers to the bridge of her nose and pinched, seeking relief. The little trick didn't work and the pain descended, moving into her cheeks. And, the top of her head hurt, too. That, plus the little hot and cold flashes— it was almost like having the flu.

It's as if my immune system has gone nuts, she thought, touching her nose with her tissue. She'd been feeling rotten for every minute of, how long? She calculated. Eight weeks, she knew. Eight weeks felt like an interminable, unendurable amount of time.

That was probably only because it was so hard for a healthy person to be sick—it felt like it would never end. And she guessed it really had been eight weeks that she'd felt like this. Marc had been feeling kind of like this when she first met him on the telephone. He'd sounded so . . . Marc. Why did he creep through her mind at such odd times? Bro'Man didn't do it. Atlanta didn't do it. Neither Milt nor Deb Thomas did it. Only Marc. When would he stop? Even Butch asked about him.

It's been eight weeks since I gave him the boot, she thought. *Eight weeks since I tossed him out of my life, and I wish I could say I'd never given him a second thought.*

As it was, she'd given him second, third, and twenty-fourth thoughts. His hoarse murmurs, hovering close to her ear brought tears to her eyes, in her dreams. "Good night, Marc," she caught herself whispering to a phone that hadn't rung. Too often, she found herself hugged up in the middle of her Rice bed, arms wrapped around her legs, face resting

uneasily on her bent knees, and her body throbbing with need—
hungering for a man who wasn't there.

Picturing him bent over his drawing board, his fingers stained with
chalk, his neck arched over his work, and his face fixed in rapt attention
to detail, her heart ached until she thought it would shatter. It was
hard enough to dream of him as a sexual being, but Davida couldn't
help seeing him as more, as what he really was—a good and simple
man. A man whose touch, thought, and presence she craved more
than she would have ever believed possible.

And to think, I thought he was the wrong man, she caught herself
thinking over and over.

It had been too long. A quick look at the desk calendar confirmed
what she'd known in her heart. It was almost as though her body,
missing his voice, missing his touch, missing everything that made
up Marcus Benton, had gone into mourning for him—*right along with
her mind.* And it really had been two full months of feeling flat out
rotten. Nothing seemed to be working right. First it was sleep—she
couldn't seem to get it together, there. Then came the light headaches,
sore throats, and nagging little dry coughs. It had been like that since
. . . Almost since Marc's last visit.

Why, she wondered, *does everything always seem to lead me back
to him?* And, at the heart of it, everything really did. Like last night
. . . Davida hated that late last night, when the wind rocked the nearly
leaf-bare trees outside her windows, she found herself looking to the
telephone, thumbing the button on her Caller ID, wondering where
he was, what he was doing, and worst of all, why he was doing it
without her.

She could call him. She could bite back all those bitter and ugly
things she'd said to him. She could do that, and hope he was a better
person than she was. She could call, and hope he could find a way
to forgive her. That might work to at least preserve a friendship.
Another tear, too quick for her to catch, fell, staining her desk blotter.
She didn't want to be just his friend. She wanted to be so much more
than that, but did she have the right? Did she have the right to ask
him for anything more? Especially a big thing like his trust?

In her office, Davida used her fingers to press back a spill of tears.
She swallowed more tea from the Styrofoam container. If she were
him, she didn't know that she could ever trust her again. If she were
him, she would always wonder . . . It was too easy to imagine. Marc
would wonder forever, or at least for whatever time they had together,
when she would seize her child as a shield again and push him away.

Oh, but last night, when the cold night wind rose, calling like a
lonely old woman around the corners and eaves of her house, she'd
tried to ignore the feeling. Butch was right, sort of, though she would

never admit it. He'd always cautioned her that one day she would wake up alone and regret it. Pulling her old gray sweater closer, wandering through the house, turning out lights and setting things to rights, her only comfort was that when she noticed her isolation, it was night not day, and she was already awake—at least he wasn't completely right.

Finding herself alone in the space of her large house, with Destiny sleeping soundly across the hall, Davida tried not to feel useless or unwanted. It had never been that way while Marc was in her life. With Marc, she was always sexy, vivacious, and scintillating—or at least she felt like she was. If she hadn't sent him away, she could call him, tell him how she felt, and let his voice wrap itself around her like a pair of strong arms—caressing and protective. She could even, be Boo, if she wanted to.

Turning to her bathroom, Davida had idly lifted the bottle of pear nectar bubble bath. Turning warm water on full blast, she spilled a generous amount from the bottle and watched the bubbles form in the deep tub. The scent evoked memories that ached like physical wounds. *I bought this in Atlanta,* she noted, capping the bottle. Outside, rain began to tap at her windows. Any other time, the sound would have been soothing, but last night it grated on her last nerve, leaving her emotionally raw and psychically bruised.

It seemed right somehow to do this bath in the dark, like a closing ceremony, a final mourning for something she might never have again, and she switched off the electric lights.

Barefoot, still in her jeans and old sweater, she brought the boxes of tiny votive candles she'd stored, from her room. The heavy forest green robe she'd bought, with the intention of giving it to Marcus as a Christmas gift, lay folded on the floor near the foot of the tub. Setting her candles along the sink, the edge of the tub and the mirrored vanity, she took her time, lighting the candles one-by-one.

She should have music for this. When no theme song suggested itself, Davida elected silence and the sounds of the storm.

Her lips trembled as she slipped her arms free of the old gray sweater. Reluctant, barely manageable, fingers found the hem of her T-shirt, and she lifted her arms to pull it over her head. She stood with the shirt twisted, binding her arms to her chest and remembered another T-shirt, and the man who'd freed her from it. The man who'd freed her from so many things—she let the shirt fall to the peach tiled floor. Her fingers were suddenly stupid, incapable of reason as they clumsily tried to undo the buttons of her jeans.

Finally stepping free, forbidding herself to rush, Davida approached her tub. The water was warmer than she'd anticipated, sending heat spiking through her body. An orgasmic thrill raced from her feet, up her legs and her spine, tracing her nerves, bringing a climactic gasp, that might have been his name to her lips. Her breasts were swollen so tightly they hurt, aroused by nothing more than the echoing sound of his too familiar voice ratcheting through her mind.

Easing herself into the gently moving water, laved by the lick of foam and wetness, Davida wondered at what she was feeling. Never in her experience, had the absence of any man shaken her the way Marcus Benton's had. Of two minds, she wondered if she should feel shame or pain at the reaction to the empty space Marc left within her. Feeling hollow, she scooped a handful of water and watched it pour along her skin, forming a tiny river—like a tiny river of tears. Lifting her hand again, she let the water fall along the drift of her arm and the flow of her breast to pool at her navel and the juncture of her thighs. Watching, she hurt with an indescribably almost unendurable pain.

Finally seated, breast deep in steamy heat and bubbles, Davida had looked to the frosted pane in her bathroom window. The tip of a branch tapped there, etching the sound of loneliness into her heart. Every time there's a storm, for the rest of her life, was she going to regret being nervous and stupid? Every time it rained, was she going to hear his voice and cry because she sent him away?

She'd never wept before. Even when she lost Skip, she didn't weep. She shed tears of loss and sorrow, but as much as she missed him, she never felt this empty. Maybe because with Skip she knew her loss was irretrievable, but with Marc . . . she didn't know. She blotted tears from her face with a bubble-shrouded hand and leaned back against the terry bath pillow. Wanting to throw her head back and wail, she closed her eyes and pressed her lips tightly together, instead.

She'd never felt like screaming before. She'd never thought it would help, but right now, she almost felt like she'd die if she couldn't let some of this pain out. Water splashed impotently, overflowing the tub when she slammed her palms to the surface. Only the fear of breaking her foot kept her from lashing out with both long legs. Heavy strands of her coarse hair clung and curled against her moist cheek, and Davida Lawrence had to remind herself that as angry as she was with herself, she would die without air. She would die without food. She would manage to live without screaming, and she would live without Marcus Benton, but what kind of life would it be? She knew she didn't want to know the answer.

She could always call him. And say what? *Marc, I was wrong, and I miss you so much I hurt.*

It was hard not to slam her hands against her desk in useless frustration. This was not what she wanted do this morning.

She hung her head at her desk and tried to imagine the most eloquent and expressive words she could use. She hadn't come up with them last night, and she was doing no better this morning. Two fat tears landed in her lap and shimmered before sinking into the soft wool of her pink dress. Davida used the back of her hand to brush away the tear that hung at the base of her lashes. She was too hard on him, and he didn't deserve it, but she was so wrapped up in the moment, in what was happening to Des. She couldn't find a space for him . . .

It was no excuse, and useless to try.

The ringing telephone brought her back with a start. The little blue bar was blinking on her computer: e-mail. Still at work—this was not where she was supposed to sit mooning over someone she'd thrown out of her life using both hands and a foot. Lifting the telephone receiver was the last thing she wanted to do. Whoever it was, it wouldn't be Marcus, of that she was more than certain.

"Good morning, Davida Lawrence. How may I help you?" Her voice was steady and poised—the immediate composure was an act, but a good one.

"Hello?" It was Quita. "I wanted to be sure you still wanted to have lunch, because I'm taking an hour of leave time. Famous-Barr is having a sale today."

"No problem, Queen of Sales. I'm still planning on lunch." Davida grinned, then sneezed.

"Bless you," Quita offered. "You know, you need to see a doctor about that little cold you've got. It's been hanging on for an awfully long time."

"Yes, but to tell you the truth, I've had enough of doctors to last me for a lifetime, thanks." Davida sneezed again, passing a hand across her face. She felt warm, even to her own hand.

"Still, it's not like you to get sick. I mean, for as long as I've known you, you've never been prone to . . . ooh, girl!"

Davida made a face on her end. "What?"

"You know," Quita said slowly, "the last time you carried on like this was when you . . ."

"Oh, no. That's not even a possibility, here."

"You know, you are so good at denial. Davida, have you seen a doctor?"

"For a cold, Quita? No, I think, not." Davida's fingers found busywork on her desk top. Signing off on several vouchers, she continued. "This is only a cold, or sinusitis. Either way, we have a long weekend coming up, and Des is spending Thanksgiving with Mama Lou. I'll be fine."

"But, I'll see you today for lunch?"

"Of course," Davida said. Hanging up the telephone, she wondered if seeing her doctor was really a bad idea.

* * *

Still at her desk, Davida pressed a palm to her face. Nobody should have to this. Her chest rose and fell heavily with her breathing, and her head was pounding like half the NFL was in there holding practice. Maybe Quita was right. Davida flipped through her rolodex to find Dr. Belinda Reed.

"Oh, my darlin', Davida. What a surprise." The doctor answered her own phone, her voice warm and welcoming over the telephone line. "Long time no hear from. Melanie tell you I asked about you last time she was here? We never get to see you unless something is really bothering you." She waited. No answer. She tried again, "What is bothering you, Cookie?"

Davida sniffed. "I'm just not feeling like myself, Belinda. I've had a cold for almost two months, now."

"That's not like you," the doctor agreed.

"So, people keep telling me." Davida shrugged.

"What seems to be the problem?"

"Ah, nothing, B." Davida sighed. "Actually, everything. Nothing hurts, but I'm generally miserable. Like I told you, I seem to have a never-ending cold, and I just don't feel like myself."

A sharp tapping came over the line, and Davida knew Belinda was thinking, using the eraser end of her pencil against the phone. *She used to do the same thing when she was a kid,* Davida recalled. You never outgrew some habits, it seemed.

"Any other complaints?"

"B, if I were some kind of Victorian woman, you'd probably call what I have 'malaise.' " She propped an elbow on her desk and dropped her chin against her fist. "Do you think, maybe I'm starting menopause?"

"Davida, you know I can't diagnose you over the phone . . ."

"I know," she said thoughtfully. "I just thought it would give me a little time to prepare myself if I knew."

It was the doctor's turn to grow contemplative. "How do you think you'd feel if this were related to menopause?"

"Sad," Davida said immediately. "I mean, it would mean . . ." She had a mental flash of the beautiful and vibrant women who stood so prominently in her life. Her mother, her aunt, and her mother-in-law had all experienced menopause, and seemed to have thrived. In fact, that trio could have been the poster models for postmenopausal pride. She sighed, and rethought her answer. "You know, B, menopause is really just another state of being, isn't it? I don't guess that would bother me at all." She shrugged. "I just want to know for sure why I'm feeling like this."

The doctor hummed a response, then the pencil tapped again. "You know," she finally said, "the last time you complained of not feeling like yourself . . ."

"I know," Davida interrupted. "I know."

"You still need to come in. Friday at three thirty, okay?"

Davida nodded. "I'll be there."

"Is there some reason these rooms always have to be so cold?" Davida complained. "Like, is there some doctor law that says you have to raise x number of chill bumps on a tired black woman in a white paper gown before your exam is official?"

"See?" Belinda Reed drawled, smiling. She pushed the pastel blue door closed behind her. "That's why I miss you, your sparkling wit." She reached up to give Davida a swift pat on the shoulder as she walked past. Her glasses slid dangerously near the square tip of her broad nose as she flipped through the lined pages on the chart she held. "How's the wonder child doing these days?"

"Fine. She no longer wants to be a princess, a ninja, or a singer. She's talking about becoming a doctor."

"Oh." The doctor beamed over her steel rimmed bifocals. "Have her come see me sometime, though I'm sure she's seen her share of doctors' offices. It might be fun for her to see one and not be on the receiving end for a change. Besides, if you bring her here to the Women's Group, she'll get to see real women as real doctors." Belinda smiled. "We make great role models, you know."

"Good idea. She might enjoy that," Davida said through chattering teeth. "Really, B, could I at least have my jacket? It's cold in here."

"Big baby." Belinda grinned, passing the jacket to her reluctant patient. Perching on the white enamel-coated stool at the foot of the table where Davida shivered, the doctor reviewed her notes, then looked up. "So, what's up, Cookie? Talk to me."

Davida shook her head and sniffed. "Like I told you on the telephone, just a cold that won't go away." She shrugged.

"Not exactly like you," Belinda said, frowning. "Let's have a look."

Pulling out the tools of her trade, the doctor provided a thorough examination. Then, pulling off her rubber gloves, she rolled them into a neat, disposable ball and tossed them into the metal receptacle. "I'm thinking this isn't a regular cold, at all, Davida."

"Well, I don't think I have any more blood for you to take," Davida said miserably, rubbing her arm, fingering the Band-Aid.

"We can work with what you've already given us." Doctor Reed raised her eyebrows and tried to look older and wiser than even her gray hair made her appear. "I'm thinking of doing some other tests on you."

"You ran an allergy series on me about two years ago, remember?"

"Yeah, I did," the doctor agreed slowly. "But we haven't done a pregnancy test in quite a while."

"A what? Why?"

Dr. Reid sat heavily on the enameled stool and crossed her legs. She took a deep breath and let it out slowly, as though preparing herself for an ordeal of monumental proportions. "Your temp is above normal. Your immune system seems to be breaking down under no more than normal stress, along with the nausea and dizziness. And, I'll tell you"—she sucked at her teeth—"during that pelvic, you looked a little . . ." She nodded.

"Oh, come on, B. We were talking about menopause when I made this appointment, and now you're suddenly talking about pregnancy tests—that's totally opposite ends of the spectrum. You're joking, right?"

"No. No joke, my dear."

"But, a cold can make . . ."

"Your symptoms are perfectly logical for around nine weeks. Making a baby is hard work, Cookie, and that can take a toll on you." The doctor shook her head negatively. "I really don't think this is a cold we're dealing with."

Eyes moving frantically, Davida counted mentally. *This is not possible!* "This is not possible," she said aloud. "My period is not, hasn't been . . . It's regular," she announced as though the knowledge would fend off all other possibilities.

"We both know that regularity is not absolute proof of anything." She gave Davida's knee a solid pat. "Think of it this way, if it's not a pregnancy, we'll look at other factors, other options—but I'm betting you're pregnant."

"I'm forty years old. I'm not married."

"Davida. Cookie. Who said that has anything to do with getting pregnant?"

"I don't have a father anywhere out there on the horizon!"

"Davida. Sweetie. Of course, you do. You've got a somebody out there, somewhere, or we wouldn't be considering this possibility."

"It's not a possibility." Davida couldn't control her features, and it took several minutes for the shock to run the course of her body. The tears and trembling were simultaneous. "Oh, no. Belinda, uh-uh."

Belinda Reed did the only medically feasible thing she could. She stood and folded her patient into a hug. Patting Davida's heaving back, she began asking questions. "Any soreness of your breasts,

Cookie? Any vaginal dryness during intercourse? Are you more tired than usual?"

Davida cried harder, stuffing her fist against her lips to muffle her sobs.

Finally quieting, she knuckled her eyes, ruining what was left of her makeup. "Now what?" she hiccupped.

"We do the test," the doctor replied.

Shivers wracked the patient. "How long does it take? I mean today is Friday, so Monday? Tuesday?" Davida accepted a handful of tissues and sniffed again.

"It has been a long time for you, hasn't it?" the doctor said, kindly. "We've managed to speed up the process a little since Des. If you want to wait, we'll have your results in about an hour."

"Hour?" Was that like, sixty minutes? An hour was all the time she'd have to revise her entire life? She took the cup of water from Belinda's hand and tried to swallow slowly. "But, it could be negative, right? It could just be a cold, right?" She sipped more water, but settling in her throat, it refused to go down.

Dr. Reed patted Davida's knee again. "Let's just wait and see."

Davida finally managed to swallow. Sliding off the table, she reached for her clothes. "Yeah. Might as well not buy trouble when there's so much available for free—right?"

Her practitioner grinned at her. "Come see me when you're dressed," she said, easing from the room.

Crunching the little white pleated paper cup into a ball, Davida tossed it toward a waste paper basket and missed. Bending to retrieve it, she wondered how this had happened. How had this happened? *How do you think, Davida?*

She'd made love to a man who made her feel like a very young woman again—that's how it happened. She'd made love to a man who brought back all the promises of youth and tenderness, and the vulnerability she'd thought she would never feel again. Her hands rushed to her face, and she hid her face behind them, trying to breathe and remain upright. *Lord, I remember trying to explain where babies come from the first time Des asked, and it had nothing to do with making love to a fantasy.*

She closed her eyes behind her hands, and tried to imagine herself holding a new baby again. Feeling it close to her body, sharing her body with an infant, someone who needed her in ways that Destiny never would again. Pregnancy was a big jump from menopause, and not necessarily even a part of her future. *It's going to be all right,* she assured herself. *Whatever the tests reveal, it's going to be alright.* She began to dress.

The band of her pantyhose settled neatly at her waist, and made

Davida pause. Looking down at her sleek brown belly, she wondered what it would look like fully distended, fully pregnant. *Like this,* turning sideways she puffed out her stomach. Checking her reflection in the mirror above the sink, she hooked her thumbs into the band of her hose. *I, we,* she corrected, looking down at the space she'd made, *we would fill all that up.* She remembered the silhouette, and how pleased and *ripe* it made her feel the first time around.

From the time she'd begun to show, Davida had marveled at how curvy her form became, with her navel sitting jauntily upturned, saluting the baby to come and the world at large. It still made her smile to see other proudly pregnant women, especially when they parked that hand on top, like they were comforting their babies.

Maybe being pregnant, if she was pregnant—maybe it wouldn't be so bad. Once she found a way to explain it to Des, and could look her mother in the eye without feeling like a bad child herself, maybe it wouldn't be so bad.

She wondered what this baby would look like. Who he or she would take after? Which side of the family would . . .

She found the long, navy pleated skirt to her J.G. Hook suit and stopped where she stood. Her hand found the exam table, and she fumbled backward looking for a place to sit. Her eyes grew large and intensely dark. Hearing herself for the first time, Davida had to remind herself to breathe.

Marc.

Lord, she was drifting along here in her own little fool's paradise. She was dreaming of cuddling this soft little perfect baby, dreaming of what it'd look like, and where was her mind? She couldn't find the words to tell Marc she was wrong. Where in the world was she going to find the words to tell him he was going to be a father?

The skirt slipped from her nerveless fingers and hissed into a pile on the floor at her feet.

They'd talked about this—sort of. He liked children, he wanted children—but with her? He said "some day," but he didn't say right away. This man was five years younger than she was. Some day for him could be in ten or twenty years. He had a whole future planned for himself, and she knew that it included his work—not a baby!

Marc's world was filled with colors and shapes. He was working on something that he'd waited his entire life for. What was she supposed to say to him, "excuse the interruption, but here's your baby"? Now was the time for him to celebrate a major artistic achievement, not for him to be pushing a baby carriage. Davida probed the inside of her tip of her tongue. It didn't help, not even when she traced her lips with the tip of her tongue. The dryness persisted.

He'd warmed up to Des calling him daddy really quickly, but it

took time to be a parent, and that was hard enough when it was
planned. And Lord knew this was not planned. Surely, when he did
get around to having children and parenting, he didn't plan on doing
it with a senior citizen.

She closed her eyes and wished away the incipient nausea. And
what about the sickle cell? She thought he said he'd been tested. She
thought he said he was negative. She thought he said . . . Damn! She
should know this. Why didn't she know this?

She grabbed the skirt from the floor and stepped into it. Jamming
her arm into her blouse, Davida tried to calm herself when a button
came off in her hand. She was probably overreacting. It wasn't a baby.
She was not having a baby. This was probably just the flu, just like
she thought in the beginning. It was either the flu or menopause. After
all, at forty, there was very little chance of her even being . . . The
soft knock on the door stopped the flow of her thoughts.

The door opened just enough for Belinda Reed to stick her head
in. Davida heard another button pop off her blouse and go rolling
invisibly across the exam room floor. "Ready? We've got your
results." Her arm came through the door holding a steaming mug of
lemon scented tea. "Thought this might warm you up if you're still
cold."

"You're nurturing me." People always sought to nurture when
they had bad news. The corners of Davida's mouth turned down.

"Just finish putting your clothes on and come on out," the doctor
said.

Fumbling in her purse, Davida dug out two safety pins. Her shaking
hands nearly stabbed her own flesh several times before she succeeded
in closing her pale yellow and navy striped blouse. She pulled the
jacket on, then off as she gathered her coat and scarf. Slipping into
the navy leather pumps was an afterthought. Her primary thought was
nearly paralyzing. *How to tell Marc?* Fully clothed, she tugged the
door open and trudged through it. The azure and blue corridor before
her looked endless.

"I'm right here," Belinda called cheerfully.

Davida slowed at the corner, her eyes entering the space first.
Belinda was seated on a soft deep green and yellow print love seat
tucked into an alcove. The tiny area had been made to look almost
like a mini-sitting room, complete with a small Sheridan coffee table,
brass lamps, and potted plants. She had more of the lemony tea ready
for service in a pretty silver pot. A small china plate held Pepperidge
Farm cookies. "Come on, sit." She laid a welcoming hand on the
cushion beside her.

"You're not fooling me, you know." Davida let her coat, scarf, and purse slide onto a chair across from where her doctor sat. "You're sitting there all cozy and cute, trying to soothe me into trusting you."

It was true. Belinda Reed was tiny in stature, dressed in embroidered denim, and built like a cuddly teddy bear. Her little round brown face showed light traces of makeup and crinkled with fun. "Now you don't trust me? That's okay, I took pretty good care of both you and Butch whenever I had to sit for you two monsters." She pushed her glasses higher on her nose. "Of course, I was only a teenager, a mere child myself, but I took care of you then, and I guess I can still do it." She patted the cushion again. "Have a sit-down, old friend."

Davida sat. "I'm dying, right?"

Belinda chuckled. "Just the opposite, you're fine. The test is back." She lifted the silver teapot and poured carefully, then offered the cup to Davida.

Accepting the cup, Davida closed her eyes. "I'm pregnant?"

The doctor nodded, waiting for the other shoe to drop.

When the richly chocolate eyes opened again, Dr. Reed was puzzled by the mixed expression she saw there. "So, I'm pregnant with a child who very well might have his beautiful golden, long-lashed eyes, his precious dimples, and my sickle-cell trait." Davida's lips trembled, and she set the cup aside, covering her mouth with the back of her hand. "B, I don't know what I'm going to do here."

"What are you asking me, Cookie?"

Davida's eyes cleared dramatically as she looked up. "Come on, B, you've known me since all my babies were dolls." She wrinkled her nose. "I just don't know how this happened. We were so careful about . . ."

"Protection?" Belinda lifted her head and gave the other woman the benefit of a wise nod. "No form of birth control is ever one hundred percent certain, Cookie. You already know that." She blinked, and her mouth dropped suddenly. "What about the father? You're still, uh . . ." She waited.

"On good terms?" Davida colored, her dark skin suddenly infused with a dusky rose tint. "No, we're not." She dropped her eyes. "I have no clue how I'm going to tell him tell him about this, B." She sniffed and cleared her throat. Her eyes ranged about the room, taking in everything but Belinda Reed's face. "The last time I saw him, I told him to get out of our lives, and pretty much expected not to ever look back." Liar. At least, she didn't really tell him to get out of our lives. She looked down at her lap.

Belinda cocked her head. "Did you mean it?"

"I thought I did," Davida whispered.

"And how do you think he felt?"

"B, I thought your specialty was gynecology."

"Don't you think he'd like to know, deserves to know, about your pregnancy?" the doctor asked softly.

"Maybe." Davida brought the cup to her lips and sipped to avoid speaking.

"If you were willing to give him the chance, do you think he'd be willing to co-parent with you?"

The gold-rimmed china cup rose to her lips again, and Davida jumped when she accidentally slurped against the rim. She lifted and lowered her shoulders.

Co-parent? Of course, he would. He would be there, hovering and being conveniently responsible, if he had to be. Marc would probably put his dreams and, in fact, his whole life on hold for this child. And then spend the rest of his natural life hating her for causing the detour in his life plan. Maybe it would be better never to mention the child, to run off and hide somewhere in a place where he could never find her. Like that could happen! If she had to share this child's life with him, every time the opportunity arose, he would look at her with those beautiful eyes, and try not to hate her. Every time he turned those fascinating eyes on her, Davida knew she would feel about as guilty as any one human being could. She drank again.

Belinda Reed lifted her own cup and sipped, a tiny, ladylike action, then touched her lips with the white cloth napkin. "I'm thinking that you might want to take some time to get used to the idea of this baby, and then you might want to talk to him. I don't need to tell you how hard it can be, being a single parent." She inclined her head and raised her brows. "You might want to talk to him and to the rest of your family."

"My family? Not to sound too cavalier, but they're all adults, I guess they'll all adjust. I have only one real worry."

The kind smile was a sweet touch, and any other patient might have bought it at face value. Davida knew it was meant to encourage her to keep talking. "What am I going to tell Des?" she asked.

"That she's going to be a big sister." The doctor grinned mischievously. "Unless you think she's got more specific questions."

Lowering her eyes, Davida's fingers rose to worry a spot behind and beneath her right ear. "You know my child."

"My advice is to answer *exactly* what she asks you, and no more. If you don't embellish, her imagination won't roam—too much. Drink your tea."

Finishing the cup obediently, Davida held it forth for a refill.

CHAPTER
TWENTY-ONE

The creamy, sand-colored walls of the corner office, with its practical gray carpeting, neat ranks of filled bookcases, and broad-leafed, fluorescent-light-nourished plants, seemed to be closing in. The fact that the office seemed unbearably hot didn't help, either. Essie Cofing was determined to get on her last nerve, and from where Davida sat, she was doing an awfully good job of it.

"Now, Dee, I think we've finished almost all of our business." The little brown, birdlike woman fluttered, arranged a neat row of pens, then leaned over her tightly folded hands. She blinked and seemed to have to refocus her brown eyes behind the brown frames of her thick lensed glasses. Fumbling, she selected a pen from her row and twirled it along her fingers like a dwarf baton. "There's just this one last thing, Dee. You want to tell me, how advanced is your condition?"

My condition? Oh, this was way too much. Davida shook her head. "No, Essie, I don't want to tell you."

"And you're not together with the father, are you?" The IRS manager looked very sad.

"Essie." Davida looked down, trying to ignore the stridency she heard in her own voice. "You called me in here to check some personnel problems, and we've done that. My 'condition' is no problem. Not for me, and certainly not for you." She stood and raised a warning finger to her supervisor. "Essie, you're trying to get to a very bad place in my life. Don't go there."

"Oh! Uhm, well, Dee." Esme Cofing stood and tugged at her brown wool sweater. "Dee, I really didn't mean to offend you—and I'm sorry that I did." She crossed her arms tightly across her chest and pursed her lips. "I don't know what to say."

Collecting her folders, Davida was tempted to feel sorry for the embarrassed Essie. She was, after all, only acting on the impetus of office gossip That's what I get for relying on Quita's ability to keep her mouth shut.

"I really didn't mean to offend you." Essie fluttered, dropped her pen, and apologized again. "It's just, I know that it's been hard for you, being alone, with Destiny and all. I just thought that if we were able to plan a little bit ahead . . ."

Davida patted the air between them in a conciliatory motion, and nodded. "I understand," she said. "It's okay." She managed to reach the door while Essie twisted her sweater down and over her knuckles.

"Dee, really . . ." Essie's eyes were lost in the glare of overhead lighting.

"It's really okay, Essie. Nothing's come up that I can't handle."

"I almost believe that," Essie whispered.

Davida tried not to meet the other woman's eyes as she eased through the door into the hall, and hurried toward her own space. The last thing she wanted right now was to have to endure the carefully phrased congratulations or sympathy of another coworker. She turned a short corner, cutting past the copy room, avoiding Anne Laird in the process, and applauded herself on meeting the challenge when she reached her office unaccosted. Closing the windowed door behind herself, she kicked her foot against the short-napped carpet.

"I don't know what possessed me to think I could tell Quita anything, and not have it meet me coming around a corner," Davida said, and kicked her pump at the carpet again. "I don't know why I'm getting so angry. It must be that hormonal thing Belinda warned me about."

As if summoned, the telephone rang on cue. Davida pressed her lips together and took a deep breath. "Good afternoon, Davida Lawrence speaking. How may I help you?"

"Oh, Cookie, I was afraid I'd missed you!"

"No, you got me, B." Something in the vicinity of Davida's stomach executed a barrel roll, and she bent her knees and reached for the nearest chair. Sitting, she held the phone to her ear. "What's up?"

"I'm thinkin'." Belinda clucked. "I'm thinkin' I'd like to take a closer look at that little guy of yours," she said. "I'm thinkin' we might like to try an ultrasound."

"An ultrasound?" The barrel roll happened again, and Davida felt the emotional shift of about a ton of fear. "Is there any special reason?"

"No," the doctor said lightly, too lightly for Davida's comfort. "I was thinkin' you might like to get an early photo for your family album, and maybe we should go ahead and schedule you for amniocentesis while we're at it."

Davida wanted to scream, she wanted to kick something, but didn't know how to do it and retain a little dignity and a little sanity in the process. "It's the sickle cell, isn't it? You're worried that the baby's affected by . . . or is it because of my age? Tell me, B, because I'm too afraid to cry."

"Cookie, amnio is a personal decision. We only do it so that an appropriate decision can be made by the parents . . ."

". . . if something's wrong—right?"

"Listen, sweetie, I'm not there, I can't give you a hug right now. But I can tell you that at fourteen weeks, your little baby is really a baby, and doing fine according to our last little look-see. That little guy's got a brain, and fingers and toes, and if we tried, we could get a great heartbeat. All we want to do with this test is to make sure he or she is as healthy as we can. You want to know that, don't you?" She got hiccups for an answer. "Then, don't be afraid, just tell me when we can schedule the amnio."

Still holding the telephone, Davida covered her mouth with the other hand and felt the slow and steady slide of tears along her cheek. Damned hormones. She seemed to cry at everything these days. She'd cried almost all morning over something Destiny asked last night.

Sitting in the den, watching the screen of her computer, Des had suddenly twisted in her seat. Drawing her leg under her, cocking her head to the side, she watched her mother. Feeling the weight of too curious eyes, Davida looked up from the shirt in her lap. Something about that look made her set the buttons aside and park her needle in the fabric of the shirt she was working on. Pulling her gold-rimmed glasses from her face she looked at the child.

"Mom?"

"Yes?" Sudden indigestion threatened.

"Do you know what a bastard is?"

The indigestion, hot and burning, stabbed Davida's chest. "A what?"

"A bastard." Destiny's eyebrows furrowed and lifted in emphasis. "Is our baby gonna be a bastard?"

"A what?" The tears began to boil up from somewhere behind Davida's eyes.

The child's lips tightened and twisted. "I want to know. Is our baby gonna be a bastard? Tawanna Mallory says the word is a social term, not a criticism. She says that's what her mother says. She says that when you don't got . . ."

"Have," Davida corrected automatically. She felt sick, sick and angry, and knew it was wrong to direct that anger at either Destiny or Tawanna. They were children, and had made no judgment until one was provided for them. The definition included in the comment was more than enough to prove the words had been overheard. For a long instant, Davida hated Yvonne Mallory for corrupting both children. When her stomach lurched, and the heartburn sent gorge higher in her throat, Davida amended her anger—Yvonne's gossip now troubled three children.

Des stood up and wiped her hands on her jeans. Flexing one leg, she rolled her foot to the side and knotted her fingers behind her. The picture of vulnerability, she came closer to confront her mother. "Mom? Is our baby gonna be a bastard?" She planted her knees on the sofa and sat on her heels looking at her mother.

"No, sweetie." Davida opened her arms and Destiny crawled into the opening. "Our baby is not a bastard. Our baby has a mother and a father, and a big sister. Okay?"

Des looked up and blinked. "So Marc is going to marry us, all three of us, and we're going to be a family? Tawanna Mallory said that was the only way to not be a bastard—if the mother and father got married." She snuggled close, laying her head against her mother's full breast.

"Sweetie, that's something Marc and I haven't discussed yet. But I'll let you know as soon as we decide anything, okay?"

"Okay." Des grinned, her smile cutting her mother's heart. She laid her palm against the slight swell of her mother's stomach and watched the delicate movement as Davida breathed. "It's going to be alright," she whispered.

And Davida knew she would give her life to keep it so.

"So, when do you want to schedule it?"

"It?" The question brought Davida back to the here and now.

"Yes. Stay with me, Cookie," the doctor insisted. "When do you want to do the amnio?"

"Where would I have to do it? Could it be done there, at the Women's Group?"

"Absolutely. The only problem is that the earliest we can get you in here is on the eighth of December, say two o'clock."

Frowning, Davida fingered the pages of her desk calendar. The eighth was a week away, but if it was the best she could do . . . "Two o'clock, on the eighth is okay," she said finally.

"Okay, we'll get you in," the doctor agreed happily. "And, you're going to want to bring someone with you, just for moral support. Why don't you bring the dad? I'd love to meet him, and besides, they usually like being included, getting to see the baby. You two can even learn the sex, if you want to."

The big sniff carried over the phone line. "Still having those shifts in your immune system?" Belinda sounded leery. "Or, are those tears?" She waited and got only another sniff in response. "Have you told him about the baby, yet?"

"Not yet." Davida pulled tissues from the box and crushed them to her nose, then dabbed at her eyes.

Doctor Reed sighed heavily. "You really ought to tell him before this baby starts college, or joins the military, or gets married."

"I know, but, I've got until the eighth. I'll see you then, B." She hung up so quickly the doctor had no chance to respond.

Pulling more tissue from the box, Davida touched her nose again. She stared at the suddenly ringing telephone and wondered who in the world it was, this time. And, why in the world are *you* calling me? She touched the speaker button. "Good afternoon, Davida Lawrence speaking. How may I help you?" She didn't sound too bad, she thought. A little stuffy, but otherwise nonhormonal.

"Hey, Cookie."

"Butch." She knew Quita hadn't gone and called her brother. "What's up?"

"I just got in from Quebec, and I have something for Des. I wanted to ask about the transfusion program you're trying to get her into. I heard about a similar program while I was away."

She sniffed. "Availability has closed on several of the hospitals, so right now we're looking at Rainbow Children's Hospital in Cleveland, Ohio, and the Medical College of Georgia."

Glenn Morrison stretched, and groaned in the process. "I thought you were considering that hospital in Atlanta, too. What's the name of it?"

"Emory University," she said dully, "they have an opening, too."

"That sounds like a good bet." Glenn stretched and sniffed. "What are you going to be doing while she's going back and forth for these transfusions?"

"Oh, you'll be glad to hear this," Davida sat a little straighter and prepared herself for a lecture. "I've decided that I'll look into a temporary transfer to whatever city Des needs to be in."

"You'd consider moving?" Surprise was evident in his voice. "Which one looks best so far?"

Davida squinted and tightened her shoulders. "Emory. There's a region IV agency opening, too."

"Region IV is the Southeast, isn't it? And Emory is in Atlanta, isn't it?"

"Marc's still in Atlanta, right? Be nice to be in a city where someone cares about you."

"You sound just like Mom," Davida sniped. "That's why I stay in St. Louis, Butch."

"Mom told me you had some other news," he said abruptly.

Of course it would have been too much to ask of Jewell Morrison to keep the news of a new grandchild, even a five inch, yet-to-be-born, grandchild to herself. "Yes, I'm expecting," Davida confirmed.

"Then, maybe there's someone who cares about you in Atlanta, and you ought to give him a chance. Maybe you ought to consider being somewhere where you and your children will be special, too."

She hung her head and tried not to imagine Marc's face. It was difficult, and she nearly succeeded, then it seemed she could almost feel his hand, firm and gentle at her cheek. "Marcus Benton and I have too many differences, and I can't force my way into his life. It wouldn't be fair to him or this child."

"Force?" Glenn Morrison blew air harshly across the receiver. "What are you talking about, Cookie? Marc would gladly walk back and forth between Atlanta and St. Louis every day for the rest of his natural life, if it would get him to you. How do you figure you have to force anything on him?"

"Marcus has plans for his life, Glenn. Remember how single-mindedly you approached law school? How absolutely nothing was going to keep you out? And how determined you were to go to the one school you'd always dreamed of?"

"Yeah . . ." He drew the one word out.

"Well, that's how Marc is. That's how his art is. He's waited for the break that allows him the freedom to create Bro'Man just the way he's always wanted to. I love . . ." She caught herself. "I care too much for him to take that away."

"Cookie, sometimes the concept of heart's desire is overrated."

"I don't think this is one of those times."

Glenn made an odd clucking sound with his tongue, and his sister had the distinct feeling of chastisement. "Have you talked to him?"

Pulling more tissue from her box, Davida sneezed loudly. "Sorry," she said.

"That's not an answer."

"Okay. No."

"In my considered opinion, you've made an inappropriate rush to judgment. Destiny already adores this man. From what Mom says, Des has pretty much elected him to Daddy status. And you . . ." Her brother sighed, and the creak of his leather chair punctuated his concern. "Cookie, I've seen the way you look at him. I've seen the way you make moves to include him in your life. He's good for you."

And, he used to call me, Boo. The tears began in earnest. *And, I liked it.*

"You're a fine one to talk," Davida tried. "The only people you seem to hang out with are your clients."

"Hey, we were talking about you, remember? Cookie," Glenn pressed his advantage, "I've seen you come alive when he's near—and it's better than you've ever been alone."

"I'm not up to this today, Butch," she said tiredly. "I still have to talk to Dr. Saylor."

"Okay." She could almost see him lifting his hands in surrender. "I'm not trying to get into your business, because I know you'll only tell me that you're a grown woman and quite capable of making up your own mind."

"I appreciate your understanding. Talk to you later?"

"You bet, just remember, I'm on your side—and, by the way, I agree with Mom. The man's in Atlanta—you need to go to Atlanta." And he was gone, but the telephone was ringing again.

"Hellooo." It was Quita, too happy and too spunky. One word and she was already making Davida's head hurt. "I just wanted to check, to see what you've done since lunch. Have you told him, yet?"

"No."

"Are you going to?"

A shrug and very humble nod. "I guess I have to," Davida said. "What kind of choice do I have?"

"Well, what have you been doing in the meantime, I mean, to get ready? To get your nerve together?"

"Avoiding Belinda Reed for one thing."

"Avoiding? Why avoiding?"

"I got a call from her earlier today. She said . . ." It was hard, and the tears were imminent. "She said she'd like me to have am—, amni—, amnio—"

"Amniocentisis?" Quita finished for her. Davida nodded, stuttering over the affirmative, and the tears were there, hard, fast, and threatening to last forever. Quita clucked with concern and love and Davida had the frightening realization that she was being nurtured, and nurturing was always the precursor to something you didn't want to know about.

"So, what is this amnio thing supposed to do?" Quita asked, her voice low and curious.

Davida felt her body sag, and knew this was neither the time nor the place for this particular explanation, but with Quita, she also knew the question could not be put off for long. "It lets the doctor see the baby, test the fluids for content." She closed her eyes, not wanting to think of the other things the test would forecast.

She imagined Quita's eyes growing wide as she focused on Davida's words. "Well, did you schedule it, the test, did you schedule it yet?"

"Yes."

"When is it?"

"On the eighth, then I'll be out for a few days."

"Oh. Are you not coming in to work on the Monday after?"

"No, the doctor says I should plan on being out for about three days after the test." Davida caught her breath and held it for a long time. "Quita?" Who else was she going to ask? If the news was bad, and there were problems, her mother would probably faint, and Aunt Wesie and Mama Lou would probably try to stage a beat down on the doctor. She didn't feel right asking Butch, so . . . "Would you go with me? I don't think it'll take long, but I know I can't do it alone."

"Go with you? Oh, Davida, yes. Yes, I'll go. When?"

"Two o'clock on the eighth."

"That's a week," Quita said quickly. Her breath caught with an audible hiss. "So soon." Davida heard the question before it passed her lips. "When are you going to tell him? It would be a good idea to do it." Her voice slowed. "He ought to be there for this."

"I know. I just don't know how." Collecting another fistful of tissue, Davida sneezed twice.

"Dee, he really needs to know and he deserves the opportunity to be there with you when the test is done."

"I know." She folded her hand, still full of tissue, over her face.

"I know what," Quita volunteered, "I could call him for you."

"Don't you dare! You, stay away from the phone," Davida warned, "I have to do this on my own, and I will. But, not now. I'll do it later, after I've had a chance to think."

On her end, Quita's round body sagged immediately. "You would disappoint me . . . I mean him like that?" She pursed her lips and tried very hard to look hurt.

"Forget that, Quita. He's not . . . he's not part of the big picture, not for me. I have some things to do, and I'm just going to do them. What I'm going to do first though, is stop crying, because I can't face Des like that, and then I'm going to do this test."

"Okay, then," Quita agreed, "I'll be there with you."

With the line dead at her ear, Davida wiped her nose a final time. Hanging up, she pitched the ball of tissues into the nearby wastebasket. It felt like a good omen when the crumpled tissue flew true, landing neatly. *Well, as long as I've got good omens working for me . . .* Davida's finger shook as she punched in the Atlanta numbers.

* * *

Pounding through the purpling night, Marc watched the sky gray with what passed for fall in Atlanta. Crunching through strewn leaves, he hardly noticed the hexagonal flagstones lining the sidewalks. His path carried him along Highland Avenue, parallel to the Freedom Parkway, then turned slightly, curving across East Avenue and Ralph McGill Boulevard. The rhythmic slapping of his feet against the city sidewalk did little for him this night. His heart pumped, hard and heavy, and at any other time, he would have enjoyed his run.

He usually followed this path because it was never boring. If he'd felt better, he might have laughed—it was important not to be bored. The cool thing about his path was that always, there were other runners, bikers and skaters, no matter what time he ran, there were people doing something. Always, there was something to see, but for tonight, his eyes were empty and blind. Tonight, not even the changing flow of community, ranging from hardworking to upscale, registered with him.

Crossing Boulevard, then North Avenue, nearing Ponce, Marcus barely noticed the traffic. Headlights pouring determinedly toward midtown held no fascination for him, and he wasn't even tempted to make a detour down Ponce for a quick visit to the St. Charles Deli. He didn't even worry about the possible dangers inherent to darkness as his Reeboks carried him closer to Piedmont Park. His shirt and shorts were already damp, and he shook his head to knock off the drops of sweat dangling at the tip of his nose. "A ten-mile run will do that to a man," he muttered, picking up the pace.

The one thing a ten-mile run wasn't doing for Marcus Benton this night, was clearing his head. "I'll never understand how something that can start out so right can wind up so wrong," he said jogging in place, waiting for the light to change. Lifting a hand to wave at a carload of pretty happy hour goers, he finally crossed the street, shaking his head at their whistles and cat calls.

Maybe, that was what was wrong. She was tired of putting up with "women things." If he'd been pressed, Marcus knew he couldn't have identified a "woman thing" if his life depended on it. But, that still didn't explain her call yesterday. She'd called to say she was pregnant, and somehow, it seemed she was absolving him of any responsibility for it—but even in absolution, there was rejection. Did that count as a "woman thing"?

He shook his head again, and ran harder. The pumping of his legs, his firmly muscled thighs lifting and lowering mechanically, meant little to him. *Maybe,* he told himself, *it was just about her and family.*

Maybe it was initially a "mother/daughter thing," something mysti-
cally bonding, applying only to herself and Destiny, that a man was
never meant to understand—but the thudding knot in his stomach
promised that wasn't it. Logic told him that it was fear that made
Davida turn on him, and that only made things all the more painful.

"I know it was fear, and I guess I don't really blame her, but why
couldn't she trust me?" he muttered. "What have I done to convince
her that I've changed, that I'm less than worthy of her trust?"

He couldn't think of it yesterday either when he sat on his stool
in front of the drawing board, struggling to maintain focus, trying
desperately to meet a deadline. Marc had been reworking Bro'Man—
something about his expression bothered Marc, it was too tense, too
knowing. Working with charcoal, blending carefully, Marc tried to
make the changes he saw in his mind, and they refused to happen.

He looked at the background. There was something off there, too.
It was too flat. All of the colors looked like they were straight out of
a crayon box. They just sat there on the page, doing nothing, expressing
nothing of the story he'd developed with J.B. Maybe that was why
Bro'Man only looked like a two-dimensional drawing to him. It had
been like this since his return from St. Louis.

"I hate this," he said flipping the blending stick onto the board.
Separation, being sent away, was the last thing he expected when he
stood in the hospital looking at the woman he'd begun to see as the
realization of his future. "Somehow," he whispered to his drawings,
"I thought she would understand my feelings. I thought she would
expect me to feel connected to her and Destiny. I thought"—he stood
and walked to one of the tall windows—"I thought . . . I don't know
what I thought," he admitted to the Atlanta skyline.

The ringing phone was a distraction, and Marc wrinkled his brow.

The phone rang again, and he hoped it wasn't Feng Shui with more
of his "words of wisdom." The rap artist had been there earlier, and
noticing Marc's unusual funk wanted to know what was happening
with him. "Nothing," Marc replied.

"When a man of the arts has been denuded of words, I suspect the
finely drawn hand of a woman in the mix," the big man postulated.

"No, it's not like that," Marc tried.

"But, my brother, I have been there. I feel your pain, I know your
vision." He nodded sagely, shuffled his feet in an absurd little dance,
and Marc's heart sank. When he lowered himself to the futon in his
studio, his eyes met Milt's, and Milt just shrugged. *Now, why did I
think he would offer any help?* Marc wondered, knowing he didn't
want to hear any more from the "rap master" who considered himself
a neo-humanist prophet.

The phone rang again, and Marc counted it as three. One more and the machine would pick up. Even though he knew he needed to talk to him, he hoped it was not Milt. Man, he really didn't want to talk to him—at all. If he talked to Milt, he knew Milt was going to try to set up another meeting with Feng Shui, and Marc couldn't take it!

Fourth ring, and the message began. Reciting with the machine, Marcus wished he had some small amount of control over who the caller might be. "I sound like some kind of fool," he berated himself. "A weak, little wimpy, wishing it would be . . ."

"Marc, this is Davida." Her voice was breathless. The rush and whisper of her voice touched his soul and he grabbed for the receiver like it could save his life. Closing his eyes, trying for a composure his heartbeat denied, Marc stood with his hand covering the mouthpiece.

"Hello? Hello?" Even in confusion, her voice stirred him.

"Hello?" Bringing the phone to his lips, surprised at the huskiness of his tone, Marc forced himself to speak slowly.

"Marc, this is Davida."

As if he wouldn't know! "Hello." It was weak, but he couldn't trust himself to say more, to give her any more power than she already wielded.

"Marc, there's something I need to talk to you about."

"Really?" Closing his eyes, wanting to hope but not daring to commit to what he feared might be a foolish act, Marc tried to hold on to the texture of her voice, the memory of her thickly lush lips pressed against his. Her voice was cool, and he missed the warmth that was so much of his fantasy woman. He tried to smile, and it hurt his face. "No, how are you? No, how've you been?"

"No, Marc," she said quietly. The softness in her voice was brittle, challenged with anxiety, and it made Marc afraid. "I'm afraid this is not that kind of telephone call," she said.

But, it could be, Boo. It could be if you'd meet me just part of the way, he wished he could say. "What kind of call is this?" Too late, Marc realized his tone. Too late to take back the chill of offense, and when she spoke again, he knew Davida heard and recognized it, too.

Sounding sullen and dull, almost anaesthetized, she began slowly. "I called to tell you . . . something." Her breathing was suddenly labored and he imagined her with the intense look she'd worn standing over Destiny's bed. "Marc, I'm not sure if there's any right way to tell you this."

Then just say it, dammit! What was she going to say, and how bad could it be? Hadn't they already been through the worst? Why was she hesitating? *I don't know how to make anything easy for you, Boo. Baby, if you'd come with a set of instructions, I swear, I'd still be lost.* "What is it, Davida?" He hoped his tone was even, unbiased, and nonthreatening.

"You sound like you think I'm about to take a leap off a tall building, or something." The unexpected flash of wit came out of nowhere, and for the first time, Marc smiled. She sounded like the woman he'd met and learned to love through the miracle of fiber optics. Maybe this was going be alright, after all. Seconds later, his hopes took a left turn. "I'm not planning on doing anything desperate, but we definitely need to talk. This concerns both of us," she said, "and it would be wrong to leave you out."

The small hairs on the back of his neck rose, alert to approaching danger. "Is Des alright?"

"Yes, she's fine."

"Davida"—Marc pressed his back against the wall and slid down to a squatting position—"can we cut to the chase on this? You're beating around the bush, and I don't know why."

"You're right." Her voice was distant but rushed. "Marc, I was at my doctor's, and I'm pregnant."

"Pregnant? With a baby?" No, man! Pregnant with a guppy—of course she was pregnant with a baby. His baby! He shook his head to clear it. "When? How did this happen?"

"When? I can't pinpoint the time for you, but it happened in the usual man/woman sort of way, I presume." Davida covered the phone with her hand and bit at her lips to keep herself from screaming. Why did he sound like that?

Somehow, she wondered at her own surprise. *He sounds like I knew he would*—surprised and shocked. And why wouldn't he sound that way? She closed her eyes and used the heel of her other hand to wipe the hot tears that threatened to dissolve her resolution. He was either thinking she was lying to get him back into her life, or that she somehow found a way to get pregnant. Either way, he thought she'd trapped him.

Her stomach turned violently, washing her in sudden sweaty nausea, and she would have sworn the baby turned and jumped in protest. Laying her hand on the slight rise of her belly, she began to take deep breaths. *It's going to be alright,* she told her child. *Just remember, you have a mother and a big sister who want you desperately, and who can't wait to love you.* Her stomach quieted—waiting.

"Davida?" He waited. "Did you hear me?"

"I, no. I didn't hear you."

"How many, uhm . . . I don't know how you measure it." He sounded sheepish. "I guess I could ask Renee, and she'd be glad to tell me, but . . ."

"No!" Davida closed her eyes and tried to assess her feelings. Not embarrassed, not entirely ambivalent, she knew that she wasn't ready to have Marcus sharing their baby with the world. "I guess, uhm, it's weeks."

"And this baby is . . . ?"

"Fifteen weeks." "This" baby? Why couldn't he say, "my baby" or "our baby"? Davida used the tips of her fingers to massage her forehead. She needed to get off the phone. She couldn't do this. She shook her head in abject denial, but couldn't shake the feelings of loss for the fantasy this man had once been.

"So, when should we plan to get married?"

Oh, now she was dreaming. She thought . . . "What did you say?"

"I asked when you wanted to get married. You know, to give the baby a name, and . . ."

"And what? Make an 'honest woman' out of me?"

"Why not?" He smiled into the phone.

"Marcus Benton, that is the lowest, most insulting . . ."

"Wait a minute," he said flatly. "You're mad at me?"

"And insulted," she spat.

"I've been down this road with you before. You get ticked off at the drop of a hat, don't give me a clue as to why, and it's my fault. What, honestly, what did I say this time?"

"Marc, I've been married before, and I know something you probably don't."

"Here we go," he groaned, shielding his eyes with his hand. "You're going to give me the benefit of your vast knowledge and ancient wisdom. This is where you tell me all the stuff I'm too young to know, right?"

She talked right over him. "When two people come together, when they decide to marry, it shouldn't be the result of an 'accident,' and that's what you think this baby is. Well, I've got something to tell you. This child deserves better than being thought of as an 'accident.' I didn't set out to trap you into anything, and I only called you because it seemed right. I told you before, we don't need you—so you can keep your marriage proposal. I don't need that, either."

"Davida, let's be reasonable . . ."

"I don't have to be reasonable, I'm pregnant," she snapped.

"So, does that mean I have to get Milt to start looking into child support and visitation rights?"

Her gasp of surprise sliced his ear like a surgical stroke. "Do whatever you have to, Marcus." She was gone before he could protest.

That was yesterday, and a day of careful thought had gotten him nowhere in terms of clarification. Calling her had done no good, she was obviously using a Caller ID or some other method of screening her calls. Marcus ran faster, turning into Piedmont Park. Disconnectedly, he wondered where a man signed up for answered prayer or a fairy godmother. He had the distinct feeling that one or both of those was what it would take to clarify whatever it was he had left with Davida Lawrence.

"All I'm saying is, the girl is almost drowning in denial." Quita licked her fingers and reached for another Buffalo wing. "So, I see nothing wrong with helpin' a sister out."

"Don't do it," Mel warned. She was busily cleaning her fingers with a spare cocktail napkin.

"Well," Anne lifted another wing and carefully separated the meat from the bone of the drumette. "Teacake and I talked about this." She paused when the other two looked at her in surprise. "We did. He's big on communications, and I was concerned." She lifted her brows and the dainty morsel dangling from her fingertips. Chewing, she held her piece. "Anyway"—she finally swallowed—"I just want you to know, 'my name is Wes, and I ain't in this mess.' "

The other two women frowned. "You went through all that to tell us that?" Melanie sucked her teeth in disgust. "It wasn't worth it." Quita nodded slow agreement.

"I do think it was a good idea for you to volunteer to accompany her to the doctor's," Anne said, selecting another wing. Quita smiled.

"Girl, you know she was going to volunteer," Mel grinned. "How else was she going to get the four-one-one? And you know she needed it firsthand." The grin worked its way into a guffaw.

"Say what you will, I'm just going to do what any *real* friend would do." Quita held her confident smile on her lips, but an inscrutable shadow wended its way behind her eyes.

Both Anne and Mel saw it. "What are you going to do?" they asked together.

"I'm going to commit an act of friendship, just as soon as I can figure out a way."

CHAPTER
TWENTY-TWO

Texture. *That's what it's about,* Marc realized suddenly. His mouth dropped partly open at the discovery. Pushing away from his drawing board, he ran to the kitchen, grabbing a stray *Atlanta Journal* along the way. In his kitchen, ripping the newspaper into strips, Marcus dumped flour and water into the basin. Mushing his hand through the gray papier-mâché mixture. He watched it thicken as he washed his hands. Cardboard, he remembered, with a finger snap as he headed to his bedroom.

Returning to the kitchen with backing from several of his drycleaned shirts, and a metal ruler, working with a deft quickness, he tore the cardboard into rough shapes, glued them together and seemed well pleased with the results. He didn't know why he hadn't seen it before. *Guess that's what happens when you try to wear too many hats,* he thought. His breath came in a harshly ironic blast. He'd waited his whole life to do this, why hadn't he seen it? The background needed more texture.

Starting across the kitchen again, his impassioned eyes glowing with a creative fire, he paused in midstep. A base. His eyes darted from side to side. He needed a base. When he remembered the crating from his last shipment of canvases, he smiled. The wooden flats were still on the floor of his closet where he'd left them earlier in the week. Covering the raw wood with muslin, he knew this was going to work, felt it in his bones, and it thrilled him.

Now that he was looking at it, the answer was so simple, had been there all along—texture.

There was a cartoon, an old one Marcus remembered from childhood. It had real buildings, real trees, what seemed to be a moving sky. Animators had worked their magic over and around the sets. Everything had the clarity of real life and the flow of fantasy. The perfect visuals had thrilled him, charmed his childish mind, and filled his dreams for years afterward. That texture, that touch of "stretched" reality, was the ideal setting for Bro'Man.

How did I forget? How did I lose sight of . . . ? He sighed and shook his head. Man, forgetting? It all came back to Davida Lawrence, of course. Boo came into his life, and every sane thought went right out of his head.

That's not fair, he warned himself, *it's wrong to blame my forgetting on her.* The truth was he really had taken on a big chunk of a big project. Writer, animator, director, producer—man, he'd taken on everything but trying to be the voice talent. He grinned wryly. It really was funny, the stuff a man took on himself when he was trying to follow one dream, and forget another.

Setting the first of his miniature buildings atop the base, Marc stood back critically. It looked right. He set another beside it, and felt his focus return. Another idea, this one not fully formed, made him head for his kitchen cabinets. Pulling a can of coffee from the shelf, he dumped a handful into a saucepan, adding water and heat. Wetting several sheets of cardboard, he shook them nearly dry, tore them in half, leaving them in a glass bowl. He picked up the bottle of mustard and the bottle of catsup, unsure of which one would give the desired effect. "Mustard," he decided, and shook the contents into the glass bowl.

Using his hands to scoop mustard over the wet paper, Marc nodded contentedly as the paper yellowed. The scent of boiling coffee filled the kitchen, and he lifted the pan from the burner to cool. Tearing more paper, feeling the inventive thrill of directed movement, Marcus began to dip squares of cardboard, leaving them on the drainboard to dry. The cardboard, laid out straight, began to curl at the edges.

This is working, this is working! Marc was almost ready to sing the charmed words out loud. He was back in the flow, 'cause this was working, this was working . . . Marc pumped his fists in the air, feeling like he was finally beating back the ennui that bogged him down over the past weeks. The drying paper shaped nicely over his fingers, giving him the rounded, softened edges he sought. Setting them on his makeshift board and fabric base, he was well satisfied. The condiment aging would give his buildings a validity that flat paint could never approximate. A little spackling, maybe mixing a little tempera with sand or gravel for a further touch of reality. Then, he could add some miniature plant life, maybe even set up a permanent miniature nursery in a terrarium so that . . .

The ringing telephone interrupted his flow of thought. Annoyed, he decided to let the machine pick up as he used his hip to push a chair clear of the table, just enough to sit. Bending his finger to shape the cardboard, he imagined the yellowed paper combined with other colors and lighting. *This is going to work. Fixed outdoor sets will lend continuity to my story line,* he thought with satisfaction.

The telephone rang again.

Marcus cast an annoyed glance over his shoulder *I'm not answering that,* he thought stubbornly. Turning back to the tiny buildings forming between his rapidly moving fingers. This was fun. He grinned. It was like origami, and as he worked, it was very much like the Oriental art of paper folding with slightly less natural results. This was going to be great for the outdoors, but what about indoors?

The telephone rang again.

Buy a clue! he thought angrily. *I'm not answering!* Narrowing his eyes in concentration, Marc began to picture reworked interior sets and how they would affect the scheduling already in place for the filming of Bro'Man's first episodes. The problem was how to keep them static without losing the freshness that this kind of work demanded . . .

The telephone rang again.

Good, the machine would get it now. Whoever the caller was, they were obviously determined to "reach out and touch." Surely there'd be a message—for later. Marcus bent back to his work.

Seconds later, the telephone rang again. Disgusted, Marcus left his kitchen table and walked to the answering machine. He stood with tightly crossed arms and narrowed eyes as the phone completed the requisite four rings, stopped, then began again. Who did he know who was this determined? And, why? Tucking the corner of his lip between his teeth, he snatched the receiver from the cradle.

"What?" he growled.

"Whew! Something told me that if I just kept hitting the redial button, I would finally get you! Have you been there all along, just not answering?"

"Who is this?" Obviously some nutty woman with a redial fixation who'd settled on his number, and didn't have a lot of respect for answering machines.

"You don't know me, but you do. Well, let me clarify that." Marc's heavy breathing crossed the line. "I'm Quita Wilson," the woman admitted hurriedly. "I met you in St. Louis."

"St. Louis?" In spite of his resolve, Marc felt an irreverent bubble of hope flutter in his chest.

"Yes. I'm a friend of Davida and Glenn's." She waited. "I met you at Culpepper's, and again at Davida's house last summer?"

"Oh. Oh!" With just a little thought, he put a pertly rounded, sleekly groomed cinnamon face with the voice on the line. "Yeah." He rubbed a hand across the lower half of his face. His eyes narrowed again. "Why are you calling me? And, how did you get my number?"

Certain she had his attention, Quita thumbed the button on her speakerphone, more than four hundred miles away. "I'm calling to tell you that you need to be on your way to St. Louis, and if I were you, I would be flying somebody's friendly skies, with a serious quickness."

"What?"

"Look, Buddy, your Boo really needs you."

"Davida?" That bubble of hope was a turncoat, and it brought friends—little evil acid bubbles rushing through his stomach. "What about her? Or is this about the baby?" Turning to the wall, Marcus switched the phone to his other hand.

"Calm down. I don't think it's anything scary, 'course I'm no doctor, and all I know is what I'm told."

Marc's hand crossed his forehead and held there. He swallowed hard. "What are you told, Markeda?"

"Just Quita," she corrected acerbically.

"Quita," he amended.

Placated, she continued. "Davida's doctor called her the other day. She wants her to have a test called amniocentesis. She, the doctor, says she doesn't suspect that anything is wrong with the baby. She says it's a normal thing to do when the mother is more than thirty-something, and I guess you know . . ."

"Yeah, yeah . . . When?"

She sighed heavily. "I wish you'd let me tell this my way."

"Sorry." Marcus closed his eyes and prayed for deliverance from this willful woman.

"Anyway, the test is going to be done December eighth, at two in the afternoon, at the St. Louis Women's Group. They're over on Grand, not far from Soulard, and . . ." She paused, then asked, "Marc, do you think you want to be there?"

Did he want to be there? Marc's tongue touched a molar before he bit his lip. He sucked in a big draught of air and held it in his emotion-bound chest. He let it out slowly, trying to calm himself. "Quita, I'd sell my left . . ."—then he remembered he was speaking with a lady. "I'd sell my soul to be with her, but she doesn't want me."

"Humph! That's what you think?" Quita made a convincingly

disgusted tsk'ing sound. "The only thing that woman doesn't want is to be without you." She paused, then continued slowly. "I don't mean to be talking out of school . . ."

It was Marc's turn to tsk. "That never seemed to stop you before."

"Anyway." Marc imagined the hand she might have thrown up to stop him, had they been face-to-face. "Whether you know it or not, there's a really good chance that Destiny is going to wind up in a special medical program, there in Georgia."

Marc's heart leapt, and that shameless bubble of hope was back.

"Uhm-hmm. How far from you is Athens? That's where the University of Georgia is, right?" Before he could answer, "Never mind. Do you know where the, uhm, the Summit Building is? Anyway, I had to go in to see Essie Cofing—you don't know her, but she's Dee's immediate supervisor, here in St. Louis. She had a bunch of stuff on her desk when I went in there this morning, and I saw the thing on her desk. Just lying there. I read it, upside down, but I read it and I knew—I knew I had to call you."

"What thing?"

Quita sighed, and managed to sound thoroughly put upon in the process. "The transfer request."

Marc switched hands with the phone again, and it came nowhere near helping. It was easy to slide down to the floor, to squat into a near sitting position, thanks to the lack of support offered by his knees. He felt dizzy and sick. The quick, hot sweat beading his face, ran into his eyes and burned. This couldn't be right. He was having trouble breathing, and the pain in his heart seemed to radiate sharply. "What transfer request?"

"I told you," Quita said slowly, "but I'll repeat it. Destiny has been accepted for a program in Georgia. Davida is her mother. Because Destiny is only eight years old, her mother needs to be with her. Davida works for the IRS, and she's asking for a temporary, emergency transfer to be with her daughter. I did some checking, and there is an opening—in someplace called the Summit Building, in Atlanta. Now, do you understand?"

"Oh." Marc blinked at nothing in particular. His open palm massaged his chest, and he felt the comfort of instant recovery. Davida wasn't running from him, fate was sending her running to him. "I got it," he said.

"Okay, Mr. 'got it.' Now that I've stepped out here on thin air, risking my little round brown butt, what are you going to do—because you do know my life is not worth two dead flies now—she's going to kill me really dead when she finds out I called you—what are you going to do?"

"I'm going to see you very soon, Quita." Marc stood, amazed at his renewed stability. He found a pencil tucked beneath the phone. "Give me your number."

"Are we about to synchronize watches?" She giggled.

"Something like that." He smiled—for the first time since he'd answered the line.

"Quita, I still don't understand why we had to drive with the top down." Davida pulled the fuzzy collar of her coat higher, and looked a little more miserable. "It's cold." She sniffed.

"Please, Dee. It's December eighth. How many more decently warm days can we expect to have?" She opened her arms wide, and smiled expansively. "Besides, what's the sense in buying a convertible if you never put the top down?"

Eyeing her suspiciously, Davida pulled her coat tighter. "It's forty-nine degrees and we're in a moving car. The baby is cold," she muttered.

"Oooh! Right! The baby." The fingers of her leather glove moved over the Mustang's console. "That any better?"

"Much," Davida agreed. She stretched her gloved hands to the heat. "Nobody, and I mean I can't think of a single living soul, nobody else would put the top down and the heat on, but you."

Waving at a smiling man in a passing Mercedes, Quita tossed her head lightly. "Is that what you want to believe, or would you rather be cold?" Davida pressed her lips together, and Quita looked satisfied. "That's what I thought." She wheeled expertly down Olive, heading for Grand and the Women's Center offices. Minutes later, pulling the car to the curb, she looked at her friend. "Are you nervous?"

Davida appeared to think about it. "I'd be lying, if I said I wasn't." Her gloved fingers tugged her white angora hat lower over her short hair and cold ears. Pulling her matching scarf tighter, she said, "I hadn't really thought about it before, but Belinda did say this is an invasive procedure."

Quita turned in her seat. "You mean like surgery?" When Davida nodded, Quita leaned across the seat and patted her arm. She closed her eyes briefly, hoping. Stirring beneath the comforting hand, Davida snapped her door open and stepped from the Mustang. Quita shifted into park and hurried behind her, rushing through the door before it closed. Fingers on the door edge, she scanned the street and saw nothing and no one out of the ordinary.

Okay, that's good, she placated herself. *It wouldn't do to have things happen too soon.* She looked at her watch and prayed for timeliness. Everything depended on timing. Rounding the corner, she watched Davida gather her paperwork from the receptionist, then followed her into the waiting room.

The Women's Group offered a waiting area that reminded Quita of her mom's "sitting room." On the walls, gilded frames held everything from mirrors and numbered prints, to the original art of the Women's Group staff. Two corners held neatly cluttered whatnot shelves, filled with china figurines. Intrigued, Quita found herself standing, her back slightly bent, peering at the miniatures behind the glass doors. She straightened immediately when the door to the Women's Group swung open, then sagged in relief when a tall, golden-skinned woman swung into the office, and waved, throwing her black leather coat across her arm.

"That's Valerie Simmons," Davida whispered. "She's the perinatologist I'll be seeing."

Quita breathed a hasty sigh of relief. Okay, so it wasn't who she was expecting. She smiled as the woman strolled past.

Delicate floral wallpaper and creamy plush carpeting combined with what Quita's mother and aunts always referred to as "heavy" good furniture to give the room a pleasantly feminine and soothing feel, but it wasn't working on her. Hanging her coat and Davida's on a carved wooden stand took a couple of minutes, and settling into a chair beside Davida used up another. While it didn't feel like enough time, it also felt like too much. Quita stole another glance at her watch. "Hope we're not running behind here," she muttered.

"No," Davida replied, making Quita jump. "Belinda is nothing if not punctual. We've still got a few minutes before . . ."

Doctor Belinda Reed looked more like an affable children's television show hostess than a medical practitioner as she smiled her way into the reception area. Her bright red corduroy jumper was a festive touch beneath her white lab coat, and the bell and ribbon festooned pin on her lapel did nothing to dispel the image.

"Good to see you, Cookie, you're right on time, and don't you look cute. I love that outfit! That navy velvet is beautiful! A shirt and pants, umph, nice, nice choice for this kind of weather, and it looks comfortable, too." Without missing a beat, she turned to Quita. "Are you here to keep her company? I'm Dr. Reed, and Dr. Simmons will join us shortly." She offered a hand and Quita took it, impressed to meet a woman who talked faster than she could.

"Oh"—Belinda turned slightly to look over her shoulder—"before I forget, I want you to meet Lydia Case." She looked over her shoulder at the empty door, then took a quick step backward. "Lydia!" she hissed, then smiled when she was rewarded by the head that popped around the door.

"Honestly, Dr. Reed." Lydia Case straightened her pink and lavender smock over her lavender cotton scrub suit. "I was running as fast as my two little feet could take me." She pulled a stethoscope from her neck and tucked it into her pocket, then patted her short Afro to locate her glasses, which she also tucked into her pocket. "Which of you is Mrs. Lawrence?"

Davida raised her hand and wiggled her fingers. "Me?"

"Oh. Cool."

Belinda winced. There was something a little disconcerting about a medical professional who still used the word "cool" with the ease of Lydia Case. But what were you going to do? She was damned good at her job.

Lydia Case took Davida's hand in a professional press. "I'm going to be your tech today, and if you've got any questions for me or Dr. Reed, feel free to ask 'em." Davida gave her a quick headshake, and Lydia nodded. "Nervous? I know I was when I went through mine."

Davida's eyes came up quickly. "You've had this done before?"

"Oh, heck yeah." A tall and rangy, slow-speaking woman, Case fanned a hand and made the sentence sound like one word. "I mean it was my choice and all, but"—she shrugged—"it was a decision that gave me and my husband a chance to come to grips with some choices, you know, options ahead of time. For me, it was the only thing to do. You know, amnio can detect about seventy different metabolic disorders, and in my case there was some suspicion of trisomy because of my family history."

She grinned at the confusion on Davida's face and fanned her hand again. "I know, I know, what's trisomy, right?"

Davida nodded tightly.

"That's cool, it's a valid question. Look at it like this, most people have forty-six chromosomes, in twenty-three pairs, but some have an extra copy of one chromosome. That's called trisomy. The most common trisomy is Down's syndrome, and then there's a whole slew of sex-linked disorders like hemophilia or varied types of muscular dystrophy."

Davida's hand went protectively to her stomach as she listened. Her brown eyes were darkly suspicious as they swept the room. "How does it relate to sickle-cell anemia?"

Tempted to suggest that they move the conversation from the reception area to a consultation room, Case looked into her eyes and realized this was an answer the other woman couldn't do without, and she needed it right now.

"The test is pretty accurate for detecting blood disorders like sickle cell. Hey, don't let that put you off.'' Lydia Case shook her head when Davida's shoulders drooped. ''As it turned out, all my tests were negative, and the only thing they didn't warn me of was that a three-year-old could be as busy and as noisy as my little Justin.'' She pulled a key ring from her pocket and fumbled through to display a small photo charm. ''Here he is,'' she preened, obviously pleased with Davida's appreciation.

''Wait a minute.'' The name caught Quita off-guard. She turned her whole body to slowly face the technician, still adjusting to the child's name. ''You named your child, 'Justin Case'?''

Lydia nodded happily.

''No. Really? You really named that adorable little boy, Just-in-case?''

''At least nobody will ever forget him.'' Lydia laughed.

''No.'' Quita's head bobbed in agreement. ''You've got a point there.''

''Well, ladies, I guess we should get this party started.'' Belinda smiled again and extended a hand to the open door at her back. None of the women seemed to notice Quita's darting and nervous study of the front door.

Belinda bustled along, talking all the while. The three women followed her, nearly colliding when she stopped abruptly outside the pastel blue door of an exam room at the end of the long hall. ''This is the room we're going to use, Cookie. We'll get you settled and . . .''

Lord, Quita prayed, *I can't stall this for much longer. Help me!* ''Doesn't she have to change or get prepped or something?'' She looked at the doctor with suddenly jittering eyes. ''Doesn't she?''

Belinda and Lydia looked at her with matching confusion. Belinda moved to open the door. Still holding the door handle, she looked first at Quita, then Davida. ''Just go on in, Cookie. Make yourself comfortable, and like I told you before, you'll just need to adjust your clothes—pull them down enough to expose your womb, and we'll go from there.'' A gentle push from her hand ushered Davida into the exam room.

Pulling the door closed Belinda blocked Quita's following. ''You,'' she said sternly, ''I want to talk to first.''

Oh, Lord, please don't let her kick me out! That would ruin every-thing . . .

Belinda tugged the sleeve of Quita's gray sweater, forcing her into the next room. ''Now, you listen to me! I have had just about enough of whatever this peek-a-boo thing is that you're playing. Cookie is already nervous enough, without you scaring her. You were supposed to be here as her moral support, not the one we have to get the smelling salts out for, so calm yourself down. This test isn't going to harm Davida, alright?'' Belinda frowned. ''Are you listening to me?''

Quita turned her head slightly, blinking fast. ''No. I'm trying to hear.'' Satisfied, she looked away from the door, then gripped her shoulder bag like a shield and shrank before her questioner.

''You're trying to what?''

''I told you, I'm trying to . . .'' *She doesn't have a clue what you're talking about,* an evil little gremlin cackled in Quita's brain. Facing the irritated doctor, she patted the air between them. ''I was sort of expecting someone else,'' she admitted guiltily. Squeezing her face into a touchy little pie of expression, Quita offered a weak little smile. ''I guess you know, Davida and the baby's father are not together.''

Dr. Reed nodded tersely, crossing her arms beneath her ample bosom. ''Uh-huh. And?''

''And even though she won't admit it, she really still cares about him.'' Quita crossed her hands protectively in front of her body. ''And father's need to know about stuff like this—right?'' She tried another short-lived smile.

Belinda's brow rose and the corners of her mouth turned down.

Quita tried a tight little laugh. ''Well, you see, sometimes these things need a little help, a little push.'' Her hands rose and fluttered uselessly before twining themselves in front of her again. ''So, I pushed. I called him.''

The look on the doctor's face changed. Her eyes widened and her mouth softened. ''I see. What did he have to say . . . No, wait a minute, I don't even want to know.'' She threw up both hands before Quita could respond. ''I don't even want to know, because it's a cinch you didn't tell her that you called him, or I'll bet she never would have shown up here today, and I can't say I would blame her. You had absolutely no right to invade her privacy like that, young lady. And then to come in here peeking around corners, trying to make us your unwitting accomplices . . .''

Dr. Belinda Reed reached across the small space between them to tap Quita's chest sharply, then waved the offending finger with authority. Quita had the good sense to cringe and try to look contrite. ''Whatever you did, I don't want to know about it, and you'd better not upset my patient any further. You are going to stop peeking around corners in my office, and I mean stop it right now. You take your merry little butt in there and do exactly what you came here to do. You are going to give her all the support and empathy you can muster, but you don't mention that man, you don't show out, and you don't add to her nervousness not even a little bit. Have I made myself clear?''

Quita cast her eyes low and her bottom lip quivered. "Yes, ma'am," she whispered.

The doctor brushed past indignantly, then paused with the tips of her fingers gripping the door. "And one last thing, if he's late, it's his loss."

CHAPTER
TWENTY-THREE

"Okay, Mrs. Lawrence." Lydia stood in the doorway. "This is where we're going to do the test. You know"—her lips pressed, then lifted at the corners—"I think I like your given name better, it has a kind of elegant ring to it. You mind if I call you Davida?"

"Fine with me, if I can call you Lydia."

The technician grinned and stepped back. "Actually, most of my friends call me Dee, you can, too, if you want to."

Davida's step faltered and she had to place her hand on a nearby metal cabinet to catch herself. *How many times in a lifetime will that happen?* she wondered, looking over her shoulder. *First my brother and I share childhood names with a stranger on the telephone, and now I get to share another nickname with this lady.* There was way too much synchronicity here.

"What happened?" the technician asked' "did you trip?"

"Just a misstep," Davida covered. *Synchronicity?* That wasn't a word she could ever remember using, but it did have a ring of familiarity. Now, where had she heard that word before? She had an odd sense of déjà vu, and probed the memory for details. *Marc,* she suddenly realized. That was his word, and the realization throbbed like a sore tooth.

"You, okay?" The technician still looked worried.

"Oh, yeah, Dee. I'm fine," Davida lied. She was anything but fine. She should have called him. She should have taken the chance that maybe one day he would understand the choices she'd had to make, and the reason she'd had to make them. She should have swallowed her pride and called him. "Where do you want me?" she asked with forced brightness.

"How about right here for a few seconds, while I finish setting up?" Lydia Hill pointed to a low metal stool. Davida walked over to it, sat, then stood and twirled it counterclockwise to raise it higher. The technician grinned broadly. "That's usually where Dr. Reed sits. I guess you can tell, huh?"

"A tad low." Davida nodded and grinned back. "She is a bit vertically challenged, isn't she?"

"I like you." The technician giggled with a hand on her monitor.

"Ahh, Dee, I like you, too." Davida looked around, really seeing the exam room for the first time. "You know, I'm really glad you're a woman, and that you've had this done before. To tell you the truth, I don't know what I would have done if I'd walked in here and met someone who treated me like a statistic or something less than human. With you, I feel a little, I don't know . . . safer? Is that the right word?"

"Well, right or wrong, it's cool, and I can relate." Dee Case moved a few steps to her right, and patted the exam table. It was like a regular paper-sheeted exam table, with a small pillow to prop the patient up. Dee slid a small tray-like extension from the end of the table, then pushed it back. "Why don't you have a seat up here, and I'll call Dr. Reed." she patted the table and slipped from the room.

There was a phone on the wall, right there, Davida noted. She wondered why she didn't use that one. Maybe she was trying to give her some privacy, a few minutes to rethink all of this, just in case she wanted to back out. Or maybe she thought she'd feel self-conscious hauling herself up on that table.

Feeling self-conscious was the least of her problems, Davida noted as she lifted herself, one hip at a time onto the exam table. Hauling and lifting was exactly what it felt like. The twelve pounds she'd gained since becoming pregnant all seemed to reside in her hips and behind. And she still had about sixteen or seventeen weeks to go. She squeezed her thigh and tried not to despair over the excess she found there. *That's a whole lot of StairMaster time,* she thought.

Belinda promised the test wouldn't take long once they actually got started. Davida swung her feet and tried to hold onto the fact that B had never lied to her before—that she knew of. Belinda also told her that from all outward appearances, the baby looked healthy. That was a good thing, and today's test would confirm that. But she said Davida would have to wait ten to fourteen days for the test results. That was an awfully long time. Catching her hands in the hem of her shirt, she twisted them into the fabric. Reminded her of Essie Cofing's eternal fluttering, Davida freed her hands and sat on them.

Still looking around, Davida tried to guess the use of the arcane equipment surrounding her. Belinda said they would do an ultrasound first, then the amniocentesis. B had promised it wouldn't hurt. Davida looked around and tried not to shake too much. Belinda said that when the procedure was done she should plan on not lifting or walking for three days. That was funny. How could anyone manage to parent an active almost nine-year-old child and stay off her feet for three days? But, she'd find a way, because B said running around would increase her chances of miscarrying.

From where she sat, trying to imagine the procedure, Davida couldn't stop shaking. She could almost see Dee Case, the technician, standing to the right, almost parallel to the exam table. She would have control of a computer system, complete with what looked like an attached television monitor. Davida leaned forward, wondering what the tech would see. Looking up, she saw another screen. This one looked like a television, too.

Maybe that was for her, so she could see what's going on with her baby. Without thinking, her hand went to her belly and massaged slowly. *I don't know why I'm so nervous,* she telegraphed mentally, *you seem to think everything is fine.* The baby gave a light reassuring flutter that made the mother smile. "As long as you think so," Davida said, quietly patting.

When the door from the hall opened, behind her, slightly to her left, Davida turned. Relieved to see Quita trailing Belinda Reed and Lydia Case. "Whew!" she breathed. "I was beginning to feel a little lonely in here."

"No need to feel lonely," the doctor soothed, sending a nurtured chill up the patient's spine. "Why don't you lie back, and we'll take a few pretty pictures, okay?" Her eyes narrowed behind her glasses. "Miss girfriend?" She pointed to Quita. "Why don't you just stay there, where you are?"

"Yes, ma'am." Quita took a few steps backward and pressed her back to the door. When Davida looked back, over her shoulder she could still see her friend, but she felt an awfully long way away.

"Let's get you ready for this." The doctor and technician helped Davida to lie back and move her clothing into place. Pulling out the little tray at the end of the table, the one she'd noted earlier, they helped her settle her feet and legs more comfortably. "Are you alright?" the doctor asked. "You're a little long, you know."

Tipping her head, Davida looked up into the cherubic round brown face. "You know what's surprising?" she asked, conversationally. The doctor raised an eyebrow in question. "That I'm managing to lie here and not having to make a break for the bathroom." Davida held her face straight. "That fifty yard dash seems to be my favorite sport, lately."

"Well, Cookie, that goes with the territory, you know?"

"That part I remember from the first time," Davida said, staring up at the white fluorescent lighting. She tried to remember to breathe, and vaguely heard Belinda tell her she was doing fine, and to remain calm. *Remain calm?* she thought. *Why don't you let me stick you?*

Unsure how she managed to remain silent, Davida dismissed the random thought, and jumped when Lydia touched her skin with the cold betadine soaked swab. "This is just a disinfectant," the tech explained. "We'll do the ultrasound, then the amnio, just like we discussed. Dr. Simmons will be in for the second part. Are you sure you don't want a local?"

Davida shook her head. "No, I'll pass. You said it would only put the nerves in the outer skin to sleep, right?"

"To sleep'? You've been talking to Des, haven't you?"

"Don't laugh at me, B," Davida grinned back. "I'm doing the best I can, under the circumstances." She could still smile. A little joke was still funny, maybe this wouldn't be so bad, after all—she hoped. *Lord, please don't let anything be wrong.* She should have at least called him back, but she thought she had time . . .

And that was what it had always been about with them. Time. If the timing had been better, they might never have met. Then there were the differences that time had wrought between them in age, in experience, in responsibility. Those were differences Davida had never found the time to resolve, and now . . . What if something was wrong with the baby, and there was no more time . . . ? She closed her eyes and tried to turn off her senses and her fear, as cold, clear surgical jelly was spread across her skin. *Don't think about it,* she cautioned herself, concentrating on the in and out of her breathing rhythms.

Electrodes connecting her to the monitor suctioned against her tight skin, and Davida tried to hide her fear beneath deep and measured breathing. If she worked at it, she might succeed in ignoring her surroundings and hearing only the end results—that her son or daughter was fine.

It's not working, she finally conceded, pulling the breath in and holding it for a long moment. Try as she might, she still heard the low, cautious voices around her, along with an odd tapping sound. *That must be the monitor coming on,* she told herself, unable to rationalize the odd chill that struck her. Was that tapping coming from behind her?

"You can open your eyes," Dee Case said from across the room. "We've got a nice picture up here."

Opening her eyes slowly, Davida remembered to look up at the monitor, where her baby tilted its head upward. She felt the matching motion in her womb. "Oh, Quita"—the first tears gathered in her eyes—"I should have called him."

"I know, girl." Quita sniffed.

Dee watched her instruments and made adjustments. The sound of the baby's steady, rapid, healthy heartbeat filled the room.

Hands at her lips, Davida watched breathlessly. "Quita, you hear that? The baby's heartbeat . . ."

"Yeah, girl, it is." Quita sobbed softly.

Dee Case made more magic with her computerized keyboard and the picture sharpened significantly.

"Oh," Davida breathed in awe. "The baby's sucking his, her, the thumb." she laughed. "I have a thumb-sucker."

"Correction, Boo. We have a thumb-sucker." The hand touching Davida's hair was one she knew instantly, and would never have mistaken for that of any woman.

"Marc?" Her eyes moved from the screen to the man who stood just behind her shoulder. "You're here? Really here?"

"I'm here, Boo." He squatted low, his lips at her ear. The crown of his head touched hers, then moved away as he kissed her cheek. "I'm right where I want to be, Boo. The only place I can be. Nothing and no one in this world is more important to me than you and our baby, right now."

Davida moved her elbow, needing to sit higher, to see him more clearly. For that first dizzying second, while he held her eyes magnetically, she felt pinned by the stunning aura of sensuality that surrounded them. He was so close, she felt his breath against her cheek. "What about your project? What about Bro'Man? You waited all your life for . . ."

"You." He brushed his lips softly against hers. "I already told you, Boo, you're the chance I've always waited for. There is nothing more important to me than you, this baby, and Des, and I dare anybody to stand in our way." He grinned and nuzzled her ear. The baby wiggled slightly on the screen. "Boo, do you know I would kill a rock for you?"

"A dead rock, Marc?"

"A dead rock, Boo."

"Oh, this is way too much synchronicity," she whispered, reaching back to press his face closer. Placing his hand over hers, he reached out with his other hand to touch her hair again. His fingers, light and cautious, moved across her forehead to sooth and comfort, then moved back to her hair, sealing their connection.

Belinda Reed cleared her throat noisily, drawing all eyes to her diminutive personage. "We do have work to do here," she announced.

"This is so cool," Dee whispered to herself as she went to work with betadine soaked gauze and swabs, cleaning and recleaning Davida's exposed skin. As if to make the job a little easier, the baby made a quick little move, adjusting what they now knew was *his* hand.

"Omigod," Quita blurted. "He's not only a thumb-sucker, but look what he does while he sucks his thumb!" She pointed.

"Oh, Quita." Davida squeezed her eyes shut in the face of her friend's observation. "That's a horrible thing for a godmother to notice."

"Officially?" She cut her eyes at Marcus.

"Officially," he concurred.

"Then, I didn't see a thing," Quita promised, loyally lifting her right hand.

The door opened silently on oiled hinges. "You guys ready for me?" Valerie Simmons edged into the room holding Davida's chart. Her hand went immediately to the well-defined curve at her waist, and she stood, looking for all the world like an *Ebony Fashion Fair* model. "I was out looking at houses this morning, and time got away from me," she apologized.

"Cool. You're right on time, Do. We got the monitors in place already. I've got the needle ready, and the baby is lying to your left, so we're going in on the right, okay?"

"Okay, Dee, that sounds right. Just remember, we might have to do it over if this little guy decides to move." Dr. Simmons pulled on surgical gloves as she looked at Davida's bared stomach, then the monitor and back again. "You're looking real good, here, Davida." She turned to Dee Case. "Can I have the needle, please?" Smiling at her patient, the doctor waited a beat. "Ready?"

"How long is that needle? That thing's got to be every bit of six or seven inches." Quita breathed from her corner. "It's so skinny . . ." She raised a hand and fanned herself rapidly. "Oh, I think I need some air. It's so warm in here." She rushed from the room without a backward glance. Belinda Reed closed the door behind her.

Toying with the idea of jumping up from the table and running down the hall to join her retreating friend, Davida balked. Marc's fingers touched her hair again, and she nodded. "I'm ready," she said shakily. Refusing to watch herself, Davida concentrated on the screen above her and the man at her side.

"This is going to be just like drawing blood," Valerie Simmons said.

"Uh-huh. When's the last time you had blood drawn this way?" Davida quipped.

"Oh, you got jokes, huh?" The doctor's golden skin lit up with her smile as her hand moved precisely across Davida's skin. "Know what you call a sheep with no legs?"

"You're as bad as Des," Davida said on the edge of a sharp gasp when the needle slid beneath her skin. Not daring to move, her eyes grew large as she saw on the screen exactly what she felt moving through her body. "Please don't make me laugh."

Marc's fingers traveled again through the soft strands of her hair, close to her scalp, this time, trailing warmth. "Tell us, doctor," he asked softly, almost as though it mattered. "What do you call a sheep with no legs?"

"A cloud." Simmons looked up quickly, gauging the patient's nervousness. "Hang in there, Davida. We're just about there."

"Cool," Dee Case nodded from her station. "How 'bout this one, doc? Where does a bird go when it loses its tail?"

"This had better not be about cocktails," Belinda grumbled.

At her side, his cheek nearly touching hers, Marc grinned at Davida. "I've got to admit it," he said. "I really did think Des told some bad ones, but I'm having second thoughts now."

"Come on, you guys! This one's not that bad. Where does a bird go when it loses its tail?"

"We give up," Davida said, her eyes fixed on the screen.

"To the retail store!" Dee smiled bravely in the face of resounding boos.

"Those are pretty bad, but I have one for you ... oh ..." Her eyes went to the screen of the monitor above her. The long needle neared the amniotic sac in her womb and Davida stared. Transfixed, she watched the needle press, then puncture the sterile sac she carried in her body. Her gasp was the only sound signaling the short, mild cramp she felt. When Marc's hand closed over hers, she wanted to look at it, to see them joined at the time of their son's first touch of the world. She intended to look, but couldn't tear her eyes away.

"It is like drawing blood," she said to the awestruck man at her side.

Marcus nodded silently. This was the beginning. He still had to get through Lamaze classes, learning to diaper, and God help him, labor. *Whatever you do, man, don't blink,* he told himself. *You know there's gonna be questions later!* And that made him smile. *Boo and I really do have a later to look forward to,* he thought. 'Course he'd learned his lesson about springing things on her. He'd learned that he'd have to take her timing into consideration. But there was time for that, too.

His dimples flashed, and Dee Case hoped nobody caught her sneaking a peek at them. *He sure is a good-looking man,* she admired, *such pretty eyes with those long lashes.* It sure would be nice to have him look at her like he was looking at Davida.

He really dressed cool, too. That vest buttoned up so high, still it managed to show off his chest and arms. She tilted her head and smiled professionally. She would bet he lifted weights or something . . . It took her a minute to remember that she was the one who was supposed to accept the fluid for testing.

The doctor handed off the second tube of fluid and prepared to remove the needle. "Okay, Davida, we're coming out, and I want to hear that joke . . . in . . . just . . . a . . . second." She freed the needle and deposited it in the prepared sterile tray. "Okay," she applied the Band-Aid. "Now, tell me the 'better' joke."

Marc managed to link his arm with hers and to clasp Davida's fingers. "I'll still love you," he promised, "even if it sucks."

"Gee, thanks for the vote of confidence." *I never said "gee" before this man came into my life,* she noted. Taking a deep breath, Davida also noted a distinct absence of discomfort.

"I'm still waiting on this 'better' joke," Valerie Simmons grumbled, snapping off her rubber gloves.

"Okay. If good people go to heaven and bad people go to hell, where do prostitutes go when they die?"

"What?" Simmons looked blank. "It's a trick question, right?"

"No," Davida said simply. "There's no trick. Guess."

"I don't know," the people in the room chorused.

Using her elbow, Davida pushed herself higher, a secret smile teasing the corners of her lips. "They go to the Virgin Islands, for recycling."

Both doctors stood with their backs against the wall staring at each other, then burst into laughter. "The Virgin Islands," they screamed.

"For recycling," Dee hooted. "Now, that's cool."

"You can sit up now," Valerie said around a series of simmering chuckles. "If you want to clean up a little, there's a bathroom over here in the corner. Just don't forget what I told you. No lifting, no walking for three days because . . ."

"It's an invasive procedure. I remember." Davida smoothed her shirt, and realized Marc was still laughing. He'd almost stopped, then caught her eye and started anew. Hysteria? That could happen to prospective new fathers, couldn't it?

"What's going on in here?" Quita's head appeared through the open door. "I could hear you laughing all the way out in front."

Belinda removed her glasses and dabbed at her eyes. She shook her head and cleared her throat. "I'm not telling."

"So, what did I miss? Anything good?" Quita had a serious emotional need to know.

"My patient is entitled to confidentiality," Dr. Simmons stated. "Dr. Reed and I have agreed. You want to know what's going on, I suggest you stay in the room next time."

"Fine way to treat a godparent," Quita sulked.

"Okay," Dr. Simmons turned to Davida and let her grin calm itself. "I just want to go over a few things with you before you get out of here." She pulled a typed list from her pocket and smiled when Davida and Marcus looked on together. "I want you to pay close attention to these four items," her tapered nail tapped the page. "I can't overemphasize it, now. The three days of not moving around are very important. It's going to give your body the time it needs to heal from this procedure. You will remember to call us if any bleeding or discharge occurs—right?"

Her eye was firm, and Davida nodded obediently. "I don't like the idea of you being alone, though. Is someone going to be with you?"

Quita and Davida opened their mouths, but Marcus was faster. "She'll never be alone again," he said.

"Spoken like a true new father." Dr. Simmon's looked well satisfied. The medical staff withdrew tactfully, shooing Quita before them.

Folding her fingers into his, Marc studied them closely. "I meant it, you know."

Tears welled in Davida's eyes, triggered by the poignancy of his simple words, and her heart filled her chest almost to bursting. In that moment, she knew she was lost, had been from that first telephone call. It was one thing to be attracted to the man's physical appearance, or to be touched by the painful vulnerability his words and talent sometimes failed to conceal, or even to see how gently he treated her child. But to be the open and willing recipient of the simple passion that defined and qualified his heart caused Davida's world to tilt on its sternly fixed axis, spinning her off into worlds of unexpected emotion.

I love this cute little man, I really do, she realized *I love him hopelessly, totally, and willingly.* The baby moved gently, and Davida had the blessedly intuitive thought that the baby loved him, too, and that it was right beyond all reason.

In a flash of clarity, she realized this was the shape and feel of love she'd hoped for with Skip. This feeling, this connected oneness was instinctively more real than what she and Skip built over their years together. It wasn't Skip's fault, he'd given her all that he had, and at the time, it had been enough. He'd given her fidelity and security. He'd been proud and solid, steady and never wavering, always the man she'd married, and asked only that she give him the same. And she had.

But Marcus Benton was different. With the inventive passion of his youth he offered all the things Skip had and more. He was light and laughter, speed and intellect. He was invention and charm of the most fascinating kind. He was romance of the hearts and flowers type. And now, as she sat looking into his eyes, Davida knew he was also the love she'd sought all her life. It didn't matter how fate had stepped in to miswire the telephone lines and accomplish what neither she nor Marc had ever been able to find on their own. It didn't even matter that he was fairly short, or that she would probably outweigh him before their son made it into the world.

To top it all off, it didn't matter that she certainly hadn't come here today looking for love. It was just there and that was good enough.

CHAPTER
TWENTY-FOUR

"Come on, Marc. Please. Just one more."

"Des, that's what you said fifteen minutes and six boxes ago." Marcus Benton planted one hand in the small of his back, groaned, and held one finger up in front of the little girl's face. "You do know that one is this many, don't you?"

She broke into a gale of childish giggles, danced on her toes, and reached out to squeeze his finger in her hand. " 'Course I do, Marc."

He wouldn't have taken her weight in gold for the moment.

Davida leaned on the banister. "You know, Marc, you can still escape if you need to."

Looking up, Marcus was struck by the beautiful changes pregnancy had brought to this already lovely woman. Her ebony skin glowed with a flush that reminded him of the fine sweet, wet, magenta velvet found on the inside of a fresh ripe peach, right near the living heart of the fruit. The brown of her eyes had taken on a new light that swirled and sparked with her mood, picking up and reflecting the world around her. Her glossy hair, black as night, touched her face like licks of midnight fire—a suitable frame for the smile that Marc wanted to be the first and last one he saw every day for the rest of his life.

"Oh, it's not going to be that easy to get rid of me, Boo. I intend to stick around here, lift, tote, and do anything else I have to do. I'm going to be here when those tests come back on the baby, and I'm going to help you and Des celebrate your last Christmas in this house.

I'll even move a few more of these Christmas boxes, if I have to.'' He leaned slightly backward, his lips puckered and waiting.

"You know, I like it when you beg.'' She grinned, meeting him halfway with a loud wet smack of her own lips.

Destiny dropped to the lowest step, and buried her face in her hands to sit giggling at her mother's feet. "So mushy,'' she declared.

"But it's such good mush.'' Davida moved carefully down the last few steps to stand in the midst of the red and green rubble of Christmases past. Looking down, she noted ornaments she'd bought when she and Skip first bought the house. There were others from Destiny's first Christmas. She bent slightly to retrieve a twirly, handcut, glitter-sprinkled spiral. "Remember this?''

Des stood and moved closer. Her mouth opened and her red and white barrettes swung as she nodded. "I made it when I was little,'' she recalled, looking at Marc. "That was when I was first grade''— she looked at her mother—"or kiddy-garden?''

Davida turned the ornament to check the date she'd neatly recorded. "It was kindergarten, Des.''

"So long ago.'' The child sighed as she dropped to her knees. "You think next year we could get a real tree?''

"Would you like to help us pick out a real one for here?''

Des grinned, her tongue sweeping the edges of her front teeth. "That would make the best last Christmas.'' She thought about it. "It would smell good, too, wouldn't it? Like at Aunt Wesie's?''

Her mother nodded. Eloise Davies was widely known for her choice in what she insisted was traditional Christmas greenery. She annually draped her house in evergreen finery, and the scent lingered long after the wrapping paper was gone.

One hand on the wall, the other on Marc's arm, Davida lowered herself to sit on the floor. Marc sensed something was happening and didn't want to be left out. He sat, too.

"You know, things will be different next year,'' Des said, nodding wisely. "Next year, we'll have a new kind of Christmas. Not like what we had before—a just-us-two Christmas, and not like this year, a now-we've-got-Marc Christmas. Next year, we'll be four. Even our Christmas cards will be different. Changed for good.'' She sounded a little sad.

"But change can be a very good thing, Destiny,'' her mother said. Doing the mother thing, Davida wet her thumb and scrubbed at a dark splotch on the child's cheek.

"Ugh!'' Marc and Destiny choked together. Davida looked up in amazement. She was not even married to the man yet, and he was already related to her child!

"Why you gotta spit on her?" Marcus demanded, laughing as Des scrubbed at her cheek.

"You two needn't think you can gang up on me," Davida replied, haughtily patting her belly. "He's on my side."

"Only 'til you spit on him," Des offered. She stopped rubbing long enough to squint at Davida then Marc and back again. "What's his name gonna be, anyway? We can't just go around calling him 'he,' or 'him.' " Screwing up her face, she paused almost long enough for a breath then bounced over her crossed legs "I know. I know what we could call him, he could be DaviDesti-arcus!" She looked around. "You don't like that one? That's okay, I can do better, uhm . . . What about . . . Lawrence Benton?"

"Maybe we could talk about that one," Davida said thoughtfully.

"I don't know," Marc countered, "DaviDesti-arcus is kind of growing on me." Destiny rolled onto her side, laughing harder when Marcus draped a spill of silver tinsel over her head. Davida added the cord of a bright red lacquered apple over the child's left ear and the little girl batted it to make it shimmy against her dark skin.

"Next year, there'll be a baby, so we can't have stuff that might break and hurt him. Maybe we have to get different decorations, or put the tree up real high." Des was suddenly bright-eyed and curious "In Atlanta, I'm going to have my special blood fusions. . ."

"Trans-fusions," Marc and Davida corrected as one.

"Trans-fusions. I'm gonna have a new doctor, and even though Tawanna's mother said she could come an' visit, I'm gonna make new friends. I'll have a new school, and Mom has a new job. What are you going to do until the baby comes, Marc?" She blinked.

"I forgot." Marcus brought the heel of his hand solidly against his forehead. "I don't know how I forgot to tell you. In my e-mail, today. Feng Shui's got the financing—we're a go! Bro'Man will be a BET fixture for next fall, and we're looking at a full-length animated feature for the following Christmas. Milt is sending the last of the contracts first thing Monday."

"This is all so fast." Davida opened her arms to accept his hug. "I'm so happy for you. It's like this happened so fast."

"Fast? You, the Speed Queen, thinks I did something fast? How about you arranging for your transfer and then the Renaissance Square condo—long distance?"

"Marc!" Davida made a deliberate eye and brow gesture to the studiously listening child . . .

. . . who noticed immediately "Oh. This is some of that stuff that you and him still have to work out isn't it?" Des stood and pulled tinsel from her hair, shook the bundle, and laid the apple on top. She straightened, and shoving her hands into the deep pockets of her jeans, looked at them appraisingly. "I can go get a cookie or something and come back."

She started across the foyer, then turned to look back. "Long as you're workin' stuff out, could you please decide when we're going to get married? I think we should wait for the baby so we can all be there, and it should be when he has a name so we can call him something." She spun on the toe of her pink Reebok and headed for the kitchen.

"See what you started," Davida whispered

"Not me, but about your job?"

A puff of air lifted her bangs from her forehead, and Davida pushed her legs straight out in front of her. "I already told you. When I got the acceptance for Destiny, I contacted Emory's hospital, Egleston, it's called. The counselor suggested I might want to stay busy, so I asked about an emergency transfer at work. The guy I talked to in Atlanta, a Mr. Harris, told me the job was three months, temp-to-perm. I'll work three months, have the baby, and in five months be available when it converts to a permanent position." She shrugged.

Marc looked in the direction Destiny had gone. "Still think that condo's a good idea?"

Davida nodded. "Until Des fully understands our commitment and has the reality of our marriage to look at yes, I think we need to live separately."

"But we do get the house in Buckhead?"

She knew the one he had in mind. It was a perfect little southern dream of a house with a big yard, and a carriage house in the back that could be converted into an ideal studio. He was already seeing it with the addition of skylights, and was fully in love with it. "We still get the house in Buckhead, but I've got problems with the idea of a crimson and cream nursery."

"But, Boo"—he leaned close enough to press his warm lips to hers in a brief, tantalizing promise—"the boy's father and uncles are all Kappas. He's not even born yet, and he's already a legacy—it would only be right. He needs to be immersed in . . ."

"We'll . . . talk about it . . . later." Davida felt the blush begin between her breasts and rise.

"Okay, but what about this wedding of ours?" Marc's eyes went to Destiny's path again, but his hands went elsewhere "You know we're under strict orders to figure something out. I want to go on record as suggesting Atlanta. The Botanical Gardens there are gorgeous . . ."

"Marc, St. Louis is the only logical place. Think about it. Your family is here, my family is here." She spread her hands, touching his shoulders.

"But Milt and Deb . . ."

". . . would probably love the plane trip."

"Not in January." He brushed a finger across her parted lips.

"I want to be a June bride. I didn't get to be one the first time, and with you, I want all the romance I can get."

"From me?" His dimples emerged slowly as the grin bloomed into a full-blown, dazzling smile, heart-wrenching in its open splendor. "You do know how to charm a man. June it is."

Davida suddenly moaned and reached for her lower back. Marc moved closer and took over the massage, his hands making long slow strokes.

"Marc? Did you forget?"

"What? Oh, you mean Des staying over with Tawanna Mallory tonight?"

"Well," Davida said slowly, her body moving with his hands, "that's part of it."

"What's the other part?"

"Pregnancy makes you feel . . ." Her smile filled in all the blanks. With each long stroke of his hands, Davida felt his caress move through her body, touching the peaks of her breasts, between her thighs, even the sensitive balls of her feet. She could swear her toes curled when he leaned closer, his breath touching her ears. She moaned helplessly.

"What happened?" he asked innocently, doing it again.

"You know."

His warm breath touched the spot and she went limp. Marc chuckled and leaned closer, touching the spot with his tongue.

"I guess I'm gonna have to get real used to this mushy stuff when we get married, huh?" Des stood grinning in the doorway. "It's okay with me though, 'cause there's worse stuff than being in love." She shrugged. "Love is a good thing, for all of us."

She crossed her arms and looked oddly grown-up. "Guess y'all are just meant to be."

Out of the mouths of babes.

EPILOGUE I

"Alright, Anne, admit it. Just go on and say it right out loud. I did the right thing for the right reasons when I called Marcus in Atlanta, things worked out, and as a result I will always have the best news."

"Well." Anne reached and missed the envelope by inches. "If I admit it, will you quit playing and let me see what it is, for myself?"

Quita waved the tiny white envelope under her friend's nose. "I don't know." She smiled broadly, showing bright teeth. "Maybe, if you beg."

Anne's lips twisted to the side. Then, a vaguely conniving look crossed her face. "How about if I invite you to dinner, instead?" Quita took a deep breath and started to speak. Anne held up a hand to forestall the words "And, oh, by the way, did I mention Glenn Morrison will be there?"

Quita handed over the envelope.

"Thank you." Anne plucked the envelope from the other woman's manicured fingers. It bore an Atlanta, Georgia, postmark and Davida Lawrence's handwriting. Knowing what the envelope was bound to contain, Anne smiled. *One of the best reasons in the world for having a Sister Circle is times like this,* she thought, pulling the pastel card free, and reading:

> Davida Lawrence and Marcus Benton
> proudly announce the birth of their son

John Mathew Benton,
Born at Crawford Long Hospital
Atlanta, Georgia, on April 15th at 7:47 AM
Weight: 8 pounds, 7 ounces
Length: 23 inches

First Anne cooed, then she grinned. Tipping the envelope, she laughed out loud when the small color photo fell into her hand. The tiny baby wore a blue stocking cap and an Atlanta Braves bunting. "At least Marc didn't talk her into putting the baby into crimson and cream."

"Yet." Quita laughed. "But, you know it's coming." Looking over Anne's shoulder, she, too, admired the baby. "Oh, look," she slipped her index finger into the envelope. "There's a little note."

Anne pilled it free and read aloud.

Quita,
    Please tell everyone hello for me. I'm moving a little slow right now, but I'll get announcements and photos to them all. I sent yours first, 'cause you've got the biggest mouth (smile)! John's doing wonderfully—I'm almost afraid to put him in the dark, every time I look away, he seems to grow. Renee says he looks like former Atlanta mayor, Maynard Jackson. Marc says all babies born in Atlanta look like Maynard Jackson! The baby's been home less than a week, and he and Des have already bonded into some kind of sibling mutual admiration society. Gotta go. Someone here is demanding lunch.
    We're all fine, hope you are, too. Talk to you soon.

                                                              D

"I think this means we raised our girl right." Anne sniffed.

"Yeah, girl," Quita said, touching the moist corner of her eye. "I was kind of scared for her back there near the end of December, when we were waiting for the results of the baby's tests. I know for a fact it made her last Christmas here a much happier one when she found out the little fella was negative for any birth defects."

"Do you think she'll ever have him tested for"—Anne looked up, then lowered her eyes—"you know."

"Bone marrow?" Quita shrugged. "I don't know. He's still awfully young, but I can't see why not. You'll have to ask her and Marc." She paused. "On the other hand, Des is a terrific kid, and can you imagine being able to help her out and not doing it? I can't. Maybe this little brother will make a decision on his own, in time."

Anne lined her arm with Quita's. "So much in this life depends on time."

Fingering the sheer silk of her white scarf, Quita tossed the ends of the square over her shoulder as she and Anne walked toward her golden Mustang. "I know," she said.

EPILOGUE II

From *The St. Louis Post-Dispatch*, Sunday, July 24.

Lawrence and Benton

Davida Morrison Lawrence of St. Louis and Marcus James Benton of Atlanta, Georgia, were married June 25 at First United AME Church in St. Louis, at 7 in the evening. The Reverend Carlton D. Reese officiated the ceremony.

The bride is the daughter of Mrs. Jewell Morrison of St. Louis, Missouri. The groom's parents are Mr. and Mrs. Richard L. Benton, also of St. Louis, Missouri.

Given in marriage by her brother, Glenn Morrison, the bride wore a sleeveless, empire waist gown of silk organza with a chapel length train. She carried a cascading bouquet of gardinias, calla lillies, and stephanotis.

Quita Walton served as the bride's honor attendant. Bridesmaids included Renee Johnson, Anne Laird, and Melanie Baker.

Milton Thomas of Atlanta, Georgia, served as best man. Groomsmen included Herbert O. Jenkins, George Johnson, and Clayton Jasper.

Special readings during the ceremony were given by Louise Lawrence, the bride's aunt Eloise Davies, and Destiny Lawrence, the bride's daughter.

Alan Burnis served as the organist while accompanying

music was provided by Jeffery Rowser with George Drake as soloist.

Following the ceremony, the bride's family hosted a formal reception at the Regal Riverfront Hotel in St. Louis, Missouri.

Following a honeymoon in Bermuda, the couple lives in Atlanta, Georgia.

Author's Note

I hope you've enjoyed this story and the characters as much as I have. While the characters and situations I've presented are fictional, please know that there are many children and adults who, like Destiny Lawrence, have sickle-cell anemia. These people are bright, interesting, articulate, and maybe even related to you.

The bone marrow and blood donation and transfusion programs featured in this work are real and accessible. The book Marcus presented to Destiny, *Puzzles,* by Dava Walker, is real. Emory University in Atlanta, Georgia, does indeed have a pediatric sickle-cell program, and your local Red Cross can provide further information.

I have elected to become a bone marrow donor, and encourage each of you to at least become more familiar with the disease. After all, as people of color, "... if not us, who ..." will be there for these members of our global village?

Think about it.

With much love and respect,

Gail McFarland
P.O. Box 56782 Atlanta, GA 30343
E-mail: GmcFit@Yahoo.Com

ABOUT THE AUTHOR

Gail McFarland is a native of Cleveland, Ohio, but now lives in Atlanta, Georgia. She has worked as a teacher, a case worker, and a Peace Corps Volunteer recruiter, as well as in a residential shelter for abused women and their children. She is now an aerobic instructor and Fitness Trainer. She has been writing and publishing short fiction since 1990.

COMING IN SEPTEMBER ...

REMEMBER ME   (1-58314-032-8, $4.99/$6.50)
by Margie Walker
DNA lab technician Layla Griffin made a discovery could clear a man awaiting lethal injection for one of Texas's most sensational murder trials. She seeks out the detective assigned to case, Sergeant Paul Diamond, but an assault leaves her with amnesia. In order to uncover the real murderer, Paul helps Layla recover her memory—and thus finds love.

INTIMATE SECRETS   (1-58314-033-6, $4.99/$6.50)
by Candice Poarch
Johanna Jones returns to her hometown of Nottoway, Virginia as the owner of the town's only hotel, only to fall head over heels for the town's most eligible bachelor and owner of an aerospace company, Jonathan Blake. But there is a threat to both of their businesses. Together they find solutions and strengthen a love they didn't know existed.

FOR KEEPS   (1-58314-034-4, $4.99/$6.50)
by Janice Sims
Cheyenne Roberts is summoned back home to Montana to restore her family's ranch. Her neighbor is Jackson Kincaid, whom she is attracted to. With an injured leg, he finds himself alone with Cheyenne in a snowed-in cabin. He can only let her nurse him back to health. Trapped, and in close contact, they must confront their undeniable passion.

RETURN TO LOVE   (1-58314-035-2, $4.99/$6.50)
by Viveca Carlysle
Four years ago, Trisha Terrence left a perfect love for her career. But her partner in the bed and breakfast she owns gambled away his share to dangerous men. Seeking refuge, she can only think of Kaliq Faulkner's Wyoming ranch. He has mixed emotions about Trisha staying at his ranch, but spending time together once again, they rediscover their love.

Available wherever paperbacks are sold, or order direct from the Publisher. Send cover price plus 50¢ per copy for mailing and handling to BET Books, c/o Kensington Publishing Corp., Consumer Orders, or call (toll free) 888-345-BOOK, to place your order using Mastercard or Visa. Residents of New York, Washington D.C. and Tennessee must include sales tax. DO NOT SEND CASH.

LOOK FOR THESE ARABESQUE ROMANCES

AFTER ALL, by Lynn Emery   (0-7860-0325-1, $4.99/$6.50)
News reporter Michelle Toussaint only focused on her dream of becoming an anchorwoman. Then contractor Anthony Hilliard returned. For five years, Michelle had reminisced about the passions they shared. But happiness turned to heartbreak when Anthony's cruel betrayal led to her father's financial ruin. He returned for one reason only: to win Michelle back.

THE ART OF LOVE, by Crystal Wilson-Harris   (0-7860-0418-5, $4.99/$6.50)
Dakota Bennington's heritage is apparent from her African clothing to her sculptures. To her, attorney Pierce Ellis is just another uptight professional stuck in the American mainstream. Pierce worked hard and is proud of his success. An art purchase by his firm has made Dakota a major part of his life. And love bridges their different worlds.

CHANGE OF HEART   (0-7860-0103-8, $4.99/$6.50)
by Adrienne Ellis Reeves
Not one to take risks or stray far from her South Carolina hometown, Emily Brooks, a recently widowed mother, felt it was time for a change. On a business venture she meets author David Walker who is conducting research for his new book. But when he finds undying passion, he wants Emily for keeps. Wary of her newfound passion, all Emily has to do is follow her heart.

ECSTACY, by Gwynne Forster   (0-7860-0416-9, $4.99/$6.50)
Schoolteacher Jeannetta Rollins had a tumor that was about to cost her her eyesight. Her persistence led her to follow Mason Fenwick, the only surgeon talented enough to perform the surgery, on a trip around the world. After getting to know her, Mason wants her whole . . . body and soul. Now he must put behind a tragedy in his career and trust himself and his heart.

KEEPING SECRETS, by Carmen Green   (0-7860-0494-0, $4.99/$6.50)
Jade Houston worked alone. But a dear deceased friend left clues to a two-year-old mystery and Jade had to accept working alongside Marine Captain Nick Crawford. As they enter a relationship that runs deeper than business, each must learn how to trust each other in all aspects.

MOST OF ALL, by Louré Bussey   (0-7860-0456-8, $4.99/$6.50)
After another heartbreak, New York secretary Elandra Lloyd is off to the Bahamas to visit her sister. Her sister is nowhere to be found. Instead she runs into Nassau's richest, self-made millionaire Bradley Davenport. She is lucky to have made the acquaintance with this sexy islander as she searches for her sister and her trust in the opposite sex.

Available wherever paperbacks are sold, or order direct from the Publisher. Send cover price plus 50¢ per copy for mailing and handling to Kensington Publishing Corp., Consumer Orders, or call (toll free) 888-345-BOOK, to place your order using Mastercard or Visa. Residents of New York and Tennessee must include sales tax. DO NOT SEND CASH.

ROMANCES THAT SIZZLE
FROM ARABESQUE

AFTER DARK, by Bette Ford   (0-7860-0442-8, $4.99/$6.50)
Taylor Hendricks' brother is the top NBA draft choice. She wants to protect
him from the lure of fame and wealth, but meets basketball superstar Donald
Williams in an exclusive Detroit restaurant. Donald is determined to prove
that she is wrong about him. In this game all is at stake . . . including Taylor's
heart.

BEGUILED, by Eboni Snoe   (0-7860-0046-5, $4.99/$6.50)
When Raquel Mason agrees to impersonate a missing heiress for just one
night and plans go awry, a daring abduction makes her the captive of seductive
Nate Bowman. Together on a journey across exotic Caribbean seas to the
perilous wilds of Central America, desire looms in their hearts. But when the
masquerade is over, will their love end?

CONSPIRACY, by Margie Walker   (0-7860-0385-5, $4.99/$6.50)
Pauline Sinclair and Marcellus Cavanaugh had the love of a lifetime. Until
Pauline had to leave everything behind. Now she's back and their love is as
strong as ever. But when the President of Marcellus's company turns up dead
and Pauline is the prime suspect, they must risk all to their love.

FIRE AND ICE, by Carla Fredd   (0-7860-0190-9, $4.99/$6.50)
Years of being in the spotlight and a recent scandal regarding her ex-fianceé
and a supermodel, the daughter of a Georgia politician, Holly Aimes has turned
cold. But when work takes her to the home of late-night talk show host Michael Williams, his relentless determination melts her cool.

HIDDEN AGENDA, by Rochelle Alers   (0-7860-0384-7, $4.99/$6.50)
To regain her son from a vengeful father, Eve Blackwell places her trust in
dangerous and irresistible Matt Sterling to rescue her abducted son. He accepts
this last job before he turns a new leaf and becomes an honest rancher. As
they journey from Virginia to Mexico they must enter a charade of marriage.
But temptation is too strong for this to remain a sham.

INTIMATE BETRAYAL, by Donna Hill   (0-7860-0396-0, $4.99/$6.50)
Investigative reporter, Reese Delaware, and millionaire computer wizard, Maxwell Knight are both running from their pasts. When Reese is assigned to
profile Maxwell, they enter a steamy love affair. But when Reese begins to
piece her memory, she stumbles upon secrets that link her and Maxwell, and
threaten to destroy their newfound love.

*Available wherever paperbacks are sold, or order direct from the
Publisher. Send cover price plus 50¢ per copy for mailing and
handling to Kensington Publishing Corp., Consumer Orders,
or call (toll free) 888-345-BOOK, to place your order using
Mastercard or Visa. Residents of New York and Tennessee
must include sales tax. DO NOT SEND CASH.*